I0610439

FRACTURE

ZIVA PAYVAN LEGACY • PART 1

EJ FISCH

Transcendence
Publishing

FRACTURE

Copyright © 2019 E.J. Fisch

All rights reserved. No part of this publication may be reproduced, distributed, or transmitted in any form or by any means, including photocopying, recording, or other electronic or mechanical methods, without the prior written permission of the author or publisher, except in the case of brief quotations embodied in critical reviews and certain other noncommercial uses permitted by copyright law.

First edition: October 2019

If you would like to use material from the book, prior written permission must be obtained by contacting the publisher at transcendence.publishing@gmail.com.

The Transcendence Publishing name, imprint, and logo are trademarks of Transcendence Publishing.

Publisher's note: This is a work of fiction. Names, characters, places, and incidents are a product of the author's imagination or are used fictitiously. Any resemblance to actual people, living or dead, or to businesses, companies, events, institutions, or locales is completely coincidental.

ISBN-13: 978-1-7334772-0-8
ISBN-10: 1-7334772-0-9

WHAT'S COME BEFORE

The distant world of Haphez is located on the edge of populated space. The planet's native superhuman race is feared and respected by neighboring civilizations. Their military and police forces are unmatched.

DAKITI: ZIVA PAYVAN BOOK 1

Ziva Payvan was one of the Haphezian Special Police's finest operatives. Along with special operations squadmates Skeet Duvo and Zinni Vax, she was tasked with some of the most daunting missions in agency history. When ordered to bring a field operations agent named Aroska Tarbic on board during a new assignment, her world was turned upside down; two years prior, Aroska's younger brother had been one of her targets, and unbeknownst to HSP's administration, Aroska knew she'd carried out the hit.

But a sinister plot against Haphez forced the two of them to set their differences aside and cooperate with one another. The plan, put in motion by the semi-amphibious Sardons and a Haphezian woman named Saun Zaid—with whom Aroska had been romantically involved—consisted of using genetic information from captured Haphezians to create an army of hybrid Haphezian/Sardon super soldiers, which would then be used to forcibly take valuable resources from Haphez. Ziva and her team, along with Aroska, traveled to the Dakiti Medical Research Center on the Sardon homeworld to put a stop to the facility's operations and discovered that Aroska's former teammates, Jole and Tate, had been among the captive Haphezians there. Both agents were rescued, but Aroska was captured by Saun.

Breaking protocol, Ziva made a solo venture back into Dakiti to extract him and, in the process of saving his life, ended up revealing a long-kept secret: she wielded Nostia, a forbidden telekinetic ability used by a sect of Resistance fighters who had rebelled against the Galactic Federation decades prior. Aroska was shocked by the display and placed her under arrest, but once Dakiti was destroyed and the team made it safely home, he convinced HSP Director Emeri Arion to drop the charges and tell no one about Ziva's power, since she had used it to save his life. Ziva and Aroska parted ways amicably, though the lingering memories of Aroska's brother left a rift between them.

NEXUS: ZIVA PAYVAN BOOK 2

Two months later, Ziva was framed by a fellow HSP agent for the assassination of the Haphezian Royal General. Hunted by Diago Dasaro—the very man who'd framed her—she sought help from Aroska, who had been on leave since the Dakiti mission. While the pair's relationship was still tenuous, Aroska aided her in staging her death, at least long enough to keep Dasaro off her back while she attempted to find out why she'd been framed. But before she and Aroska could leave Haphez, Ziva stepped in to rescue Kade Shevin, a young HSP agent who'd been targeted by Dasaro after assuming her innocence in regard to the assassination. With Kade in tow, Ziva and Aroska escaped to the seedy world of Chaiavis.

While on Chaiavis, the trio met Kat Reilly, a Haphezian Defective who'd been banished from Haphez as an infant due to genetic abnormalities. As it turned out, Kat had been using her limited resources to remotely look into Dasaro's activities, suspecting his involvement in the massacre of citizens in her hometown of Argall. Using clues from Kat and information Kade had stolen from his supervisor before leaving Haphez, the group discovered that Dasaro had framed Ziva because she too had been digging into his involvement with Argall. The little mining town was known as the origin place of niobi crystals, which were commonly used in weapons development, and it was revealed that mercenaries under Dasaro's control had overrun Argall and were distributing the crystals to the black market. Armed with this knowledge, Ziva, Aroska, Kade, and Kat made a plan to return to Haphez, confront Dasaro, and stop the mercs' operations in Argall.

Before their departure, however, Kat confided in Ziva that she was dying from a mysterious illness, something caused by an entity called Ronan, and asked that Ziva investigate.

Upon returning home, the mission to liberate Argall was successful and Ziva was able to kill Dasaro, but not before he severely wounded her. With her innocence in the assassination all but proven, she was granted a stay at the Haphezian military's renowned rehab facility and requested that Aroska join her team in her absence while Skeet took command.

RONAN: ZIVA PAYVAN BOOK 3

On the final day of Ziva's rehab, a downed aircraft released a mysterious gas into the military base. She returned home to help HSP investigate the crash and learned that Aroska had discovered the information Kat had given her about Ronan. He and Skeet were currently out searching the galaxy for Zinni, who had been captured by Ronan's soldiers several weeks prior. Enraged that the agency hadn't alerted her to the situation, Ziva set out to find her team and, after striking a deal with mobster Tobias Niio, located Aroska and Skeet on the desert world of Aubin. There, she narrowly thwarted the two agents' execution by a man named Taran Reddic, who was also hunting Ronan and thought the Haphezians were employed by the mysterious entity. Reddic informed the team that he and his squad had been commissioned by the Federation and that Ronan was in actuality the leader of the Resistance.

Having hit a dead end in their search for Zinni, the group returned to Haphez and learned that those who'd been exposed to the gas at the base were presenting with adverse neurological symptoms, yet Ziva remained healthy. Thanks to her newfound knowledge about Ronan, she deduced that the gas had been an experimental form of nostium, the chemical used by the Resistance to produce Nostia in their soldiers. It was discovered that the Resistance was planning to expose Haphezians to nostium in hopes of drawing Federation forces out to the edge of the galaxy to deal with them, thus leaving the Core worlds vulnerable to Resistance incursion.

Throughout the course of additional Resistance attacks, Ziva and Aroska began to acknowledge the emotional bond that had inevitably formed between them during their past experiences together. Ziva finally confessed to Aroska that his brother's death had essentially been an accident, and, armed with the truth, he found it in himself to forgive her. Having cleared the air, they managed to rescue Zinni and gain critical Resistance intel, but not before Aroska's other brother was killed by enemy soldiers.

Even as HSP and the military worked together to form a plan of retaliation, the Resistance fleet arrived in Haphezian airspace. Ordered to remain planetside as a strategic advisor thanks to her knowledge of nostium, Ziva could only watch helplessly as Aroska stole aboard a military craft en route to the battle. After escaping HSP custody, she joined the battle as well and discovered that Taran Reddic and Tobias Niio had both arrived with fleets of their own to assist Haphez. She tracked Aroska to the Resistance flagship and, after joining forces with some of Reddic's men, stormed the bridge to confront Ronan.

After defeating the Resistance leader and disabling the ship, Ziva transmitted Resistance information to the Federation, but despite the fact that she'd never been an official member of the rogue faction, the data listed her as a Nosti. She and Aroska escaped the vessel, though her own ship sustained damage in the process. Upon returning to Haphez, Reddic placed her under arrest, having seen her name in the transmitted files. Preparations were made for her to surrender herself to the Feds, but as she attempted to pilot her damaged ship up to rendezvous with a Federation escort, the vessel exploded.

Mourning their loss, Aroska, Skeet, and Zinni sat down that evening to read farewell messages she'd composed, and Aroska couldn't help but notice his message had been sent one minute *after* the explosion...

THE
ZIVA PAYVAN
SERIES

A full dramatis personae and glossary of series terms can be found at
www.ejfisch.com/glossary

PROLOGUE

Don't look back. Don't you dare look back.

She clenched her hands into fists and stopped at the base of the *Intrepid's* boarding ramp, taking a quick look over her shoulder in spite of herself. If she included the squads of HSP guards, a dozen faces stared back at her from across the landing platform, but only the four nearest to her really mattered. As expected, the sight of them made her eyes and nose start to sting, and she forced herself to continue moving up the ramp before she could do something ridiculous like change her mind.

She ducked inside the ship and pressed her back against the wall long enough to take a couple of deep, calming breaths before hitting the ramp controls and sprinting for the cockpit. Every second counted from this moment forward. She slid into the pilot's seat and swiveled around to face the control board, ignoring the warning lights that already flashed in response to the damaged hull.

The ignition sequence was initiated with the flip of a switch, and she watched on the monitor as the liftoff repulsors powered up. The boarding ramp locked into place and the airlocks activated as the repulsion reached one hundred percent power, and the ship began to lift off.

An alert appeared on the console immediately. "WARNING: Hull breach detected. Starboard thruster core temperature rising."

"I know, I know," she whispered. "Just hold together for a couple more minutes."

Two green blips appeared on the scanner, representing the fighters Reddic and Mae piloted. A nav transmission came through from the first one, showing her the location of the Federation flagship she was to rendezvous with. She nodded to herself and entered the coordinates into the *Intrepid's* nav computer.

"WARNING: Starboard thruster pressure loss detected. WARNING: Starboard thruster core temperature twelve percent above safe threshold."

"Sorry," she said, giving the control panel a gentle pat. She took one more look at all the readings before activating the autopilot system and leaping from the chair.

The biggest problem with this supposed plan of hers was that she had no idea how much time she had. At least there'd be plenty of warnings, but how soon those warnings would appear was the real question. Klaxons already blared as she jogged down the corridor to the cargo bay, and a monotone feminine voice relayed fresh warnings over the comm system. The ship had attempted to transfer power to the port thruster and had overloaded it.

Great—just what I need.

She entered the cargo bay just in time to see the wall-mounted comm console hum to life. A quick glance at the screen told her it was Skeet calling, and as a registered secondary user of the ship, the system would let him through regardless of whether she accepted the transmission. She muttered a rough curse and opened the line.

"I hope you're not going to try to talk me into coming back down." She had hoped to sound good-natured, but the thought of wasting valuable time had given the response a harsh edge. She left the transmission open and moved over to where the three jet suits hung in their case.

The desperation was apparent in Skeet's voice. "You have to, Z! The ship's not stable. You'll blow before you hit five klicks. Even if you don't, you'll never break atmo."

You think I don't know that? She pulled one of the bigger jet suits down and stepped into it. "*Sheyss*, Skeet. I told you everything would be fine. I've got it under control."

"Don't be stupid, Zival!" another voice shouted in the background.

She froze for a split second before reminding herself to keep moving. Aroska. Of all people, he should trust her to have the situation handled.

"I'm not going to debate this." Heat flooded her cheeks as she stormed back over to the comm console and ended the transmission.

The voices of her teammates were replaced by another alert from the ship. "WARNING: Starboard thruster core temperature forty-three percent above safe threshold."

"I know what I'm doing, I know what I'm doing, I know what I'm doing." She was trying to convince herself of that just as much as she was trying to drown out a new warning about the starboard engine running hot.

She manually locked the comm console as another transmission from Skeet came through. The jet suit she'd grabbed was a bit baggy even after she'd tightened the clasps as far as they'd go, but it would have to suffice; there was no way she'd obey the ship's current suggestion and initiate emergency landing procedures.

A quick look at the scanner above the weapons lockers told her she was still on course to rendezvous with Colonel Matney's ship, as were Reddic and Mae. She moved toward the port airlock, opting to stay as far away from the faulty starboard thruster as possible, and glanced around as a new alarm began wailing. The ship was looking for her, waiting in vain for her to take action at the helm.

The comm console continued buzzing as she took up the jet suit's helmet and moved into the airlock. According to the altimeter beside the outer door, she'd just broken thirty-five hundred meters. The jet suit could only operate up to about a kilometer in altitude, and even then, its boosters were designed to lift its users from stable surfaces, not stop them from hurtling downward from multiple klicks at terminal velocity. She wasn't entirely sure if it would stop her before she reached the ground, but there was only one way to find out.

A loud beep echoed through the airlock and she looked up at the wall display to see that the ship's thermal scanners had located her there. There was nothing it could do aside from pester her with prompts, but it was treating her absence from the cockpit as an anomaly and began checking the system for further internal inconsistencies.

"Stop it, just stop," she muttered through her teeth as the comm system chimed once more. She set about securing the inner airlock door and overriding the pressure lock on the outer one. The scanner alarm stopped blaring but was immediately replaced by a new one—louder and more insistent—that signaled the inevitable failure of the starboard thruster. The starboard engine wasn't far behind, and the ship listed sharply to one side, throwing her against the airlock wall. She steadied herself and staggered toward the hatch, patting the jet suit's utility pocket to ensure the data pad she'd brought was secure. She hoped it—and her, for that matter—would survive the trip back to the ground.

She took one last look at the timestamp on the wall display as she hit the controls to open the outer door; her plan might still work after all. A blast of frigid, moist air hit her, and she only had a split second to stare out into the swirling clouds before the ship lurched and a ball of fire propelled her through the opening.

FRACTURE

ZIVA PAYVAN LEGACY • PART 1

CHAPTER 1
PRESENT DAY · DELATORI

Just go. Run.

The front door of the house was just a few more strides ahead. His legs were pumping as fast as his heart was beating. He wasn't even sure if his pursuer was still behind him, but he dared not pause to find out. To his delight, the door was already unlocked; he punched the controls and slipped inside, taking a moment to catch his breath.

There was no doubt in his mind that this hunter was hoping he'd lead them to his father, the true target in this situation. He was merely a decoy, a distraction to occupy this assassin while the rest of his family fled the city. So far the plan seemed to be working, but the thing about fishing was that it never worked out so well for the bait. If he failed, the assassin would not hesitate to kill him, regardless of whether he was the quarry. The only consolation was that he'd been off-world for the past several years and knew very little about his father's situation or the people hunting him. He clung to a shred of hope that plausible deniability could work to his advantage.

Once his racing heart slowed a bit, he carefully turned and risked a look out the window. The clearing outside was bathed in brilliant silver-blue moonlight that seemed nearly as bright as the daytime sun. He scanned the tree line for several minutes, watching for any movement or shapes that seemed out of place. Just as he'd made up his mind that he was safe, a shadow detached itself from the foliage and stepped into the clearing, then began striding purposefully toward the house. He shuddered and his heart collapsed into his stomach. This was the same shadow that had just pursued him for three kilometers through the forest, the one that had already killed his sister in an attempt to reach their father.

He was unarmed, and the assassin knew it. Otherwise he doubted they'd be so quick to expose themselves. If they were trying to get inside his head, it was working; intentionally presenting as such a vulnerable target was just a reminder of how powerless he was. He had no idea who this house belonged to, but chances were slim that there were any weapons available. Anything that could be used for self-defense had likely been taken during the evacuation. He at least had the presence of mind to lock the door, and he stood there listening with bated breath as footsteps approached outside.

This house seemed bigger than others in the area and appeared to be furnished with high-end decor. The owners were probably wealthy and had no doubt been some of the first to leave the city. Large pieces of furniture were stacked up nearby, giving him the impression the front door had recently been barricaded against attackers. He considered trying to reestablish that barrier, but even if he could move all the furniture himself, there was no time. He slowly began to back away, looking wildly about for some other means of escape.

A soft clicking just outside sent him scurrying down the hallway. Based on the skill the assassin had shown throughout their pursuit, he didn't doubt their ability to breach the lock. Even so, the sound of the door sliding open came far too soon for his taste. He darted into the first room he came to, some sort of study or sitting room. A plush sofa and matching armchairs were arranged around a low table, and a desk and large cabinet were positioned against the far wall. He ran to the cabinet and flung it open, finding it empty except for a couple of deactivated data pads and an old blanket. The bottom shelf was clear, so he ducked down and crawled inside, pulling the door shut as quietly as he could behind him.

There in the confined space, each breath and heartbeat sounded horrifyingly loud. He leaned forward and rested his head on his knees, watching the room outside through the narrow crack between the doors. The moonlight poured in through the window, giving him a clear picture of the area. He strained to hear, willing his pulse to slow. He'd been able to hear nothing but himself since leaving the front door. The assassin could be anywhere by now.

A cold sweat coated his forehead and he shivered, though whether it was due to nerves or an actual drop in temperature, he wasn't sure. The idea of having been left behind was beginning to take its toll on him. Per his father's plan, there was a small shuttle waiting for him at the spaceport, but the trek through the forest had taken time he didn't have, and he doubted the pilot would have waited this long for him. Most of the personal transports had either been destroyed or taken during the evacuation, but maybe there'd be something left that would at least get him up to the orbital transfer station. The trick now would just be to make it to the port in the first place.

An unfamiliar shape caught his eye and he leaned over to peer through the crack again, shuddering when he realized the assassin was standing in the doorway of the room. The galaxy only knew how long they'd been there. He swallowed against the bile rising up in his throat and clamped a hand over his mouth to keep himself from crying out. His skin crawled as the shadowy figure took a couple of slow, silent steps farther into the room. The moonlight turned their black clothing a silvery-gray and illuminated severe facial features, and he was surprised to see that the person was a woman. She kept her dark hair pulled back and surveyed the room with eyes that appeared just as dark in the shadows. She wore a long combat knife strapped to one thigh, and in her left hand she gripped a suppressed pistol.

The woman stood so still that for a while he wondered if she was simply a figment of his terrified imagination. But then her head moved, and she turned to look directly at the cabinet. It was all he could do to keep from squirming. Surely there was no way she could actually see him, but although he didn't have a clear view of her face, he was almost positive the two of them were making eye contact.

She knows you're there, and she wants you to know it. After everything he'd seen, he wouldn't put such a manipulation tactic past her, but he sat there shaking his head as discreetly as possible, hoping she couldn't sense the movement and trying to convince himself there was no way she could possibly know where he was.

He nearly wet himself when he saw her take a step, but she simply pivoted and strode from the room as quickly and quietly as she had entered. He leaned forward, straining to see through the crack and hoping he'd catch sight of her passing by the doorway as she searched the remainder of the house. He held his breath and listened for her footsteps but was met only with silence. Then, after what felt like hours, he heard a beep followed by metal scraping on metal. The front door had opened and closed. She was gone.

He was torn then between waiting to make sure she didn't come back and rushing to a window to see if she was setting up an ambush outside. He settled on a happy medium and sat there counting under his breath for three minutes before easing the cabinet door open. When he was sure everything was still quiet, he crawled out, crouching until the circulation returned to his legs. He moved across the room centimeter by centimeter, half-expecting the assassin to appear in the doorway again. But the journey out into the hallway remained uneventful, and he breathed a sigh of relief when he saw that the path to the front door was clear.

He stepped out, mentally running through all the possible routes to the spaceport from here. He dreaded the thought of going on foot, but he hadn't a clue how to break into a car and doubted he'd find one available for breaking into anyway. Running wouldn't be so bad; it would enable him to hide and maintain a lower profile. But running would also require him to cut back through the same forest he'd just been chased through, and there was no way to know where the assassin had gone.

He wasn't entirely sure which came first: the explosion of pain at the base of his spine, or the realization of *exactly* where the woman had gone. Perhaps he had heard a sound or seen something in his peripheral vision. He couldn't remember, and the next thing he *did* remember was striking his head on the floor.

Something warm and wet began spreading at the small of his back, and he could feel it dribbling down his sides and pooling under him. But there was no more pain. He didn't think he could feel his legs.

The floor behind him creaked and the rough tread of a boot sole came to rest on his shoulder. He drew a sharp breath in through his nose and was blinded by hot tears as a powerful leg flipped him over onto his back. The woman was nothing more than a dark shape hovering above him, distorted by his swimming vision. Though he still couldn't see her face, he could once again feel her icy gaze drilling into him.

She stood there observing him silently for several seconds before bending down and shining a small spotlight directly into his face, blocking his view of what—if anything—she was doing. He did his best to keep his eyes open, not wishing to be caught unaware again, but the light burned and sent pain stabbing through his head, so he eventually allowed his eyelids to shut. He wanted to beg for mercy, offer to disappear and tell no one about this incident, but his throat seized up and the words eluded him. He guessed the effort would be futile anyway.

The light shut off after a moment as if she'd finished studying him. He thought he heard her release a disappointed sigh, though it was difficult to hear over his own raspy breathing.

"You shouldn't have run," she said. Her voice was a far cry from what he'd expected. It was low and smooth, and despite the circumstances, he couldn't help but be soothed by it.

I know, he wanted to say as tears spilled down his cheeks. *I know that now.*

"Please," he managed as she rose back into a standing position. The moonlight glinted off the casing of her pistol as she took aim for his head.

He shut his eyes again, reveling in the darkness. There was a soft pop followed by a brief burning sensation in his skull, and then...

Nothing.

CHAPTER 2
ENTERTAINMENT SECTOR - NORO, HAPHEZ

"And how's life in logistics?"

"Oh, you know." The words were said around a mouthful of food. "Same old grind."

Aroska Tarbic looked across the table at Jole Imetsi, unable to help but laugh a bit at his old friend's response. It was the same answer the man always gave when asked how work was going, and it was a running joke dating back to when they'd still worked together in the field operations division of the Haphezian Special Police. Their work and caseload had changed so often that the proverbial 'grind' was virtually nonexistent.

Tate Luver laughed as well from his place on Aroska's left. The three of them had made a point over the last couple of years to get together semi-regularly and share a meal, and no matter how many times they did it, being in the company of his former teammates still felt surreal to Aroska. The period of time when he'd thought them both dead haunted him to this day. Even once they'd been rescued from the vile Dakiti Medical Research Center on Sardonis, he'd had his personal problems and then had gotten caught up in the whirlwind of special operations, making it nigh on impossible to catch up at the time. His work schedule was more unpredictable now, but he still managed to make time for them these days. In a way, being with them made it feel like nothing had ever changed.

A quick glance around, however, revealed just how much *had* changed. Four solid years of spec ops had given Aroska a different view of the world, made him more cynical and wary than he'd been even after some of the things he'd endured in field ops. Spending time with his old friends brought him a surprising amount of comfort, and regardless of how long they'd been apart, they could always pick up right where they'd left off. But he'd never been sure whether he had the same effect on Jole and Tate. He often wondered if they felt any bitterness toward him, as neither of them had ever been cleared for active duty. He had to remind himself he hadn't actually done anything to hurt them, but the thoughts plagued him all the same.

Jole was slender, having never been able to gain much muscle mass after being subjected to Dakiti's sick experiments. Tate spent most of his time in a hoverchair and was still undergoing periodic physical therapy for the same reason. Neither of them had ever earned a coveted spot at the Na Facility, the Haphezian military hospital renowned for its rehab programs, but considering the circumstances surrounding their disappearance and subsequent rescue, the agency had footed the bill for their recovery and had even found in-house jobs for them. Aroska was glad; as former members of the Alpha field ops team, they didn't deserve to be cast aside.

"Someone's got to keep Adin and his team out of trouble, right?" Tate said with a chuckle.

Jole nodded and swallowed another bite. "I'll say it again: back in our day, I never had as much respect for the logistics division as I do now."

Aroska smiled, glad his friend seemed to be content with his work. The logistics analysts represented a crucial behind-the-scenes element of field ops, handling everything from traffic data to communications in order to ensure investigations ran smoothly. As an ex-field ops agent himself, Jole provided unique insights that had turned him into an invaluable member of the logistics team.

He turned to Tate. "And how are classes going?"

The former intelligence agent had originally been asked to help out with several of the classroom courses required for recruits in the field ops track, but having specialized in crime scene investigation during his prime, he'd eventually become head instructor for one of the forensics classes. The hoverchair only served to accommodate a loss of mobility, not a loss of expertise.

Tate dipped his head and grinned as if the question were humorous. "You know, with the number of smartass kids who think they know everything coming through the basic training program, I'm sometimes not sure how the ops divisions ever function as well as they do."

The three of them shared a laugh. "The combat phase thins them out," Aroska said.

"Or their lieutenants whip their asses into shape if they make it through selection," Jole joked to Tate, shooting Aroska a good-natured wink.

A melancholy silence followed as they each contemplated what Jole had just said. It seemed that he too could easily forget just how much had changed. Although Aroska enjoyed working in spec ops and meshed well with his current team, he missed his friends. Deep down, he knew he would always be their lieutenant.

"What about you, *boss*?" Tate finally asked. "How's life in the fast lane?"

Aroska couldn't help but wonder if the man was merely playing on Jole's mistake or if he was being spiteful. "I've told you before—you guys don't need to call me that anymore." He took a sip of water and shrugged. "But life is good. Skeet and Zinni are doing well, and we stay plenty busy. You know there's a lot I can't talk about. We leave in the morning for our independent service term, so the rest of the evening is just downtime."

"That's good," Jole said. He grew quiet for a moment and pushed his food back and forth across his plate. "You seeing anyone?"

In a psychiatric or romantic capacity? Aroska couldn't help but bristle a bit, and his answer was the same either way. "Nope." He stuffed a bite of food into his mouth.

"Hear that, Tate? Noro's most eligible bachelor still hasn't found a new girl." The man laughed, then sobered somewhat. "It's been four years, man. You don't think it's time to move on?"

Romantic capacity, then. He'd told them a little about his relationship with Saun Zaid following their disappearance and the way he thought he and his new partner had shared something special...at least until she'd betrayed him to the Sardons. Hell, she'd been responsible for Jole and Tate's capture in the first place. After hearing stories about the depressed slump he'd fallen into following that whole debacle at Dakiti, both men had expressed an immense concern for his emotional well-being, even going so far as to introduce him to a few of their female acquaintances. He was glad to an extent; they were simply fulfilling their duties as his long-time best friends. He'd even indulged them and tried meeting up with some of those lady friends, but a sense of distraction and insincerity had led to him breaking things off every time, complete with a stale 'it's-not-you-it's-me' line and an awkward, hasty goodbye. In light of all that, these inquiries were getting old.

"I'm fine. Really. You asked me that last time we got together."

"That was three months ago. I just thought something might have changed since then."

It had really been that long? In a way, Aroska was glad, as it meant he'd stayed busy and content enough that the passage of time had hardly been noticeable. But it also terrified him, because that was another three months that...*she*...had been gone.

"I appreciate the sentiment," he said, "but like I told you, I'm fine. I'm doing better now than I have in a long time."

It was at least a partial truth. He was fine because he believed *she* was still out there somewhere. He'd never confessed to his friends that *she* was the reason he couldn't bring himself to move on. For all they knew, he was still hung up on what had happened with Saun, no doubt the reason they continued to tease and press him on the matter. All they knew about *her* was that he'd done some work with her and then had joined her former team on a permanent basis following her disappearance. *No*, he corrected himself, *her death*. Like the rest of the agency, the rest of Haphez, and hopefully the rest of the galaxy, Jole and Tate believed she was dead.

He'd at least told Skeet and Zinni about the timestamp and had showed them her final message because it was only fair, but they'd remained skeptical. At least they believed his theory that staging her own demise was the only way she could have saved herself from the Federation—they claimed to, anyway, and Zinni had been the one who'd suggested she leave in the first place. But both of them still seemed angry that she could have been selfish enough to go without telling them, to play with their emotions by making them believe she was dead for the second time in nearly as many months. He'd tried to explain, tried to make them understand what a self*less* deed it had been, because her actions had protected all of them from the Feds as well. Their anger was merely a coping mechanism; he was sure of it. The feeling of utter helplessness left him overcome by frustration sometimes, too. They at least indulged him when he tried to explain his suspicions about her status and whereabouts, though he often got the sense they thought he was crazy.

In the back of his mind, Aroska was aware of Jole and Tate speaking to one another, discussing their own love lives, or lack thereof as the case may be. He wasn't comfortable telling them he thought she was alive. Sure, they'd met her way back during basic training, but they didn't *know* her, not the way he did. He hadn't shared anything he'd learned about her history or any details of what all had transpired since Dakiti either. It wouldn't mean as much to them, and there was no way they could understand, mostly because he himself still didn't fully understand how he felt. Besides, a very small part of him was leery about getting his hopes up. The timestamp discrepancy could have easily been caused by a damaged comm array—there was no shortage of those after the Resistance had destroyed half the city—but as always, he reminded himself she wouldn't have asked him about the time if it hadn't been significant.

"—to get that?"

He blinked and met Jole and Tate's inquisitive gazes before reaching for his buzzing communicator. It had been weeks since he'd allowed his mind to wander so severely with regards to *her*, and the thought of having faltered was disappointing.

The incoming comm code was Skeet's. Aroska gave his friends an apologetic nod and accepted the transmission. "Yeah, Skeet."

"Emeri is requesting a meeting with all of us," the Alpha spec ops lieutenant said. "Says we've already got a contract for the service term. I don't have details."

"Got it. I'm on my way."

He pocketed the communicator and pulled out his credit chip, paying for all three of their meals before Jole or Tate could protest. "Sorry, gentlemen. Duty calls."

Jole lifted an eyebrow. "I thought you had the rest of the night off."

Aroska sighed. "So did I."

CHAPTER 3
HSP HEADQUARTERS - NORO HAPHEZ

The headquarters of the Haphezian Special Police was an establishment that never truly slept, but if it had what could be considered 'business hours,' they had ended for the day by the time Aroska arrived at the campus's operations wing. He made his way through security, a process usually rendered quick and painless by his spec ops status but currently facilitated further by the lack of personnel coming through at this hour. As he moved through the wide lobby toward the elevator bank, he couldn't help but pause in front of the long wall overlaid with matte gray tiles, tiles bearing names he'd honestly never paid much attention to until a very specific one had been added four years ago.

His eyes went to work counting—tenth row down, sixth column from the right—until they fell on *her* tile, almost perfectly at eye level. She'd been granted five stars for her contribution to the battle against the Resistance and the sacrifice she'd made to protect Haphez from the Federation, as well as for a remarkably successful career. It was one of the highest honors among HSP agents and Grand Army soldiers alike and was almost always awarded posthumously. The world—or at least the agency—regarded her as a hero, despite the revelation that she had wielded the Resistance's forbidden telekinetic power, the Nostia, from a young age. He'd always felt a measure of pride about that.

He continued on his way, riding the elevator to the ops wing's top floor. The only illumination in Director Emeri Arion's office was provided by the natural evening sunlight streaming in through the picture window across the room. When Aroska thought about it, he wasn't sure if he'd ever seen it any other way. He'd been in this office more times during his four years in spec ops than he ever had during the ten he'd spent in field ops, but it always looked the same. He liked it that way; it gave the office a more relaxed atmosphere, a sense of calm, a good thing considering the reasons behind his presence there were often stressful on some level or another. He wondered if the director kept it like that for exactly that reason.

He found Skeet Duvo and Zinnarana Vax already waiting through the open door as one of the director's aides showed him in. Emeri himself was nowhere in sight.

"Contract already, huh?" he said. The two agents merely shrugged in response to his questioning glance. "That's new."

"We don't know anything more than we did when I called," Skeet replied. "Apparently the Royal House has been briefed, so this must be something big. Emeri said to meet him here, but he has yet to make an appearance."

Aroska stuffed his hands into his pockets and moved over to look out the window, something he always made a point of doing when he was in this office. Even after four years, it was hard to get used to the way Noro's skyline had changed due to the repairs following the Resistance attack. Once-familiar shapes and silhouettes were all different now. He could barely see the Tranyi River from here these days due to new construction, and that had always been his favorite part of the view.

As he studied the way the city's shadows shifted with the approach of darkness, it struck him that he *had* been here at night. He'd stood before this very window the night after the *Intrepid* had blown, studying the ruins of the city in the waning light. Both the grievous view outside and the harsher lighting within the office had seemed appropriate then, perfectly complementing what he'd come to consider one of the worst days of his life. It was hard to believe how much time had already passed.

Aroska sighed, shook his head, and turned back around to face Skeet and Zinni. He hated to admit that blocking out these memories had gotten easier as the years went by. But there were times he still made himself miserable *wondering*, and today certainly seemed like it was turning into one of those days. Missing her came in waves. The majority of the time, he could keep himself afloat with no trouble at all, but sometimes the uncertainty made him feel like he was drowning. He knew both of his squadmates felt the same.

Skeet stopped his pacing and Zinni rose from her seat when Emeri entered the room with a man Aroska didn't recognize. A whiff of body odor told him the stranger was human. He was well-dressed, probably wealthy, but looked exhausted. Movement drew Aroska's attention back to the door, and he saw a pair of what appeared to be personal security detail take up positions just outside before it was shut and locked.

"Pahl Starcer," the director said, extending a hand toward the three of them, "meet the agency's Alpha special operations squad. You requested the best of the best, and it doesn't get any better than these three."

They all exchanged a glance. The majority of their independent service terms were spent thwarting dangers to Haphez, many of which were posed by humans. But now there was one here, to do what…recruit them? The fact that the man was present in Emeri's office meant he— or his proposal, at least—was somehow significant, especially if the rumors of the Royal House's involvement were true. And the fact that the team was just now learning about him meant his arrival was either classified or had been on very short notice. Perhaps a mixture of both.

"What can we do for you, sir?" Skeet asked, motioning for everyone to go gather around the conference table across the room.

"Mr. Starcer has a problem that is—how did you put it when we spoke—uniquely Haphezian in nature," Emeri explained. "The Royal House recommended the three of you, and when he found out you would be departing soon, he insisted on arranging a meeting before you could do so."

Starcer nodded. "I understand you're preparing to leave for an independent service term. I know the term hasn't officially started, but time is of the essence and I couldn't afford to chase you halfway across the galaxy. Consider my contract in effect as of this moment. Rest assured you will receive additional compensation for your trouble."

"Trouble?" Zinni said. "Trust me, sir, it's anything but trouble."

Aroska had to agree. It was no trouble because it saved them a trip to Aubin, the desert world they usually called home for the duration of the service term. Ordinarily, they would have traveled straight there to set up shop before looking into any HSP intel and pursuing cases on their own, but for the past few terms, going there had been...difficult, to say the least. Every time he'd looked out at the sprawling desert, he'd had to fight away memories of his near-death at the hands of the Durutians. Based on the amount of time Skeet had spent gazing out over the sand, he felt the same. And, of course, thinking of that close call in turn sparked memories of their subsequent rescue by *her*.

Damn it, he couldn't get her out of his head today.

"We're listening," Skeet said, leaning over the table and giving Starcer his full attention.

"I run a materials development center on Delatori," the man began. "Carbon composites, flex-steel, heat-resistant plating, you name it. Our primary buyers are vehicle manufacturers, specifically combat vehicles, both land- and air-based. It's one of several centers in the area, and Delatori as a whole is known for its high volume of materials exports."

"Delatori," Skeet mused. "That's Niiosian Mob territory, right?"

Starcer winced. "It is. And, admittedly, many of our buyers have direct ties to the Mob. But it makes for good business. They pay well for our products, and we're able to keep producing and expanding. So, yes, you could say we've been absorbed into their network."

"And where exactly do we come in?" Aroska asked.

"How much do you know about the Ibarra Cartel?"

The name sounded vaguely familiar—Aroska felt he had become more attuned to galaxy-wide events since transferring to spec ops—but Starcer's tone almost made the question seem rhetorical. Skeet and Zinni remained silent as well.

"Ibarra has been encroaching on our...the *Mob's* territory for the past few years, though things have escalated more recently. They're a bunch of gun runners, and they do all of their own manufacturing, so they've got considerable firepower and have gained the support of all the smaller groups they supply. Their leader is a man named Manes. Alastair Manes. Young, charismatic, ambitious. Apparently, he inherited the position when he killed his own father. Word is he's got his sights set on Tobias's spot too."

"A gang war?" Skeet said, unimpressed. "I'm still not sure if I see how this affects us."

Desperation flashed through Starcer's eyes. "Manes recently made a push for Delatori. He targeted many of the development centers, including mine, and threatened to destroy them if we didn't start producing for him. I thought if he wanted the materials he wouldn't actually go through with that threat, and I was stupid enough to lead a revolt. Most of the other distribution managers are still loyal to Niio—Tobias may not be an upstanding citizen himself, but he takes care of us. I had a good following, but Manes had an army, and he decided if he couldn't have our materials, no one could. His men came through and decimated everything they didn't need, and now that there's less resistance, they're there trying to salvage whatever they can. Delatori is a war zone right now. Most of the settlements have been evacuated."

He stopped to take a deep breath and gripped the edge of the table to still his trembling hands. "As if that wasn't enough, Manes put hits out on all the managers. He claims it was to stop the revolts at the source, but I believe he's just doing it because he can. Most of the others have been killed already. It's possible I'm the only one left."

That still didn't tell Aroska why the man needed *them* specifically, and he watched as Skeet's eyes narrowed. "With all due respect, sir, personal protection detail is a little below our pay grade," the burly lieutenant said.

Emeri stepped forward as if to intervene, but Starcer continued without assistance. "It's not just that. Manes's assassin, the one who's been carrying out all of these hits...she's Haphezian."

The three of them shifted and threw each other curious looks.

"I've heard the old saying 'it takes a Haphezian to kill a Haphezian,' so I knew I would need to come straight to the source for aid, and I'm grateful to your superiors for recommending a team of your caliber.

See, Manes himself doesn't concern me at the moment, at least not on the level this woman does. I have a set of schematics—a physical copy of specs stored in a secure location—that I was due to deliver to a Niiosian manufacturer, and I think it could help give Tobias an edge over these Ibarra thugs. I need the assassin dealt with so I can return to Delatori and see to it that those plans don't fall into the wrong hands."

He paused, and in that instant, Aroska saw his composure wilt away. "Please. I'm the one Manes wants, but he had my daughter killed in hopes of getting me to surrender, and I haven't heard from my son in four days. He was supposed to leave Delatori just after I did. He stayed behind to run interference and throw this assassin off my trail, but—" his jaw trembled "—I don't think he ever made it off-world."

Both Skeet and Zinni were standing up a little straighter than they had been initially, and Aroska's interest in the story had suddenly been rekindled as well. "What more do you know about this woman?" he asked.

"She's a ghost. She made quick work of the other managers, and she knows how to stay out of the spotlight. I've never had the misfortune of encountering her myself, but those who have seen her—the ones who are still alive—describe her as brutal. Savage. Rumor has it she goes by Matia Moryi."

The four Haphezians in the room exchanged a glance. "*Matia kahn zymoryi*," Skeet said.

"What?"

It was an archaic phrase that had to do with heavenly bodies and was specifically used in reference to solar eclipses; with five moons, they were fairly commonplace on Haphez. But based on what they'd just learned about this assassin, Aroska guessed the name had a darker meaning. He cleared his throat. "Literal Standard translation would be 'she who brings the night'."

Starcer's face turned ashen, and he finally settled into one of the chairs surrounding the table. "She certainly does that, doesn't she."

"Per Royal Officer Ganten, you are to find Moryi and investigate her," Emeri instructed, allowing Starcer a few moments of respite. "The crimes she has committed, however heinous, have not been against

Haphez, so we currently have no grounds for arrest or prosecution. But anyone with her skills is either ex-military or ex-agency, and the Royal House agrees that neither the GA nor HSP needs our names sullied by a rogue individual. Look for something we can bring her in on, and bring her in alive. Lethal force is to be used only as a last resort."

"Pardon me for asking, sir," Zinni piped in, "but what good will it do to take Moryi out of play? Manes will just keep sending assassins until he gets what he wants."

"The key is to buy me some time," Starcer said. "The Niiosians have other development centers at their disposal. If I'm able to return to Delatori and recover those specs, I can help provide the firepower and defenses they need to keep the Cartel at bay. But right now, Moryi is the biggest barrier. Manes knows I had extra projects going on the side and that the work was connected to Niio. He may be rather enigmatic, but he's notoriously tenacious, *and* manipulative. He'll just send Moryi back to Delatori to wait for me to show my face, to wait for me to think the coast is clear. If she's out of the picture, I'll have time to do what I need to do." He paused and took in a shaky breath. "Please. I don't want my children to have died for nothing."

For involving neutral worlds, the situation was starting to feel awfully political. Pledging too much allegiance to certain independent systems was nearly as bad as falling under the Federation's control, and Aroska dreaded the idea of having HSP associated too closely with the Niiosian Mob. Taking sides in such a large-scale gang war seemed unwise. But it wasn't like they were allying themselves directly with Tobias—their actions would merely enable someone else to *maintain* a preexisting alliance, and an unofficial one at that—and it wasn't like the agency itself was taking a stance. The Royal House had delegated this case to a spec ops team for a reason; they would complete their mission, remove the threat posed by this Matia Moryi in one way or another, and the agency could always maintain deniability if things took a turn for the worse, especially because it was an independent service term. Besides, after Tobias's contribution in the battle against the Resistance fleet, doing him a tiny favor couldn't be all that bad.

"Do you think Moryi is still on Delatori?" he said. He expected his next thought to be harder to articulate, but the words came out with surprising ease. "Would she have just stayed there to wait after she killed your son?"

Starcer's eyes had glazed over as he stared ahead at the table. "She could be, but I was the last of the managers in that particular region, and my son...he bought me enough time that I doubt she knows where I went. She's either still following my trail, trying to figure out where I am, or she went back to report to Manes. He's currently based on Panuco. The Cartel has several major outposts, but Panuco is..."

Everything after the word 'Panuco' was garbled noise in Aroska's ears. His heart rate quickened and a chill surged down his spine. Out of the corner of his eye, he saw Skeet and Zinni both turn and glance at him, though he didn't dare showcase his thoughts by meeting their gazes. He cleared his throat and shrugged, hoping to direct their attention back toward their client. "Find Moryi and look for a reason to bring her in. Seems simple enough."

"Mr. Starcer will remain here in protective custody until you have completed your assignment," Emeri said. "He'll be waiting for an all-clear signal."

"And please," Starcer said, "I hope you'll move as quickly as possible. I'm prepared to offer additional compensation if this is all over within ten days."

Ten days was pushing it. It would take between four and five to even reach Ibarra-controlled space, leaving them only five more to investigate Moryi, let alone find her. But if they went straight to Panuco.... It gave Aroska an idea.

"We're on it, then," Skeet said.

The director turned his attention to Starcer. "The agency and the Royal House thank you for bringing this issue to our attention. Unless you have any other information you believe would benefit us, you are dismissed. My aide is waiting outside and will show you to your accommodations."

The man nodded and drew his hands down over his face before rising to his feet. The air of gratitude he projected didn't quite conceal his defeated posture and the vacant look in his eyes. "Thank you all for your work on this," he managed.

They watched as he made his way to the door, moving as if he were in a fog, and met up with his two security guards outside. The door shut behind him, casting the office into silence.

Aroska glanced to Emeri, aware the team hadn't been dismissed but intrigued by the look on the director's face. The man leaned over the table, his focus directed downward as if he were trying to gather himself. Both Skeet and Zinni seemed to notice this as well and shifted uncomfortably.

Skeet cleared his throat. "Sir?"

"As you all know, ops division hierarchy has been...volatile for a while now," Emeri answered without looking up.

It was all he needed to say for them to understand the sudden melancholy. Ever since the Resistance attack four years earlier, there'd been a shift among not only HSP agents but the Grand Army and, frankly, the entire Haphezian population. While numbers were currently back to being relatively normal, the year or so immediately following the battle with Ronan had seen a staggering three-hundred-percent increase in recruitment for both HSP and the GA. In the agency's case specifically, a high percentage of recruits were actually passing elite training, which meant ops team rosters were continually full. That in turn created a system of competition among teams, which meant the team hierarchy was changing almost constantly. Aroska did the math for a moment—his team had held Alpha status for six years now if he counted the time before he'd joined. Once upon a time, that would have been a fairly average stint, but considering the circumstances now, he was sometimes surprised they'd been able to hold on to the Alpha title for as long as they had.

It wasn't that their team had gotten worse, not by a long shot—they'd been just as motivated as everyone else, perhaps even more so thanks to their personal stakes in the fight against the Resistance. It was merely a matter of now having a number of other teams who were so close to matching them in skill that the differences were growing nearly indistinguishable. Obviously that was something to be proud of from a patriotic standpoint, but it also meant there was an ever-present threat of losing their title. 'Threat' was probably too strong of a word, though Aroska couldn't help but think of it in that manner.

"Does our Alpha status hinge on this mission?" he asked, positive he was voicing what Skeet and Zinni were both thinking as well.

"Evaluations are taking place this quarter, yes," Emeri answered. "Your independent service term as a whole was going to be the deciding factor, but…"

Skeet crossed his arms. "Will we *lose* Alpha status if we fail this mission?"

Aroska hadn't wanted to be so blunt, but there it was.

"I wouldn't put it in those exact terms," the director said. He straightened and looked them each in the eye, having apparently recovered from the initial displeasure of bringing up a difficult topic.

"As I mentioned earlier, Officer Ganten has ordered that Moryi be brought in alive, with lethal action to be used only as a last resort. I realize that seems a bit uncharacteristic when your role is often to permanently neutralize threats, but so far there's been no indication that she's a Defective, and a Haphezian citizen working for an organization like the Ibarra Cartel is cause for concern. The goal is to deliver her to Haphor and learn everything we can about her to ensure we're not dealing with a breach of security. Letting her die will be considered mission failure except under very specific conditions, such as a drastic self-defense situation."

"I can only assume such a case would at least warrant a review," Zinni said.

"Of course it would. But with the state this division is in now, there's just no guarantee a review would help. It will simply depend on the exact circumstances."

While Aroska could feel his resolve strengthening already, another part of him couldn't help but be apprehensive about all of this. They'd dealt with the looming threat of a downgrade for nearly four years now, so it wasn't like this was a new issue. But there was something generally unpleasant about the word 'failure,' and he didn't want to see it as the documented reason for said downgrade.

To top it all off, the idea that had formed after Starcer's mention of Panuco was slowly taking hold, digging its roots deeper into his mind. It was an insane thought, and he needed to mull it over somewhere other than here when he was supposed to be actively engaged in the conversation. It was growing harder and harder to focus as the minutes passed.

"Listen," Emeri continued, "I'm not under any illusion that this won't be an incredibly difficult task. Obviously it would benefit us to have Moryi taken out of play as quickly as possible—Starcer's timetable is tight, albeit not unattainable. But as far as I'm concerned, you have the entire service term to get the job done as long as you do exactly that. I'm prepared to do everything in my power on this end to help you succeed."

The corners of Aroska's mouth curled upward. "You favoring our team, Director?" he asked, well aware such a thing was strictly forbidden.

Emeri's face didn't change, but the amusement was clear in his eyes. "Absolutely not. I don't want to see any of my operatives fail. What kind of agency head would I be otherwise?" Then the amused flicker vanished, and he cast his gaze downward once more. When he spoke again, his voice was low, his tone flat. "I want you three to be incredibly cautious with this. There's not a lot of intel on this Manes character aside from what Starcer has told us, but from the looks of it, the man's a manipulative bastard. Whether he has a way with words or whether it's his actions that keep people in line, I don't know. What I do know is that not just anyone can unite an entire sector of independent Fringe worlds and maintain sufficient control over them. I would advise against dealing too closely with the Niiosians and their allies for the same reason. You're already treading on the brink with this mission— the last thing we need is to get dragged any further into this conflict."

"Understood, sir," Skeet said.

"I'll provide you with the full report Starcer submitted to the Royal House regarding Moryi. It mainly reiterates what he told you here, but it goes into more detail about his project and work on Delatori if that's where you want to start your inquest. Under the circumstances, I'm requesting a daily sitrep so we can give Starcer regular reports and he can pass any more pertinent information on to you. Other than that,

I'm afraid I don't have anything else for you. The mission is all yours, Lieutenant Duvo."

The director gave them a deep nod of acknowledgement before moving off toward his desk. Aroska and Zinni watched him go before turning their attention to Skeet, who shrugged and checked the time.

"Take an hour to prep," he said. "Go home, grab anything you were planning on bringing in the morning, then rendezvous back here. We leave tonight."

CHAPTER 4
HSP HEADQUARTERS - Noro, Haphez

By the time they left the office, night had fallen. The three agents were silent as they made their way down to the parking bay. Torn between not wanting to waste valuable time and not wanting to seem like he was rushing, Aroska trudged along behind Skeet and Zinni, his mind abuzz. Unless he was mistaken, his teammates were quiet for the same reason he was. None of them were currently contemplating the mission itself; instead, they were each reflecting on the implications of the information they'd just learned and what failure could mean.

Getting killed would obviously be the worst-case scenario on any mission—that, or sustaining some sort of debilitating injury that put a permanent end to your days of field work and disbanded your team. But a status downgrade was often treated as a close second. Receiving Alpha status in the special operations division—and in field ops, for that matter—was one of the highest honors a group of HSP agents could ever have bestowed upon them. The title came with mission priority and enhanced benefits and pay, not to mention simply having the *distinction*. It wasn't that any of the other ops teams were bad or unskilled by any means, but Alpha status simply wasn't something one wanted to let go of, especially after all the work it had taken to get there in the first place. There'd been some hard feelings among other spec ops agents when Aroska had first joined their ranks on a permanent basis, but after learning he'd been directly endorsed by a woman who was widely regarded as one of the best operatives in agency history, they'd calmed down.

The three of them reached the bay level and stepped out of the elevator, and it was like the chime of the bell snapped them all out of some sort of daze. Aroska opened his mouth to speak, but Skeet turned to face him and held up a hand for silence, orange eyes imploring him to listen.

"Look. I know you want to be excited, and believe me, Starcer got my attention when he mentioned Panuco too. But you can't get your hopes up."

"I know."

"How long has it even been?" Zinni asked quietly.

"Almost a full year. I know it's a long shot, but maybe we'll at least find a clue."

"I can't have you distracted," Skeet said, though his tone remained surprisingly soft. "Maybe we can head to Panuco for a couple of days after this mess is cleaned up, but for now I need your focus on this mission where it belongs."

"And that's where it will be."

Skeet sighed and gave him a faint smile of understanding. "I don't suppose it would do much good to tell you to get some rest once we're underway."

"Probably not."

"Well then, both of you go get prepped. Report to the situation room in one hour."

They continued on their way, each of them moving off toward their own vehicles. Aroska picked up his pace, some mixture of apprehension and genuine excitement propelling him forward. Skeet was absolutely right; he shouldn't be getting his hopes up, but it was hard to *not* be eager in this situation. The feeling of simultaneously wanting to know everything and not wanting to know anything left his stomach tied in an uneasy knot.

It took him a mere ten minutes to reach his new apartment downtown. It could hardly be called 'new,' considering he'd lived there for over four years, but he'd lived in his previous house since leaving his family and beginning his career, so this place still felt new by comparison. He rode the elevator to his floor and let himself through his front door, pausing a moment to take a deep breath and admire what he could see of the Noro skyline through the massive window across the living room. Opting to leave the lighting panels off, he moved silently through the kitchen and into the hallway, guided by the glow of the city lights.

He'd never been a man of many possessions, and he'd chosen to leave many of his belongings behind when he'd moved. Too many sour memories. That left him with excess storage space, something he'd been concerned about at first—the apartment had felt so empty. But throughout the past four years, he'd found a way to fill the void, both figuratively and literally.

His bedroom was dark as well, though with a large window similar to the one in the living room, ambient light from outside still allowed him to see without trouble. He veered toward his closet, a space twice as big as his old one and thus only half as full. He wasn't entirely sure why he felt obligated to keep this project hidden—Skeet and Zinni obviously knew what he was up to. Still, there was a certain intimacy about it that compelled him to keep it private, locked away in this tiny space rather than left in the open.

As he parted the closet doors, he had to squint against the greenish-blue light emitted by the screens and monitors he'd set up inside. His clothes had all been pushed to the far side to make way for the mobile workstation. The sleek terminal mounted on it had been running constantly since about two weeks after the destruction of the *Intrepid*. On a screen above it, images and video feeds flashed by so quickly he could hardly see them while a set of algorithms searched for familiar physical features. Beside that screen, two smaller ones displayed lists of saved files. Ship manifests. Med center records. Law enforcement chatter. Not just from Haphez, but from all over the Fringe. The algorithms were all agency-grade, and he'd surely be reprimanded for using HSP resources for personal purposes if anyone besides his teammates found out about it, but he didn't care. When he'd received *her* note, been led to believe she was still alive, sitting idly by had been the last thing he wanted to do. She'd told him not to come after her, but that didn't mean he wasn't going to do everything in his power to find her from afar. This system did all the work and allowed him to go about his life, check in every so often, and not let the search itself consume him. A win-win scenario.

He'd sorted the data into three categories: useless, potentially useful, and legitimate clues. There were only two of the latter, and 'legitimate' was a bit of a stretch. Both were surveillance photos taken from a distance and too grainy to actually see clearly, but he had a gut feeling. Those remained fixed at the top of the screen while the system continued combing through a seemingly endless string of other images looking for similarities, and any corresponding data had been bundled together and attached accordingly.

He would let the machine continue doing its work while he was gone, he decided, in case he didn't find anything during the trip—that seemed like a satisfactory balance between optimism and realism. He unlocked the strongbox up on the closet shelf and began to rifle through it, allowing his fingers to briefly come to rest on the weapon it contained—a certain melee weapon he should by no means have in his possession and which he'd in fact lied about having. With a sigh, he found the secure memory stick he sought and copied all of his current findings over to it, thinking it wise to keep all of this information close under these circumstances. Then, heart racing for reasons he couldn't explain, he reached out and tapped one of the screens, expanding the cluster of files attached to the more recent of the two surveillance photos. His eyes pored over the material within, studying it as if he hadn't already spent countless hours and sleepless nights doing so. There was a tightness in his chest, an excitement that threatened to seize control of his entire being, but it was immediately countered by what he could only describe as dread. This internal battle was something he'd grown accustomed to during his hunt for clues, but the thought of all his labor finally producing some fruit made it exponentially worse. All of the data in this file pointed to a place he would never have expected and never imagined going himself, until now.

Panuco.

Chapter 5
Commercial Sector - Tabaco, Panuco

The drunken voices around her had all morphed into a single, deafening roar. She'd been waiting there for half an hour, and the resulting headache made her wince. The bar seemed twice as crowded as it normally was at this time of day, accounting for twice as much noise. According to what little she'd heard of a coherent conversation earlier, most of the patrons were gamblers who had just won various bets at some sort of sporting event. A race, maybe. She didn't really care.

All the other stools at the serving counter where she sat were occupied. The man on her right let out a hearty laugh and toasted with his friend before turning to stumble away, elbowing her in the shoulder in the process. She drew a deep breath in through her nose and released it slowly, not in the mood for confrontation. The idea that she could snap his neck if she wanted brought her plenty of comfort, and she once again let her gaze flit over to the door at the back of the establishment. She checked the time. They never made her wait this long.

She watched the door for a few more seconds before lowering her gaze to the glass of liquor she'd been absentmindedly pushing around on the surface of the counter. The bartender had simply left it there and nodded toward a man several seats down. He'd been eyeing her flirtatiously for a while and trying to carry on a conversation from a distance, but all the noise had made it impossible to hear him and easy to ignore him. Out of curiosity, she turned to see if he was still there and was startled when he slid into the now-vacant seat beside her.

"What do you say you and I get out of here?"

Well, he didn't waste any time. His breath reeked of alcohol as he rattled on. She shut her eyes and heaved another sigh; as much as she hated walking through that back door, she almost welcomed the thought now. It wasn't too hard to brush off his continuous advances—she was no stranger to the concept of waiting at this counter amid the establishment's more...*unrefined* clientele. But given the current circumstances, he was trying her patience.

"Come on, baby. What do you like to do? We'll do whatever you want."

She tensed when she felt his hand come to rest on her thigh and pictured herself wrenching his arm around backwards before slamming him down against the bar and driving her knife through his shoulder. Or maybe it would be better to just shoot him. Her left hand slid from the counter and came to rest on the cold metal casing of the pistol holstered against her leg. The sensation sent a series of images flashing through her mind. Shafts of silver moonlight cutting through the dark forest. That sitting room with the ornate cabinet. The man lying on his back in a pool of his own blood.

She was drawn back to the present when the stranger's hand slid around the small of her back. She forced herself to relax and finally turned to face him, putting on the sincerest smile she could muster. "Whatever I want?"

The man's face brightened, and he seemed to take her sudden openness as an invitation to move even closer. "Anything," he crooned, his breath hot and stale. "What do you like to do?"

She hummed good-naturedly and gritted her teeth behind a closed-lipped smirk. "I like to hunt," she answered, leaning toward him.

"Oh, a girl who can handle a gun," he said with a sly grin. "What's your game? Mirax? Red hoppers? Something bigger...orofins?"

She laughed as if the answer was obvious and brought her mouth to within a centimeter of his ear. "People," she whispered.

In that instant, the faux smile fell away from her face and she leaned back, returning her attention to her drink on the counter. Out of the corner of her eye, she saw the man's countenance change as well as he slid backwards off the stool and stumbled off in the direction from which he'd originally come. *Good riddance,* she thought, turning her glass in a slow circle and risking yet another glance at the back door. Still nothing. She let her gaze rove back toward her would-be suitor, hoping to catch a glimpse of whatever horrified expression remained on his face, but the moment of euphoria was a fleeting one. The man stood with two others who had been seated at a nearby table, whispering instructions and glancing her way with eyebrows drawn. Upon closer inspection, he was someone of high status—perhaps the son of some politician who was used to spending his parents' money and getting his way—and these men were his bodyguards. The two thugs watched her as their client spoke to them, silently warning her that even something as petty as hurting his feelings had been a bad idea.

She sighed and pushed her glass down the counter as she rose to her feet, certain someone would gladly finish it for her. As she'd expected, the two bodyguards rose as well, positioning themselves to intercept her regardless of which direction she headed.

As much as she wanted to avoid a fight, she felt a certain part of herself come alive in response to their movements. She watched the rest of the crowd in her peripherals; despite the heavily inebriated state of most of the bar's patrons, many of them had begun to cautiously back away upon sensing the impending conflict.

She wasn't entirely sure where to go. Remaining seated would only draw the bodyguards toward her, and if interaction with them was inevitable, she preferred to do it on her own terms. Leaving the building would just make her late for her meeting. She wondered if perhaps letting herself through the back door would work, but entering uninvited could very well land her in worse trouble. It was her only real choice at the moment though. That, or neutralize the two thugs right here in the middle of the crowd. With as foul a mood as she was in, neither option seemed the least bit appealing.

She hadn't made it two steps before the nearest bodyguard began to approach. Her hands curled into fists and she veered toward him in return, taking slow, methodical steps and maintaining eye contact. Her muscles twitched, ready to be put to action, but she willed herself calm and held her arms loose at her sides, focusing on keeping her breathing even.

As she came within a meter of the man, she took a slight step to her left in hopes of showing him she had no real interest in a confrontation. He apparently had other plans; he mirrored her movements and took up a stance in front of her, forcing her to either face him or turn back the way she had come.

She stopped, drawing a deep breath in an attempt to quell the wave of raw rage she felt welling up inside of her. After botching her latest mission and enduring the long wait and harassment for the past half hour, her patience had officially run out.

She ran her gaze up the man's body, starting with his boots where they were firmly planted on the floor and ending with his shaved head that almost seemed too small in contrast to his thick neck and bulging traps. *Built for strength, not for speed.* He wore a cross-draw holster in a harness under his left arm. *Even slower.*

The man gazed at her through narrowed eyes, jaw set as he completed his own assessment of her.

"You're in my way," she said, voice low. The crowd around them had quieted to the point that she was sure he could hear her. The way some of the onlookers squirmed told her *they* certainly could.

"You think you're funny?" the thug growled, jerking his head toward his client. He crossed his arms, reinforcing the barrier his thick body had already formed. The second bodyguard took up position several steps behind him, prepared to intercept her if she somehow made it past the first man.

"I've been informed many times that I have no sense of humor." She angled for the narrow space between the man and the edge of the counter, wondering if he might by some miracle be intimidated by a sudden advance.

He wasn't. He shifted his weight and turned slightly to keep his body perpendicular to hers, then his hand shot out and closed around her right bicep. She ground her teeth and glanced down at his meaty fingers, silently noting that this was his dominant hand.

Allowing him to maintain his grip on her, she pivoted and ducked under his arm, yanking it around behind him. The muscular limb gave her some resistance, but it was no match for the speed with which she'd moved. A grotesque pop emanated from his shoulder. She jabbed the heel of her boot into the backs of his knees, forcing his forward momentum to send him down against the bar. With her left hand, she pinned the now-screaming man to the counter, keeping his arm folded at a severe angle behind his back. With her right, she drew the combat knife from the sheath on her thigh and drove it through the back of his shoulder, just as she'd fantasized about doing to his employer.

All of this had transpired in *maybe* two seconds, and she knew it wouldn't be long before the second thug reacted, assuming he wasn't coming at her already. She stepped back from the writhing man and, in one fluid movement, drew both her pistol and his on her way down into a crouch. One round from the confiscated plasma pistol went into the second bodyguard's right kneecap. A round from her own suppressed projectile pistol went into his left. The man collapsed onto the floor and hollered, grasping desperately at both blown-out knees. A dark pool of blood began to spread under the leg the bullet had penetrated. His own gun, another plasma pistol, lay on the floor beside him, forgotten for the moment.

She rose up slowly, holstering her weapon and sweeping the commandeered plasma gun between the two thugs. The one on the bar wouldn't be going anywhere soon; the long knife blade had passed cleanly through his locked shoulder and had embedded itself in the surface of the counter. He could only scream and flail his left arm at the bartender, who had stood motionless and watched the scene unfold with a horrified expression. The man on the floor had gone pale but still managed to snarl a curse at her as she bent down to retrieve his weapon. She was tempted to respond with one of her own, but the back door opened—*finally*—and drew her attention.

"Moryi!" barked the woman who had emerged. Kimbra Soto was big—tall, broad, muscular—and, though she hated to admit it, unmistakably Haphezian. There were some things about a person that never changed, regardless of how long they'd been away from their homeworld, and her build and posture were prime examples. Her sage-green eyes tended to take on an icy-blue quality given the right lighting. They certainly did now as she stood there surveying the room with her hands on her hips. The look on her face shifted from one of shock to one of anger and disgust, and her thoughts were displayed clearly: *Not again.*

Kimbra watched as she tucked each of the pistols into the spacious cargo pockets in her tactical pants. She moved toward the back door, eyeing the man who had started all of this as he cowered under the table his bodyguards had been seated at. He watched her pass from behind trembling hands.

She pushed past Kimbra, shooting the other woman a scowl in the process, and found herself in a dim service corridor. The space opened up into a storeroom for drinks and non-perishable food, and beyond that, the door of an office stood ajar. She angled for it, pausing just long enough to heave a short sigh before stepping inside.

CHAPTER 6
COMMERCIAL SECTOR - Tabaco, Panuco

All the screens projected from the desk showed live security feeds from somewhere in or around the main bar. Alastair Manes kept his gaze fixed on one in particular even as the visitors entered his office, watching as one brutish man writhed and bled all over his floor and another writhed and bled all over his serving counter. A couple of bystanders were currently attempting to dislodge a long knife from the shoulder of the latter.

"Matia," he said. The word presented itself as more of an exasperated sigh than a name. "Matia, Matia."

The office fell silent for a moment as Kimbra slid around to fold her arms and lean against the back of his chair. Together they watched as Matia Moryi came to a stop in front of the desk, hands resting on her hips as she met each of their gazes in turn, her fiery eyes burning with a familiar defiance. She was a formidable woman, even for a Haphezian, a quality he'd had no trouble getting used to. Her perpetual scowl combined with a wild hairstyle and the war paint she wore on her face made most people—sober people with control of their faculties, anyway—think twice about giving her and, subsequently, him trouble. It made her a useful tool, albeit one that had certainly not been necessary in this instance.

He sighed again and pinched the bridge of his nose between his thumb and forefinger. "Sometimes I wonder if you're worth all the trouble you cause." He gestured at the screen. "This? This is bad for business."

She gave the security feed a disinterested glance before easing into the chair opposite him and draping one leg over the other. Asserting herself, as always. Damn but she could be infuriating.

"Did I invite you to sit?"

"No," she answered, "no you didn't. But you did tell me you'd make sure all your customers know to keep their hands off of me."

"I have. Trust me, all of my regulars know to steer clear. But when we have visitors from the illustrious Core in our midst, the rules change."

There was a palpable shift in the room as all three of them stirred uncomfortably at the mere mention of the Core. These people here today were simply tourists; he'd had them watched the moment reports of their arrival began flooding his office, then followed for the duration of their short visit. Some rich, rebellious chump had apparently hired a couple of goons to accompany him as he made his first excursion out into the Fringe, almost as if he were on safari. He was harmless but stupid, and while Manes didn't blame Matia for reacting the way she had, the last thing anyone around here needed was to have garnered the attention of any of the Federation-controlled Core worlds.

"I do not want to see anything like this happen again," he went on. "Is that clear?"

Matia clenched her jaw and watched him for a moment as if waiting for an 'or else,' but it never came. And if Manes was honest with himself, it never would. He'd never admit it directly, but he needed her. He'd demanded her loyalty as penance for killing her predecessor, his favorite enforcer, but over time he'd granted her a certain level of autonomy in order for her to perform the full scope of her duties, a level of autonomy that meant she could walk away at any moment. He'd once threatened to send the full force of Ibarra after her if she ever tried to leave, but realistically he knew she was skilled enough that such a venture would be a monumental waste of resources. She was a valuable tool, just as he'd been contemplating a moment earlier, a weapon he did not want to lose. And as the head of a cartel that specialized in the creation and movement of weapons, he liked to think he knew a thing or two about taking care of them. Ergo he found himself cutting back on the threats more and more often so as not to drive her away, resorting instead to speaking to her like a child.

He reached over and minimized the security feeds, though not before he noticed someone had managed to dislodge her blade from the bodyguard's shoulder. "Tell me about Delatori," he said, folding his ring-adorned hands on the surface of the desk.

She leaned back and brought her elbow to rest on the top of her chair. "I went to the development center as you ordered. A man fled when I arrived, and I pursued him on foot out into the forest. There was a small, isolated neighborhood and he took refuge in one of the deserted homes. I cornered him and killed him." She paused and met his expectant stare, shifting her attention up to Kimbra for a moment as well. "It wasn't Starcer."

Manes sighed and lowered his gaze, raking a hand back through his greased hair.

"A search of the body indicated that it was his son," she continued. "I believe this man purposely stationed himself there in order to throw us off Starcer's trail. His comm logs revealed that he was due to meet a shuttle in the city, presumably so he himself could escape, but by the time I made it to the rendezvous location, the ship was already gone."

She didn't blink as Manes lifted his head and scowled. "You didn't—oh, I don't know—*ask* him where his father went?"

"He wouldn't have told me," Matia retorted, narrowing her eyes. "This was the second time one of Starcer's children volunteered to act as bait for us, or else the second time *he* forced them to act as bait. The man is a coward, and these people obviously knew how high the stakes were when they chose to defend him. They've both clearly been willing to die for him and I wasn't going to waste my time with an interrogation after I'd already chased this man for three kilometers on foot."

Kimbra shifted against the chair behind him. "You losing your touch, Moryi?" she scoffed. "It shouldn't be this hard to kill one man."

Manes turned long enough to send her a scolding glare, then hurried to continue before the two women could launch into one of their all-too-common rounds of bickering. "Matia is right. Pahl Starcer has already demonstrated an extraordinary aptitude for self-preservation, and the probability is high that he's no longer on Delatori. The most important thing is that we've once again kept him from accessing the schematics he was planning to provide the Niiosians with. If he wants to recover them, he'll have to return to his office. We'll know the moment he does."

Across the desk, he saw a brief flicker of disappointment in Matia's eyes before she straightened and stood. "I'll leave right away, then."

"No, you'll stay here. We have spies on Delatori who are more than capable of relaying information. You've done excellent work throughout the past couple of weeks. Stay here and unwind, but be prepared to depart again if our contacts discover where those specs are stored. I'll arrange for proper payment to be transferred to your account."

She looked him in the eye for a moment as if searching for sincerity in his words. He *had* meant to be somewhat condescending, though his tone had betrayed that more than he'd intended. While he was perfectly sincere in his praise for the results she'd been eliciting lately, this business—or lack thereof—with Pahl Starcer was beginning to grate on him, enough to turn even a cordial conversation sour.

"You've done good work, Matia," he repeated, sensing her apprehension as she tried and failed to read him. "We may not be precisely where we want to be at the moment, but we've certainly made progress, and we still have the advantage."

He felt Kimbra shift once more. The woman was fierce, often abrasive, and was his favorite enforcer to date, but she could be so petty when it came to matters of him heaping praise on anyone but her. Truth be told, before Matia's arrival, Kimbra had been the sole recipient of much of that praise; in that sense, her behavior was justified considering how long she'd been faithful to him and how infrequently he genuinely complimented anyone.

Matia sent the woman a cold glare before returning her attention to Manes. "We done here?"

He folded his hands in front of his mouth and dipped his head.

With a terse nod, she turned and strode from the room under the scrutiny of several of his soldiers who had arrived in the hall outside, standing by to make sure she didn't do to their leader what she'd just done to the two men in the bar. She walked with squared shoulders and her head held high as she passed them, matching—if not surpassing—many of them in height. Despite the brutish physique of most of his security detail, she had nothing to fear from any of them, a fact she seemed to enjoy ensuring they were all aware of. In fact, despite the confidence she always projected, Manes was relatively sure *he* was the only person on this planet she was truly afraid of, and that was likely from a psychological perspective, not a physical one. That was fine with him. It was part of what kept her here.

His attention shifted to Kimbra as she stepped out from behind him and perched on the edge of his desk, staring down at him with her arms folded. She gnawed on the inside of her lip for a moment as if pondering how to be appropriately tactful in what she was about to say. For once.

"We've talked about this," she muttered.

"And I seem to remember telling you not to worry about it."

"But Pahl Starcer—"

"—is not currently of any concern." He forced the last syllable out through clenched teeth, tired of repeating this same old argument with her. "Our hold on Delatori has been solid for a number of weeks now. One man is not going to make a difference. Besides, one can't help but admire his tenacity."

She straightened and waved one arm toward the door in exasperation. "You know how easily she cut down the other managers," she said, lowering her voice to an agitated whisper. "No amount of 'tenacity' should have kept her from getting to him too."

Manes rose, jaw set. Kimbra still had a slight height advantage, but the way she almost imperceptibly shrank away from him made her seem smaller. He brought his face to within centimeters of hers and took her jaw between his thumb and forefinger, forcing her to look him in the eye. "If I have to speak to you again about this juvenile popularity contest between you two…"

As with Matia, he found himself unwilling to ever threaten Kimbra too harshly—she was still his most prized asset, truthfully more valuable than Matia due to the unfailing loyalty she'd demonstrated to him over the course of many years, as well as the sense of companionship she often provided in a more…intimate sense. But there were times when his patience with her personality simply ran out.

He loosened his grip ever so slightly, in turn prompting her to relax ever so slightly. She dipped her head, allowing him to lean in and brush his lips over hers. Whatever fragrance she wore didn't quite mask the underlying scents of plasma fire and blood—the perfect combination of lethal and sensual. But now was neither the time nor the place for this, and he was irritated enough with her that he couldn't quite bring himself to enjoy her company. He lingered there against her for another moment before releasing her and stepping away.

She steeled herself and held his gaze for another couple of seconds before turning and striding toward the door. "I sincerely hope I don't end up having to say 'I told you so'."

Manes watched her depart and then slowly lowered himself back into his chair, curling his hands into fists and releasing them a couple of times before bringing the security screens back up. One of the feeds depicted Matia as she exited through the service door and made her way back across the restaurant. The two injured bodyguards were currently being hauled out the front door by several Ibarra soldiers. Under normal circumstances, they would just be dumped outside and left to fend for themselves, but if they were really part of a group visiting from one of the Core worlds, he imagined he should actually spring for medical treatment just to avoid problems. On another screen, he could see their client still standing near the bar, quivering and looking bewildered as he glanced between his departing escorts and the puddles of blood on the floor.

Satisfied that order seemed to have been restored for the time being, he moved to minimize the screens again, but he paused with his hand hovering over the controls when he saw his bartender beckon to Matia. She approached and accepted a narrow bundle he offered, unwrapping it to reveal her knife, still coated in tacky blood. Flipping it over in her hand, she gave him a nod of thanks, cast the bloody rag aside, and strode toward the man from the Core.

Manes tensed, ready to call someone to intervene—or to intervene himself—if the situation escalated any further. But Matia moved with a calm grace, prompting him to relax. Nonetheless, the visitor flinched when he saw her coming and turned to run, but in his clearly intoxicated state, he ran headlong into one of the stationary bar stools. Trapped against the counter, he could only stand there with wide eyes as she moved up and silently towered over him, their bodies centimeters apart. Without breaking eye contact, she reached down and took hold of the hem of his dress jacket, wiping the bloody blade back and forth across it before slipping the knife back into its sheath on her thigh. She glanced down toward his legs, and upon closer inspection, Manes saw a wet stain spreading down his pants and a puddle forming at his feet.

With that, Matia turned and made her way across the room, disappearing from the feed as she reached the door and left the building. Manes couldn't help but grin as he closed the projection for good and leaned back in his chair. She could be so manipulative—a woman after his own heart—and whenever he began to doubt her capabilities, it was the little gestures like this that convinced him this was where she truly belonged.

Chapter 7
2 Years Ago - Tabaco, Panuco

The creak of the walls and the scrape of a door opening manually snapped her to attention. She blinked and turned toward the sound, squinting against the shaft of light that cut through the darkness of the corridor. The angle was bad; from here, she couldn't get a clear view of who—or what—might be entering. The glare of the light was excruciating anyway. After spending at least two days locked up, her eyes had finally adjusted to the gloom enough that she could make out shapes and shadows, but this new development had just sent her back to square one. Bright spots floated in her vision even when she closed her eyes, and she reached up to shield her face.

A moment of silence preceded the sound of footsteps, soft enough that she couldn't tell whether it was a futile attempt at sneaking or simply a cautious approach. She caught a whiff of human body odor, but she was aware of an unfamiliar Haphezian scent as well—odd, considering how far from Haphez she was. Two people had entered, then, but only one of them drew closer.

The cell was completely bare, leaving her body—her own hands, feet, and teeth if need be—as her only weapon. It was often an adequate weapon, at least depending on how well the opposition was armed, but here, so disoriented, she felt a pang of fear. She clenched her jaw when she felt her *cha'sen* glands start to swell, positive this was exactly the reaction her captors had wanted.

A single figure moved toward her, an undefined silhouette blurred by the light shining behind it. She blinked and squinted, desperately trying to get a better idea of what she was looking at. The person—the human, judging by the height and posture—kept one arm extended in front of them, gripping some form of weapon. It would have to be dealt with.

The cell door opened outward. Even in total darkness, she'd been able to ascertain that much when she'd probed every centimeter of the space immediately following her incarceration. She stepped forward as the man approached, ready to use the door to her advantage the moment he opened it, but the soft *clink* of metal on metal stopped her in her tracks. The weapon he held had suddenly increased in length and one end now protruded between the cell bars; she processed all of this just a fraction of a second before a stream of blue energy shot forward from its tip. She shifted, but not before the current hit her, wracking her body and sending her to the floor. He activated the stun baton again, and she rolled over in an attempt to escape the shock. It was unlike any baton she'd ever used. It certainly had the same effect, but the ability to electrocute from a distance was new. She wasn't sure if she wanted to know what kind of damage it might cause at closer range.

The current stopped, and she could only lie there and cough for a moment, fighting off a wave of nausea and flexing her traumatized muscles in an attempt to alleviate the tingling and numbness. Behind her, she heard the coded key rod being inserted into its socket, followed by the squeal of rusty hinges as the door swung open. Instinct took over as the man entered the cell, and she lay there motionless as he drew nearer, working to slow her breathing. In the light from the end of the corridor, she could barely make out the man's shadow rising up against the wall. He began to stoop down, extending the stun baton toward her once again.

The moment before the rod touched her shoulder, she gathered all of her remaining strength and whipped around, throwing herself toward him and taking hold of the arm with the baton. She yanked it down and kicked her legs upward simultaneously, catching his torso between her calves as he stumbled forward. Using his body as an anchor, she threw him down face-first and rose up on top of him, reaching into the darkness toward the place she'd heard the metal baton collide with the stone floor. Pinning him down just long enough to leap to her feet, she grasped the weapon and jammed the tip up against the back of his neck, activating it at the base of his skull. His scream was cut off after just a split second as his body convulsed. The smell of singed hair and flesh wafted through the cell, and in the blue light cast by the electric current, she saw a thin stream of smoke rising up from his head.

"Enough!" a woman's voice commanded.

She deactivated the baton and released the man, who remained limp even as she staggered away from him. She lunged for the open door, but it slammed shut just as she reached it. A low hum echoed through the corridor, narrowly preceding the full illumination of the space. Stunned, she stumbled backward against the wall, squeezing her eyes shut to quell the pain shooting through her head. Between the shock of the baton and the shock of the light, her body was left trembling, and she couldn't help but sink to the floor.

The newcomer swore, then remained silent for several seconds; a faint tapping of fingers on a screen filled the void. "We recovered your ship," she said. "The *Talon*. Nice name." A snide chuckle. "We know who you are, Matia Moryi."

Matia bristled at the sound of her name, but rather than respond, she curled her fingers around the baton once more, aiming it in the direction of the voice. The stream of electricity cut through the space, merely a blur until it exploded and dispersed just centimeters shy of the visitor's body. An energy shield. She should have known better. She let the baton clatter back to the floor.

"That's right. Don't waste your time."

She dipped her head, shielding her face with her hand and watching the woman in her peripherals, unsure if the odd rippling sensation she saw was merely the shield settling or a product of her swimming vision. This was the Haphezian she'd smelled, no doubt about it, but the woman's appearance came as a surprise. The sides of her head were shaved, and she wore the rest of her thick blonde hair pulled back over the top of her skull and bundled into a bushy ponytail. She didn't appear to bear any *gesh punti*, but the still-rippling shield and odd shadows cast by the assorted lighting in the corridor made it impossible to see her face clearly. She wore tight, low-cut leather and was armed with two pistols and a knife, at least that Matia could immediately see. This was a woman who clearly knew how to handle herself but wasn't beyond using her physical appearance to get what she wanted as well.

"Who hired you?"

Matia coughed and worked to get her legs under her, bracing herself against the wall as she settled into a crouch. "I think it's my turn to ask a question. Who the hell are *you*?"

The woman watched her through the cell bars, staring her down like a wild animal ready to pounce on its prey. "That's not how this works."

"What is this place?"

"You've caught the attention of Alastair Manes. You might not be glad you did."

Matia tilted her head, disappointed the constant flinching left her looking so vulnerable. "Who?"

"Don't play coy with me. You were right in the middle of our operation on Zenat. You're clearly familiar with Cartel dealings."

"I have no idea what you're talking about."

Okay, maybe the vulnerability wasn't such a bad thing. She could work with this.

The woman hesitated as if searching for sincerity in her response. "Six days ago, you killed a man on Zenat with his own knife. Slit his throat and left him to bleed out. That man was Manes's favorite enforcer. Why did you target him?"

"He got in my way."

"So you were hunting his target too? Why?"

"I was just following orders."

"And who might those have come from?"

"Look." Matia swallowed against a parched throat and flexed her arms to see if her muscles had stopped spasming. "If you really knew who I was, then you'd know I'm freelance. Assignments and payments are all completely anonymous. I never know who hires me. I get picked up by a client, do the job, get paid, and that's the end of it."

"Surely there are communication records."

"Even if there were, I wouldn't share them with you." Matia struggled to her feet as the lightheadedness finally began to abate, though she was still forced to shield her face from the light. "You said you've got the *Talon*? Feel free to check the comm logs. All the transmissions self-delete upon receipt."

The woman remained silent for several seconds. "You're Haphezian."

"What of it?"

"You're a long way from home."

"I could say the same thing about you."

The woman stepped forward into the better light, and Matia saw that the strange shadows on her face were in fact two large patches of scar tissue. She'd been right in her initial observation as well: no *gesh punti* were visible. Considering the size and placement of those patches, it wasn't difficult to figure out what had happened.

"The last Haphezian I ever spoke to told me I wasn't worthy of the name and left me something to remember him by," the woman said, running a thumb over one of the scars. "I came out here to get as far away from you people as possible. Can't say I'm thrilled you're here."

The way she had emphasized the words 'you people' gave Matia the impression she'd spent so long trying to blend in and start fresh that she didn't even consider herself Haphezian anymore. And with her maimed *gesh punti*, marks that traditionally denoted family lineage, it wasn't a stretch to assume the man who had disowned her was a relative.

The crackle of a communicator interrupted her train of thought. "Kimbra, status?"

Matia watched as the woman—Kimbra, apparently—reached down to her belt and removed her comm without breaking eye contact. "More talkative than I expected," she said, warily appraising Matia as she spoke. "Still a lot to learn."

The man on the other end of the transmission seemed satisfied by this and said nothing more. Matia wondered if it was this Manes person Kimbra had mentioned. The big blonde woman, however, seemed anything but satisfied, and continued glowering at her as though she might be able to simply make her disappear if she stared hard enough. Matia straightened, finally feeling like she could see well enough to put her hand down, and approached the cell door. She had a few centimeters on Kimbra, though the other woman had a broader build. The air between them felt thick, and whether it was an abstract sensation due to the tension, a real sensation due to the energy shield, or both, she wasn't sure.

Kimbra's gaze flicked briefly down to the dead man on the floor before she pivoted to leave. "We're far from done here."

Matia stepped forward and took hold of the cell bars, watching her depart. From this angle, she couldn't see the door itself, and with the corridor fully illuminated, the shaft of light from outside was all but invisible. But the sound of those rusty hinges was perfectly clear as the heavy door swung shut. Mere seconds after it did, the long hallway was plunged into darkness once more.

She stood motionless for several minutes, partially in an attempt to re-acclimate to the black void and partially because she was completely baffled by the encounter that had just taken place. If it could even be considered an interrogation, it was the strangest one she'd ever endured. No, the electrocution and searing light hadn't been pleasant, but no further consequences had come of her unwillingness to divulge any information. And then this Kimbra woman had said they weren't done here—what was that supposed to mean? What were these people hoping to accomplish?

The darkness felt heavy and oppressive after the shock of the light. The thought occurred to her that she should recover the stun baton, should search the guard's corpse for a tool, weapon, or some other means of escape. Odd that they'd left him in here. But her body was tired, her arms and legs like lead. The disorientation wrought from inability to see left her dizzy, and she began to slowly shuffle backward, feeling around behind her until she found the wall. It wasn't like she had any shortage of time in here; she could examine the body later. Right now, she just needed to rest. She pressed her back against the wall and slid to the floor.

By the time it occurred to her that this feeling wasn't normal, the darkness was already consuming her.

The door at the end of the hallway opened every day for what felt like weeks. Or at least she assumed it was weeks. As much as she'd tried to keep track of the time, it was nearly impossible in the dark, and the odd, suspiciously timed bouts of unconsciousness after each visit certainly weren't helping. She could at least say lengthy chunks of time had passed between each incident. Whenever she became lucid again, the dead body would be mysteriously gone from the cell, and some meager food and water rations would be left in its place. Then she'd sit there for hours.

The same routine ensued every time. A guard approached in the dark, shot her from a distance with the stun baton, then attempted to enter the cell. She wasn't sure what their goal was. If they were trying to demonstrate that they had absolute control over the situation, it wasn't working. Even while stunned and sick, she still had the advantage so long as she could get them onto the floor. Several of them she fried with their batons just as she had the very first time. Then they learned their lesson and started wearing protective helmets; she stabbed a few in the throat with the batons' sharp emitters and broke all the others' necks, preferring efficiency over creativity.

Then came the intervention. The lights would come on suddenly, blinding her, and the woman called Kimbra would appear outside the cell to repeat the same interrogation regarding what had happened on Zenat. After the second or third round of arguing that she knew nothing about her employer, Matia had found it simpler to just sit on the floor and remain silent. Their first encounter had been enough to tell her she and Kimbra shared no common ground, so there was no point in interacting. The lack of compliance always seemed to fluster the blonde woman anyway, and she would check in with the man on comm and leave after only a few minutes.

Matia dispatched this current guard just as she had all the others, unable to understand why they kept coming. At this point she knew they weren't trying to restrain her. She wasn't sure exactly how they'd been sedating her after each interrogation—most likely some form of odorless gas—but why not just use a similar process every time they came to her cell and avoid the unnecessary bloodshed? Not to mention the waste of resources…if they wanted her to keep killing their soldiers, then that was their problem. But no, there was something else at play here. One time she'd tried *not* fighting back just to see what would happen, but the guard just kept hitting her with the stun baton until it had been legitimately difficult to bring him down. As much as killing them was a simple reflex, it had also become necessary from a self-preservation standpoint.

She had to admit that after days of this routine, she'd come to dread the sound of the door opening. Despite knowing precisely what to expect, she felt a certain part of herself involuntarily come alive when she heard those screeching hinges. She'd tried to subdue it, wondering if perhaps her captors were intentionally activating this instinct for some reason, but it was exactly that: an instinct. Suppressing conditioned reactions she'd developed over a long career wasn't something that happened easily.

With a sigh, she stepped back and rested against the wall, waiting for Kimbra to appear and repeat the same series of questions. On the bright side, she'd developed a method over the course of her incarceration that allowed her eyes to adjust to the lights faster, so when they came on this time, it only took her a few seconds to focus on Kimbra…and the strange man standing with her.

He wasn't old, probably not even forty. His dark, greased hair hugged his scalp and shimmered in the corridor's harsh lighting. He wore a short, neatly trimmed beard peppered with the slightest hints of gray, and his dark eyes were like shadows, hollow and emotionless. This was without doubt Alastair Manes.

The corridor fell completely silent for several long seconds as the two of them stood there observing her. She got the sense that his presence meant something had changed, that they had deviated from the routine, and she wondered if it meant she'd actually get out of this cage. Either that or she'd be dead in a few minutes.

"Matia Moryi," the man finally said. "I should be impressed, but part of me wants to just kill you now."

She looked him in the eye as best she could past the glare. "Well, I'd appreciate it if you decided promptly."

He smiled softly, and she had to admit he was rather handsome in a sort of eerie way. Based on the subtle creases lining his face, he smiled like that often, but she got the impression it never indicated good intentions.

"Don't worry," he said, "I've already made my decision. You passed."

Kimbra threw him a quizzical glance as if she too were waiting for an explanation. "Passed?" Matia said.

This time he didn't smile, and she got the feeling that was somehow worse. "Here's the thing, Moryi," he said, stepping past Kimbra and stopping with his face centimeters from the cell bars, "you killed a man named Jerrick Taan, one of my best people. His position is now vacant because of you. Under normal circumstances, I'd be forced to replace him with someone of a lesser caliber. But luckily for me—" he looked her directly in the eye "—you possess the precise skill set I need."

A cold tingle shot through her body and the hairs on the back of her neck stood on end. Without any further elaboration, she understood what he was saying: she *owed* him for what she'd done.

"I've seen what you're capable of," Manes continued, gesturing at the dead man on the floor. "You are both willing and able to kill without thought and without mercy. And, objectively speaking, taking Taan out was no easy feat."

He paused as if a thought had come to mind and reached into the pocket of the long leather coat he wore, removing an object which Matia recognized after a moment as the knife she'd used to slay the man he spoke of. He slid the blade from its sheath and held it up where she could see as he examined its razor-sharp serrated edge.

"So, here's my proposal," he continued. "You take his place. Stay here and work for me, employing all the same skills you've used during your freelance endeavors. Circumstances are such that I can provide you with a steady stream of work, and you will be well compensated. However, there will be consequences if you refuse."

He stood and let his gaze linger on her for a moment longer before the corners of his lips turned upward ever so slightly. "Think about it awhile."

Knife still in hand, he turned and strode away, Kimbra hot on his heels like a domesticated guhr hound back on Haphez. Matia watched until she could no longer see them, then she eased back against the cell wall, waiting for the familiar fading sensation as she lost consciousness again.

And then the routine continued. Soldiers came for her. She killed them. Sometimes it was multiple soldiers at once. Then Manes would arrive, and his presence would put a stop to whatever struggle might have still been taking place within the cell. Matia had never minded killing, particularly as a means to an end or if her own survival depended on it, but this was senseless. She was *tired*, both physically and mentally, and she began to welcome Manes's presence if it meant the madness would stop, even just for a moment. He would question her, though the inquiries had gravitated more toward her background and skill set than the incident on Zenat. Then he would just stand there silently for a couple of minutes with Kimbra at his side, waiting to see if she had a response to his offer. If the silence dragged on too long, he would leave, and the cycle would repeat.

She'd completely lost track of how many days had passed since he'd made his proposition, or of how many men she'd slain. But here she was again, standing on shaky legs over a corpse while Manes repeated the same old questions, including whether she was willing to work for him. His visits had gotten progressively less cordial—if the first one could have been considered cordial at all—and she was beginning to wonder if his offer came with an expiration. She didn't have any particular interest in working for him or his organization, but she was getting to where she desperately wanted out of this cell.

"Wait," she finally said just as he turned to leave again.

It was difficult to tell whether his dark eyes brightened ever so slightly or if it was just her imagination.

"What would my role be here?"

"You would be protecting the interests of the Ibarra Cartel," he replied coldly, "a task that is apt to take on many forms."

"Will I be a prisoner here?"

"I think it would be fair for me to utilize a certain measure of caution, at least initially. But once we establish a healthy, working relationship—" he said the words almost sarcastically "—then you'll be free to move about and carry out your tasks however you see fit. I was perfectly serious when I said I could provide you with enough work to keep you occupied and financially comfortable for months or even years to come."

Matia couldn't help but notice the way Kimbra stared at her as the man spoke, as if she disagreed with every word coming out of his mouth but knew better than to argue. Manes may have been eager to recruit her, but this woman certainly was not.

"I get access to your arsenal," she said, looking Kimbra in the eye and making her bristle further. She shifted her gaze to Manes. "I'm not an idiot. I know the Ibarra Cartel is into weapons dev."

Whatever shred of amicability had found its way into the man's demeanor vanished instantly, though he appeared more thoughtful than hostile. "Perhaps in time."

She drew a deep breath, unable to believe what she was about to say. "When do I start?"

He smiled, that same cold, empty smile she'd seen the day he'd first visited the cell. "That's better." He produced a coded key identical to what all the soldiers had carried and inserted it into the cell door. The energy shield shimmering just outside the bars vanished, and the locking mechanism popped open with a *clang*.

Matia stepped into the corridor, feeling oddly liberated just being outside the confines of the cell. She turned to follow Manes as he began to move toward the exit, but Kimbra stood fast in the center of the hall, staring her down.

"Don't think for one second that you're welcome here," she hissed.

Matia held the woman's gaze for a moment then brushed past her, not about to stoop to that level right now.

Kimbra scoffed and fell into stride behind her. "*Shouka.*"

She couldn't help but smirk as she fixed her attention on Manes and moved toward the door. Toward relative freedom. "You have no idea."

Chapter 8
THE TUNNEL - Tabaco, Panuco

The long rows of crusty apartments lined the path on either side of her, creating a dark gauntlet that always gave her pause. There weren't any hiding places or alcoves, at least none big enough to fully conceal someone, but there were doors positioned every four meters or so that anyone could emerge from at any time. While not a direct part of Manes's compound, the majority of the complex's residents were other Ibarra personnel or allies. But even though Manes had essentially taken her under his wing, two years later there were still members of his network who weren't thrilled by her presence and resented the fact that he'd allowed her into his inner circle so quickly. Kimbra was a prime example. It wasn't that Matia couldn't handle herself; this was just dangerous territory. Relations were fragile. While she preferred keeping it that way over forming an all-out partnership with Manes and his people, it often elicited extra stress she could do without.

While not technically indoors, the long hallway was still covered by a roof, or more accurately, the floor of the shady club built above it. The majority of her fellow tenants simply referred to the space as the Tunnel. The walkway was kept relatively clear, and there'd even been some repairs done after the Ibarra crew had kicked the previous occupants out. All the leftover graffiti coating the walls actually served to liven the atmosphere of the place—the dreary gray concrete wasn't much to look at. Still, she always stopped a moment to watch and listen before entering, unsure who or what might be lying in wait within.

Satisfied that there were no threats awaiting her today, she continued forward with her gaze fixed on the sixth door on the right. Taking the total length of the Tunnel into consideration, she technically lived on the outer edge, but it was still a good distance from the entrance. Nonetheless, she was glad she didn't live any further inside. The ten or so apartments on either end had windows facing the outer street, and while she always kept hers shut and locked, she liked the idea of having an alternate means of escape should the need for one ever arise.

The sounds of faint music and distorted voices reached her ears as she drew nearer to her door, and she felt the corners of her mouth twitch upward when she caught sight of the ragged, muddy boots belonging to the person from whom those sounds originated. The young man sat on the ground with his back to her, leaning against a short stack of containers someone had left outside the apartment next door to hers. His attention remained directed downward at the small viewscreen in his hand. He bobbed his head in sync with whatever music blared in his earpiece and murmured lyrics under his breath, completely oblivious to her presence.

Drawing the very knife she had wielded at the restaurant minutes before—Taan's knife, bestowed upon her shortly after coming into Manes's service—she closed the distance between them in two silent strides and pressed the blade to the back of his neck. He started then froze, letting the viewscreen clatter to the ground. With her free hand, she reached up and removed his earpiece. "You're dead," she whispered.

The young man relaxed immediately in response to her voice. Recovering the viewscreen, he scrambled to his feet and brushed himself off. "*Pazska*, Matia. You've got to stop doing that."

"And you've got to stop leaving yourself so vulnerable," she said. "Your lack of vigilance is going to get you in trouble one of these days, Blain."

"I'm a valuable asset to Manes. People know better than to mess with me."

"He has told me the same thing. Doesn't stop me from being cautious."

"You're too paranoid."

"And it wouldn't kill you to be a little *more* paranoid."

He merely shrugged in response. As argumentative as Blain Reed always was, she knew he usually at least tried to take her words to heart. That's what you did when you looked up to someone.

He studied his dangling earpiece for a moment before inserting it back into his ear, albeit with the music muted. A metallic disk shrouded his other ear, a device of his own invention that fed him a constant stream of nearby comm chatter. The galaxy only knew how many transmissions he was tapped into at any given moment, eavesdropping, gathering secrets. 'Information broker' was the title he liked to go by, but in all reality, he was a glorified snitch. Manes kept him around for the sole purpose of informing on any treacherous Cartel members, identifying threats to his rule, and sometimes even just maintaining the peace—relatively speaking—around the city.

"Why are you here?" she asked, continuing forward toward the door of her apartment.

"Same reason I always am," he answered, adjusting the disk on his ear and fiddling with the straps of the backpack he wore. "Any further into the Tunnel and the music and interference from the comm arrays upstairs make it impossible to get any work done."

She turned and began to work on the door lock so he couldn't see the smirk spreading across her lips. He was there for the same reason he always was all right, but she knew it wasn't the reason he'd just given, at least not completely. He was there because, contrary to what he told himself and everyone else, he was an outsider here, just like her.

She'd looked into him after meeting him for the first time and had found no official ties to the Ibarra Cartel. Roughly eighteen years old, he was the orphaned son of someone who had once done Manes a favor, and thus he had spent the majority of his life scraping by on the streets of Tabaco, looking for ways to make himself valuable and trying to convince himself he belonged. In a sense, she was doing the exact same thing, just in different ways. She wasn't one to ever have anybody tug at her heartstrings like this, but there was no denying the common ground they shared. Neither of them wanted to admit their situations aloud, but each could sense the alienation and desire to connect in the other. That was the real reason he always showed up at her door, and the reason she always put up with him being there.

"You want to come inside and work?" She turned and found him fixated once again on his viewscreen, trying hard, she knew, to feign disinterest. If she was honest with herself, she was legitimately concerned for his well-being, what with all the time he spent sitting in the Tunnel with his surroundings completely tuned out. She wasn't sure if she'd go so far as to call him a friend, but he was certainly one of the only people in these parts whom she considered an ally.

He glanced up as if he hadn't even noticed her go in. "Hm? Oh yeah, sure."

She led him inside and gestured toward her meager little dining table, barely big enough for the two of them to sit at. He promptly removed his backpack, withdrew a small portable computer, and slumped down into the chair as if that had been his plan all along. The music volume increased, and his gaze zeroed in on the computer screen as he bobbed his head. Just like that, he was gone again.

Unsure how he could possibly stand to have so much noise—much less two different types of noise—in his head and still focus, she sat down and removed from her pockets the two pistols she'd confiscated from the bodyguards in the bar. Both were very basic, making her wonder whether the two men had simply been hired guns rather than personal security detail with an employer who had a decent arms budget. Not that it mattered. Even low-quality weapons were still useful in the hands of someone like her. She could spruce them up and add them to her arsenal.

Plasma pistols like these couldn't be disassembled to the extent that projectile weapons could, but she set about doing it to the best of her ability. With stolen weapons, you could never tell what kind of care their previous owners had taken of them, and the last thing she wanted was to continue using a gun with a broken cooling rod and have the plasma cell explode in her hand.

She finished breaking down one of the pistols and laid out what components she could, pleasantly surprised to find that everything appeared to be in order. This particular model was of a higher caliber than what she typically liked—she preferred precision and subtlety to shock-and-awe—but she imagined this weapon would still come in handy at some point. She'd never been sure whether Manes had people trying to keep tabs on her armament, but she liked the idea of staying a step ahead if they were.

Movement caught her eye, and she saw that her little project had managed to pry Blain's attention away from his work. He watched the remaining intact pistol warily as if he were afraid it would jump up and attack him. She'd never been sure where his aversion to guns had originated, and it was difficult for her to even fathom such a distaste for an object that felt so natural in her grasp that it might as well be an extension of her hand. Perhaps he'd suffered some traumatic experience, or maybe he merely had no understanding of weaponry. Well, she knew the latter was true, which had always surprised her given how long he'd spent living amid a cartel of arms dealers. So perhaps it was a mixture of both.

"I wish you wouldn't do that here," he murmured, muting the music and comm receiver. His face turned ashen and he shifted his gaze back down to his tiny computer. He may have consistently projected an air of fearlessness as a self-preservation tactic, but if one thing could make him wilt, it was a firearm.

"This is my house, Blain," Matia said, leaning back in her seat and unable to suppress the annoyance in her tone. The majority of the time she and Blain spent in each other's company was downtime between jobs, so she imagined she appeared relatively non-threatening in his eyes compared to when she was fully equipped for a mission. But the few times they'd interacted while she was packing more than just a basic sidearm—and sometimes even then—they'd argued incessantly. He'd complained about how uncomfortable it made him, and she'd tried to convince him the weapon couldn't hurt him on its own, she posed no threat to him as its owner, and as a matter of fact he should be carrying himself for protection in a city like this. But so far, they had yet to compromise. She'd given him a knife as a gift once and it had taken long enough just to convince him to carry that.

She set about polishing up a few of the pistol's internal components before piecing it back together, stealing glances at her young companion as she did so. He'd resumed his work but made a point of not looking at her, and she could feel the vibration of his leg bouncing nervously under the table.

Irritated, she got up and took both weapons over to the cabinet where she kept the half of her arsenal that didn't permanently live aboard the *Talon*, making a mental note to be sure to check the second pistol later. It wasn't so much empathy for Blain or even a desire to respect his wishes as it was a selfish need to keep their little alliance intact, however unorthodox it may be. As much as he sometimes got on her nerves, his skill set had turned him into an asset of sorts, and his company never failed to be a welcome reprieve from that of people like Kimbra and Manes himself.

She went to shut the little cabinet, wincing a bit as the sound of the door's squealing hinges triggered a brief memory of her imprisonment upon being brought to Panuco for the first time. Her situation had changed drastically—for the better, objectively speaking—in the two years since her arrival, but conversations with Manes like the one she'd just come from at the bar sometimes made her feel like she was in an entirely different kind of prison. She wasn't sure what to make of it. She knew he had never fully trusted her, and unless she could rewind time, be born on Panuco, and grow up within Ibarra's ranks, she didn't expect him to start.

But despite his amiable demeanor, she could sense whatever trust he had toward her dwindling. Whether it was due to prodding from Kimbra—that *shouka*—or a product of his own inference, she wasn't sure. What she did know was that she needed to stay in good standing with him for as long as she possibly could. The handsome pay she received for her work was good incentive alone, but she got the sense he would have no trouble disposing of her if he finally decided he'd had enough, regardless of how many times he told her how valuable she was or how she was free to come and go as she pleased. She didn't doubt her abilities to escape in such a case, but trying to function in her line of work while spending the rest of her life hunted by Ibarra didn't sound the least bit appealing.

Angered and unnerved by the mere thought, she opened the cabinet door again and slammed it three times in quick succession, startling Blain and leaving her own ears ringing. It was something she'd gotten in the habit of doing whenever she put her weapons away, citing a sticky latch whenever her young companion was present. In reality the door was merely an outlet for whatever fury she happened to be feeling on a given day. That, and forcing herself to listen to the groaning metal over and over was her way of reminding herself she was free and in control of things. Or so she told herself.

She secured the cabinet and considered doing a little weightlifting to blow off steam, but a small blinking light on the comm console beside the locker caught her eye. That light usually indicated an unopened message, but a quick glance at the screen revealed empty incoming transmission logs. She stole a peek at Blain and, upon finding that he had thrown himself back into his work, took a closer look.

Sure enough, there was a message there after all, hidden behind a partition she'd created to filter out anything that wasn't from Manes or the third-party contact who had handled all of her freelance contracts before her Cartel days. The message was text-based but the file was minuscule; she accepted it and found that it only contained a single, affirmative binary value. Other than the fact that it had come through a deep space comm relay in this sector, there was no data regarding the sender's identity or where the message had originated.

Heaving a sigh, Matia stepped back and responded with a message of her own that contained nothing but the same single-digit affirmation. With that, the indicator light stopped flashing, and her inbox cleared out for good.

"I'll be over here," she said, heading toward the meager pile of fitness equipment on the other side of her cramped living quarters. "Feel free to work as long as you'd like."

For a moment she thought Blain had actually acknowledged her with a nod, but upon closer inspection he was only bobbing his head to the music that once again blared in his earpiece. She picked up a rusty barbell, unable to help but smile to herself. She may have chastised the young man for tuning out his surroundings when he was outside, but she didn't mind if he did it within the walls of her home. And today—she took one last glance over at the comm console—she preferred it.

Chapter 9
Saber - Deep Space

Stealing a glance back toward the cockpit, Aroska turned away from the massive viewscreen displaying Pahl Starcer's reports and slid into the chair at one of the comm room's workstations. All the pent-up excitement he'd been trying to contain since the previous evening was finally taking its toll, and it was becoming harder and harder to focus. He pulled out his memory stick and inserted it into the terminal's socket, taking another moment to listen for approaching footsteps. All remained quiet except for the hum of the FTL drive reverberating throughout the *Saber*, the unregistered *Infiltrator*-class ship the agency had provided the team with. Drawing in a deep breath, he navigated to one of the files saved on the stick and hesitated for a split second longer before opening it.

He hated himself for watching the recording again. It had been— he thought about it for a moment—months, actually, since the last time he'd viewed it. He'd come to think of it as a way to gauge how well he was doing moving forward with his life, but at this point, after an evening of not being able to keep *her* out of his head, he couldn't help it. Part of him—the part that actually listened to Skeet and Zinni's continual warnings—didn't believe he would ever see her again, didn't believe she could have survived the *Intrepid's* explosion. That part of him simply wished to ensure his memory of her remained one hundred percent intact, and watching the vid always made him feel like he was reliving their last moments all over again.

But another part of him, the part that believed wholeheartedly she was alive and was hell-bent on finding her someday, knew that watching the recording would only increase his agitation. She'd been gone for four years; if she'd wanted to make contact, she would have. He respected her too much to try to chase her down if she didn't want to be found. Besides, he still couldn't risk exposing her to the Feds. He would be content with simply knowing where she was and maybe looking out for her from a distance.

And so he hated the vid for the same reason he loved it: it made it seem like she was right there, that he needn't search for her any longer. The realization that he had to continue looking was always disheartening.

On the screen, he saw Skeet and Zinni file out of the holding room, leaving him alone with her. He watched himself place his hands on her waist, recalling the way she'd stiffened a bit in response to his touch. He'd seen the recording several times before stopping to wonder if she always reacted that way because she was so used to being touched harshly, whether by Jak Gamon, the Cobian pirates, or in everyday combat situations. On Kat's balcony...up on the hill outside of Salex...that night in his apartment...she'd done it every time. The thought made him sick.

Aroska's heart rate quickened as he watched himself cradle her face and bring his lips to hers. He'd really only meant for it to be a genuine gesture after what he'd done in Kat's garage, so he'd been surprised when she'd reciprocated, however timidly. There were times when he still wondered if he should have pulled away so quickly, and whether trying to make light of the situation had only driven her away faster. But as with every other time, he convinced himself that was foolish thinking. She would have left regardless, and though he was still saddened by the circumstances, he knew that by doing so she had saved them all.

These workstations were in close enough proximity to the cockpit that he kept the vid muted. Most of the conversation it portrayed had been whispered or murmured, so it was difficult to hear anyway. Not that it mattered; he'd memorized the dialogue long ago. A smile spread across his lips as he recalled the way they'd joked about her threat to castrate him if he ever kissed her again, and he cringed when he saw himself begin to shed tears at the thought of losing this person he'd become so inexplicably connected to. In the face of someone who showed so little emotion—or else showed it in such unconventional ways—he looked ridiculous.

The floor creaked somewhere behind him, snapping him out of the trance the vid had put him into. He froze, aware he was under scrutiny, and paused the recording. Despite the forewarning, he was still startled when he swiveled in the chair and found Skeet leaning against the bulkhead. He had no reason to be embarrassed—he knew both Skeet and Zinni had viewed the recording several times themselves—but he still felt his shoulders sag significantly in response to the lieutenant's look.

"Sorry," he murmured, well aware of how many times Skeet had suggested he leave the vid alone.

The man merely sighed and remained motionless. "You know, there must really be something special about you because I knew her for over ten years and I never saw her smile like that."

Confused, Aroska shifted back around and realized he'd paused the vid on a frame that showed her looking down at her feet, her lips parted in a sheepish but undoubtedly genuine grin. He'd just told her she was crazy, he recalled, something she'd once informed him she took as a compliment, and something he'd *meant* as a compliment. He hadn't even considered her response at the time, but now that he thought about it, he realized he'd never seen her smile like that either.

"You love her?"

The question caught him off guard and he spun to find Skeet's fiery eyes locked on him in a quizzical manner. The lieutenant's tone was gentler than expected.

Aroska stole another glance at the frozen frame on the screen. He'd asked himself that same question on several different occasions. After a lifetime of superficial relationships and after spending so long convincing himself he had to keep hating her for what she'd done to his family, it was still sometimes hard to realize there were other options. She'd done some things—was capable of some things—he wasn't sure if he'd ever be able to wrap his head around, and they'd both hurt each other in so many ways, whether they'd meant to or not. But despite that discomfort, her absence certainly left a hole, an emptiness, somewhere inside of him. The connection they shared was stronger than anything he'd felt in a long time, and the thought occurred to him that perhaps it was her version of love.

Regardless, he'd finally come up with an answer over the past couple of years that he thought made sense. "Yeah," he replied. If nothing else, objectively speaking, the way he'd chosen to allocate his spare time and energy in recent months was an affirmation of sorts. "Yeah I do. In one way or another."

The corners of Skeet's mouth twitched upward in a half-hearted smirk. "She's a bit of an acquired taste, isn't she?" He sobered and shifted his weight to his other leg. "She cared...*cares* a great deal about you. This may sound strange, but that's why she always treated you the way she did, why she often came across so cold. She was protecting you."

"From what?"

"From herself."

It never ceased to amaze him how things she'd said in the past continued to make more and more sense. She'd tried to keep him at arm's length so she wouldn't become attached and therefore wouldn't compromise herself emotionally or expose him to the perpetual suffering and chaos her life seemed to consist of. And now, having fallen in with her and her team, and having spent the past four years doing much of the same work she'd always done, he'd experienced firsthand the very things she'd been trying to shield him from.

Skeet hummed in amusement. "I just didn't think I'd ever see that."

Aroska couldn't help but snort as well. "I know. There was a time when I never would have imagined saying any of this."

"You were the source of a lot of emotional turmoil for her over the years. I've never seen anyone affect her the way you have."

"*You're one of the few people who gets under my skin, and I kind of hate you for that...but thanks.*"

"You think she...?" he began, pausing a moment. After some of the trauma she'd endured over the years, she certainly coped and showcased her feelings in unique ways, so he wondered if she was even capable of love in any sort of traditional sense. In many ways, this connection she'd formed with him—and with Skeet and Zinni, for that matter—almost transcended that.

This time, Skeet's chuckle was genuine. "Man, the day I know what she's thinking will be the day the galaxy implodes." He grew quiet for a moment. "I don't know if this answers your question, but I think you've earned a spot on her list."

"Her list?"

"Of people she'd do anything for. Kill for. *Die* for."

Aroska nodded. That explained some of her behavior, namely escaping HSP's lockdown to come find him aboard the Resistance flagship. She demonstrated her feelings with actions, not words.

"Well," Skeet sighed, straightening and raking a hand through his hair, "she's lucky to have you. She's always had people who care about her, but she's often been too blind and stubborn to see it. Just..."

"Don't let it affect my work," Aroska finished for him. "I haven't thus far, and I don't plan on starting now. You can trust me, Skeet."

"Well, yeah. But I was going to say just don't get your hopes up. The chances of actually finding her are slim enough, but the chances of her running to you with open arms are probably nonexistent. In fact, I wouldn't expect her to react in any way you might consider normal. She's *not* normal. And if we do find her, she may not even be the same person you knew before."

"You think so?"

"Are you the same person you were when she left?"

Aroska snorted. "Good point."

Skeet dipped his head and turned to leave but hesitated for a moment in the doorway. "You just have to realize there's a good chance we'll never see her again."

Although Aroska was determined that wouldn't be the case, he nodded anyway. Even if he did find her, he knew it would be difficult to convince her to come home. Or, considering it was likely still too dangerous for her, keep *himself* from trying to convince her to come home. She'd left in order to protect them, and as much as he hated to admit it, he needed to leave her alone in order to protect *her*.

"You should get some rest," Skeet finally said, resuming his journey out the door. "We'll all need to be on top of our game for this. Zinni and I will handle things for a while."

Aroska acknowledged him with a nod and turned back to the screen, listening to the lieutenant's footsteps fade away down the corridor. Skeet was right; he needed to rest, but at the moment all he wanted to do was comb through all of his collected data for the umpteenth time and imagine what would happen if it was actually accurate. The idea that had presented itself during the briefing with Starcer still plagued him as well. If they acted on it, it could potentially make the mission a hundred times easier and help ensure their success, but they risked exposing delicate information that could put them all in jeopardy. If they *didn't* act on it, taking Moryi down might be more of a challenge, but they would also keep certain secrets intact and maybe even avoid potential bloodshed. He had opted to keep his thoughts to himself until he'd had time to mull them over further, but now here they were on their way to the opposite side of Fringe Space and he still hadn't decided on the best course of action. Perhaps it was time to bring Skeet and Zinni into the loop after all.

He rose to his feet and headed down the corridor in the direction the lieutenant had gone, contemplating how best to address a subject neither of them were fond of. A direct approach would be most efficient, both in terms of the mission and team cohesion, and the thought prompted him to pick up his pace.

In the cockpit, neither Skeet nor Zinni were at the ship's controls; the former stood with his elbows resting on the back of the pilot's seat, while the latter sat sideways in the copilot's, her legs draped over the armrest. Aroska's sudden arrival triggered an abrupt silence and wary glances, something he'd grudgingly grown accustomed to. The two of them talking about him behind his back was nothing new, especially when it came to matters related to *her* and his little side project. He knew they were only concerned for his well-being, but it still set him on edge.

Might as well be blunt. "We need to go to Panuco," he said, crossing his arms and settling against the back wall.

Skeet began to speak, paused, appeared pensive for a moment, then shut his mouth and gave Aroska a single nod, inviting him to continue his thought.

"We need to go to Panuco, and we need to find her." Aroska hesitated, sure he knew what they were thinking, and reminded himself that he wasn't just basing this proposal on his own interests. "I'm not an idiot—I know if we try to establish contact, we risk exposing her to the Federation. Believe me, I'm not suggesting we do this just for the hell of it. We have a very limited amount of time here, and we might as well be running blind. She could help us."

Neither of them made any move to agree, but neither did they immediately shoot him down. Zinni glanced up at Skeet then hoisted herself out of the chair, moving around to lean against the back of it. "I have to admit it's not the worst idea."

"You've told us that lead is almost a year old," the lieutenant reminded them. "Assuming it was even her, what are the chances she's still there?"

"Low," Aroska answered, "but the point is she *was* there. Even if she's not around anymore, there was obviously something there that was important enough for her to pay a visit in person." He turned and faced Skeet directly. "You were there on Aubin. She said she owed Tobias a favor after he helped her find us. Said she 'sold her soul' to the Niiosian Mob. If she went to Niio after the *Intrepid* blew, if she found work with Tobias, chances are she's very familiar with the Ibarra conflict, if not involved directly. If that was her on Panuco, she could have been there investigating Manes or even hunting Moryi herself. I mean, who better for the Niiosians to use against someone like that?"

He paused, out of breath and feeling as though he'd been rambling. So rarely did he get the opportunity to share his thoughts about all of this that when he did, he tended to have trouble articulating them in an organized, linear manner. That of course did nothing to improve Skeet and Zinni's opinions of it all. They were currently watching him as if he'd been speaking a foreign language.

It was Skeet who responded first, if lowering his gaze and massaging his forehead counted as a response. "So," he began, face contorted in such a way that it was difficult to tell whether he was disgusted or merely trying to wrap his head around all of these ideas, "all of this hinges on the assumption that she actually went to Niio to escape the Feds and made good on her agreement with Tobias."

"Right."

"I won't lie—it does make sense. Niio would be a perfect place to disappear, and the Mob could offer her a measure of protection and a steady stream of work. But still, it's all just based on an assumption." Skeet paused and smiled to himself as if amused by a thought. "A likely assumption. She always did have a strange sense of honor."

"Have you searched Niio specifically?" Zinni asked, folding her arms.

Aroska nodded. "They don't have much material available for me to tap into in the first place, but if she was there under the circumstances we're assuming, she probably would have done her best to stay off the radar. And in the event the Niiosians have been actively hiding her, it would be virtually impossible to find any information there." He took a moment to rub his eyes. "I think I've got a couple pieces of data from Niio saved, but the only real promising clue besides Panuco was from a small spaceport on Kais a little over two years ago. And 'promising' is relative."

Zinni hummed to herself for a moment. "There's still a good bit of distance there, but Kais is close enough to Ibarra space that it's likely under Manes's control. At the very least, that area of Fringe Space is probably contested between Ibarra and Niio." She glanced at Skeet and shrugged. "Could be legitimate."

As with the lieutenant, Aroska found it difficult to tell whether she was making an actual suggestion or merely playing along for his benefit. Logically, he knew they were both professional enough—and the situation with Matia Moryi dire enough—that they'd never intentionally string him along, but uncertainties like that came from a more sensitive part of his mind that, while easier to subdue these days, could never be deactivated completely.

Skeet let out a sigh reminiscent of a father whose children had just asked to keep a stray pet. "What physical features are your algos looking for?"

Both of them knew Aroska had tapped into agency resources for his project—in fact, he'd gotten help from Zinni in masking his digital footprint initially—but he'd never gone into detail about what he was doing with those resources, partially because he wanted them to be able to maintain deniability, and partially because they'd never actually asked. He knew they were curious, but they were better at hiding it, and he imagined maintaining deniability had crossed their minds too.

"I've got several running at once," he answered. "Facial recog is the primary and would be the most accurate, but I've never gotten a hit. It's probably a combination of me not looking in the right places and her knowing better than to show her face anywhere the Feds might see it. Both of my best leads are too far away to get an accurate facial reading."

"So what are those based on?" Zinni asked.

He turned back toward the corridor and beckoned for them to follow. "Here, let me show you." He took off for the comm room where he'd been working, pleased by the sounds of their approaching footsteps after a brief hesitation. Sliding into the chair at the work-station, he minimized the recording from the holding room—still frozen on the frame depicting that smile—and brought up the two best images, enlarging the one from Panuco in the center of the screen. Skeet and Zinni came to a stop behind the seat, waiting in silence for him to continue.

"In lieu of facial features, I've ended up focusing more on height and stride." Aroska waved a pair of additional dialogs onto the screen, showing them how the algorithms had analyzed archived footage from HSP Headquarters, the HSP med center, Noro Spaceport, and other familiar locations from home where she could be seen in the feeds. Using those as a baseline, the system was able to study the constant stream of data coming in from around the Fringe, searching for similarities and calculating match percentages.

"There wasn't enough movement in the footage from Kais to get an accurate stride reading," he said, pointing, "but the height and posture of this person are a ninety-four percent match."

Zinni leaned in to get a better look. "You've told us Panuco was the best match, but that sounds pretty damn good to me."

"I've been leery about getting too excited because it's just not much to go on. Statistically speaking, the percentage of humanoid races who even fall into this height category is low in the grand scheme of things, so any hit is worth checking out. But at this point, it's difficult to even tell if this person is male or female." He stared at the grainy image a moment longer before shaking his head, waving it off the screen, and shifting his focus to the one from Panuco. "Again, this one is from a little less than a year ago, and it's got the opposite problem. Algos calculated an eighty-nine percent match in stride, but the height is off."

"Too short?" Skeet asked.

"Slightly too tall, actually. Not by a lot, but enough to make me doubtful." Once again, he took a moment to just stare at the image, suddenly feeling doubtful about *all* of it. Maybe it stemmed from speaking out loud about something he'd kept to himself for so long, and now that he was voicing his thoughts, he realized how severely he'd been grasping this whole time. The logic related to the Niiosians and locations made sense, but just as Skeet had cautioned, it was all based on assumptions. Assumptions that, if Aroska was honest with himself, had still mostly come from his heart, even if the reasoning was sound.

He reached forward and minimized all the screens. "You know what? Forget it," he said, leaning back in the chair and dragging his hands down over his face. "This is crazy."

There was only a brief silence before Skeet spoke. "No, it's not," he said, his tone surprisingly upbeat. "We'll go to Panuco."

Aroska swiveled in the chair and found Zinni looking at the lieutenant with the same incredulity he himself was feeling. "You sure?"

"Yeah, why not. No better place to look for information about Moryi than the heart of Ibarra territory, right? Emeri merely suggested we start with Delatori, but it sounded to me like Starcer didn't think she'd be there anymore. Panuco might be the best option anyway. Besides—" he reached past Aroska and brought the surveillance image back up "—we could very well be looking at Moryi right here. You said the stride was a close match but not perfect, and the galaxy only knows someone like that is going to move in a similar fashion."

Zinni lifted an eyebrow, some mixture of skepticism and pleasant surprise in her face. "I'll go plot a course, then."

"Do what you can to shave off some time. Panuco's at least a couple more days' journey than Delatori would have been."

She gave him a mock salute and disappeared into the corridor, leaving the two men in the silent comm room. Aroska looked up and couldn't help but be relieved to find Skeet's gaze focused on the screen instead of on him. As eager as he was for a chance to potentially make good on all the work he'd done over the past four years, there was something about the lieutenant's tone that still made him feel as though he was simply being catered to, being reluctantly indulged. It would be stupid to turn down an opportunity to act on all of his work, but he'd always imagined such a venture happening under more noble and independent circumstances.

"If she's out there, I'd like to find her just as much as you do," Skeet said quietly, finally peeling his eyes away from that image. He leaned back against the desk and folded his arms, staring down at the floor as he spoke. "It may not always seem like it, but Zinni and I both miss her like hell too."

"I know," Aroska said.

"I've always just felt like dwelling on the idea that she's out there would make everything worse. It has almost been easier to just pretend she died in that explosion, you know?" He forced a stiff chuckle. "Besides, I figure she's the type of person who would want all of us to move on. Live our lives. Do our jobs."

Aroska was sure of that, though he liked to think he'd done a decent job balancing the 'moving on' part with his tedious inquest. There were just times—like now—when it seemed like he'd been emotionally whisked back to square one.

"You were right," Skeet continued. "If by some miracle we're able to find her, she could be an incredibly valuable asset." He straightened and began moving back toward the door. "Just remember what I said earlier."

Aroska stood abruptly. "Skeet?"

The lieutenant stopped.

"You have my word that my focus will be one hundred percent where it needs to be until this thing is over, but I appreciate the opportunity to potentially find some closure. So thank you for that."

Skeet appeared mildly amused for a moment before moving back over to shake Aroska's hand, drawing him in close and knocking their shoulders together in a brotherly fashion. "I don't know if she'd think you were an idiot for doing all of this or if she'd admire your tenacity." He broke away and resumed his trek toward the door. "We'll sit down and come up with a game plan for when we reach Panuco, but in the meantime, I thought I ordered you to get some rest."

He disappeared through the opening, leaving Aroska alone once more. Taking one last look at the grainy image on the screen, he removed and pocketed his memory stick, plagued by the same mixture of excitement and dread he'd felt as he'd returned to his apartment to gather his things. The situation was full of so many unknowns, but he suddenly felt readier than ever to face them.

CHAPTER 10
THE TUNNEL · TABACO, PANUCO

The hinges hadn't squealed to alert her this time, so the sudden feeling of the stun baton's emitter digging into her back was a complete shock, even without the electricity wracking her body. How had she not heard anyone enter the corridor?

He's coming, her mind warned her.

He's already here, you idiot.

She'd let her guard down—had fallen asleep—and this was her consequence. They'd taken her by surprise, and now she was stuck. Couldn't move. Couldn't react. Couldn't even speak. This wasn't fair. They always allowed her to fight back. Wanted her to, even. That was the whole point. See how easily she could kill.

Something solid pressed down against the entire back of her body, with the sharp emitter hitting her just below the right shoulder blade and rendering her arm numb. But nothing touched her face—or chest, or stomach, or legs—the way it usually did when she was pinned to the floor. It occurred to her that she was on her back...but also being impaled in the back. It made no sense.

The conscious sense of confusion jarred her awake. She lashed out with her legs, the move she always led with in order to take the guards by surprise and drag them down to her level. Rather than a man's chest, they caught only empty air; her knees knocked together with an audible *clack*, and her feet came crashing down against something too soft to be the floor and not quite soft enough to be comfortable. The soldiers weren't usually quick enough to avoid her initial attack like that.

Something semi-solid touched her arm as she flailed, and she turned and slammed her fist into it, followed by her elbow. Then she flung herself from her bunk, her hand finding the pistol on the bedside table by pure reflex. Movement behind her. She whirled, leveling the weapon at empty space she was certain had contained *something* just a split second earlier.

You're in your apartment.

That wasn't true, and if it was, it didn't matter. Danger was all that mattered.

Nothing is happening to you.

Then why did her shoulder still hurt? Damn it, he should have been here by now. He always came. Part of her feared him, but whenever he arrived, the pain stopped. She wanted the pain to stop.

She swept the pistol around the room, charging toward the hallway when she saw nothing. Someone was here. Someone was coming for her. Someone had been there, trying to shock her.

You're in your apartment.

Movement! She pivoted and fired three rounds at the figure standing at the end of the hall, center of mass. Glass shattered. A loud crash followed, but no bullet-riddled body hit the floor.

You're in your apartment. You're in your apartment. You're in your apartment.

Matia shuddered as the feeling of familiarity jolted her to her senses. The kitchen and living area were both dark and still, just the way she'd left them before going to bed. Her gun cabinet. Her comm console. The table. The weights. Nothing looked out of place. She lowered the gun, hand trembling as she did so, and moved toward the mirror she'd just shot all to hell. She'd positioned it so she could see the front door from her bedroom, a primitive security measure, and now here she was shooting at her own reflection. In the apartment's faint ambient light, she could barely make out her silhouette reflected in the shards, distorted and broken.

She began making her way back toward the bedroom on wobbly legs. It had been two very long years since her incarceration and the miserable vetting process the Cartel had put her through, but that didn't stop her mind from conjuring up these memories, some of the most vivid she could ever remember. This was disappointing—she'd been doing so well lately in terms of avoiding these nightmares.

Probably because she hadn't been sleeping much.

She arrived in the bedroom doorway and stood staring at the filthy, cramped space in the light seeping through the little window. The sharp emitter? That broken spring that had finally poked through the mattress and jutted out when she rolled over too far. The movement she'd first sensed? The odd tilt in the mattress caused by that broken spring. And the solid form she'd attacked? Her own pillow. The rest of the room remained empty. There was nobody there, no one coming after her. She was alone.

She returned her pistol to the table beside her bunk and moved over to the window. The narrow backstreet outside was also empty, with an assortment of colored lights visible along the main boulevard farther out. The latch remained fastened—nobody had gotten in or *could* get in this way, short of breaking the glass—but she knew it could get sticky at times, and if she needed to get out in a hurry, that would be a problem. She reached out and unlocked it, sliding the bolt back and forth several times until it moved smoothly in its track. *There.* She locked it back up then stood and stared at it for a moment, unsure if she felt any better.

The apartment remained silent as she made her way to the lavatory. If not for the fact that the tiny room was pitch black, she would have opted to just leave the lights off; the momentary blinding glare of the single light panel sent her right back to the cell block, the very place she felt she'd just escaped from. She reached out to open the storage compartment behind the mirror, hesitating a moment to study her own reflection. This mirror may have been intact, but she appeared just as broken. Bloodshot eyes enveloped by dark circles peered back at her from between squinting eyelids. *So tired.* She'd gotten some decent sleep on the trip back from Delatori, but that was a relatively short journey when traveling at FTL speeds, much of which she'd needed to spend making other preparations for her return to Panuco. She was often able to sleep well when she was alone aboard the *Talon* in the solitude of deep space; here in the apartment, not so much, partially thanks to the nightmares and partially because even after two years here, she still hated to let her guard down for any extended period of time. Couldn't leave herself vulnerable like that. Needed to be in control.

She opened the compartment and selected a tiny autoinjector from the tray within, touching it to her neck and wincing at the sharp pinch she'd never quite managed to get used to. She'd always considered it a punishment of sorts for using stims like this. At least they were high quality, the real deal rather than some homemade concoction that would give you a nice rush and then send you crashing back down a few hours later. Besides, unlike some of the Cartel's other nefarious side products, these stims had no real harmful side effects.

No physical ones, anyway.

She leaned down over the sink, gripping the edges and shutting her eyes against the glare of the lavatory light as she waited for the cocktail's effects to take hold. She didn't enjoy living like this, stuck in a bad habit and mental prison, but even if there was someone within the Cartel who had the expertise to help her, she wouldn't have trusted them to. Besides, if she was completely honest with herself, all of this pain—despite the misery and discomfort—*drove* her. She may not have liked it, but she thrived on it, and those were two different things. It made her jaded, made her feel like she had nothing to lose, and that was what it took to survive out here. She had a job thriving on pain only made her better at. Deep down, she still maintained a large enough shred of self-awareness to hate herself for thinking this way, but there was no going back now.

The stim kicked in after just a few moments. Feeling energized, Matia tilted her head back and forth, cracking a neck stiff from sleeping on that horrible mattress. Money was no object—Manes paid her well enough that investing in some nicer furniture and even in nicer digs would have been no problem at all. But the desire to avoid putting down any permanent roots on Panuco kept her living in this squalid hole and the majority of her finances tucked safely away in off-world accounts, out of Ibarra's reach.

She made her way out to the kitchen and activated the lights, looking around at the space and disgusted with herself for thinking she'd been anywhere but her apartment. The time display on the comm console across the room revealed she'd only been asleep for a couple of hours; normally when she was awake at this time of night, she'd either go prowl the streets of Tabaco—finding it beneficial to understand the inner workings of the city after dark—or she'd clean her weapons, reveling in the silence and the steady, methodical project. The thought occurred to her that she'd never had a chance to examine the other pistol she'd taken from the bodyguard at the bar the previous morning, and she angled toward the gun cabinet.

The locker door squealed open as usual, though the sound made the hairs on the back of her neck stand on end and left her cringing for a split second longer than normal after what had just occurred in the bedroom. For a moment she could only stand there and stare blankly at the collection of weapons inside, grinding her teeth as she envisioned shadowy figure after shadowy figure creeping toward her down the detention corridor. She'd learned some time later that these men hadn't been guards at all, but rather Cartel prisoners Manes had promised to favor if they were able to subdue her. It explained the seemingly endless supply of expendable soldiers and why they'd all been relatively easy to bring down; she imagined real Ibarra soldiers would have refused to keep coming after her—especially one-on-one—after learning she'd taken out a couple of their predecessors. And of course Manes's promises to these people had been beyond empty. He'd sent them in knowing full well they wouldn't succeed, so he had tested her abilities, worn her down, made her dependent on him, and cleared some of the refuse out of the Ibarra network's prisons, all in one fell swoop.

Hot rage surged through her and she slammed the door shut, then again, and again, continuing well past her customary three slams until the grating noise echoed all throughout the apartment. The fury wasn't even about killing those prisoners so much as it was merely disgust at the way she'd been manipulated, and even then, it was less about that than it was at her own damn mind for constantly sending her back to those days. She was in control now, damn it. She was tenacious and callous and resilient, favored—and well paid—by perhaps the most powerful man in this sector of Fringe Space. There was no way she should still be letting the past bother her like this.

She gave the locker door a few more hard slams for good measure, wincing as a sharp edge sliced across the heel of her hand. She swore under her breath and stepped back, sucking on the cut while she waited for the ringing in her ears to die away. A shallow dent had appeared in the center of the metal door thanks to the uneven distribution of force, and for a moment she felt a pang of guilt. Of the few things she owned, this gun cabinet was something she took pride in, something that physically represented the control she kept reminding herself she had, and here she was tearing it down.

The thought occurred to her that in her fit of anger she'd completely forgotten to retrieve the commandeered pistol, the very task that had brought her over to the locker in the first place. She heaved a sigh and checked the cut on her hand, wiping it across her pant leg before proceeding to open the cabinet again. She lifted the latch almost reverently this time, offering a silent apology to this construction that protected her valuable tools, and fetched the gun. Her anger gave her energy and made her good at what she did, and the hellish experiences she'd endured formed a protective shell around what had otherwise become a very...empty persona. The trick was simply to channel both of those things rather than allow them to consume her.

As she examined her pistol, the thought occurred to her that something now felt off about the locker. She looked up, brows furrowed, and swung the door back and forth a couple of times. No squeal of hinges. Perplexed, she bent down to take a closer look. The dent she'd just created had in turn reshaped a warped section on the door's interior edge, subsequently straightening the segment where the faulty hinge was attached.

For the briefest of moments, she almost felt disappointed that this tool she'd used to combat her suffering was no longer functional, but it occurred to her that anger *about* that suffering was what had ended up fixing it. "Hm," she said aloud, stricken by the appropriateness of it.

With that, she secured the door, took her new weapon to the table, and made herself comfortable.

I'm in control.

CHAPTER 11
MARINA - TABACO, PANUCO

The briny ocean air stung Skeet's eyes as he moved forward down the quiet wharf near Tabaco's docks. A thick, swirling fog had rolled in after nightfall, reducing his visibility to what seemed like only a few meters. The sea was nothing more than a black expanse somewhere off to his left, rumbling and crackling as it met the jagged coastline. It was too dark and cloudy to see it, but he could still feel the space, the openness, and despite all the traveling the team did, it made him uncomfortable after being so accustomed to the cities and forests at home on Haphez. He felt exposed.

Zinni and Aroska moved silently along about half a stride behind him, flanking him slightly. None of them said a word; the decision to stay quiet had been unspoken and unanimous. Not only were they in unfamiliar territory and dealing with unfavorable weather conditions, but if intel about this Ibarra Cartel was accurate, they'd just landed in perhaps the most dangerous place in this sector of Fringe Space.

The *Saber* remained docked on a beach on the outskirts of town, with all stealth and security systems engaged. It wouldn't keep anyone from seeing the ship with their naked eye and poking around, but no instruments from Tabaco's Port Control should be able to get a fix on it. There were plenty of other smuggling vessels lurking on the edges of the city in a similar fashion, so it was unlikely anyone would pay it any special attention, but the fog would help conceal it this evening anyway. They'd secured a car for ground transportation during their stay, and now here they were making their way into the heart of the town.

The first step in gaining information in a place like this was to simply listen, so that's what they did. Each of them peered into the fog, prepared to face whatever or whoever might emerge. Their path was illuminated by glowing orange panels mounted on tall poles, though those panels were hardly more than bright spots surrounded by warm halos in the dense mist. Having enhanced eyesight was pointless in these conditions, and the overwhelming saltiness of the air made it difficult to pick up any unfamiliar scents. An involuntary chill crept down Skeet's spine, though whether it was due to the nippy fog or the apprehension, he wasn't sure.

A shape—revealed to be the outline of a building as they drew nearer—became visible through the fog ahead and his ears picked up the sound of murmuring voices. Aroska and Zinni heard it too; he held up a hand and the three of them slowed to a stop, listening. As far as Skeet could tell based on the muffled dialogue, the voices simply belonged to fishermen or dock workers. Most of the people in this area of the city were likely average citizens with no direct ties to the Ibarra Cartel, but if the organization bore as many similarities to the Niiosian Mob and had as much reach as they thought it did, there was no telling who might still be watching, listening.

The buildings grew more numerous as they continued on and the walkway led them into a narrow street, too small for anything more than foot traffic and the occasional hovercart. People milled about, their movements slow and silent as if the fog were subduing more than just the light. It was easier to see here in the street where the lights were closer together and the structures helped keep more of the damp cloud at bay, but Skeet still felt as though he were viewing everything through some sort of fuzzy veil. He blinked rapidly several times.

A door opened somewhere up the street, drawing their attention. Light spilled out, along with the sounds of music and laughter. A tavern, probably to serve dock crews and traders coming through the port. The three agents exchanged a glance; it was as good a place as any to begin their search. They would certainly attract attention by going straight to such a public venue, but it wasn't like someone of Haphezian stature could remain inconspicuous in a city like this for very long anyway.

A series of nods indicated they all agreed the place was worth checking out. Skeet jerked his head toward the door. *Let's go.*

They proceeded forward, drawing no more attention from anyone outside than they had thus far. But the moment they set foot inside the bar, everything changed. Nonchalant glances to see who had entered transformed into permanent, leery stares. The noise didn't stop, but there was a palpable shift in the atmosphere of the place as raucous conversations turned to wary murmuring and the music became slightly less peppy.

Well, that hadn't taken long. Skeet paused and took in the scene, meeting the gazes of those who looked his way and compelling them to lower their eyes again. Like everyone they'd passed outside, the people here all appeared weary and weather-beaten, a perfect match for the surrounding architecture in this coastal Panucan capital. None of them seemed ready to cause trouble, at least not yet, but Skeet had already identified a couple who looked like they'd have no difficulty handling themselves.

A subtle shift in body weight was all it took to capture Zinni and Aroska's attention, though they both kept their eyes on the crowd as well. Without a word, the three of them split off, with Zinni moving around the perimeter to the left while Aroska went up the center of the room and Skeet himself turned right. They weren't really sure what they were looking for at this point—perhaps anyone who took too much interest in their arrival or tried a little too hard to ignore it. Better yet, maybe someone who would willingly share the information they sought.

Skeet took slow, methodical strides around the edge of the room, hands held loosely at his sides in an attempt to appear casual while still remaining prepared to react. Those seated ahead of him stayed engaged in normal conversation until he got too close, then they would watch him in silence as he passed, turning and muttering to each other once he'd gone by. He could hear a similar sound pattern rippling across the establishment as Aroska and Zinni elicited the same reactions.

A moment of walking brought him up to the bar itself; it was dinner time so most of the patrons were seated at the regular dining tables, but a few grizzled dock workers sat hunched over stiff drinks at the serving counter and watched him pass by out of the corners of their eyes. The bartender himself stood cleaning a vacant section of the bar and froze mid-wipe to scrutinize him. Skeet hesitated and met the man's questioning stare, offering him a firm nod to signify the team meant no harm but did mean business. For a moment, the barkeep acted as if he were considering interaction, but then he pointedly continued his cleaning, prompting Skeet to move on.

He continued down the length of the bar and shifted his attention over to his teammates as they both completed their circuits. The three of them converged against the back wall, where they found a vacant table with a decent view of the entire floor and seated themselves. They all spared each other a brief glance before returning their attention to their surroundings, a silent signal that their initial trip through the building hadn't yielded any interesting results. Now all they could do was wait.

"We'll give it an hour," Skeet said, speaking Haphezian so quietly that any humans nearby likely couldn't hear him even if they could understand him. "Watch and listen."

He settled back in his chair, resting his left arm casually on the table while bringing his right hand to rest on his thigh just a twitch away from his holster. The only problem with watching and listening was that most of the conversations that were of any consequence had ceased upon their arrival. News of their presence was probably spreading through the city like wildfire, which unfortunately meant it would reach Cartel ears before long if it hadn't already. But it also meant that if *she* was here, or had been here, it probably wouldn't take her long to find out about them either. After Aroska's spiel and demonstration with the surveillance images on the journey here, he couldn't help but think about her, despite the fact that he'd become relatively proficient at blocking thoughts of her from his mind. *If* she was here and *if* she knew as much about the Cartel as they hoped she did, then it was true that she could prove to be a great asset.

But at the same time, part of him didn't want her help. It had taken him a couple of years to admit he'd be okay with her not coming back, regardless of how much he missed her. It wasn't the fact that she'd left that bothered him, but rather the fact that in doing so, she'd misled them once again. Granted, Aroska had wasted little time in sharing her final message, but even thinking she was dead for a single day was too much after the things she'd already put them through, the things she'd already kept from them. She'd *abandoned* them, at a time when he was already feeling like he barely knew her anymore, no less. No matter how many times he'd been reminded by others—and himself—that her departure had been for purely selfless reasons, he still found himself going through phases of complete and utter bitterness, perhaps due more to the somewhat rocky state of their relationship when she'd disappeared. Now was turning into one of those times; curiosity about whether they'd find her here had morphed into a hope that she wouldn't be here. This was his team now, damn it, and if she was going to just desert them all like that, then there was no reason for her to be a part of it anymore. He and his squad were perfectly capable of solving problems on their own.

It almost broke his heart to even be thinking this way.

And of course all of this hinged on the fact that she'd actually survived the explosion and that all of Aroska's clues hadn't been complete coincidences. *Sheyss*, he did not need to be dealing with this uncertainty right now, and maybe the real reason he hoped she wasn't here was because he didn't want to acknowledge these negative feelings. He returned his focus to the floor.

As the minutes passed, Skeet couldn't help but notice the way the tables nearest to them were being vacated more frequently than those on the far side of the room. Most of their occupants stopped to send the three of them distasteful glares before departing, with some even pausing on the way out to have a word with the bartender. The man could be seen looking in their direction every few minutes, still standing stiffly and allowing his gaze to dart around as if he wasn't sure whether he should initiate contact. Out of the corner of his eye, Skeet could tell Aroska and Zinni were also looking toward the bar; they too recognized these things.

Their hour was almost up when the bartender finally slinked out from behind the counter and approached. All the tables but those in the farthest reaches of the restaurant had been cleared, despite the early hour, and mere observation hadn't yielded any useful information, so

Skeet found himself excited by the prospect of interaction. The barkeep advanced toward them with a steady stride, but based on the way he kept working his throat as he swallowed repeatedly, he was just as uncomfortable as his patrons.

"You speak Standard?" he demanded, coming to a stop in front of their table with his arms folded across his chest.

None of them said anything, but Skeet responded with a single, slow nod. He'd taken to resting his chin in his hand with his elbow propped up on the table and made a point of maintaining that posture rather than straightening, creating an impression of boredom that clearly set the man on edge.

"Well listen, unless you have some legitimate business here, you'd best get the hell out of my bar. I'm losing paying customers."

Once again, none of them spoke. Skeet studied the man as he stood there, chest puffed out to create an illusion of confidence. Judging by his haggard appearance, he had plenty of experience dealing with unruly customers and was trying hard to treat this encounter as merely that. But Haphezians were a rare sight out here, which meant his approach wasn't entirely applicable. It also meant he was likely to know something about Moryi, considering she was probably one of the only Haphezians in this sector of space.

The silence dragged for several long, uncomfortable seconds. "Can I help you with something, then?" the bartender asked, unfolding his arms and taking an aggressive step toward the table.

This time Skeet turned, looking first to Zinni then to Aroska, receiving silent confirmation that they'd each completed their appraisals of the man and had deemed him potentially useful. He returned his gaze to the bartender and lowered his hand to the table. "Matia Moryi."

For a moment the man looked perplexed, then the confusion morphed into concern. But no defiance. At least he wasn't going to waste all of their time by denying he knew anything. "What about her?"

"We'd like a word with her."

"Why?"

Skeet waved his hand dismissively. "Haphezian business."

"You know her," Aroska piped in, a statement rather than a question.

"Don't know that I've ever spoken to her, but I know who she is. Most folks in these parts do. She's one of Ibarra's top enforcers."

"Tell us something we don't know," Zinni said.

The man's posture loosened a bit, though a thin sheen of sweat still glistened on his forehead. He turned and looked around before pulling out a chair and easing up to the table opposite the three of them. Several of the remaining customers threw him curious glances.

"First of all, does Manes know you're looking for her?"

Skeet tilted his head, feigning incomprehension. "Manes?"

For just the briefest of moments, the man's eyes widened and his mouth hung slightly agape, though it was difficult to tell whether the reaction was one of fear or merely of shock. Regardless, the expression vanished a second later when he forced out something that sounded like a cross between a scoff and an incredulous chuckle. "Oh, you have no idea what you've gotten into. If Manes doesn't know you're here—"

"That doesn't concern us," Aroska said.

Well, that wasn't accurate. Manes might very well be more of a concern than Moryi, at least when it came to power and resources. But Skeet recognized what the sergeant was doing, projecting an air of confidence—potentially false though it may be—that would hopefully rub off on the bartender and keep him talking.

This time the man let out a full laugh, though his eyes still showed more apprehension than amusement. "I think you'd all change your tune if you actually knew any better."

Once again, the three of them remained silent, allowing him a moment to calm down and recognize they were perfectly serious about their intentions. The moment he did was obvious; the forced smile fell from his face, and he clenched his hands into fists and lowered his gaze to the table.

"Is there something we can call you?" Skeet asked.

The man swallowed and sighed before responding. "You can call me Adler."

Whether or not it was his real name didn't really matter. "All right, *Adler*, let's try this again." Skeet sat upright and leaned forward, staring the man down across the table. "Matia Moryi."

"Listen, there's not much I can tell you just 'cause I don't know much about her. She keeps to herself and is one of Manes's pets, which makes her ominous enough. But folks steer clear of her for other reasons. That lady's nasty. Got some real issues, from what I hear. Just a few days ago, she stabbed one guy and shot another in one of the other local haunts—word was the two of them just got in her way. I was just glad none of that *pazska* happened in my place."

He gestured at the space surrounding them, then leaned forward and lowered his voice. "I've heard stories. One time she was supposed to take out a target right here in Tabaco. Shot someone else instead, but only to wound. Waited 'til the real target came out into the open and tried to help, then killed both of them. Nasty, I'm telling you."

So Moryi was skilled but volatile. A lethal combination indeed. Adler's description of her reinforced Starcer's and the way she had hunted down and destroyed anything that stood between her and her targets on Delatori. Bringing her home alive could prove to be a challenge.

"If you give me a little time, I can try to get you some more information," the bartender continued. "I know some folks who might be able to tell me something, and they'd be more apt to talk to me than to you people."

Skeet leaned back in his chair again, once more adopting a neutral-verging-on-bored countenance. "Why would you do that?"

Adler's eyes widened in confusion and his gaze darted back and forth between the three of them for a moment. "That's why you're here, isn't it?" he exclaimed, forcing out that same cross between a scoff and chuckle. "That's what you asked for."

"Yes, but what reason would you have to comply?"

The confusion slowly hardened into suspicion, then into the barely concealed fear the man had shown upon their arrival. "Look, if Moryi's got some baggage that could jeopardize her position in Manes's network, or worse, jeopardize Manes himself, he's going to want her gone. And—" he paused as if unsure how far to elaborate "—if that's the case, I'd like to be the one to bring that tidbit of information to him."

Skeet nodded. "Seems reasonable." It didn't, really, but it felt like the appropriate thing to say given the circumstances. Anything to keep Adler cooperating.

"So tell you what. You three clear on outta here and let me run my business, then I'll see what I can dig up for you later tonight and we'll arrange a meeting tomorrow." He pulled out a communicator.

The key now was to agree but wait just long enough to make the man feel like this was somehow a contest he was winning. Skeet made a show of appearing pensive for a moment before pulling out his own comm and waving an encrypted code over to the device Adler held. "You can reach us with that."

"Good," the bartender said, checking the code. He then stood abruptly, once again drawing the attention of the few customers remaining in the tavern. "Now, I'd be much obliged if you'd get the hell out of here."

Skeet dipped his head respectfully as Adler turned and made his way back toward the serving counter. He stood, as did Aroska and Zinni, and the three of them began to move toward the exit, keeping a wary eye on their surroundings just as they had on the way in. The patrons remained completely silent as they passed, no doubt unsure what to think about the fact that Adler had initiated contact and had even been relatively friendly with them. Of course the chances anyone had heard the specifics of their conversation were low, but if these people's demeanor was any indication, merely speaking to strangers was enough to arouse suspicion.

The thought drew his attention back to the bartender himself, and he began to search for Adler in any reflective surfaces they passed. In the last second before they cleared the doorway, he caught sight of the man standing behind the bar, watching them depart with a communicator pressed to his ear.

Chapter 12
Saber - Tabaco, Panuco

"Thoughts?"

None of them had spoken for the duration of the journey back to the *Saber*, once again unsure who might be watching or listening, particularly after their encounter in the tavern. The fog made it easier to move about unseen, but they still took a circuitous route back to the ship, taking extra precautions to ensure they weren't being followed.

"That was too easy," Zinni replied immediately.

She'd remained silent throughout much of the conversation with Adler, focusing instead on the man's tone and demeanor while Skeet did most of the talking. Aroska had done the same, and while his field ops training made him much more qualified in the realm of behavior analysis, she was confident in what she'd seen. There'd been a measure of genuineness behind the bartender's offer to assist them, a bona fide enthusiasm, and yet it felt...elsewhere. Applied to something other than their meeting. Combined with the fear he had demonstrated of them, Alastair Manes, *and* Moryi, it left her skin crawling.

Skeet nodded in agreement where he stood leaning over the table across from her in the *Saber's* armory. "Tarbic?"

Aroska stood staring at the surface of the table as well, brow furrowed. "Here's the thing. *If* we could just have Moryi handed to us, that would obviously be ideal, and I think it's reasonable to at least cautiously pursue that lead." He looked up and gave Zinni an affirmative nod. "But you're right—I don't think it's as simple as that."

She offered a nod of thanks in return. "Adler made it sound like if we're coming after her because she's carrying baggage Manes doesn't know about, the Cartel might be more willing to hand her over, if not ready to kill her themselves. But we're after her *because* of the work she's done for the Cartel. There's not actually any baggage."

"Manes doesn't know that," Aroska offered. "Nobody does. For all anyone here knows, this is Haphezian business, just like we told Adler."

It was a reasonable point. "I suppose there's a measure of truth behind that," Zinni said.

"Well, I'm glad we're all on the same page." Skeet appeared thoughtful for a moment. "We'll go through with the meet tomorrow. Get there early and scope out the location once we know where it is. Proceed with the utmost caution. If any little thing seems out of place, we bug out. Maybe grab Adler and see if we can still get some information out of him. We'll just have to do it the hard way."

"Sounds good to me," Zinni replied, moving over to the holoprojector and opening up a secure comm channel. The timing was such that it was the middle of the night back home and she doubted there was any chance they'd catch Emeri live, but he'd requested regular check-ins, and the current developments seemed significant enough to warrant a report despite the irregular hour.

"Alpha, 40319," she said in response to the automated prompt once the connection was made. "Sir, Officer Vax here. We've touched down on Panuco and have made contact with a local who claims to have intel regarding Matia Moryi. The current objective is to meet with this man first thing in the morning. We plan to take every precaution and should have an update for you in—" she glanced up at Skeet, who mouthed an answer "—eight hours. Alpha team out."

She disconnected and double-checked that the transmission had been sent successfully before turning to her male counterparts. "And now we wait."

"I'll take first watch," Skeet said. "You two see if you can catch some sleep. Tomorrow's going to be a busy day."

Chapter 13
Industrial Sector - Tabaco, Panuco

"We're ahead of schedule with the current batch so the buyer requested an additional fifty units. I informed them the rush job would include a sixty-percent price markup, and they're still willing to pay. I'm anticipating having the current order plus the additions ready for shipment within the next three days."

Alastair Manes struggled to focus as the floor manager rattled on about inventory, fixated as he was on the lingering mental image of the three Haphezian visitors he'd received news of less than an hour prior. Their presence here was troubling, to say the least. To begin with, Haphez was located as far on the other side of the galaxy as you could get from Panuco, so he doubted they'd have come all the way out here without a specific reason. Secondly, to his knowledge, Kimbra and Matia were the only two Haphezians to have ever set foot on Panuco; due to the women's non-traditional appearances for their race, he may not have even recognized these visitors as Haphezian save for the research he'd done into their culture when Kimbra had first come into his service.

Oh, and then there was the fact that the very shipment of weapons currently being discussed had been developed using replicated tech based on a collection of crystals Ibarra had acquired through black market channels a few years prior. Niobi crystals, he believed they were called. They had originated on Haphez, and they had made him a lot of money.

It suddenly occurred to him that the floor manager was watching him expectantly, as if waiting for him to answer a question he hadn't been paying attention to. Rather than respond, he picked up a rifle stock from a nearby conveyor belt and examined it. "What of the shipment of zocrum from Delatori?"

The manager stammered for a moment as he struggled to adapt to the sudden change in topic. "Six tons have been recovered as of yesterday and are being prepped for delivery to our facilities. There was enough damage done to the repository during the fighting that it may take a number of weeks to recover the rest."

It was news Manes normally wouldn't have wanted to hear, but at the moment he was so preoccupied that he couldn't bring himself to care. As if on cue, an echoing screech filled the assembly floor as the main door opened. Two of his soldiers entered, escorting a middle-aged, balding man whom he presumed to be the bartender who'd reached out to him with information about the strangers. He waved his people toward an office space on the other side of the floor, somewhere they could talk away from the noise.

"I expect an update when the sale goes through," he said, setting the gun stock back on the conveyor as he turned to leave. The manager offered a respectful nod.

Manes turned and made his way across the floor; most of the manufacturing process was automated or done by bots, but he was aware of the few workers' eyes following him as he went. It was difficult to tell whether they were afraid or merely curious as to their recently arrived comrade's impending fate. He was fine with both scenarios— either way, it kept them in line.

He ascended a set of rusty steps and strode across a short catwalk, letting himself into the office. His two soldiers had seated the bartender in the desk chair and sat perched behind him on the desk itself. They straightened immediately, and their visitor hesitantly leaned forward as if he were unsure whether he should stand.

"Thank you for your service," Manes said, repeating what had become his signature phrase whenever one of his citizens performed a valuable deed or brought him a useful piece of information. "Mister...?"

The man had been beaming in response to the greeting and rushed to compose himself. "Adler, sir. I'm the evening barkeep at Haddon's Tavern down by the marina."

Manes nodded and pulled a small holoprojector from his pocket, displaying one of the images the man had sent him along with his request for an audience. It appeared to have been taken from one of the surveillance feeds in the tavern, depicting the three strangers as they moved toward the door to leave. "Tell me about this," he said, leaning back against a small cabinet beside the chair.

Adler shifted and cleared his throat. "They showed up about halfway through my shift. Two men and a woman. They were big, they were armed, and they moved like they were military. Maybe cops. They went and sat in the back like they were waiting for something, but nothing happened. After a while I noticed they were scaring my customers away, so I approached and asked how I could help them."

"And what did they want?"

"They told me they were looking for Moryi."

Interesting. Manes had found himself hoping Panuco had just been a pit stop for these people, as it had been for the young man from the Core a few days earlier. But they were here for a reason, just as he'd initially feared. And it was a reason he definitely hadn't expected.

"Did they say why?"

The man shook his head. "Only that it was 'official Haphezian business.' Can't say I've ever met any Haphezians, 'sides your girls, and after tonight, I can't say I'd ever want to again. Way I see it, if Haphezian cops are here looking for one of the only Haphezians on the planet, it can't be good."

One of the only Haphezians, indeed, and one who had a virtually nonexistent past at that. Kimbra had always been quick to remind Manes that they knew nothing about Matia, but he'd dismissed her complaints the majority of the time in favor of the assassin's immensely useful skill set. It didn't matter who she was or where she'd come from as long as she could perform in her role and perform well. But if her elusive backstory was going to start causing problems for him, well, that was another matter entirely.

Still, it was tempting to give her the benefit of the doubt. Despite a somewhat rocky start within Ibarra ranks, the woman had thus far done nothing to make him think her disloyal and, despite occasional instances of characteristic antagonism and brazenness, had seemed perfectly content to remain in his employ so long as he provided a steady stream of work and income. There was more information to be gained here, and if these people were hunting for her, she may very well be grateful to have the Cartel at her back.

"What did you tell them?" Manes asked.

Adler appeared chagrined for a moment, hesitating as if he wasn't sure how or if he should answer. "I told them I knew who Moryi was," he said. "If they knew enough to track her down here, I figured it would be a waste of breath to say I didn't know anything—everyone in this town has at least heard of her. I was cooperative and told them I would try to get them some more information about her, but I swear it was only to buy some time. You have to believe I never planned to actually tell them anything. I transmitted to your tip channel as soon as they left."

Manes smirked at the sight of the sweat that had become more prominent on the man's forehead the longer and faster he talked. "Take a breath, comrade," he said, placing a hand on the bartender's back. "You have done nothing wrong."

He felt the tension in Adler's shoulders release all at once as the man sighed and sank back in the chair.

"In fact, I would commend you for your integrity and ingenuity. I believe you have just paved the way for us to move forward in dealing with these people."

"I have?"

Manes stood and moved over to the large observation window, getting lost in the rhythm of the assembly lines below as he considered all of his options. "I have an important task for you, Mr. Adler. I want you to contact these people and tell them you've gotten that information about Moryi for them. They will undoubtedly want to negotiate a meeting place—indulge them, but get them to agree to this spot at the shipping yards." He retrieved a data pad from a nearby drawer and brought up the location he had in mind, waving it over to the wrist-mounted unit Adler wore. "They should find it to be a suitably neutral location."

"And if they don't agree?" Adler asked, studying the proposed meeting place on the map.

"The likelihood is low, but we'll deal with that situation when and if it arises."

"What do I tell them?"

"You needn't tell them anything." Manes moved back to the window, clasping his hands behind his back as he once more gazed down at the floor. "You only need to keep them in the open and stall them long enough to give my strike team time to move in and take them out. If you keep them positioned correctly, they should pose very little risk and should not be difficult to subdue. You will of course receive adequate compensation when the job is done."

"Not to question your methods, but wouldn't you like to find out why they're here first? See what Moryi knows?"

They were legitimate questions. Manes turned from the window. "Leave Matia to me," he warned, taking care, however, to keep his tone soft. "Regardless of the reasons behind their presence here, they are a threat, not only to one of my most prized assets but to our entire operation as well. They should be treated as such."

Adler nodded and relaxed again. "I understand. It's your call, sir."

"You've done this organization a great service tonight, comrade, and what I have asked of you is no small feat. Go now and arrange your meeting. One of my people will be in touch with you tomorrow to process your payment."

The bartender dipped his head and rose from his seat, followed by the two soldiers who had escorted him in. One of them ushered the man out the door; the other hung back, respectfully waiting for any further orders.

"Bring Matia and Kimbra to me immediately," Manes said without even looking at him.

The man strode out, leaving the little office in relative silence. It would never be truly silent, not with the racket of the machines below seeping in through the old walls, but that was noise that could easily be tuned out. Manes found he couldn't hear much at all as he stood there revisiting the same thoughts he'd been mulling over upon beginning the conversation with Adler. If Haphezian police were here hunting Matia, it certainly meant she was guilty of something—perhaps whatever incident had prompted her to leave Haphez in the first place—but whether that 'something' was a threat to him remained in question. Even if whatever she'd done hadn't been meant to hurt him, having these people here poking around in Ibarra business could be detrimental, especially if they found out about the niobi technology, so they needed to be dealt with either way. The way he saw it from where he stood now, regardless of what was going on, this was her mess to clean up. Her reaction to that idea would be telling, and if he was honest with himself, he was curious to see how Kimbra would react to these agents' presence as well.

Manes pried himself away from the window and went to sit at the desk, steepling his hands in front of his mouth while he stared at the smooth metal surface, just as he so often did in his office at the restaurant. So rarely did he have to deal with this sort of thing within his own organization. The only people he'd ever had issues with were independent contractors who either hadn't been vetted adequately or thought they could get away with double-crossing him. Matia had been with him long enough at this point that, despite the fact that she technically fell under that category, he no longer thought of her in that capacity. She'd done plenty to prove her loyalty to him over the past couple of years, so he was surprised when he considered how deep his suspicions currently went. He wasn't yet convinced she had intentionally lied or deceived him, but if she had baggage in her life that could compromise her position or Ibarra operations, then at the very least, she'd withheld information.

His main question right now was *why*, and if the plan he'd just set into motion panned out, he'd have answers soon enough. In the meantime, it wasn't much of an exaggeration to say he hated this feeling of uncertainty more than anything else in the known universe. Uncertainty and indecisiveness caused hesitation, and hesitation caused mistakes. Hesitation meant lost opportunities. And in his world, a world where only the most resilient individuals thrived, hesitation caused death. It had been his father's downfall, after all—Oron Manes had hesitated when presented with the opportunity to expand Ibarra's territory, to take command of new resources that would allow the Cartel to flourish. Only a weak man would have done that, and Ibarra needed someone strong to lead it. Someone who would do whatever it took to survive and maintain control. No hesitation. No uncertainty.

Manes couldn't shake the feeling that he was failing in that department at the moment.

He sat there in silence until he heard the same groan of the massive door opening downstairs. Boots ascended the rusty steps, and he looked up to find Kimbra and Matia entering the room, followed by the soldier he'd sent to summon them. Both women regarded him warily, no doubt confused by the secrecy and urgency surrounding their presence here. Their mutual concern seemed to have temporarily put a halt to their otherwise constant bickering.

"A situation has been brought to my attention," Manes said, glancing between the two of them as they came to a stop in front of the desk. Kimbra swallowed, looking entirely uncomfortable with the fact that she was stuck standing beside Matia rather than scrutinizing the other woman from her usual place behind his chair.

He set the tiny holoprojector on the surface of the desk, displaying the clearest of the images from the bar. The three strangers dominated the shot, their facial features unmistakable. The two women stepped forward to take a closer look.

"Haphezians," Matia murmured, her brows dropping into a scowl. "Who are they?"

"And what do they want?" Kimbra said, her expression mirroring that of her counterpart.

"I was hoping one of you could tell me," Manes answered, wincing inwardly at the accusatory edge that had found its way into his tone. No need to deploy that just yet. "To my knowledge, you two are the only Haphezians in this sector, and Kimbra hardly counts."

He watched as Matia stole a glance at the patches of smooth scar tissue on Kimbra's face before leaning in to study the hologram, taking in every detail of the visitors' faces. Even in the still images, the intensity in their eyes was clear. The cunning. The intelligence. They observed their surroundings warily, and even in the relatively confined space of the tavern, they managed to move and position themselves strategically, the same way she often did.

"They're here for one of us?" Kimbra asked.

"I've received an update from one of my men at the port," Manes said, nodding. "Rumor has it they're searching for Moryi specifically." He shifted his gaze back to Matia, and this time the accusatory tone wasn't an accident. "So, what can you tell me about them?"

She swiped through a couple more of the images before stepping back and crossing her arms, continuing her examination from a distance. "A three-man team like that? I'd guess they're HSP. That's Haphezian Special Police. Probably from one of the operations divisions."

"And?"

"And what do they want with me? I don't have a damn clue." She flung her arms up in an exasperated shrug before bringing her hands to rest on her hips. "I've been gone a long time. Years. There's no way anyone from Haphez should be looking for me at all, much less here." She scoffed and shook her head slowly as her gaze settled on the holo again. "Of all the places..."

Manes studied her silently for a moment, unable to pinpoint whether her flustered state could be best attributed to mere confusion or a deeper agitation. Perhaps only time would tell. Anyone who didn't know her might think her perfectly calm, and while she was, relatively speaking, he wasn't sure if he'd ever seen her this ruffled in the two years he'd known her.

Kimbra had calmed significantly upon learning she was neither the subject of this meeting nor the target of these Haphezian agents. "What's our plan of action?"

Manes couldn't help but notice the way she'd begun edging around the desk toward his chair. "I received a tip this evening from a bystander at the eatery where these images were taken." He waved through the images and paused on one that clearly depicted Adler conversing with the agents. "Apparently the bartender at this establishment took an interest in these people and willingly initiated contact. According to the conversation that was overheard, this man—Adler is his name—disclosed information about you and promised to meet these agents again tomorrow morning with more intel."

The way Matia's features hardened brought him a measure of delight and, he had to admit, relief. It reminded him of the early days she'd spent in his service, the days where she'd trusted no one and self-preservation had been her number one priority. Not that either of those things had changed much in more recent days; it was just good to see that same defiant anger in the current context.

Still, if there was one thing the two of them had in common, it was that there was no one—perhaps with the exception of Kimbra—whom he fully trusted either. He wasn't yet one hundred percent convinced she truly knew nothing about these strangers. There'd been something about the way she studied the images, something verging on longing in her eyes that made him wonder if she'd actually divulge any information even if she did know why these people might be here. He wasn't sure what the circumstances were surrounding her departure from Haphez, but unlike Kimbra, he'd always been under the impression she'd like to return to her homeworld someday. So perhaps what he was seeing—assuming he *had* seen something and wasn't simply being paranoid—was merely nostalgia. Given the relative fondness he'd developed for this woman and her sensational ability to wreak havoc on his enemies, he found himself willing to remain objective for the time being.

"What's our plan?" Matia asked, parroting Kimbra's previous question.

"I'm having this Adler watched tonight," Manes lied, not giving a second thought to the fact that he was blatantly using the barkeep as a pawn after the man had taken pains to bring this situation to light. "As soon as we know where tomorrow's meeting will take place, I'll pass the information along to you. I want you on the ground in the morning to deal with this situation."

Her facial expression didn't budge, but she swallowed quickly before nodding. "I'll take them out."

"No, not *them*. Only the informant."

"What?" Kimbra said, stepping back around in front of him and placing her hands on her hips. "Why not them?"

"I have other plans for them," Manes answered.

Matia bristled visibly and her scowl deepened. "Meaning what, exactly? I don't want these people on my tail any longer than necessary."

He shot her a glare that warned her to stand down. "First of all, an example needs to be made here. Our entire network needs to look at Adler's dead body tomorrow and see what happens to people whose loyalties lie in the wrong places. He made a mistake he must be punished for." The chair scraped along the cold concrete floor as he stood up, compelling Kimbra to retreat a step. "Secondly, assuming you're being completely forthright, none of us have any idea why these agents are here. I have my suspicions, but I would also like some definitive answers."

Manes placed his palms flat on the desk and leaned over it, staring at the hologram of Adler speaking with the Haphezians without really looking at it. This was a test, he decided. For him, a test of nerve, one he'd already passed by making the decision to have Adler executed. For Matia, a test of loyalty. He already felt better about where she stood after this conversation, but in this case, actions would speak louder than words. If she truly believed Adler planned on betraying her to the Haphezians, she should have no trouble following orders. And that would only be the beginning of her trial.

"No, we'll keep them alive," he continued quietly. "Let Adler and these agents believe they have the upper hand for just a bit longer. Then see how they react when their informant is taken out of play. Make them believe they were your targets as well, but ultimately do not harm them. I want to see what they're willing to do—and capable of doing—while they still think they're in control. If our observations don't give us any conclusive information within a couple of days, we'll bring them in."

Matia shrugged, apparently satisfied with the suggestion. That, or she knew better than to argue further. "Whatever you say."

"Keep your comm on tonight and I'll have someone get in touch with you the moment we have details." He slid one hand over and shut down the hologram, clenching the tiny projector within his fist. "Dismissed."

She watched him a moment longer as if she were unsure whether the conversation was truly over, then pivoted and left the room, followed by the soldier who had been waiting outside for the duration. Neither Manes nor Kimbra moved until the echoes of retreating footsteps on the stairs became indistinguishable from the noise of the factory floor. The blonde woman stepped around in front of him and folded her arms, leaning against the desk as she awaited the follow-up discussion that inevitably ensued after a conversation with the assassin.

"Adler's not guilty, is he," she said, a statement rather than a question.

Manes lowered himself back into the chair. "Put together a team," he said quietly, chin resting on his fist as he continued staring toward the doorway. "The meeting place I've arranged is optimal for a strike. The moment she takes Adler out, send them in. I want these agents captured and brought to the compound."

Kimbra scoffed. "So all of what you just said was—"

He cut her off. "You're the one who keeps insisting Matia isn't to be trusted. Now is your chance to see. This is simply a two-pronged approach to testing her. I am confident in her abilities to take Adler out of play, especially if she believes she's protecting herself. How she reacts to the strike team's presence will be...informative." He turned and looked up at her. "And as much as I *do* want these agents brought in alive, your people are authorized to employ lethal force, but only if they pose such a threat that it becomes necessary."

His gaze shifted back toward the doorway, and he folded his hands in front of his mouth once more. "As for Matia and whether she poses a threat to us as well, I suppose we will see."

CHAPTER 14
CITY CENTER - TABACO, PANUCO

For as much money as the Ibarra Cartel brought in, they certainly did a poor job maintaining any infrastructure other than their own primary facilities. The Tunnel was a perfect example; Manes and many of his top lieutenants frequented the club upstairs—sometimes for business, mostly for pleasure—so it was kept in good condition. Swanky, even. But the same couldn't be said for the apartments just below, despite many of them housing Ibarra personnel.

Matia studied the block of buildings before her, hands on her hips. If the Tunnel was bad, she wasn't even sure what to call this area of the city. The golden light from the early morning sun was actually deceptive, casting these structures in a warm glow and giving the walls—worn white after years of being pelted with sand particles stirred up by the marine wind—an almost pearlescent shimmer. Looking past that, however, these places were falling apart. The building directly in front of her had had the glass broken out of all its windows save one, and even it was on the verge of shattering thanks to a series of what appeared to be bullet holes. The facade was crumbling, and ugly yellow fungus that released a horrid stench spilled from the resulting crevices. Word was this group of buildings had been used for a variety of things throughout the years, but in its decrepit state, it was currently a haven for tweakers who'd gotten their hands on the various products Ibarra manufactured and sold on the side, as well as a number of homeless citizens and oddballs who just wanted to be left alone.

It was also the only place she knew she could find Blain on a reasonably consistent basis, at least when he wasn't camped out by her apartment door or lurking outside the compound's main gates. She couldn't understand why he—this young man with such an aversion to violence and confrontation—would willingly sleep and spend most of his time in a place where such things were almost guaranteed to be the norm, but he claimed the space was actually quiet and people left him alone. A bit of investigating on her part had revealed a small alcove where he and several other young people had set up shop. They seemed satisfied enough, but the way she saw it, this was just one more example of how Manes had everyone in this town—hell, on this planet— wrapped around his little finger. Sure, someone like Blain was low on the food chain anyway, but he was willing to continue slaving away in this hovel every day if he thought he could gain an ounce of favor from the man in charge. If Manes really favored him, he certainly wouldn't be living here.

She sighed, exasperated by her own train of thought, and moved toward the door of the building before her. This was all something she'd argued with her young companion about on countless occasions. He just didn't see the problem. Nobody around here seemed to. Panuco was a place where winning was everything. Survival of the fittest and all. Any prospect of winning, however small, propelled people forward, motivating them to pursue a prize that always remained just out of their reach. Or, rather than the desire to win, maybe it was the fear of what losing could mean. The way Manes was dealing with this Adler character was a prime example. Someone had passed information about the bartender's treachery along to Manes—and was probably being compensated handsomely for it—and now the man was slated for execution without another thought. She simply didn't know what to make of it.

Well, no, that wasn't true. She knew exactly what was going on. By engineering this endless power struggle in an environment where only a handful of people controlled that power, Manes had ensured his subjects' loyalty. Blain's sole purpose was to eavesdrop and rat people out. If even half the Panucan population was like him, willing to stab each other in the back and step on anyone it took to stay on top, then that was enough. Manes used them all to his own ends, and none of them cared. That is, if they even noticed in the first place.

Maybe it was just the outside perspective that kept her from falling into this trap. That, and the fact that she'd spent a good number of years working for—and more often against—scum like Manes, so she knew exactly what he was playing at. Aside from Blain, she didn't really care how anyone else here was treated; it was more a matter of just wanting to be right when the rest of these people were wrong. If they didn't want to acknowledge the fact that they were being manipulated, then fine, that was their own damn fault. Even she wasn't completely unscathed by Manes's tactics. Every so often, she'd catch herself pondering or, galaxy forbid, even feeling grateful for the work he'd *given* her, the refuge he'd *provided* her with. But at least she had the self-awareness to recognize that, nip the thought in the bud, and remind herself she was only here to do her job.

Matia pushed these thoughts to the back of her mind and continued forward, but stopped after a single stride when she caught sight of the scrawny man sauntering from the building. He walked unsteadily and rubbed at his single eye. It was hard to tell whether he'd just awakened or was high on something, but it didn't matter. By the time he noticed her and tried to bolt, she was already upon him.

"What have I told you?" she demanded, seizing the front of his shirt and slamming his frail body up against the building's outer wall.

"Matia," he said, dragging out the last syllable of her name and flashing a discolored smile that did nothing to conceal the tremor in his breathing. He went by Ratt, and whether it was his real name or not, it was befitting. "I wasn't...I swear...I was just—"

She pulled him away and slammed him once more. "What did I say?" she repeated. "I told you to stay away. If you *ever* come near him again..."

"Come on, Matia," Ratt whimpered, writhing in her grasp. "I haven't touched him. I just crashed here for the night. I ain't even got any product on me."

As much as Blain's poor decisions often irritated her, one of his merits was that he'd somehow managed to stay clean, despite living in this sty. It made him a target for lowlifes like Ratt who were looking for new prey to sell to—though he was likely too oblivious to realize it—but she'd always gotten the feeling this man had other foul intentions for the boy aside from getting him hooked on slag.

She drew the knife from her thigh without removing her gaze from Ratt and pressed the tip of the blade into his upper cheek, drawing blood. "If I ever see you again—and I don't care when or where—I will carve you open and let the birds at you before you're even dead." She drew her blade across his cheek, opening up a fresh cut in a silent threat to take his remaining eye. Behind his other mangled eyelid, the empty socket gaped, still scabby from their last encounter.

He had yet to stop trembling but offered a stiff nod of under-standing. "Where am I supposed to go?" he murmured.

"I don't give a damn. Get out of my sight." She threw him aside and stood motionless until he recovered and stumbled away down the street.

With a sigh, she stepped into the building, pausing a moment to let her eyes adjust to the dim interior. She didn't anticipate much trouble, but there was no sense in strolling in unprepared. Even with keen Haphezian eyesight, the place remained shrouded in shadows. Based on some of the noises—human and otherwise—she could hear around her, that was probably for the best.

She stepped over a prone form on the floor, skirting around a pair of junkies arguing loudly but incoherently as she made her way toward the stairs. She took the steps two at a time, once again pausing at the top to take stock of her surroundings. It was still early enough that most of the building's tenants—if they could even be called that—were still asleep, but blue electronic light spilled from a room at the far end of the corridor, and she could hear faint stirring within.

A few curious sets of eyes watched her as she approached, but no one spoke or reacted otherwise, either because they knew she never came here as a threat, or because they were familiar with her role in Manes's inner circle and knew she *was* a threat. They'd no doubt heard stories from Ratt and his cronies too.

She reached the door and paused in the opening, looking over the scene within. The blue light she'd seen originated from a series of holograms and screens projected above a single, tiny desk on the far side of the room. Blain sat hunched before them, merely a silhouette against the harsh glow. She rolled her eyes upon noticing his back was to the door.

The room was lit just well enough to reveal a couple of other young people lounging on filthy cots. Both appeared groggy but looked up as she stepped into the room. They'd been present several other times she'd come to call on Blain, so the mere sight of her was enough to snap them to attention, and a single jerk of her head was enough to get them up and slinking out the door. She kept her eyes on Blain as she listened to their departure; he once again had both ears occupied and had yet to acknowledge her arrival.

As tempting as it was to stand and lurk in silence until he realized she was there, she didn't have time for such a thing. She moved up behind him, wishing she could cast a shadow that would at least give him some advance warning, and repeated her usual routine of plucking his earpiece out. "You're killing me, kid."

He started so violently he nearly fell out of his seat. The panicked mash of a button minimized all the projections and subsequently pitched the room into darkness. Realizing his mistake, he fumbled for a portable lighting panel that flickered on after a moment, a substitute for the one mounted on the ceiling that probably hadn't worked in years. Its soft yellow glow illuminated his agitated facial expression as he glared up at her and sucked in deep breaths.

For someone who was so tightly wound, Matia could not for the life of her understand why he constantly allowed himself to be taken by surprise, and this morning she didn't have the patience to chastise him about it again. "I need a favor," she said, bringing her hands to rest on her hips.

As he looked her over in the better light, he averted his gaze and shrank away ever so slightly upon realizing she donned full tac gear. "You think I should help you after you pull *pazska* like that?" he demanded, rubbing his chest.

"Don't be a *bashqe*."

He gave her an unimpressed look, apparently uninterested in standing around exchanging curses in various languages. "I don't even know what that means."

"Those Haphezian agents who showed up last night," she said without further fanfare. "I want to get in on their comms."

"Haphezian agents...?"

She reached across him and brought all of his screens back up, revealing surveillance shots and comm logs from the very three agents she spoke of. The thought suddenly occurred to her that he hadn't been up early working on this—he'd been up all night.

He hung his head and swiveled back around to face the workstation. "I just wanted to get Manes some information he could use."

Was he disappointed that someone else had beat him to the task of first reporting these people's presence the previous evening? "And you can do that by getting me what I need. They're supposedly here looking for me, so Manes says this is my mess to clean up. If I can listen in, I might be able to figure out what they want, what their plan is." She paused. "And I'll make sure Manes knows you helped me."

He stared absently at the display for a moment, gnawing on his bottom lip as he mulled her proposition over. "What exactly do you need?"

"I want in on their channel," she answered, fixing her own gaze on the projections, studying the faces of the two men and the woman. The sight of them stirred something inside of her, something she instinctively quashed before she even had a chance to consider what it was. The after-effect left a sour taste in the back of her mouth and made her skin crawl.

"It'll be one way. Listen-only."

"That's fine."

Blain kicked off the floor and rolled his chair over to his bunk, the old-fashioned wheels thumping and bumping as they struggled to cross the warped, uneven surface. His backpack lay on the cot, and he rummaged through it until he found a small metal case. From that case he removed an earpiece, which he then brought back to the table to program. "I've got their comms grouped, so I'll add you to that group. They've changed channels a couple of times since they got here, but I can track those changes, so your connection will adapt as well. Might be a slight delay though."

She nodded her understanding, then lifted an eyebrow. "They're not using any sort of encryption?"

He cracked his knuckles. "Oh, they are." The corners of his lips turned upward and a familiar cocky glimmer appeared in his eyes, wiping away all signs of the moping and disappointment he'd exhibited just moments before. Normally that overconfidence was obnoxious, but in this case, it was backed by legitimate skill, skill that was proving to be very useful at that.

He finished with the earpiece and passed it to her. It was unremarkable, just large enough to fit cleanly inside her ear and be undetectable at a glance. "You're in," he explained, pointing to a small list on one of the projections. A new comm signature appeared below the three he'd already been tracking. "There probably won't be constant chatter—they're not usually on comm unless they're out and about. But if you don't hear anything within an hour, let me know."

Matia cupped a hand over her ear, attempting to block out the sudden cacophony of incoherent yelling in the hallway as she listened to the silence coming through the earpiece. Hopefully that silence wouldn't last long.

"Well," she said, "I'm headed down to the docks to set up. With any luck, this job will be easy and this circus will be over as fast as it started." She bristled when the yelling outside intensified—it was probably the pair of junkies she'd passed on the way in, now engaged in a full-blown tussle. "Sounds like the riffraff are starting to wake up. About time you made yourself scarce, eh?"

He minimized the screens and began packing his little collection of equipment back into his pack. "Yeah," he sighed. "I'll find somewhere to lay low and maybe stop by your place when you're done this morning."

She was already headed for the door and was once again glad he couldn't see the smirk on her face. "Fine," she said, putting conscious effort into sounding indifferent despite being utterly relieved by the thought of him being anywhere but here. In fact, if everything went according to plan, her apartment would be the best place for him to be.

She paused at the door and listened—the argument seemed to have moved outdoors. She saw no reason why the job this morning wouldn't go smoothly, but in her experience, thinking such a thing almost always ensured something would go wrong. Being prepared to adapt was a requirement, and she wasn't sure what all that would entail.

"Blain, do you trust me?"

Even without looking back, she heard the chair squeak as he sat up straighter and regarded her for a moment. It was probably the most serious question she'd ever asked him, and given the current context it no doubt left him confused.

The silence dragged on for several long seconds before he gently cleared his throat. "Sure."

"Good. I want you to remember that."

She continued out the door without another word. The moment she rounded the corner and was out of sight, she reached up and dug her earpiece out, studying the tiny device in the dim light as she descended the stairs. She hadn't been entirely truthful with her young associate just then. It wasn't quite time to go to the docks—she had one more stop to make first.

CHAPTER 15
SHIPPING YARD · TABACO, PANUCO

The surrounding landscape looked drastically different in the daylight. A thin fog drifted along the ground right near the waterline, but beyond that, the sky was cloudless and the sun shone unhindered. The dull roar of the sea still filled the air, but rather than a sinister black void, it was a shimmering expanse that by most accounts would be considered beautiful.

It wasn't that Aroska didn't think it was beautiful—it was just that there were other things he needed to be looking at, and he feared the pleasant sight would lull him into a false sense of comfort. Comfort would be nice right about now; the collective tension he, Skeet, and Zinni felt was thick enough to be sliced with a blade. But no, he didn't dare succumb to that desire.

The three of them had discussed this development at length, this meeting with the bartender. There was still something about it that rubbed them all the wrong way. They'd been planetside for barely twelve hours; as Zinni had put it the night before, this was too easy. And yet, if Adler really did have information that could benefit them, this was the simplest—and fastest—way to move forward in their search for Moryi.

The man had contacted them not too long after their initial meeting with a suggested rendezvous location. There they waited now, having been present there since sunrise to keep an eye out for suspicious activity. So far they'd seen nothing of interest, a good sign. The area was wide open, with good sight lines in all directions and few places that could fully conceal anyone setting up an ambush. There were a couple of spots that made Aroska nervous, though at this point he couldn't tell if they were of legitimate concern or if he'd just spent too long looking at them. He checked the time, glad the moment had nearly come to get this show on the road.

Behind him lay a shipping yard, where bots and dock workers oversaw the movement of assorted pallets and containers from nearby watercraft. A commotion drew his attention, and he turned to see that a large cylindrical crate had toppled and broken open. A flock of enormous gray birds that had been circling overhead descended upon it immediately, gobbling up its contents—some sort of shellfish—even as workers beat at them and fended them off with shock batons. It made Aroska wonder if the shipment was really that precious or if the shellfish were simply a front for something more illicit. Given Panuco's notoriety, the latter wouldn't have surprised him at all.

He swept his gaze over the entire yard once more. It was the same group of people who had been there since he'd arrived, all going about their business and paying little—if any—attention to their surroundings. The stacks of shipping crates would provide some cover, but anyone who chose to take that cover would be putting themselves at a tactical disadvantage with their backs to the ocean. No decent means of egress. And unless an enemy took an amphibious approach, the likelihood of an ambush coming from that direction was low.

As satisfied with the state of things as he thought he'd ever be, Aroska slid down from the tall shipping container he'd been perched on under the shade of a scrubby tree on the edge of the yard. The warm sun felt nice after sitting still for so long in the shadows with the cool sea breeze coming through. He flexed his chilled fingers, turning his attention to the relatively empty parking area where the meet with Adler would take place. Skeet arrived from his post down the street where he'd been watching for any movement amid the nearby buildings, and after a moment Zinni approached from where she'd been waiting in the team's car, scanning the open land in the opposite direction.

"It almost pains me to say that everything looks good," Skeet said, stealing a glance back over his shoulder toward the buildings he'd been scouting. "All the more reason to be doubly cautious."

Aroska and Zinni nodded in agreement. "We'd be able to see anyone coming from a long way off over there," the intelligence officer said, shielding her eyes as she took a look back toward her post as well.

Skeet looked in the direction she had indicated, letting his gaze linger on the empty stretch of land before turning and focusing on a lone figure approaching on the otherwise unoccupied street. He shifted, cracking his neck as he brought his hand to rest on his holster. "Keep your eyes open, huh?" he said, nodding toward the man.

Aroska jerked his head toward Zinni, moving to the far edge of the street and positioning himself to flank Adler while she did the same on the other side. The man faltered for a moment when he saw them moving to intercept, but he continued forward toward Skeet with his hands out where they could see them.

"Hold up," Aroska called the moment Adler was flush with him and Zinni. The bartender flinched but complied, remaining still while the two of them closed in. Aroska took hold of his arms, ensuring he kept them raised while Zinni came up behind him and began patting him down. The team had already concluded that they didn't mind if he was transmitting—and that they fully expected him to be—but nobody was comfortable with the idea of him carrying.

Zinni ran her hands up and down his torso, paying special attention to his waistband before moving down and checking his pant legs and ankles. "Clean," she announced.

They turned and found Skeet already making his way up the street toward them. Adler stood tall, but the effort it was taking for him to swallow gave Aroska the impression he wasn't as comfortable being here as he'd seemed when he'd first suggested the meet. It was difficult to tell whether he was apprehensive simply because he didn't trust strangers, or for reasons yet unknown. If the things he'd already told them about Matia Moryi were true, he had every right to fear Haphezians.

"Mr. Adler," Skeet said. He had yet to remove his hand from his sidearm. "You have information for us?"

The man glanced around as if he were uncomfortable despite being in a wide open, breathable space. Or perhaps it was the openness itself making him uneasy. Or perhaps he simply didn't want to make eye contact. A dozen possibilities spun through Aroska's mind and he took a step back, giving himself a full view of Adler's body and any unspoken language it showcased, purposely or otherwise.

The bartender nodded in response to Skeet's question but refrained from speaking for a moment longer. The thick tension they'd all been feeling returned instantly.

"Moryi's been quiet since she floored those guys in that other bar. It's typical of her to lay low for a few days when she gets back from a mission, so maybe she's been gone somewhere recently." He paused and chuckled. "Not like she comes out and socializes much in the first place."

Aroska ground his teeth but said nothing, letting Skeet take point. If they'd gone to all this trouble only for this man to tell them he didn't have any more information...

The lieutenant voiced his thoughts exactly. "Mr. Adler, I hope you have more than that."

It wasn't like they were losing anything if he refused to talk. They'd taken a gamble with Adler and would just be back where they started upon arriving on Panuco. The issue was that Aroska could tell the man wasn't telling them everything. Like the previous night, he was holding a lot of anxiety—no, anticipation—just beneath the surface. His gaze shifted not only between the three of them but to his surroundings as well. Based on how quickly he would return his focus to them, Aroska could tell he was trying not to look around, but it was happening all the same.

"Well," Adler said, "I did tell you no one knows much about her."

"You seemed eager enough to help us bring her down last night," Zinni said. "What happened to wanting credit for that?"

Another subtle glance up the street. Aroska swept his gaze around as well, wondering what the man was looking for. They'd approved this suggested meeting location because, aside from the shipping yard, it was relatively free of pedestrian traffic. But now the street wasn't just quiet; it was deserted. Once again, his mind cycled through the possibilities. This could just be a time of day with little foot traffic, and they'd happened to be here during a particular lull. But things were rarely that simple. The more probable scenario—the one they needed to be prepared for, at least—was that anyone wandering outside had been sent away, or else had fled for some reason. Something was about to happen.

"I know where she spends most of her time when she's planetside," Adler finally said, drawing out his words as though he were putting extra thought into each and every one of them. "Outside Manes's primary compound, there's a small residential sector..."

Neither Skeet nor Zinni seemed to be paying any more attention to him either. Both looked to Aroska and then around, eyes wide, backs straight, muscles tense, suddenly hyper-aware of their surroundings.

An eerie silence preceded the *thwack* of a bullet striking bone, followed almost instantly by the distant crack of a rifle somewhere behind them. Aroska was on the move before Adler's body had even hit the ground. He slid in behind a nearby parked car, sacrificing a couple of seconds to wipe his sleeve across his face and clear away the bartender's hot blood spatter. A look back revealed that Skeet and Zinni had fled in the opposite direction; the former crouched behind another vehicle and the latter hunkered down behind a low wall that separated the street from the shipping yard.

The spit and sizzle of plasma fire drew his attention back to his immediate surroundings, and he caught sight of a figure in full tactical gear moving into cover across the street. Beyond that, a field of long beach grass stretched for two hundred meters or so, sloping gently upward until it transformed into some rocky foothills and cliffs that no doubt concealed the sniper.

"Got foot soldiers," he said into his earpiece as he caught sight of another armored man slinking through the tall grass. He raised his pistol over the top of the car, squeezing off several blind shots that would keep these thugs at bay long enough for him to slide to his right and dive behind the next parked vehicle. It carried him further from his teammates, but the extra space decreased the chances of getting surrounded.

"Two more down here," Skeet replied. "This was an ambush."

By whom, Aroska could only guess. From what little he could see when he risked another look over the car, their attackers' garb was all identical and they moved as a unit. The safest bet was that Alastair Manes had sent them; the man was undoubtedly aware of their presence on the planet. He wasn't sure if Matia Moryi was high enough up in the Ibarra food chain to have any thugs at her disposal, but that was still an option. Regardless, based on Adler's behavior, the man had been expecting this and had blatantly led the team to this spot so these soldiers could take them out. Aroska doubted the man had known he'd be expendable too.

Movement on the left caught his eye and he turned to find one of the soldiers advancing toward him, rifle raised and a fraction of a second from firing. Aroska lifted his own pistol and squeezed off three quick shots, aiming initially for the man's weapon rather than his unprotected head. As hoped, the rifle flew from his hands in a cloud of sparks, leaving him shocked and exposed for just a short moment before Aroska buried another plasma bolt between his eyes.

"One down," he called over the comm, peering through the grimy car windows in search of the first two men he'd seen.

"Make that two," Zinni answered. "I count six remaining."

"Everyone move for the car," Skeet said.

Aroska glanced in their direction even as he continued moving the opposite way. Putting too much distance between himself and his team would leave him exposed, but if they could hem in their attackers, they'd have a definite advantage, even without equal numbers. He could still see both Skeet and Zinni moving about and noted their positions, knowing they would do the same with him despite the fact that he was ignoring orders.

Another shot suddenly rang out from the hills across the field, similar to the one that had killed Adler but with a softer tone. There was a second shooter somewhere up there. Aroska kept his head down, unsure where the bullet had struck. He hadn't heard it hit the wall or any of the parked vehicles, which left only...the soldiers?

He peered up above the car just in time to see one of the thugs coming his way. He took aim, but before he could get a shot off, the man's head snapped to one side and he stumbled forward into the dirt. The sharp crack of the rifle registered a split second later. Another man lay newly dead in the street just behind him, no doubt the target of the previous shot.

"Alpha Two, let's go!" Skeet's voice said in his ear.

"Working on it!" Aroska replied, gritting his teeth and ducking back down as a barrage of plasma fire pelted the car. He could hear another set of heavy footsteps approaching with haste, and the thought occurred to him that if a second shooter was now targeting the soldiers, this man might be on his way over to seek cover of his own.

Determined he would receive no such privilege, Aroska watched him approach through the car window, ready to put a halt to his advance. But once again, a projectile struck, followed by the distant report of the rifle. The man hit the car, still moving full speed. His forward momentum carried him over the engine compartment and his limp body slid into a heap in the very spot he'd likely been seeking out for cover. Aroska positioned himself to make a run for it, but before he could move, the entry wound caught his eye. No blood. No exit. The flesh around the hole was scorched as if the projectile had been superheated.

The comm crackled in his ear. "You're clear, Alpha Two. Get moving."

The words—the *voice*—echoed through Aroska's mind, and he froze and fell back against the car door. For several long seconds, the only sound he could hear was the static in his earpiece. Plasma bolts continued to fly down the street as Skeet and Zinni engaged the remaining soldiers, but they had both gone radio silent as well, surely just as shocked by the voice as he was. It was *her*, no doubt about it. Part of him was ecstatic that his plan to draw her out had worked, as well as relieved that she had arrived in time to assist them with the Ibarra thugs. But at the same time, the realization that she was so close yet so far away left him numb. Struggling for air, he lifted his head and peered through the car window again, scanning the distant cliffs but knowing he would never see anything.

"Please tell me I'm not the only one who heard that," he said, reminding himself of her instructions. He worked his way into a crouch, ready to sprint back in the direction of the team's vehicle.

"Just get back here," the lieutenant replied, breathing hard.

"On my way." Aroska caught himself just before springing forward and paused to retrieve any comm devices from the body of the fallen soldier in front of him. The earpiece had been knocked away when the bariine round had struck, but the communicator itself remained intact on his belt.

Device in hand, he took off at a dead run for the rendezvous, weaving and ducking in case the first marksman was still watching. The plasma fire up ahead was dwindling, more so after the second rifle fired several more times, but it still felt like he was crossing an impossibly wide no man's land and would surely be taken out by hostile fire at any moment. When he reached the other side and was still breathing, he had to imagine a certain someone had neutralized the threat in the hills as well as the ones on the ground.

Skeet and Zinni waited just long enough to make sure he was on their heels before continuing toward their car on the far end of the shipping yard. Most of the dock workers were still cowering behind crates in response to the nearby firefight, the birds and mess from the spilled container long forgotten. They watched in half-fear, half-confusion as the three agents tore by.

A few moments later, they were piling into the car and pulling out of the area with Skeet at the controls. None of them spoke, instead working to slow their breathing and throwing each other periodic glances that spoke of utter shock and incredulity. Well, they had confirmation that *she* was here, and she obviously knew they were here. The key now was to reestablish a connection.

Aroska unclenched his fist, his fingers white where they'd been curled around the little comm module. With luck, it would lead them to Moryi, or lead them to someone else who could lead them to her. In spec ops, you typically didn't believe in luck; there was only skill. But if what had just happened back there wasn't luck, he didn't know what to call it. If she was willing to keep helping them, her knowledge plus whatever they managed to glean from this communicator greatly increased their odds of succeeding with this mission. Despite the loss of Adler, they were by no means back to square one. Now it was time to get to work

CHAPTER 16
COMMERCIAL SECTOR - TABACO, PANUCO

A commotion outside preceded the sounds of heavy approaching footsteps. Manes turned his attention away from the plate of food before him, continuing to chew the bite he'd just taken as he waited for the door of the restaurant to open. As he'd expected and hoped, it was Matia arriving; she stormed into the empty room, sweeping her gaze around and charging forward the moment it settled on him.

He wiped his mouth and slammed his utensils down, rising to meet her as several members of his entourage moved to intercept her. "What *happened*?" he demanded.

"You liar," she growled. "What the hell were you thinking sending a strike team in like that?"

"Never mind that," he said, closing the distance between them but honestly glad they were still separated by the burly arms of his men. He had no desire to be subject to the havoc she was capable of wreaking. "What I want to know is why they're all *dead*."

Drawing her weapon would be suicide in this situation, yet her hand hovered just above her holster, as steady as ever. "There was another shooter."

It was the last response Manes had expected, and for a moment genuine confusion trumped any anger he held toward her. "Excuse me?"

"I did my job," she said, her gaze unwavering, her tone low and even. "I took out your informant. The second he went down, that strike team came out of nowhere." Her eyes narrowed. "And then *they* started going down. The sniper was somewhere above me—if I would have moved, she would have taken me out, and forgive me if I wasn't too keen on dying. I was pinned down."

"She?"

"I had Blain Reed patch me into the Haphezian agents' communications so I could track them. A woman's voice came on the same channel partway through the shootout. She told one of them to move right after one of your men was shot from long range. I can only put two and two together."

Manes searched her face, unable to pinpoint any sincerity—or lack thereof—through the angry defiance he saw there. It was difficult to tell whether that anger stemmed from what had happened to the Haphezian agents or simply from being kept in the dark about the strike team. If there really had been another shooter, perhaps a fourth agent they somehow hadn't seen yet, that changed everything. But he wasn't sure if he was ready to believe such a thing just yet.

He took a step back from Matia and extended a hand, receiving a communicator from one of his men nearby. "Kimbra, status report," he said, not removing his eyes from the assassin in front of him.

For a moment that seemed to drag into an eternity, the comm unit emitted only static. Then the woman came on, the sound of her voice made choppy by the strong breeze blowing across the wharf where she was located. "I've just arrived on the scene. Stand by."

The lack of a prompt response was less than ideal, and impatience was beginning to take root. He wished he could say the tension had an effect on Matia, but she had yet to break eye contact and appeared unfazed by it all. At the very least, she was no more agitated than she'd been upon her arrival here.

"You lied to me," she said again when it became clear Kimbra wasn't going to respond in the immediate future.

It wasn't as though either of them had ever had any illusions of trusting the other implicitly, though he supposed the nature of their professional relationship had required him to be honest with her more often than not. "I merely withheld information."

"Some would argue there's no difference."

"You forget your place, Moryi."

She began to advance closer to him, but one of his soldiers responded by reaching out and seizing her by the shoulder. Two seconds later the man was down on one knee, desperately contorting his body in an attempt to alleviate the pressure in the wrist that had been locked above him. This in turn prompted the rest of the men to draw their weapons.

"You want me to do my job?" she snarled, flinging the man's arm away and ignoring the multiple gun barrels pointed at her face. "You've got to give me all the facts."

Manes wagged his head gently, not prepared to speak any further on the matter until her claims about the incident could be proven one way or another. "You said it yourself—you *did* your job."

She pursed her lips as though she wanted to say more but thought better of it. The comm finally crackled again anyway, prompting them to return to the topic at hand.

"I count eight men down," Kimbra reported. "Looks like some of them were taken out with plasma weapons."

"They were killed by the agents," Matia said.

Even knowing she preferred projectile weapons didn't bring Manes any comfort. "Do you see Adler?"

"Got him." A projection rendered just above the communicator, depicting the poor bartender sprawled on the ground, his wide eyes staring vacantly upward. A clean entry wound had pierced one temple, and blood and brain matter spilled onto the street from the opposite side of his head. It was a gruesome sight even by Manes's standards, but he had to admit these marks were consistent with the type of solid projectile Matia usually used.

"None of our people look like that, do they?"

Once again, his words elicited no response from Matia.

"Not that I've seen, no." The conviction in Kimbra's response was a plus.

"Are there any other wounds that don't match anything else you've seen?"

"Looking."

"The shooter took out three or four of our people that I saw," Matia offered. "Check around the parked cars on the east end of the street."

Kimbra's voice could be heard in the background as she barked new orders at the soldiers who'd accompanied her to the shipping yard. Footsteps echoed against the stone walkway, and a few moments later, a new visual appeared in the projection.

The wound was curious for certain. The hair and flesh on the side of the man's head was scorched, and there was very little blood, just like an average plasma blast. But in the center of the mess was a single, clean hole where it appeared a bullet had punched through. A plasma bolt wouldn't have made such an entry, and based on the lack of blood on the street beneath his head, the projectile had not exited. Peculiar indeed.

A few more muffled words were exchanged among those at the scene. "There are four guys like this," Kimbra said. "One in the back, two cleanly through the head. Another up the street, center of mass. Shooter was good."

Manes couldn't help but notice she refrained from speculating any further about Matia's involvement, despite the fact that the assassin was shaping up to be innocent. Typical—if she didn't have anything nasty to say, she tended to say nothing at all.

So instead the speculation was left up to him. He glanced up at Matia and, upon noting the way she had almost imperceptibly relaxed, nodded gently at the soldiers surrounding her. They lowered their weapons and stepped away, but none of them appeared to be willing to back off completely.

"What are we looking at here?" he asked Kimbra, turning his back on the group as he began to pace slowly amid the vacant tables.

An electronic beep told him the woman was already in the process of checking. "Scans are picking up multiple fragments within, but only one entry." Her voice rose up at the end of her thought, almost as if she were asking a question. "I'm reading traces of lead and...another metal called bariine." This time the questioning tone was even more definite.

Manes glanced back at Matia, who shrugged and shook her head.

"Looks like a form of custom frag round," Kimbra continued. "I've never seen anything like it."

The thought occurred to him that the Cartel might be able to develop a similar form of ammunition for some of its weaponry, but that was neither here nor there. "Have all the bodies brought in," he ordered. "I want them all examined, particularly the ones killed by our mystery sniper."

He ended the transmission abruptly, though not before he heard her start to mutter something in response to his verbal confirmation that Matia likely hadn't been involved.

He passed the communicator back to one of his men and stood in silence for a moment, his back still turned to the rest of the group. Regardless of who the second shooter was—a fourth Haphezian they hadn't accounted for, or a third party with some ulterior motive for taking out his men—she needed to be dealt with. And regardless of which scenario was true, the three agents might be instrumental in leading him to this person, voluntarily or not. Or, more accurately, lead Matia to this person, since she was the reason they were here to begin with.

With a subtle jerk of his head, the men surrounding him began to move away, some heading outside and some retreating to the far corners of the restaurant. Once they'd all cleared the vicinity, he turned and faced the assassin.

"I'm going to be very frank with you."

Matia's eyes narrowed and she crossed her arms. "That would be great."

"This morning was a test."

Now her brows dropped into a full scowl and she moved her hands back to rest on her hips. "What the hell is that supposed to mean?"

He decided she didn't really need to know. "I'm pleased to say you passed. Your orders were to kill Adler, and you did as you were told. The presence of this sniper was unforeseen and unfortunate, and you performed as well as you could under the circumstances." It was tempting to tell her she'd been right to keep herself hidden, but he found he wasn't entirely convinced there was nothing she could have done to stop the carnage.

"However," he continued, playing on the lie he had woven for her the previous evening, "this is still your mess to clean up. Adler's death ensured he wouldn't be able to share any revealing information about you, which puts you at a clear advantage. Now that they have slaughtered eight of our best soldiers—directly or indirectly—I am more inclined to ask that you deal with these agents in kind, but I for one would still like to know why exactly they have sought you out."

"I told you I didn't know."

"But they clearly have a reason. And I want to know what it is so I can take the necessary steps to prevent *inconveniences* like this in the future."

Matia held his gaze for several seconds as if searching for more information than what he'd just shared. "Fine," she muttered, turning to leave. "I'll deal with them."

"And Matia..."

She stopped after several strides but didn't turn to face him.

"If you ever question my methods like that again..."

His hesitation was brief as he stopped to consider the fact that he was making yet another empty threat, but it was enough for her to tell he had nothing further to say. She continued out the door without looking back.

Manes stood and listened to her departure just as he'd listened to her arrival until his men began to slowly emerge from their corners and move back toward him. He turned and went back to his table, and just like the previous evening, he felt unsure. Unsure what to do with Matia. Unsure what to do about the Haphezian agents. Normally his solution to problems like this was to immediately...*remove* the people in question, regardless of whether he had all the facts, and he couldn't pinpoint exactly what was keeping him from doing that now. He would give Matia another chance and see how everything played out.

For now, he decided, his biggest problem was that his breakfast was getting cold.

CHAPTER 17
SABER · TABACO, PANUCO

Anyone who entered the *Saber's* communications room at that particular moment might have found the scene before them humorous: three agents standing with crossed arms around the workbench, watching the tiny comm unit on its surface as if they might summon some sort of result the longer and harder they stared. Zinni's gaze flicked up to the display above the table as she checked for the umpteenth time to make sure the connection was still live. And for the umpteenth time, it was. They should have heard something by now.

Beside her, Skeet shifted ever so slightly. In the stillness of the room, she could hear the exact moment his lips parted and he drew a short breath in preparation to speak, but she held her hand up for silence, not daring to jeopardize the chance to hear the terminal signal that it had found the transmission's source, or, better yet, hear something come through the unit. If the channel was still live, it meant someone somewhere was still connected, and after what they'd all just heard down at the docks, she was very eager to find out who that might be.

It had taken her several moments to recognize the significance of the voice that had come through their comms in the midst of the shootout. On the one hand, it was so familiar that she didn't immediately realize it had been four-plus years since she'd even heard it. Secondly, it was a shock—and a relief, considering the circumstances—to hear it here, of all places. But that meant Aroska had been right. Not only was *she* here, but she knew the team was here as well. Their ludicrous plan to seek her help in taking down Moryi could work after all.

Part of Zinni—a large part—wanted to be excited. She'd been so careful not to get her hopes up whenever Aroska discussed his project, so this was all liberating in a way. She felt as though she could finally allow herself to breathe, to be genuinely happy. But at the same time, this all stirred up other memories that were, frankly, on the sour side. Secrets being kept. She and Skeet being left out of the loop in situations where she thought they should have been the first to be included. An untimely death, revealed later to merely be a disappearance. The fact that the latter issue had transpired before either of the former two could be resolved was perhaps what bothered her the most.

Lost in thought, it took her an extra fraction of a second to react when the terminal beeped. She leaned forward, her eyes poring over the information on the display. Someone was still connected, all right, and they were currently mobile.

"What does this mean?" Aroska asked, indicating a particular data point on the screen.

"Whoever's still on this channel isn't using a direct connection," she explained. "Those soldiers were all sharing one network just like you'd expect. This person is on that same network, but...removed."

"Meaning?"

"Most likely? They were tracking the soldiers. Tapped in. Eavesdropping." Zinni made a point of keeping her gaze locked on the screen, putting conscious effort into keeping the excitement from taking over. If *she* had managed to get into the team's comms, it made sense that she also would have been monitoring the strike team. Would need to stay ahead of them. Track their movements and whatnot. Yes, it made sense.

The renewed silence in the room gave her the impression Skeet and Aroska were considering the same things but were also hesitant to voice their thoughts out loud. "Can we get any chatter?" Skeet asked.

Zinni pulled up a chair and made herself comfortable in front of the comm console. "If there was anything happening on this channel, we'd be able to hear it already. But if I lock on to this signal, I may also be able to track other signals originating from or going to the same location."

A pang of doubt hit her as her fingers went to work at the console. If this was the channel the strike team had been using and they were all dead, there was no real reason anyone should still be connected...unless the source had intentionally stayed online in hopes the team would attempt a trace. The mobile signal was headed straight back into the heart of Tabaco though, which didn't make any sense if the source was who she thought it was.

The flicker of hope she'd been hanging on to was dashed when no less than a hundred additional signals suddenly appeared on the screen. At first she was positive it was an error—perhaps interference of some sort, as there was no way that many transmissions should be coming through anything short of a full-blown comm relay—but then it occurred to her that they all had the same attributes as the one they'd traced through the stolen communicator.

"What the hell?" she murmured.

Skeet leaned in and squinted at the display. "Am I reading this right? One person is tapped into all these different signals?"

"That's what I'm seeing. I can't say whether that's accurate, but I don't have a better explanation." She turned to address Aroska directly. "Recon like this seems like something she might try to do, but there's no way to know for sure if this is her."

His face appeared rather grim, but he said nothing.

"Regardless of who it is," Skeet said, "they more than likely heard what went down at the docks and are bound to know something. Anyone with access to that much information at any given time will have some answers—the question is whether they'll give them up willingly."

Zinni nodded and waved all the data from the main console to a handheld viewscreen. "Then let's go find our source."

"I want all of us wearing underlays," Skeet said. "If this goes to *sheyss* again, I'm not risking anyone taking a direct hit."

Zinni couldn't help but consider the fact that a headshot like the one that had killed Adler would render an underlay completely futile, but hopefully it wouldn't come down to that. The three of them moved across the corridor into the armory, replenishing their loadouts and taking the time to slip the low-profile vests on under their clothing. Then, armed with the viewscreen tracking the mysterious signal, they set out for the city once more.

CHAPTER 18
COMMERCIAL SECTOR - Tabaco, Panuco

Twenty minutes later they found themselves in a sector of Tabaco with predominantly pedestrian traffic not far from an area they'd previously identified as the main Ibarra compound. The signal Zinni had been tracking had continued moving as they'd travelled, but they'd managed to catch up to it and narrow it down to somewhere in the crowd. This appeared to be some sort of outdoor market; vendors and their stalls lined the narrow street, and people milled about pushing carts or carrying parcels.

"Got it," Zinni's voice murmured over the comm. "Alpha One, thirty degrees left."

Aroska peered out from his position in a shadowy alley, scanning the crowd for Skeet and then taking Zinni's description into consideration. He'd known the chances were slim that the signal would lead them directly to *her*, but he couldn't help but be disappointed when he caught sight of a young man instead. His clothes were tattered, and his ragged boots looked a couple of sizes too large. Wavy brown hair poked out from beneath what appeared to be a hand-made cap. His sagging shoulders were either the result of the impressive array of gadgetry weighing him down, or all the hours spent hunched over a table working on that gadgetry. Perhaps both.

It was tempting to confirm they were looking at the same person, but if this techie was monitoring as many comms as they thought he was, he could very well be listening to theirs. No sense in alerting him to the fact that they were watching. Aroska settled with a generic, "Target in sight."

"Likewise," Skeet said, going silent while the young man clomped past his position.

Aroska watched as the boy maneuvered through the crowd, deftly weaving and ducking despite the oversized footwear as though he'd spent every day of his life moving in a similar fashion. He wore devices over both ears, seemingly blocking out all of his surroundings, but aside from a couple of brief glances around, he kept his focus straight ahead. He was clearly headed somewhere with a purpose.

"Alpha Two, you're up," Skeet said.

Aroska waited for a pair of shoppers to pass and then stepped from the shadows, trailing several meters behind the young man. Somewhere behind him, he knew Skeet and Zinni were emerging from their hiding places as well, following in his footsteps and ready to trade places with him. There was enough variety in the crowd that they likely weren't drawing too much attention, but Aroska and Skeet in particular were tall enough that they'd be noticeable if the boy was paying his environment any mind.

After a minute or so of trailing, Aroska stepped abruptly off to the side, waiting until both Skeet and Zinni had passed him before continuing on with his head down but his eyes wide open. They repeated the same process again a minute later, with Zinni taking the lead from Skeet; the young techie had glanced behind him a couple more times, but so far hadn't seemed to recognize the signs of his evolving tail.

Aroska picked up his pace a bit when both the boy and Zinni disappeared around a corner ahead. He found himself on another narrow street branching off from the market area, but there were far fewer people here. Keeping close to the wall of the nearest building, he slinked forward and pulled up behind Zinni, who had paused in the structure's semi-enclosed entryway. Skeet arrived seconds later, and the three of them stood for a moment peering out at the young man as he trudged on through the dwindling crowd.

"No way we're going to be able to follow unseen," Zinni muttered, removing an object from the small supply pouch she wore on one thigh in place of a second holster. She held her hand out to them, displaying a small, matte-gray sphere for a moment before setting it gingerly on the ground and turning her attention to her viewscreen. "Time to get creative."

"Will he pick up this signal?" Aroska asked.

With a few taps of the screen, the tiny roller bot buzzed to life. "Non-verbal communications shouldn't be an issue," she answered.

Aroska was tempted to comment further but the steely look on her face as she directed her full attention down to her viewscreen prompted him to keep his mouth shut. Brow furrowed, she manipulated the screen for a moment, glancing back and forth between the device and the tiny bot until an image rendered on the display. She tilted the viewscreen forward ever so slightly; the bot rolled about a meter, the picture changing with it as its little cam reoriented itself.

"We can continue tracking the comm signature easily enough," she said, not removing her gaze from the screen, "but I want eyes on this kid too."

Prompted by another tilt of the viewscreen, the bot took off down the street, once again catching sight of the boy and closing the distance as he rounded yet another corner. Zinni began walking while Skeet and Aroska fell back a bit, their eyes busy searching for anything amiss while she had her attention elsewhere.

From his position slightly behind her and to her left, Aroska caught glimpses of the ever-changing image on the viewscreen as she deftly steered the bot through the remaining foot traffic, sticking to the edges of the street but somehow always managing to keep the cam oriented on the boy. The feed was almost dizzying, but as they pressed forward, he recognized his current surroundings as being where the techie had been moments before.

After perhaps five minutes of this routine, Zinni stopped short and held up her fist, eyes still fixed on the screen. Even the roller bot had stopped moving. Aroska and Skeet closed in behind her, peering over her shoulder to get a look for themselves. The young man had passed through a wide, shadowy opening beneath another building; the ground sloped off from street level, giving Aroska the impression the space was some sort of tunnel or breezeway.

Zinni carefully rolled the bot forward to the tunnel entrance, catching sight of the boy as he made his way down a long line of doors that might have been apartments of some sort. "Don't want to risk him seeing the cam," she murmured, parking the bot where it was and taking off at a steady jog toward its location.

The three of them hustled forward, pulling up with their backs pressed against the wall just outside the tunnel entrance. The bot remained beneath them, its cam pointed into the tunnel as the scene unfolded. Aroska watched on the viewscreen as the young man came to a stop several doors down and pounded a fist against the frame. His voice—more authoritative than expected, given his appearance—echoed through the space.

"Matia! I know you're in there. We need to talk." He pounded again. "Matia!"

The three of them fell completely silent, exchanging surprised glances that silently confirmed they'd all heard what they thought they'd heard. Brows knit and jaw set, Zinni took hold of the viewscreen with both hands, sending the bot zipping down the tunnel just as the apartment door opened and the boy stepped inside. The door slid shut again just as the cam managed to get a fix on it.

No one had to speak a word. Weapons drawn before the dust had even cleared, they pressed forward into the tunnel, fixated on that sixth door on the right. Aroska swept his pistol around behind them, watching for movement at the tunnel entrance while Skeet and Zinni moved up to the door controls. The intelligence officer produced another tool from her pouch, which she promptly affixed to the control panel. She and Skeet took up flank positions while Aroska pivoted and faced the door directly, waiting for the beep that gave him the green light to move.

Time slowed to half speed as the device bypassed the lock. He stormed inside before the door had even opened fully, but he only made it a couple of strides before the stench within caused him to stagger. *Stench* wasn't even the correct word, but his mind was so shocked by the scent that it could conjure up no other description. It was so familiar, yet the fact that it was present here simultaneously made it completely foreign. He forced his feet forward, staring wide-eyed into the space beyond the barrel of his weapon and suddenly afraid of what he might find.

A muttered curse somewhere behind him told him Skeet and Zinni were just as shocked by the smell, but there was no time to think about that as he rounded the corner into a cramped living area and found the young techie in his sights. The boy reacted slowly, stumbling toward the far side of the room and looking wildly about for an escape route. Aroska couldn't help but notice the way his gaze lingered for an extra split second on a narrow hallway through the kitchen, where a bipedal shadow was just disappearing.

"Got a runner!" he shouted, moving toward the hall without a second thought.

"Go!" Skeet answered. "Comms on! Zinni, circle around!"

The sound of the intelligence officer's footsteps retreating toward the front door preceded a harsh screeching sound from the end of the hallway. Aroska continued forward, heart still pounding in response to the apartment's scent, and fired a warning shot at the woman who was just disappearing through the lopsided, open window of a poor excuse for a bedroom. Given the bad angle, he didn't think he'd actually gotten a look at her face, but a series of memories conjured by the smell flashed across his vision and left him with an image that couldn't possibly be real. The landing pad at Dakiti. The dining room at his old home. That shabby safe house on Aubin. The hill above Salex. The HSP docking platform where he'd said one of the hardest goodbyes of his life.

Shaking the images out of his head, he urged himself forward and took a quick but cautious look out the window before holstering his weapon and hauling himself through. It opened onto one of the very streets the team had traveled down while searching for the source of the comm signal; they'd walked right past it, in fact. He scrambled to his feet, glad to already have a decent idea of where he was. The path on the right led to a small, dead-end square with a variety of shops. He turned his attention immediately to the left, catching sight of a tall figure moving at high speed through the crowd and leaving distressed pedestrians and angry vendors in her wake.

Aroska took off at a dead run, praying he could follow on the path she'd blazed through the crowd before it closed up completely. He had no idea where Zinni was, and considering the maze-like layout of this sector of the city, he doubted they'd even manage to find each other. The woman—Matia Moryi, he insisted—was already far enough ahead that he couldn't see her, but her trail was clear enough. He dodged a kneeling man who appeared to be assisting a woman and child who'd been knocked down, and in doing so barely avoided running headlong into a hovercart that had been pushed into his path. Over the sound of his own pulse hammering in his ears, he was vaguely aware of someone yelling an obscenity at him.

His mind continued reeling, replaying the scene from inside the apartment and leaving him with no distinction between what he *had* seen, what he *thought* he'd seen, and what he'd *wanted* to see. If the images were accurate, he didn't know how it was possible. He shook his head as the edges of his vision grew foggy.

Some part of his brain managed to warn him about a change in scenery, and he realized the crowd further ahead remained uncharacteristically calm. No crying, no angry shouts, no one on the ground. His gaze was drawn to a narrow side street just ahead, and he turned down it without a second thought. A scattering of startled onlookers turned their attention to him for a split second before returning it to an even narrower alley that appeared it would lead him back in the direction from which he'd just come. He doubted it had been an actual attempt to double back; none of these alleys ever seemed to lead anywhere except other alleys. The woman had gone in there to hide.

Aroska slowed to a stiff jog and then stopped completely, taking a moment to stare into the shadowy passage as he caught his breath. She couldn't have gotten far—he'd gained ground during the pursuit, and despite being out of his line of sight, she hadn't been that far ahead of him in the first place. His heart raced as he took a cautious step forward. He'd been so sure it was *her*, but maybe it was just wishful thinking after the incident at the docks. It wouldn't have been the first time he'd thought he'd seen her. Perhaps he really was losing his mind, just as he was sure Skeet and Zinni both thought.

He moved into the alley, trying hard to convince himself that she would never have run from him and that he was dealing with a genuine threat. His hand came to rest on his holster, though he refrained from drawing his weapon. He could smell her—the same scent from the apartment lingered in the air—and the thought of holding her at gunpoint repulsed him. A voice deep inside him warned that it was suicide to go in unprepared, so he reached a compromise by at least curling his fingers around his pistol's grip.

He crept silently along the wall of one of the buildings, unable to bring himself to call out to her. That same voice in his head reminded him that he didn't know for sure if it was her and that he should therefore not reveal his location. The horrible thought struck him that maybe he should be just as cautious even if it *was* her.

Movement in the corner of his eye caught his attention just before rough hands seized him by the shoulders. He countered and drew his weapon, but it was immediately wrenched from his grasp in the exact manner as he would have disarmed someone had the roles been reversed. The gun clattered to the ground and an expertly placed strike to his collarbone rendered his right shoulder numb. He saw a flash of red just as the assailant slammed him against the building's stone wall, pinning him there.

"What the *hell* are you people doing here?" she snarled.

Aroska held his hands up in surrender, torn between utter relief and dismay. Her voice was so familiar, but so was the indescribable anger in her eyes. It was the same way she used to look at him, back in the beginning, and whether he liked it or not, it immediately put him on the defensive. "I could ask you the same thing."

Ziva huffed a sigh and released him. Her face remained twisted, her gaze intense yet simultaneously distant, unfocused. "You have no idea what you're getting into," she snapped.

"No, I guess I don't," he said, moving to recover his pistol. "Not if you're involved."

"Leave it!"

He froze, bent halfway over as he reached for the fallen gun, lifting his hands more out of shock than submission when he glanced back and found her leveling her own weapon at his head. Damn, she was a quick draw. Frighteningly so. A mixture of confusion and legitimate alarm compelled him to comply, and he slowly eased back into an upright position.

She stared him down from behind the barrel for a moment, then she blinked and lowered the gun as if she'd just been snapped out of some sort of trance. "Sorry," she murmured, face scrunched as though she were disgusted by her own actions. She holstered her pistol and nodded at the one on the ground. "Sorry."

Aroska took a cautious step toward his weapon, not removing his eyes from her as he reached for it this time. She brought her hands to rest on her hips, hanging her head and staring blankly down at her boots while he composed himself.

When she looked up again, the vacant expression had vanished, and unless he was mistaken, some of the anger in her eyes had been replaced by fear. "You shouldn't be here."

"Neither should you." Hearing his own words struck a chord in him, and the initial shock he'd felt upon seeing her began to ebb. A lump of emotion rose in his throat, and he wanted nothing more than to reach out and embrace her, touch her, feel her. It was one thing to assume she was alive and believe she'd once made an effort to tell him that, but it was something else entirely to see her standing there in the flesh. He wanted to make sure she was real and not just another illusion, but her stiff stance and rock-solid countenance told him now would be a bad time. Not to mention she'd almost shot him...

"Damn it, Aroska," she said, lowering her voice and taking a step toward him. Desperation flashed through her eyes. "This is not a game. You need to leave. You *all* need to leave. Don't involve yourselves in this. Don't put me in this position."

"And what exactly is 'this position'? What do you know about what's going on? Why would you have any reason to be in league with Alastair Manes?" After spending four years content with the idea that she could take care of herself and had likely spent most of her time safe—relatively speaking—on Niio, seeing her here was unnerving. If not for the fact that her scent was so distinct, he doubted he would have even recognized her, at least not at first glance. She stood straight with her shoulders squared the way she always had, only now the posture looked forced. The dirty leather she wore reeked of sweat and blood. Her familiar ponytail had been replaced by a ragged braid interwoven with colored string and several cords of matted hair; the style was such that her red streaks were adequately hidden. She'd done her eyes up in an uncharacteristic amount of smudgy, dark makeup, and she wore thick stripes of reddish-brown paint across the upper part of her face and down over her chin. It made her appear uncomfortably menacing and downright savage, but after a moment, he realized it was smeared in such a way that it concealed both of the *gesh punti* patterns around her eyes.

"What happened to you?" he managed, nearly a whisper.

A new, thin scar followed the contour of her right brow and curved halfway around her eye socket, and another trailed from her right earlobe partway down her neck. He wondered if they'd been sustained in the *Intrepid's* explosion. There was no doubt in his mind that had been the source of the layer of pink scar tissue curling down her arm.

Her eyes, an odd golden orange thanks to the colored lenses she wore, seemed to have retreated deeper into their sockets. "I can't get into it now. You have to trust me."

There. Something familiar in her tone. It reminded him of the night he'd taken her up to the hill outside Salex, the night all the barriers between them had finally begun to crumble. Aroska allowed himself to relax a bit, recalling the last time she'd told him to trust her and reminding himself that she was always right.

He became vaguely aware of his comm crackling and Skeet's voice carrying through his pocket. It all sounded so far away. "Alpha Two, Three, status report."

Ziva's gaze flicked from the noise back to his face. "Let me go. Pretend you never saw me. Go back to Skeet and Zinni and tell them I got away. Let the kid go, too. You take him into custody and I'll have to come bail him out. I don't want to have to do that."

Her tone gave him the impression something worse than just 'bailing out' would happen, but he nodded anyway and mustered up a slight smile. Ziva's face softened in response and the corners of her mouth curled downward. He could only recall seeing her genuinely sad on one other occasion; the look in her eyes reminded him far too much of what he'd seen as they'd said farewell that day on the landing pad.

Zinni's voice: "Nothing on my end. Think I'm headed the wrong way. Doubling back now."

Skeet again: "Two? Anything?"

He swallowed and spread his arms. For a moment she merely stared at him as if she didn't understand what he wanted, but then, to his relief and surprise, she stepped forward and allowed him to draw her in close. She didn't relax, but still wrapped her arms around him in return. Her body was as strong and solid as ever, and the feeling—the familiarity—brought him indescribable comfort.

"I missed you," he murmured, doing his best not to wince as his hand encountered what felt like another new scar on the back of her neck.

She said nothing but responded by tightening her grip on him for just a moment before pulling away.

"Wait here for thirty seconds after I leave," she instructed. The words were firm, but her tone had lightened significantly.

He offered a reluctant nod, wishing he didn't have to let her go but reminding himself that she must have the situation under control. Granted, this was Ziva Payvan, a woman who exuded confidence in any situation. If she didn't have things under control, he'd never even know.

She backed away, maintaining eye contact for several more seconds before turning her back to him. She took off at a steady jog, and he began counting under his breath the moment she disappeared around the corner.

Those thirty seconds seemed to creep by, and by the time he made his way out of the alley and back to the street, there was no sign of her anywhere. Not that he'd been expecting to see her. If she didn't want to be found, nobody would ever find her. And yet…he'd come very close, if mostly by accident…

Either way, she was gone once more. While he had a feeling it wouldn't be long before he saw her again, he had no idea when that would be, where, or under what circumstances. Heaving a sigh, he straightened his shoulders as best he could and took up his communicator.

"Alpha Three, cease pursuit. Rendezvous with Alpha One. Moryi is gone."

Chapter 19
4 Years Ago · Niio Spaceport

An eternity passed before the door opened. She snapped awake, unaware she'd even been dozing, and took a moment to let her foggy mind process what was happening. A bright shaft of light sliced through the darkness, and she lifted a hand to shield her eyes. The motion sent fire shooting through her arm, and she felt one of her scabs tear open and start oozing again.

She opened her mouth to address the man who had entered when she saw him reach for the light control panel beside the door, but he sighed and let out a little laugh before she could speak.

"I thought I might find you here, Agent Payvan."

The door shut and a light came on within the room, but it was a dim one with a soft golden glow that wasn't nearly as harsh as the corridor lights outside. Tobias Niio stood there, as relaxed as ever, his signature antique spectacles pushed up onto his forehead. He regarded her only with admiration and pride, not the shock and wariness she'd been expecting.

He continued forward and set the items he'd been carrying on a small table. "But I guess it's not 'agent' anymore, is it."

So he'd already heard about what happened following the battle with Ronan's fleet. "You're not surprised to see me?" she managed, fighting away the faintness creeping through her head. She was reasonably sure she was feverish.

An all-too-familiar chilling twinkle danced through Tobias's eyes and he grinned. "Of course not. I knew you would never allow yourself to be killed before you were able to pay the debt you owe me."

She knew he was joking, in a way only Tobias Niio could joke.

He'd tracked the *Zenith*, of course. She'd done her best to dock it as privately as possible, and it still bore the false registration HSP had given her when she'd set out to search for Skeet and Aroska following Zinni's capture, but he could have easily correlated its arrival with hers after her previous visit.

"Right," she breathed, relieved that he seemed to be maintaining a lighthearted attitude about the whole matter. She took a cautious step out of the shadows. "So...I could use a little help."

"I can see that."

The only mirror she'd looked in since her ejection from the *Intrepid* was a tiny handheld one aboard the *Zenith*, which hadn't provided her with the greatest view. She was certain she was a mess. Her right arm hadn't escaped unscathed from the explosion, and despite the medical treatment she'd administered on the trip to Niio, the charred flesh had begun to ooze and blister. Shrapnel had sliced through the jet suit and shredded the skin around her shoulder and collarbone as well as down on her hip and thigh. A full caura treatment would have fixed her up in no time, and though the *Zenith* was fully equipped for the procedure, she'd used the majority of its caura supply on Skeet and Aroska after rescuing them from the Aubin desert. There simply hadn't been time to stock up before leaving Haphez, and even if there *had*, she wasn't sure how she would have pulled it off without getting caught.

"I'll work for you," she said, bracing herself against the back of a chair. It had been tempting to say 'I'll do whatever you want,' but she refrained. She was desperate and vulnerable enough already—no need to add verbal confirmation. "You get me some medical attention, and I'll stay here for as long as you need me. Longer than the single hit I promised you."

The mobster's facial expression didn't change. Unless it was her imagination, he looked tired. It was a far cry from that smug, calculating look she'd seen every other time she'd met with him. Perhaps here, in private, away from his entourage, he was less concerned about maintaining his facade.

"I can only assume you'd rather not let anyone know you're here."

"That would be preferable." She knew he wouldn't betray her, at least not directly to the Federation. Fed presence on Niio was as taboo as Fed presence on Haphez. Besides, she had a feeling he wouldn't be able to resist her offer. "The galaxy thinks I'm dead, and it needs to stay that way." She stopped herself before adding 'for now'; the probability that she would or *could* ever have any contact with anyone back home was abysmally low.

Tobias merely stared at her. She couldn't be sure thanks to her hazy vision, but it appeared the wheels inside his head were spinning rapidly. She wasn't sure if she even wanted to know what he had in mind for her, and she was in no position whatsoever to negotiate any further terms.

"Fine," he said, his voice distorted and echoing inside her head.

She could have sworn he followed that up with 'I'm going to need your help too,' but she lost focus when his form split in two, then three, then again and again until she lost track of how many images she was seeing. The light in the room dimmed and she reached out to clutch the edge of the table for support as the floor seemed to tilt under her feet. She caught a brief glimpse of the almost concerned look on his face before her surroundings warped, she felt herself fall, and everything went dark.

When her eyelids fluttered open, she didn't remember ever closing them, and that thought alone induced enough of a panic to bring her to her senses. She sat up, immediately regretting it as her head spun and blackness crept inward from the edges of her vision. The space she was in was ill-lit, but she did her best to gather her bearings. She lay in a surprisingly comfortable bunk on the edge of a small room. A door stood partially open off to her left, probably a lavatory. Kitchen appliances were built into the far wall above a long counter, separated from her by a dining table. To her right, a plush chair that looked like it might recline sat facing a dormant viewscreen and communications console. These were living quarters, though whose they were remained in question.

Another knock sounded at the door. *Wait, another?* It took her a moment to realize that was what had awakened her initially. She swung her legs off the bunk and stole across the room, so preoccupied with finding a weapon that she didn't notice the drip lines attached to her arm until they pulled taut and sent fire shooting up into her shoulder. She whirled just as the IV stand crashed into her; it was a narrow pole hovering on small-scale repulsors, and a cylinder mounted on top pumped minuscule amounts of clear liquid into her burned arm through multiple entry points so small she hadn't even felt them. The tiny lines had been inserted through a fine layer of sticky blue mesh stretched over her charred, cracked skin. Underneath, the flesh was already turning soft and pink, giving her the impression she'd been subjected to caura treatment.

Which meant someone on Niio had access to caura extract.

Content that the IV stand would serve as an adequate weapon, she resumed her journey toward the door just as the caller knocked again. There was no entry cam or spy hole, leaving her only able to guess who it might be. Careful not to disturb the drip lines, she established a solid grip on the pole and hit the door controls.

A lone woman stood there in the corridor, one hand resting on her hip, the other hanging casually from the strap of the bag slung over her shoulder. Upon seeing Ziva standing there with her makeshift club, her eyes widened and the corners of her mouth turned down into a frown, but her posture remained loose and relaxed.

"Oh hell," she muttered, letting herself into the room. "What are you doing on your feet?"

Perplexed, Ziva stepped back and allowed her to enter, loosening her grip on the pole but unwilling to release it just yet. The woman went to the table and set her bag down, producing a pair of vials from the padded pockets within. She held them up and checked their contents in the dim light before bringing them over to the IV stand.

"I leave for an hour and that good-for-nothing bot walks out on me," she said, seemingly talking more to herself than Ziva. She held the two fresh vials gently between her teeth as she opened the top of the IV cylinder and peered inside. "Damn it all." Her words were muffled by the vials. She reached in and pulled two empty tubes from their slots, holding them up for Ziva to see. "Would you look at that? Completely dry."

She cast the two empty vials aside and replaced them with the fresh ones, muttering what sounded like curses in a language Ziva didn't recognize. The moment the new tubes locked into place and their contents mixed with whatever else the cylinder contained, a cold, soothing sensation spread through her arm. It reminded her of rain falling on parched earth.

"What is that?" she asked.

The woman scoffed. "Of all the questions you could possibly have, that's the one you choose first?" Her voice wasn't loud, but she had a harsh accent that gave the words a commanding tone by default. She was human, average height, and middle-aged, probably about fifty. Her shaggy blonde hair reached her shoulders but was kept out of her face by a thick headband. Her wardrobe consisted of a simple shirt, tac pants, and utility vest, and a holstered pistol rode on her hip. Combined with the unimpressed look on her face, her broad shoulders and stocky build made it clear she was a force to be reckoned with.

"I know caura when I feel it," Ziva replied. "Where'd you get it?"

"You're an odd one, Payvan." The woman approached again to take a closer look at the wrinkled mesh that had been disturbed by all the movement. She reached out to straighten it. "I'd have guessed the first thing you'd want to know is—"

Taking advantage of the fact that both of the stranger's hands were occupied, Ziva pivoted and drew the woman's pistol, jamming the barrel into her chest. She lunged forward, forcing her back against the wall and pinning her there with her forearm against her neck.

"I'm taking things in stride, okay?" Ziva snarled, ignoring the pain as the IV lines ripped the rest of the way out of her arm. The mesh covering became damp as thin streams of blood began oozing from the insertion sites. "So far you don't seem so bad, but if you don't answer my question, I might start *actually* treating you like a threat."

The indifferent look on the woman's face told her this wasn't the first time she'd been pinned against a wall at gunpoint. She raised her hands in surrender and swallowed. "Relax, it's not caura. After the Fringe War, I think the whole galaxy knows better than to try to take it from you. It's a formula I synthesized myself. Different stuff, but many similar properties, although I'll admit right now it'll never be as good as the real thing. You might call it 'artificial' caura. Be glad I used it on you. Your injuries are a damn sight better than they were when you arrived, but if you want all of this scar tissue to heal up any further, you'll need more treatment."

Ziva released her—slowly—and lowered the gun. "You're a doctor?"

"Yeah, sort of. Used to be. More of a medical director now, overseeing operations at all of the local clinics. But I guess I've still got the magic touch or Tobias wouldn't have entrusted me with your recovery."

Ziva had expected as much. After all, she was hidden away in this apartment rather than lying in a med center somewhere. And if there'd been a bot watching her, it meant Tobias didn't want anyone outside of a very small circle aware of her presence, which in turn meant he was holding up his end of the deal despite their rather abbreviated encounter. It made sense that he'd leave her in the care of someone— with medical experience, no less—whom he trusted. Which begged the question...

The woman offered her hand before Ziva could even open her mouth to ask. "Serenity. Serenity Best. Though if you want to get technical, I guess it's Serenity Niio."

Ziva's planned response caught in her throat as she shook Serenity's hand. She tilted her head and regarded the woman through slightly narrowed eyes. "You—"

"It's more of a business arrangement than an actual marriage. But the man does have a sort of unorthodox charm."

Ziva could only stand there with the early stages of a smirk tugging at her lips. She usually made a point of not getting involved in other people's personal business, but in this case, curiosity was eating at her. Besides, she had a hunch Serenity was the only other person she would be in contact with for a while, so learning more about her—and, subsequently, Tobias—couldn't hurt. She never would have guessed that the head of the Niiosian Mob was married, but the idea of him doing such a thing for strategic gain? That didn't surprise her at all.

"Sounds like an interesting story there," she said, lifting an eyebrow and offering the pistol back.

Serenity accepted the gun and gave her a nod of understanding, no doubt quite accustomed to people expressing incredulity at her marital status. "Tobias takes care of his own," she responded, taking hold of the IV stand and ushering Ziva back toward the bunk. "Your presence here is a testament to that. He likes you enough—or feels you'll make a valuable enough contribution—that he's willing to allocate time and resources to get you back on your feet. It's a win for both of you."

"Is that your situation?" Ziva slid back into the bunk without fuss, already sore from being on her feet. Never in her life had she imagined putting herself in such a vulnerable position, on Niio of all places, but Serenity already struck her as someone she could trust, something that rarely happened at all, much less so quickly. She had a feeling the two of them had a lot in common.

Serenity fetched her supply bag, pulled up a chair, and went to work cleaning up Ziva's arm and re-inserting the tiny IV lines. "Yes and no." She hesitated for a moment as if searching for the right words. "Things have been rough for a while here on Niio and they've only been getting worse. Between you and me, I think that's why Tobias was so quick to take you in. He's going to want and *need* help with some things in the coming days."

"I don't doubt it," Ziva muttered, recalling what she thought she'd heard him say just before passing out.

"A lot of people have had to get their hands dirty in the name of keeping this place up and running, including me. Supplies are scarce this far out in the Fringe. Last year, I took a raiding party out to Irone to recover some medical equipment that had been part of a shipment hijacked by pirates. Most people thought we should just let it go, saying we couldn't afford to lose more resources on something that was trivial in the long run, but I didn't listen." She directed her attention to the junction where the drip line split off into three smaller tubes and fiddled aimlessly with it. "Granted, we were only reclaiming what was rightfully ours, but people got killed. On both sides. I never meant for that to happen, you know?"

"Let me guess. Tobias hadn't sanctioned the mission."

Serenity looked up and gave her the faintest of smiles. "He always said you were perceptive. No, he didn't sanction it. In fact, he was one of the people who had warned us against going. He was furious when he found out what happened, partially because of the men I'd lost but mostly because I'd been foolish enough to go behind his back. Truth be told, I was afraid he'd kill me, but I've been running the medical scene here for twenty years, and he recognized that. My expertise is invaluable. He ended up sending a team back to Irone to destroy any evidence of our involvement, and it seemed like we were in the clear.

"But then rumors got out that he'd wanted me dead for what I'd done. We still don't know who started them. Tobias had his suspicions. Even had some people executed. But anyhow, rumors started coming our way, too. Word travels fast out here. Apparently, this detective on Irone caught wind of my involvement. Without any solid evidence to pin everything that happened on me, he was planning on asking Tobias to testify against me. Figured if he allegedly wanted me dead, he'd be willing to comply."

Now it was Ziva's turn to smile. The thought of Tobias Niio bowing to the wishes of any sort of law enforcement was laughable. "You're joking."

"We assumed he was bluffing, but the man was a tenacious bastard. When we heard he was on his way here, we knew something had to be done. Dealing with him was the last thing we needed with everything else that was going on. So Tobias offered to marry me so we could invoke spousal immunity and he couldn't be compelled to testify. It's an old Federation law, but most Fringe systems still adhere to it too for consistency's sake."

"They let you do that?"

"Nobody had officially asked for a testimony yet. It was just a precaution based on the rumors we'd heard, which of course turned out to be true. For all Irone's investigators knew, we'd been married for years. And anyhow, it worked. The testimony was the only thing this detective had to go on, so he backed off. It was a win for everyone here. Tobias could focus on more important things, and I got to keep running my clinics."

"And you're still together, so to speak?"

The woman nodded. "It's only been a year, and I imagine tempers on Irone are still running hot. Don't know how long we'll have to keep up the act. It's not so bad—I'm pretty sure he's always had a sweet spot for me anyway. But like I said, it's a business arrangement. Both of us get to keep running our operations unhindered."

As odd as it was, it made sense. These people were just trying to do whatever it took to survive, a concept Ziva was no stranger to. She couldn't help but be glad Serenity was there, glad to know Tobias was the type of person who was capable of trusting people intimately, even if those people were few and far between. She wasn't sure if she'd go so far as to say she trusted *him*, despite the fact that she'd come to Niio seeking his assistance, but if what Serenity had told her was accurate, he trusted *her* to a degree. It was surprising, given that their past association had been both infrequent and tenuous, but perhaps it had something to do with these mysterious underlying circumstances Serenity kept alluding to.

"That doesn't seem like a story you tell very often," she finally said.

Serenity eased back in her chair and sighed, apparently satisfied with the state of the IV. "Oh, it's not."

"So..."

"Why did I tell you? Because I want you to understand who you're dealing with here. Believe me, Tobias is every bit as cold as he seems. Your past interactions have probably seemed downright cordial compared to what he's capable of. But he's also not one to waste lives, *or* talent. He's a firm believer that by demonstrating loyalty to his people—even if it's not always completely sincere—he will gain and maintain their loyalty in return. There are folks here who would die for him because he has helped them in their time of need. You saw the way he went to war with the Resistance over the deaths of a few Niiosian soldiers. Everyone knows what he's willing to do to protect his people and our way of life, so they gladly offer their services when he calls upon them.

"That said, he has agreed to help you because he sees something in you and believes you can help him too, and he won't hesitate to make sure you return the favor. This all goes a lot deeper than whatever deal you made with him when you came here looking for your friends a couple of weeks ago."

Ziva wasn't sure whether the chill that coursed through her body was caused by the fluid in her arm or something more abstract. "What does he want me to do?"

Serenity leaned forward and rested her elbows on her knees, looking her directly in the eye. "You familiar with the Ibarra Cartel?"

CHAPTER 20
THE TUNNEL - TABACO, PANUCO

The silence that followed the few seconds of relative excitement in the apartment was almost overwhelming. Zinni and Aroska had only been gone for a minute, though it felt longer. Skeet kept his weapon trained on the young man for the duration, finding it increasingly difficult to focus the longer he stood there. The scent of the apartment was almost paralyzing and stirred up an odd jumble of feelings inside him. Confusion, first and foremost, because he couldn't understand how it was possible. Anger, because this wasn't what he'd expected, and the implications were unpleasant. Fear, for the same reason. Finally, some measure of elation, of relief. He imagined it must be similar to what Aroska felt upon finding a promising clue, though he found himself wanting to curb his excitement until he had a better idea of what was happening.

The kid shifted uncomfortably in the corner where he'd remained after the other two agents began their pursuit. Upon closer examination, he couldn't have been more than seventeen or eighteen years old. He was scrawny and dirty, no doubt on the lowest rung in Manes's network, if he was even part of the network at all.

"Keep your hands on the wall," Skeet instructed, motioning with the barrel of his pistol. He spoke in Standard, though he guessed the bulkier of the two earpieces the young man wore might also serve as a translator. "What is your purpose here? Where did Moryi go?"

The boy reached out and placed his palms flat against the wall on either side of him as he'd been told, but rather than respond to the questions, he simply swallowed and averted his gaze. Unless Skeet was mistaken, he almost seemed more fearful of the gun itself than of the man holding it.

He could fix that. He holstered the weapon and closed the distance between them, taking up fistfuls of the kid's coat and lifting him up. His slight frame came off the floor easily, and Skeet kept him pinned to the wall at eye level. "Where's Moryi?" he growled again.

The kid flailed for a moment before his hand went to his belt, feeling around among the supply pouches there. It came away gripping a knife, which Skeet plucked and flung aside as if it were a blade of grass. "Is that really how you want to play this?" he demanded, tearing away both of the earpieces as well.

The young man finally made eye contact. "Go to hell," he muttered, though his jaw was trembling.

Keeping him flush against the wall, Skeet lowered him back to the floor and began searching him for further weapons, pulling out his own communicator with his free hand. "Alpha Two, Three, status report."

He didn't expect them to respond immediately, but with circumstances as they were, the silence was disconcerting. He completed his search without incident and stepped back, once again drawing his sidearm and motioning for the kid to keep his hands in sight.

It was Zinni who finally responded. "Nothing on my end," she said breathlessly. "Think I'm headed the wrong way. Doubling back now."

That didn't surprise him, given the maze-like layout of the narrow streets and alleys they'd traversed on their way here. Aroska had been right on...the subject's heels, and the fact that he hadn't responded yet was beginning to make Skeet nervous. "Two? Anything?"

This time the silence dragged on for so long that he had half a mind to just let the kid go and head out to investigate himself. If the situation was what it seemed based on the scent within the apartment, that would certainly explain the sergeant's long hesitation. But they didn't have all the details. There were too many possibilities.

Another minute passed before he finally heard Aroska's voice. "Alpha Three, cease pursuit. Rendezvous with Alpha One. Moryi is gone."

"Copy that," Zinni answered.

Well, that wasn't really helpful information, but if this kid was tapped into as many local communications as they thought he was, there was no telling who else might be. Skeet didn't dare ask for details over comm; the team would be back in a matter of minutes and he could get the full story then. And between the three of them, maybe they'd be able to get something out of their young prisoner.

He motioned for the kid to move over and take a seat at the pitiful little dining table. They waited in silence until approaching footsteps could be heard outside; within moments Zinni appeared in the entry, with Aroska mere seconds behind. Both stood there, breathing hard, shifting their gazes between Skeet and the kid. Then Zinni turned her attention to Aroska, just as eager for an update as Skeet was.

He kept his weapon trained on the boy even as he spoke. "What happened?" It struck him that he was almost afraid to find out. Objectively, he needed to be apprised of the facts, but given the situation, the facts had implications he was dreading.

"We need to let the kid go," Aroska replied, speaking slowly, deliberately. "We're not going to get anything out of him."

Well, that was unexpected. "What are you talking about?" Skeet said, fending off the anger he felt building in response to all the uncertainty. "We've barely tried!"

Aroska tilted his head. "Please trust me."

Beside him, Zinni appeared just as uncertain, but after studying him for a moment, she turned to Skeet and nodded.

With a sigh, he holstered his weapon and jerked his head toward the door. "Get out of here, then."

The young man scrambled to his feet without hesitation, making a quick detour to gather up his knife and earpieces before rushing for the exit and giving Aroska and Zinni a wide berth as he went. They all stood motionless until his retreating footsteps could no longer be heard, then all eyes fell on Aroska.

"It's her," he said. "It's been her the whole time."

Despite the scent in the apartment and all the things Skeet had been pondering for the past few minutes, there was something about the statement he didn't understand. Maybe because it was the last thing he'd ever expected when they'd accepted this damn mission.

He could only muster up a single word as a response. "How?"

"I don't know," Aroska answered. "She was evasive, wouldn't give me a straight answer. Just kept saying we shouldn't be here and we don't know what we've gotten ourselves into. And that was all after she almost blew my head off."

Skeet glanced to Zinni. Her face was devoid of any particular expression, but she'd gone totally pale and had her lips pressed into a thin line as if she had much to say but dared not say any of it. He felt the same, especially in light of all he'd been thinking about the night before while waiting in the bar. Not only had they confirmed Ziva was here—a shock in itself—but it was under completely different circumstances than what any of them had anticipated. Part of him wasn't surprised; everything they'd heard about Matia Moryi—her skill, capabilities, even some aspects of her nature—all made sense now. But another part of him didn't believe it at all, didn't believe it was possible. A single word reverberated through his head: *why?*

Why, why, why?

He took another look at his surroundings, stricken by the realization that this was where one of his oldest friends had rested her head for some indeterminate amount of time. Filthy and pathetic as it was, he recognized how she had made the space her own, with a secure weapon locker, weight bench, and impeccably organized kitchen area. Of course, now that they knew the truth, he also couldn't help but view it as a mercenary's nest, the hiding place of someone who had committed acts so vile that news had reached all the way across the galaxy to Haphez. The Ziva Payvan he'd once known would never have done any of those things, regardless of her temperament and often ruthless nature. Matia Moryi was the culprit here.

The thought sparked a memory, something he'd said to Tarbic during the journey here. *"If we do find her, she may not even be the same person you knew before."*

Well, this wasn't exactly what he'd had in mind.

A rambling voice reached his ears and he realized Aroska had been speaking this whole time, talking himself through what he was seeing just as Skeet had been doing silently. If his account of her actions in the alley was accurate, it sounded as though there could be a logical explanation behind her presence here…or else telling them to leave was simply her way of trying to keep them from being targeted by Ibarra. Regardless, Skeet wished very much for further explanation.

"Just so we're clear," Zinni began, her brows drawn together as she stared downward at nothing in particular, "Ziva is Matia Moryi."

Aroska stopped his rambling and met Skeet's gaze, clearly taken aback by hearing this fact articulated out loud. It sounded just as foreign to Skeet, even though the thought had been running through his mind since they had entered the apartment.

When neither of them made any move to respond, Zinni looked up and shifted her icy gaze to each of them in turn. "Ziva is Matia Moryi," she repeated, more conviction in her voice this time as though it would help her understand her own words.

"Yeah," Aroska answered, bringing his hands to rest on his hips, "she is."

"And what do we do about that?"

Skeet didn't know. He took another look around the room; the apartment contained very little to begin with, let alone anything that would give them any quick answers. The comm console against the far wall might contain some useful information, but he had no doubt it was kept secure. In light of what they'd just learned, and considering the kid with all the connections was likely on his way to tell someone what had just transpired, staying here was also a bad idea. They needed to regroup and talk things through, but they needed to do it elsewhere.

"See what you can get off of that," he instructed, directing Zinni toward the comm console.

She gave him a sharp nod and went to work.

He turned to address Aroska, but the man was already headed back down the short hallway, leaving him with little choice but to follow. Shattered glass crunched under his boots and he looked down to find pieces of what appeared to be a broken mirror that had been haphazardly cleaned up. They passed a cramped lavatory and found themselves standing in dirty sleeping quarters with a ratty bed and a few simple storage containers. Aroska went straight to a small window that opened into a back alley and stared out for a moment before easing it shut on squealing tracks. He stood and fingered the latch for a moment, then ultimately left it unlocked.

"We need to get out of here," Skeet said. "We know she's here, and we know where she lives. That's half the battle."

Aroska looked more disappointed than anything else. "I want answers."

"I know. We'll get some, but we need to come up with a plan, and we can't do it here."

The little bedroom fell silent for another moment as they simply stood and looked around at the place. Zinni appeared in the hallway, flashing her viewscreen to signal that she'd found something potentially useful on the comm console, then one by one, they all finally turned and trudged back out toward the door. Skeet cut to the front of the line, pausing in the front entrance to make sure the tunnel-like corridor outside was clear. He found himself struggling to keep his mind from running wild, something he normally prided himself on doing well. Warning Aroska to stay focused was pointless if he couldn't do it himself.

As he picked up the little roller bot and began leading them down the tunnel, the only thing he knew for sure anymore was that he had no idea what to do.

Chapter 21
COMMERCIAL SECTOR · Tabaco, Panuco

Every single report projected from his desk contained information exactly opposite of what Manes wanted to see. At the moment he could only stare blankly at them, slowly mulling each of them over as he reveled in the silence of his office in the back of the restaurant. As soon as he'd dismissed Matia and finished his breakfast earlier that morning, he'd informed his men he wouldn't be taking any audiences and wished to be left alone. The arrival of these Haphezian agents was inopportune; he had too many other matters to attend to.

First and foremost was the situation on Delatori. A fresh report had come in since the previous evening, informing him that recovery of material from the zocrum repository could take up to twice as long as initially estimated, which set his timetable back further than desired. The zocrum was a key component in upgraded weapons systems with which he'd wanted to outfit his whole fleet by the end of this quarter, and what little had been salvaged so far would only be enough to cover retrofits on his primary flagship. That, or a good portion of Ibarra's rather mismatched fighter squadron, whichever he preferred. Neither one would get the job done when it came time to advance on the Niiosians, so he would wait. Yet again.

Then there was the matter of his lead engineers on the project, who'd all been fatally wounded in an explosion in one of the workshops three days earlier. Working with volatile materials in weapons development sometimes had its price, and normally Manes wouldn't have cared too much about the loss of personnel. Everyone—usually even those he told otherwise—was expendable. But in this case, losing the project's top minds was a blow that altered the schedule even further. The curious thing was that nobody had been able to tell him what exactly happened, what precisely had caused the explosion. Typically, he wouldn't have been troubled by this either, as any answer would have involved more techno-babble than he cared to listen to. But this wasn't the first time key Ibarra personnel had perished in untimely, accidental manners, and if he didn't know any better, he'd think it was becoming a trend. He lost people on a daily basis due to the nature of Ibarra's operations, but he'd found himself needing to replace higher-ranking individuals more times than he would have liked in the four-plus years he'd been in control of the Cartel. Each of them represented a loss of momentum and increased the time it would take to expand his territory. Kimbra and Matia had probably set records in terms of how long someone under his direct command had stayed alive, and he was growing tired of it.

A knock sounded at the office door, interrupting his train of thought, and when he heard the controls beep outside, he sat forward with the intent of shooting whoever entered after he'd explicitly ordered everyone to leave him be. In walked Kimbra, having returned from overseeing the recovery of the bodies at the shipping yard. But he'd already seen the images of the carnage wrought there, and there was no way anyone would have had time to do a full examination of the corpses yet, so he had no desire to speak any further on the matter.

"Someone to see you," she said.

Manes opened his mouth to protest, but her grave features piqued his curiosity.

"It's about Moryi."

"*Pazska*," he muttered. It was barely mid-day and already this assassin he'd just been praising for her longevity was giving him more grief than any of his other problems.

He nodded at Kimbra, who stepped aside and ushered in a young man in his late teens wearing ragged clothes and a bulky earpiece. The boy was a regular in these parts and was somewhat of a technical genius, though his methods were unorthodox and he often seemed so jittery he could barely function. He'd managed to provide Manes with valuable information in the past, so perhaps he would again. His name simply escaped him at the moment, despite the fact that he recalled Matia mentioning him earlier.

"There's something you need to know about what happened at the docks, sir," the young man began, removing his earpiece and fidgeting with it as he spoke.

Manes sat back and held out a hand, inviting him to continue.

"Matia came to me early this morning and asked me to patch her into the Haphezian agents' communications. She claimed she wanted to listen in and see if she could glean any information about what they were doing here. I was already monitoring their comm channel, so it was easy to set up another node.

"The request seemed reasonable and I didn't think anything of it. But I was still listening during the shootout, and I swear I heard her talk to them. Give them instructions. I...I'm pretty sure she's the one who shot all of your men."

For a moment, Manes could only sit in silence. Why not add one more item to the list of things that were going wrong? But it only took another split second for the gravity of the situation to strike him. He rose to his feet and approached the young man, who started to shrink away until he realized Kimbra was still standing directly behind him. Reed. That was it, though Manes couldn't recall if it was his first name or last name.

"Are you able to tell how many people were on that channel?" he asked, towering over the boy.

"I thought maybe the agents had a fourth person on comm and her voice just sounded similar, but I went and double-checked before I came here. Triple-checked. The only connections were the three I'd been tracking from the start and one that matched the signature of the node I set up for Matia. The weird thing is that the connection I gave her was listen-only. She shouldn't have been able to talk to them."

"But you have an explanation for that." It wasn't a question.

Reed—*Blain, Blain Reed*—allowed his gaze to flicker away for a moment, then he swallowed as though uncertain. "I want something in return for this information."

"You'll get whatever you want, kid," Kimbra said, giving him a rough nudge before crossing her arms. "Out with it."

He hesitated a moment longer before reluctantly returning his attention to Manes. "If she had the device I programmed for her, it's possible she could have transferred the coding to a device of her choosing...say, one with two-way comm capabilities. She's got a comm console at her place with that functionality, and she could have stopped there before heading to the docks. I'm not saying that's exactly what happened, but it's the most logical explanation."

Manes raked a hand over his greased hair and pivoted, pacing slowly back to the desk and leaning over it with his back to his guests. He curled his hands into fists, pressing his knuckles into the solid metal surface and letting the pain command his attention long enough to keep himself from erupting. This information would have made him seethe under normal circumstances, but piled on top of everything else that was going on, it was about to send him over the edge.

And yet, he had questions. *If* Matia had slain his soldiers, how did that explain the different types of ammunition recovered from the scene? Two rifles, he supposed. It wasn't like the woman possessed or had access to any shortage of ordnance. He didn't think there was any way she could have known the strike team was coming, and she had seemed genuinely flustered about their presence while confronting him right there in the restaurant earlier that morning, but if she'd somehow found out, she could have brought a second gun in preparation.

She *had* killed Adler though, as instructed. Curious that she would follow orders and then allegedly commit such a heinous act against the Cartel. And what would she have accomplished by doing such a thing? She would have spared the Haphezian agents' lives is what. But why? Whatever the reason, it meant she had most likely lied to him the night before when he'd first brought the agents' presence to her attention.

"There's more, sir," Reed murmured behind him.

Manes couldn't help but smile. Of course there was.

"After I confirmed Matia had been on comm, I went to confront her about it. Wanted to give her the benefit of the doubt, see if she had an explanation. She was at her apartment, and just after I got there, those agents stormed the place. She took off and two of them went after her. One of them stayed behind and—" he sucked in a shaky breath "—waved his gun in my face and interrogated me about her."

"And you didn't tell him anything." Once again, it was not a question.

Reed scoffed. "I didn't have anything to tell him. I didn't know where the hell she went. She must've gotten away because the other two came back after a few minutes. One of them told the guy to let me go, and he did. I left, checked the comm data, then came straight here. Don't know where they went after that, or where Matia is."

Movement on one of the ever-present security feed projections caught Manes's attention, and he looked up to see Moryi herself come to a halt as three of his men surrounded her just outside the bar's front door. "Speak of the devil," he muttered.

He straightened and turned back to face Reed. The young man had exuded an air of increasing audacity the longer he'd spoken but shrank back a bit now that he was under scrutiny again. He was a pesky type, a leech who lurked in Ibarra's lowest recesses scrounging for validation and opportunities. But he also had some legitimate talent, and it could still be put to further use. Manes remained silent for a moment as a new plan began to take form.

"Thank you for your service," he said to Reed, though he locked gazes with Kimbra as he spoke. He nodded long and slow, a sign she immediately recognized as the go-ahead to conduct an experiment she had practically begged him to try on numerous occasions. The current circumstances were more favorable than any had been in the past, and if even a portion of what Reed had just told him was accurate, the situation called for it. "Comrade Soto has a project for you. You will accompany her for the remainder of the afternoon."

The twinkle of confidence in the young man's eyes faded. He opened his mouth to protest but then appeared to think better of it. Kimbra seized him by the arm and began to drag him back out the door anyway.

Manes watched them go and then returned to his desk, feeling marginally better now that he had something to look forward to. He spared another glance at the security feed outside the front door, where his men appeared to be having an increasingly difficult time keeping Matia contained. She was often belligerent and antagonistic toward his lower level soldiers, and perhaps it was merely due to the information that had just come to light, but she seemed particularly agitated in this footage. He would know for sure soon enough.

He slid his hand over and tapped the comm button on the desk's control panel. "Send her in."

Chapter 22
Commercial Sector - Tabaco, Panuco

One of the men blocking Ziva's path to the door paused and pressed a finger to his ear, then the three of them abruptly stepped to the side. She continued into the restaurant, making a point of knocking her elbow into one of them who hadn't quite gotten out of her way. The bar itself was never busy this early, but a few customers sat enjoying a mid-afternoon meal and glanced up as she came in. She paid them no mind as she made a beeline across the floor to the service room, though she couldn't help but notice Kimbra's hulking form slipping out the side door. The woman briefly glanced her way and was accompanied by a smaller person whom Ziva didn't have a clear view of, but based on the color of their clothing and the oily scent that lingered in the air, she was almost positive it was Blain.

Sheyss, she thought, doing her best to feign indifference as she reached the door and let herself into the back hall. *Sheyss, sheyss, sheyss.*

She'd always known there was a high probability Blain would hear what went down at the docks. He'd managed to get a few words in before Aroska and company had arrived at her apartment, enough for her to know that was exactly the case. But she'd gone to him for comm help because she trusted him, at least more so than anyone else on this *frouchten* planet, and he'd said he trusted her when she asked. Maybe it had been a mistake to think there was a chance he wouldn't turn her in, or perhaps he'd had every intention of hearing her out until the team showed up. But no amount of speculation could fix the situation.

None of Manes's soldiers lined the corridor today, a welcome discovery. She released a sharp sigh and cracked her neck as she approached the office, failing, she feared, to fully shake off the day's most recent developments. Damn HSP and the Alpha team all to hell for putting her through this.

My name is Matia Moryi. My name is Matia Moryi. My name is Matia Moryi. My name is—

And just like that, Matia blinked and found herself inside the office. Manes sat at his desk, staring absentmindedly at several reports projected from it. When he glanced up at her, he only looked exasperated. Maybe even bored. Either way, it was nothing like what she'd been expecting.

"You know I've never liked having to meet with the same person twice in one day," he said. "Counting last night, this makes three."

"Those agents came for me," she exclaimed, allowing her legitimate displeasure for the whole situation to give her narrative a more genuine flair. "They were at my damn apartment. It was all I could do to get away."

He blinked slowly. "How did they find you?"

"I *don't know.*"

"You were ordered to deal with them."

Matia ground her teeth; of course he would try to spin this as being her fault. Granted, until the team had found her, she had just been stalling in her apartment after stashing her rifle aboard the *Talon*, but it had only been a couple of hours since she'd last been here at the restaurant. "And when, exactly, am I supposed to have done that?"

Manes made a show of returning his attention to the projections. She knew for a fact that he'd had numerous matters to attend to lately, but this disinterest he was showing at the moment set her on edge. He should have been livid, and she almost wished he was. At least it would have given the whole encounter a sense of normalcy.

She'd also expected the man to immediately bring up the incident at the docks. If Blain had come here to speak to Manes and Kimbra, she would have thought it would be to rat her out. If he had done such a thing, she imagined she would have been dead the moment she walked into this room, so maybe he'd just fed Manes a load of *sheyss* and was looking out for her. Either that, or Manes knew everything and was playing mind games with her. Not knowing one way or the other was a mind game in itself. She hated everything.

"You will do as you were told," Manes said, voice low and firm. His dark eyes had taken on an almost predatory quality as he locked gazes with her. "Take the Haphezian agents out. I no longer care why they're here—I'm not going to risk them jeopardizing our operations any further than they already have. I want them dead. Understood?"

Alarm bells chimed incessantly inside her head, but she stood perfectly still and refused to display any outward signs of how fast her heart was pounding. Matia Moryi took life without thought and without mercy—Manes himself had once said those very words. Matia Moryi was good at her job. Matia Moryi followed orders because she was well paid and her life depended on it. But right now, Matia Moryi did not feel like Matia Moryi. She swallowed against a dry throat. Her mind felt as though it was folding inward on itself as she desperately worked to close off parts of it that had opened up today for the first time in four years.

"Understood," she muttered. Her voice sounded like it belonged to someone else.

She turned and stormed out the door.

Chapter 23
SABER · Tabaco, Panuco

The large table in the *Saber's* armory was meant to be a surface upon which to service and assemble weapons, but it made as good a conference table as any. The three of them had ended up there without even discussing it, even though the comm room might have been better suited for a meeting like this. Aroska wondered if they subconsciously felt more secure there with all the munitions, surrounded by the tools they might need to use to defend themselves at a moment's notice. He knew he certainly did.

Upon arriving back at the ship after leaving Ziva's apartment, Zinni had immediately started decrypting the data she'd recovered from the comm console there. So far, they had a three-dimensional map of the main Ibarra compound, as well as a variety of ship manifests, personnel rosters, and other tidbits of information, some of which appeared to have nothing to do with the Cartel. The compound map would be useful, though they all agreed they'd rather not make any foray into the place except as a last resort.

Once they'd all gathered in the armory, Aroska had begun by giving a more detailed account of everything that had transpired in the alley, good or bad. From there, they'd started making a lengthy list of questions sparked by their recent discovery. If Ziva Payvan and Matia Moryi were one and the same, that changed everything they thought they'd known about this mission. But in some ways, it had also changed nothing at all. If Moryi had killed Pahl Starcer's son—and all those other people on Delatori, for that matter—it simply meant Ziva had done it; the facts stayed the same, and the name of the perpetrator was all that was different.

The question now was how in the galaxy she had ever come to be in the employ of the Ibarra Cartel. As much as Aroska didn't particularly trust the Niiosian Mob, he was still grateful for their support in the battle against Ronan's fleet and had become comfortable with the idea of Ziva hiding out on Niio and doing some work for them. Not only did the exact opposite of that now seem to be true, but he couldn't help but wonder how many other deaths she had been responsible for among Niiosian ranks. Not to mention the gruesome stories Adler had told them.... He didn't even want to think about any of it, but he had to at least try to remain objective.

"I don't understand," he said. "We know she killed those soldiers at the docks. Does that mean she killed Adler, too?"

That was the other thing: she'd obviously saved their asses down on the wharf. That didn't match everything else they knew about Moryi, and it made him wonder—made him hope—there was more to the situation than met the eye.

"There could have been two shooters," Skeet replied, "though that means whoever else shot Adler probably would have known she took out the soldiers. Can't imagine Ibarra would have taken kindly to their best assassin killing their own men. My guess is she was the only one."

"How does that explain the two different forms of ammo, then? Two different rifles?"

Zinni appeared deep in thought for a moment before turning to Skeet as if an idea had come to mind. "The gun."

"What gun?" Aroska said.

Skeet nodded to himself. "She had a rifle," he answered. "Damn, that was a fine gun. Designed and built it herself. It allowed her to switch between common projectiles and those bariine rounds she loved so much." He looked to Aroska. "It's the one she shot the Durutians with on Aubin. She must still have it, or else she built a new one."

It was no wonder she had wanted to create a new bariine-ready rifle on the fly while they were on Chaiavis, Aroska thought. She'd wanted a taste of her comfort zone, a rifle that had been confiscated along with her other weapons following her arrest after Ikaro Tachi's assassination. And after returning home from Aubin, it likely would have remained among all her belongings stored aboard the *Zenith*, which had been mysteriously absent from the landing bay at her house following her disappearance. Based on the condition of the bay when he'd gone to investigate, it appeared the vessel had been stolen by looters amid the chaos of the battle with Ronan. But after receiving her message, he knew better.

"So why kill Adler?" Zinni asked. "She obviously knows who we are, so it wouldn't hurt anything if he gave us information about her, even if Ibarra doesn't realize that. Why keep him from talking?"

"Maybe she truly didn't want to be caught," Skeet muttered.

Aroska didn't care for his tone. There was objectivity—which unfortunately didn't carry too positive a note right now—but then there was all-out pessimism. Still, that suggestion could explain why she'd bolted upon their arrival at the apartment...

"I think it was a setup from the beginning," he offered. "You both saw how Adler was acting right before he died. He knew something was about to happen. He knew that strike team was coming. Maybe he went to Manes to report that we were looking for Moryi—" saying the name now made him cringe "—just like he told us he wanted to. Rather than take action against her, Manes decides to target us. He uses Adler just long enough to position us right where he wants us, then when he's no longer useful, uses...Ziva to take him out of play. Maybe she was just following orders and had no background information."

"Killing him still seems kind of superfluous at that point," Zinni pointed out. "Why would Manes bother?"

All Aroska could do was shake his head. "Don't know. Looks like Starcer wasn't kidding about how unstable the guy is."

"So Manes orders Adler to cooperate and arrange a meeting with us," Skeet said, his tone softer now. "He also orders Ziva to kill Adler once we're in position, unbeknownst to him. But did she know the strike team was coming? Were we supposed to be her targets too? I can't imagine she would have agreed to the whole setup if she'd known what was in store for us." He caught himself. "Or at least the Ziva we used to know wouldn't have."

Aroska sighed. "Switching ammo strikes me as adapting on the fly. Regardless of whether she knew about the strike team beforehand, using the bariine rounds against them was a way to cover her tracks. For all Manes knows, there were two different shooters—Moryi shot Adler as ordered, and someone else killed the soldiers, maybe before Moryi could take us out too."

"I think the truth can only come from her," Zinni said. "Not sure if we can find it on our own."

"I think a lot of what we need to know can only come from her."

There were so many possibilities right now, and focusing—or, galaxy forbid, *depending*—on any single one would result in gross oversight elsewhere. Perhaps the most basic conclusion was that Ziva was legitimately working for Alastair Manes and the Cartel; she hadn't stated otherwise during their brief encounter in the alley, after all. If this was the case, Aroska wanted very much to know how she had ever ended up out here. Freelance work might have landed her a few jobs with them, but her Matia Moryi persona was clearly something that had been a long time in the making. The thought occurred to him that his two surveillance images might be of her after all; the pattern of her makeup and the way she wore her hair were what had thrown off his algorithms, particularly in the more recent image from right here on Panuco.

If she truly was carrying out Manes's orders, she had defied him at the shipping yard by killing his soldiers, whether he realized it yet or not. While Aroska was immensely glad she had intervened—chances were high that he and the team would be dead otherwise—he couldn't help but wonder why she'd chosen to do that. The woman had always been a killer, but the stories Adler had told them about her brutal actions were disturbing to the point that he had to question whether she was even herself anymore. He wondered if she'd had every intention of following orders at the docks and then, upon recognizing them, had chosen to spare them because she'd once known them. It made him sick to think of her being so far removed. After years of longing to find her, a reunion under such circumstances was far from ideal.

Alternatively—and this seemed like the more reasonable scenario— she was working for Manes to some extent, but had actively opposed him in order to save her team. Her friends. If that were the case, it meant she was still herself, hadn't come completely unhinged, and could hopefully help them resolve all of this.

Then there was their encounter in the alley. After some consideration, he'd decided she'd been right to disarm him, though his shoulder was still a little sore where she'd hit him. She'd needed to keep him from reacting aggressively before fully realizing who she was, and he imagined he would have done the same thing if he were in her position. But her response when he'd done something as natural as reach for his fallen weapon still perplexed and unnerved him. The way she'd apologized afterward gave him the impression it had been a mere reflex, perhaps her default response to anyone going for a gun in a hostile environment like the streets of Tabaco, but she'd come painfully close to actually shooting him. He hadn't realized it until after the fact, caught up as he'd been in the moment, but he'd replayed the scene over and over in his head on the journey back to the ship. Her stance, the tension in her muscles, the cold focus in her face. Her finger had even gone to the trigger before she'd caught herself.

And how could he forget her eyes? She'd seemed so distant, almost as if she were somewhere else entirely. Then she'd blinked and realized what she was doing, and everything had seemed almost normal, or at least as normal as it could be given the circumstances. It was as though her previous actions hadn't been her own, and that unpredictability made him incredibly uncomfortable. But then she'd allowed him to hold her, had told him to trust her. The comfort of that moment made him want to forget everything else, but objectively he knew that wasn't an option.

"Listen," he finally said, "we're low on time here, and we can't exactly go to Starcer with the information we have now. We need to hear her side of the story before we can make an intelligent decision."

"I'm not disagreeing with you," Skeet said, massaging his forehead, "but we also need to be cautious. If she is Matia Moryi—if she's responsible for everything that has happened—then she has a lot to answer for. Anything could have taken place during the past four years. We can't know for sure where her allegiances lie now."

"Wherever they lie, some of them are still with us. I saw it in the alley. And she wouldn't have done what she did at the docks otherwise."

"Then why did she run?"

Aroska sighed. There were reasonable explanations for some of her actions, but still enough questions that he found it impossible to answer definitively. "I don't know."

"So what do you propose we do?" Zinni asked.

"We don't necessarily need to find her again—whatever is going on, she seems to be trying to maintain a secret, though from whom, I'm not sure. I think it's safe to say she had eyes on us before, obviously at the docks and possibly earlier, so the chances are even higher that she's watching us now. We simply need to put ourselves out there, show her that we need to make contact. Let her come to us. Better yet, let her come to *me*." This he directed at Skeet. "You know how she is. I think I can get through to her."

The lieutenant's expression softened and he glanced at Zinni, who shrugged and nodded toward Aroska in apparent agreement. The space was silent for several seconds as they all considered the benefits and potential consequences of such a venture.

"Fine," Skeet said. "One circuit through the city. Do not engage, and keep your head down. If those were Manes's men at the docks, it's a safe bet he'll send more to get the job done, especially if he knows we're still looking for Ziv...Matia Moryi."

Aroska nodded and checked his pistol, swapping his drop leg holster for a low-profile concealed one at the small of his back. "Give me an hour."

He turned and strode down the corridor toward the cargo hold, pausing for a moment to check the feed from the outer ramp cam. The area surrounding the ship looked as clear as ever, nothing but short grasses, sand, and rocks stretching from the edge of the city to the waterline. He hit the controls to lower the ramp.

Echoing footsteps reached his ears before it had even hit the ground, and a shadow in the hatch stopped him dead in his tracks. His hand went to his weapon as the thought occurred to him that the cam should have picked up anyone lying in wait outside, but the moment the intruder appeared, he knew why it hadn't—that person simply knew how to avoid it. A combination of shock and sheer relief rendered him speechless as Ziva entered the hold and angled for the ship's bow, sparing him a brief glance as she passed.

"What are you doing here?" he finally managed, having the presence of mind to retract the ramp before rushing after her.

She glanced over her shoulder as he caught up and the two of them entered the armory, much to the dismay of Skeet and Zinni. Placing her hands on her hips, she met each of their gazes in turn and then addressed them as a group. "I'm here to kill all of you."

Chapter 24
SABER · Tabaco, Panuco

Zinni froze, partially in response to those words, and partially due to the abruptness of this encounter. Aroska had given them a brief description of Ziva's new appearance, but for several seconds, she wasn't entirely convinced of who she was looking at. The woman standing in the armory doorway now was a far cry from what she remembered of her old lieutenant, and maybe it had something to do with the nature of the phrase she'd just uttered, but even her voice sounded different. Low. Threatening.

Beside her, Skeet had tensed in response to the newcomer's words. She didn't have a clear view of his right hand from where she stood, but based on the way the muscles in his arm were flexed, she had a hunch it had come to rest on his holstered pistol. Part of her didn't blame him for such a reaction and was ready to do the same, but part of her felt it was a rather extreme measure to take just yet.

Ziva seemed to note this movement as well. "Relax," she said, addressing them all but looking Skeet in the eye as she did so. She lifted her gloved hands slightly, keeping them open and visible. "Let me rephrase that. Manes sent me here to kill you, but contrary to what you probably believe right now, I don't always do what Manes says."

Aroska slipped by behind her and moved around to stand on Skeet's right. None of them had dared to loosen up yet, but neither were they willing to make any aggressive moves. Zinni assumed the desire for answers trumped all else, at least for the moment.

"What are you doing here?" Skeet asked, repeating the question Aroska had posed in the corridor.

"Finding out what the hell *you* all are doing here," Ziva said. "I told you not to look for me." This she directed at Aroska.

"We didn't," Zinni said. "We were looking for Matia Moryi. We didn't know."

The thought occurred to her that they'd certainly found Matia Moryi. Regardless of the fact that Moryi and Ziva were the same person, the former was its own entity, a new identity with its own appearance and persona. Moryi was the same imposing height and had the same hardened physique as the one-time HSP spec ops lieutenant, but her clothes and hair looked better suited to a desolate, miserable world like Duruta. It was nothing like what Zinni had expected, when or if she ever saw her old friend again.

"Matia Moryi," Ziva sighed, massaging her forehead with closed eyes. She said the name as though it belonged to someone else entirely. "This is independent service time, right? Who sent you?"

"A materials developer from Delatori named Pahl Starcer," Skeet replied. "Someone you should be very familiar with."

"Starcer." She sighed again and muttered a curse. "This isn't what it looks like."

"Then you've got some explaining to do!"

Both Zinni and Aroska opened their mouths to address him, but he lifted his hands in surrender and lowered his gaze in apology. Zinni knew he'd harbored some subtle anger toward Ziva for some time thanks to the secrets she'd kept in regards to using her forbidden Nostia to save Aroska's life at Dakiti. Hell, she'd felt the same, especially thanks to some of their former commander's other behavior in the following months. But even after learning the truth about all of it, realizing her reasoning, and being separated for four years, it seemed Skeet's anger had never fully ebbed.

"I know I do," Ziva said, unfazed by his outburst, "but that can't happen right now. There's too much at stake. You're putting me in a position I don't want to be in, and I need you all to leave before someone gets hurt."

"That's the same thing you said to me in the alley," Aroska said. "What do you mean by it?"

"I mean *this*!" She gestured around, indicating them all as a group.

"Manes knows you're here and knows you're looking for me. He wants me to take care of this problem."

"But you'd never do that," Zinni said. "You'd never 'take care of this problem'."

Her voice had risen ever so slightly as she spoke, betraying the fact that the statement had turned into more of a question in her mind. Ziva watched her curiously for a moment; it was impossible to tell whether the few seconds it took her to respond was merely consideration of that question or a legitimate hesitation. Either way, Zinni didn't like it.

"Of course not. That's why I'm here. If you leave now, I'll tell him you were gone before I arrived. But I can't pretend forever, and the longer you stick around, the harder it gets. I've already had to do too much to prove my loyalty to him."

Zinni hadn't realized how much she'd started to relax until her body went rigid again in response to those words. Beside her, Skeet and Aroska did the same.

Ziva recognized this and extended her hands further out to the sides. "That's not what I meant," she murmured, her gaze flitting to the floor.

"What are you even doing here?" Skeet asked once again, his tone conveying his increasing impatience with the fact that the conversation was going nowhere fast. "Why the hell are you working for Manes?"

"It's a long story."

Skeet shrugged and looked around the room. "And we've got nothing but time."

Ziva pressed her lips into a thin line and stared him down for a moment, her odd golden-orange eyes burning. Part of Zinni wanted to be sympathetic; Skeet was being a little too antagonistic for her taste, and driving tensions higher in an already-tense situation wasn't accomplishing anything. But at the same time, the longer her old friend remained evasive when presented with what seemed like simple questions, the more uncomfortable she grew as well.

"Did you kill Adler?" Aroska asked.

Another beat passed before Ziva broke eye contact with Skeet. "Yes," she answered with no further hesitation.

"Why?" Zinni said.

"I was following orders."

Skeet folded his arms. "But now you're not."

"No!" Ziva placed one hand on her hip and raked the other back through her ragged hair, a brief look of pure desperation flashing across her features. "*Sheyss*, how hard is it for you people to just listen to me? You have to leave before this gets any worse."

"How hard is it for *you* to just explain what's going on?" Zinni cut in before Skeet could speak, keeping her voice as calm as she could.

"And you saved us at the shipping yard?" Aroska continued as though nobody else had spoken.

"I did."

"Why?"

Both Zinni and Aroska whirled toward Skeet, who stood awaiting a response. That was the last straw. Zinni opened her mouth to address him, unable to believe what she'd just heard, but Ziva beat her to it.

"What the hell kind of question is that?"

His features remained steeled for a couple of seconds longer before he looked away, chagrined.

"I had no idea that strike team was coming," Ziva continued, the volume of her voice rising. "I was supposed to kill Adler, and that was it. When that team showed up, I had to act fast."

"Okay, everyone take a damn breath," Zinni snapped, stepping forward. Both men fell silent and averted their gazes, and Ziva appeared almost grateful she had opted to mediate. Frustration was reasonable right now, but here they were arguing like children and allowing that frustration to control the conversation.

She drew a breath and gave Skeet and Aroska one last lingering look—daring them to interrupt—before turning back to Ziva. "We have orders to bring Matia Moryi in dead or alive," she said, refraining from specifying that the 'dead' option would almost certainly result in a status downgrade. "Can't you give us some answers?"

Ziva sighed and leaned forward, placing her gloved palms flat against the armory table and staring down at the surface. She wore flexible leather spaulders and matching bracers, but the visible flesh on her muscular arms was riddled with scars and discolored tissue. The woman had endured so many traumas throughout her HSP career and even before, but whatever experiences had landed her here on Panuco in this condition were almost inconceivable.

"When I left Haphez," she began slowly, not looking up to meet any of their gazes, "I was in pretty bad shape. I needed to hide, but I also needed to stay alive. I went straight to Niio to fulfill the promise I made to Tobias, and I knew the Niiosians could probably get me the medical attention I needed."

Both Zinni and Skeet shot Aroska a glance. He in turn stared at Ziva, dumbfounded, though she saw none of their reactions with her head down. The fact that he'd been spot-on with at least part of his theory was incredible.

"Foolishly, maybe, I offered to work longer with Tobias in exchange for the Mob's care and protection. I spent almost a year with them. They got me back on my feet and brought their issues with the Ibarra Cartel to my attention. Turns out their problems have been going on for a long time, even since before they came to help us with Ronan. Tobias recruited me to be a permanent solution of sorts." She finally looked up and met each of their gazes in turn. "I'm here on his behalf."

"You're undercover," Zinni said, fearful that the statement had once again been articulated as more of a question.

It was difficult to tell whether Ziva lowering her head was a nod of affirmation or not. Either way, she didn't verbally confirm or deny.

"After I left Niio, I spent another year establishing myself, making a name for Matia Moryi in this sector of the Fringe."

Zinni shuddered to think of what atrocities that process might have entailed, given Moryi's reputation.

"And now I've been with the Cartel for two years, working for Manes, following his orders, gaining his trust. He pays me well and holds me in high esteem. Or at least he did. I think his trust is deteriorating and I'm busting my ass right now trying to keep this all from falling apart."

"What changed?" Aroska asked.

"To start with, you all showed up. He suddenly thinks I'm keeping something from him, even though that secret has nothing to do with why you're actually here. To top it off, that kid you cornered in my apartment? He was listening in on your—*our*—comms this morning. He heard my voice. He knows I helped you. I'd say he'll no doubt take this information to Manes, but I'm sure he already has. He'll do anything to gain the man's favor." She paused, and for a split second her composure appeared to wilt. "You realize what that means, don't you? Manes knows I was the only shooter, that I killed his men. But he gave me this second chance to deal with you anyway. This is a test, one I'm going to fail if you don't get out of here right now."

The armory fell silent. It all seemed like a reasonable explanation, if a somewhat vague one. If it was the truth, Zinni wondered why it had taken so long to reach it. Jumping straight to the point the moment she entered the ship would have saved Ziva the round of arguing and would have left them all in much better spirits. Now Zinni felt as though she still had nearly as many questions as she'd started with. But if what Ziva was saying was true, there wasn't time right now for further answers. They did need to leave, both for their own safety and hers.

"Z, don't take this the wrong way," Skeet began, his soft voice almost foreign after his previous outbursts, "but...twice now, you've led us to believe you were dead. You never told us you were a Nosti. Never mind all the classified work you've done for the agency. The majority of your life has revolved around secrets, half-truths, and even lies. So...give me one reason why we should believe any of this."

Zinni wanted to berate him again, despite his now-calm demeanor, but she realized it was a legitimate question. And in that instant, she understood. All the anger he'd held toward Ziva for the past few years, the uncertainty, the skepticism...it was all because he no longer felt he could trust her wholeheartedly.

Once upon a time, Ziva might have responded with 'because I told you to,' but now that was hardly an appropriate reply. "I guess I can't," she answered instead. "You just have to realize I'm on your side."

"So what do we do now?" Aroska said.

Just like that, any signs of distress Ziva had been showing vanished. She straightened and looked them each in the eye, though it felt more like she was looking past them. "You'll do as I say and you'll leave," she answered, her voice low and authoritative just as it had been when she'd arrived. "I told you before that you've put me in a position I don't want to be in. I'll say it again: you leave now, and I'll tell Manes you were gone before I got here. But I can't stall any longer."

Something about her tone suddenly seemed off, but maybe Zinni was simply imagining it after hearing Aroska's account of what happened in the alley. "But what do *we* do?" she said. "What do we do about Matia Moryi?"

"Leave the system. I'll find you later and we'll come up with a plan. But something big is about to happen here and I have to deal with it." She paused. "The less you know, the better."

Sheyss, why did she have to be so cryptic? Neither Skeet nor Aroska looked thrilled with the idea of leaving, but they refrained from arguing any further.

"Please listen to me before something bad happens," Ziva continued. She turned to leave, pausing once more in the doorway. Her hands curled into fists, but she didn't turn around when she spoke. "I hate that you came here."

And with that she went out, leaving them all standing there in shock.

CHAPTER 25
SABER - TABACO, PANUCO

The armory was completely silent for several long seconds as Aroska, Skeet, and Zinni all exchanged looks. Aroska imagined it was a combination of trying to process all the information they'd just learned and being afraid to act on it. At least that was the case for him. There were still too many things he didn't understand, and he was growing tired of it. Letting Ziva go again before she could provide him with the information he sought was the last thing he wanted to do.

He turned without another word and strode out, not caring what Skeet and Zinni thought. The boarding ramp remained lowered after she'd exited, letting the salty ocean breeze fill the *Saber's* cargo bay. He jogged down, scanning the landscape the moment his feet hit the sand below. Ziva's tall form was easy to spot as she moved across the relatively flat terrain toward the outskirts of the city. He picked up his pace. "Ziva!"

To his relief, she stopped and looked back, though she seemed rather exasperated. She remained motionless until he caught up, then she resumed her journey, not protesting when he continued to follow.

"Just talk to me," he said, taking a couple more jogging steps to match her stride.

"I told you all you need to know," she answered.

"You told us a lot without telling us much at all."

She merely shot him an unimpressed look.

"Come back with us. Tell us the whole story. We can help you here."

"What makes you think I haven't told you the whole story?" she hissed, coming to an abrupt stop. Anger flared in her eyes and her jaw twitched, warning him not to push the matter.

Aroska sighed. She was lying—he could sense it. It wasn't so much that he recognized the outward signs; she was always so careful about making sure there were no signs to recognize, and just as Skeet had said in the ship, half of her life was built on lies. This was just a time when he *expected* her to be less than truthful.

Regardless, negotiation clearly wasn't going to get him anywhere. "I'm not leaving here without you," he said, opting to cut to the chase.

To his surprise, she didn't immediately shoot him down. She merely looked at him with something verging on sympathy before shaking her head and continuing on. "You're going to have to," she answered, her voice quiet yet firm. "I still have business to take care of, and you know as well as anyone that I can't go home."

She at least had a point there; he knew she would probably never be able to return to Haphez, not safely anyway, but the desire to have her back in at least close proximity was overwhelming.

Based on their current trajectory, he guessed the small groundcar parked amid the outbuildings just ahead belonged to her. The occasional pedestrian passed by, but the area remained secluded and quiet, hopefully off of Manes's radar. It was why they'd opted to dock their ship nearby, after all.

They continued toward the vehicle in silence, with Ziva likely not wishing to say what she was thinking and Aroska simply not knowing what more there was to say. Anything he said at this point would just be repetition of previous arguments. The only way to get this woman to do something she didn't want to do was knock her out and take her by force. He felt a pang of guilt when he realized he was actually considering such a thing.

They stopped a short distance from the car and faced each other, studying one another for several seconds. "You've put me in a position I don't want to be in," Ziva said, her tone flat.

"So let us get you out of this place."

"You need to leave," she said, shaking her head. She paused and swallowed hard. "This is your last chance."

Her words carried a chill that made the hairs on the back of his neck stand on end. Something unfamiliar flashed through her eyes:

dread, with a hint of anticipation. As much as he wanted an actual explanation, for the first time he felt inclined to just listen to her.

After a brief hesitation, he gave her a single nod in response. Then, after tucking some loose strands of hair behind her ear, he slid his hand around to cradle her neck and gently pulled her to him, touching his lips to her forehead. Upon releasing her, he had to admit he was somewhat disappointed to find that her eyes were still wide open. They were out of focus, staring blankly at some unknown point beyond his right shoulder. Her mouth hung slightly agape, and a single, thin tear appeared from nowhere and slid down her cheek. Perplexed by her reaction, Aroska turned and looked behind him, but other than a pair of figures lingering a good distance away, the area remained clear.

He whipped back around and found Ziva's countenance still troubled. "What's wrong?"

She sucked in a short breath, blinked, and shook her head, almost as if she'd been snapped out of some sort of trance. The routine was nearly identical to what he'd seen in the alley. She looked down at the ground for a moment, then turned and continued toward the car. "This isn't how it was supposed to be," she muttered.

Every ounce of common sense Aroska possessed screamed at him to back off or even retreat altogether; something about her stiff stance was *off*, and a certain survival instinct—perhaps the same one she herself had often spoken of—warned him to be cautious. But despite the knots in his stomach, he found himself chasing after her. "Ziva, what's wrong?" he demanded again, rushing forward to block her path and halting her progress with a solid hand.

In the two seconds her back had been turned, the distraught look had been totally wiped from her features, replaced by an all-too-familiar stoic determination that sent up a new cluster of red flags in his mind.

She looked up and met his gaze. She was communicating with him, pleading, even, but despite the fact that he'd gotten to where he could read her fairly well, he found he couldn't understand what she was saying. In response to his question, she merely shook her head again. Stepping forward, she slid her hands inside his jacket and wrapped her arms around his torso, bringing her chin to rest on his shoulder. For the briefest of moments, the gesture brought him immeasurable comfort, but the feeling dissolved instantly when she tensed.

"I'm sorry," she murmured.

In the split second it took Aroska's mind to process the simple two-word phrase, her hand had curled around the grip of the pistol in the concealed holster at the small of his back. She drew the weapon and pressed the barrel to his chest. Pulled the trigger once. Twice. Three times.

Eyes wide, Aroska glanced between her face and the gun before taking a staggering step backward and collapsing into the dirt. The three impacts had paralyzed him to the point that the pain was left to a minimum; the only thing he could focus on was the stench of burnt material and the fact that he couldn't breathe. That, and the twisted, hateful look on Ziva's face as she moved to loom over him.

"What did I say?" she said through gritted teeth. "I told you all to leave. I told you to back off. I told you not to make me do something I'd regret. Why couldn't you have just *listened* to me?"

Aroska blinked rapidly as his vision began to grow hazy. Even if he could think of something to say, he wouldn't have been able to take in enough air to get the words out.

"I'm sorry," Ziva said again, taking one last step toward him.

He wasn't sure what he'd been expecting, but somehow one last plasma bolt to the upper abdomen wasn't it. He gasped desperately for air, the effort leaving him dizzy and numb. He stared upward at the blurry shadow that had been Ziva and watched as it was swallowed up by even darker shadows conjured by his mind. A metallic *clack* sounded somewhere nearby as she let the gun clatter to the ground. Unsure what else to do, he let his body go limp and allowed his eyes to close.

Chapter 26
4 Years Ago - Niio Spaceport

Three weeks passed, with Serenity stopping by daily to start a round of the faux caura treatment and share some basic background information on the Ibarra Cartel. The bot the woman had spoken of on the first day was never seen again; Ziva guessed it had only been needed while she was completely incapacitated. Aside from some leftover scar tissue that Serenity guessed might never fully fade, she felt rejuvenated. The treatments hadn't affected any of her older scars, but they'd healed the majority of her most recent burns and some of the smaller, seemingly insignificant injuries she'd sustained while battling Ronan and the Resistance. Three weeks of being cooped up in the tiny apartment hadn't done much for her physical condition though. She'd done her best to get some exercise in the confined space, but her options were limited. According to the former doctor, things would be improving on that front.

"You ready for this?" the older woman asked, studying the readings on a tiny device she'd just used to take a blood sample.

"To get out of this room?" Ziva responded, stretching and looking longingly at the door. "Of course. To see how the Niiosian Mob reacts to my presence here? You tell me."

They'd kept her cooped up for her own safety, Serenity had explained numerous times. Tobias's orders. Ziva hadn't even seen the man since she'd revealed herself to him upon arriving on Niio. He was protecting her from the rest of the Mob, giving her a chance to recover before announcing her presence. The situation had seemed preposterous at first, but when she'd realized that taking the time to heal and recuperate would better enable her to escape if things went wrong, she'd changed her attitude.

Serenity was quiet for a moment, but there was understanding in her eyes. "I know it may not seem like it, but we're trustworthy people. Everyone here has pledged their absolute loyalty to Tobias. If he tells them not to lay a hand on you, they won't."

That wasn't the sort of thing Ziva had ever worried about, but she gave the woman a nod of thanks anyway. It was just that usually when she came to Niio and dealt with the Mob, she had more leverage, some way for both her and Tobias to benefit from working together. That was still the case in a way, only Tobias had already done her a favor and now here she was, stuck here, with no way to know what he had in store for her. Only that it had something to do with the Ibarra Cartel.

"As far as I know, today will just be a briefing," Serenity continued. "So will the next few days for that matter. He's not one to jump into a situation without taking the time to examine all the angles. He'll make sure you have all the information you could possibly need." She paused a moment, searching Ziva's face. "And don't worry—he wouldn't have you meet with his people unless he believed they were ready too. I'm sure he's put a lot of consideration into this."

"I don't suppose you have any idea what he has planned."

Serenity shook her head. "I have some theories, but I'm not sure if Tobias himself has even made up his mind yet." She checked the time. "You'd better get going. I'll be available later if you need anything."

A car had been waiting for her outside. Without a word, the pilot had flown her into a more industrial-looking sector of the city—as if any particular area of Niio looked much different—and had dropped her off on the empty landing pad of a nondescript building. Upon entering, a single hallway had funneled her into an elevator, which began carrying her upward before she could even give it a command. When the lift stopped and the doors slid open, the gentle hum of machinery and the buzz of voices could be heard beyond.

She stepped out onto the floor and angled for the cluster of people gathered around the large control center in the middle of the room, not breaking stride despite the fact that all eyes were now on her. Tobias himself stood directly across the table, the greenish-blue light from various holograms and displays reflected in his spectacles. He regarded her with only mild concern for a moment before resuming his conversation, though it appeared most of the others present had lost all interest in what he was saying.

Some of the faces looked familiar, and Ziva guessed they'd all been in the restaurant when she'd come to Tobias just weeks earlier for assistance in locating Skeet and Aroska. Cole, the only one of them she knew by name, stood to her right, watching her with wary disbelief rather than undressing her with his eyes the way he usually did. Hyper-aware of the shock her presence had evoked, she resorted to meeting each of their individual gazes, just as she had done in the restaurant. She continued forward and around the table, sliding into a vacant place several spaces away from Tobias.

The mobster had yet to stop speaking, though he seemed displeased that the question he'd last asked hadn't been immediately answered. Whoever he'd been addressing finally managed to stammer a response and, satisfied, he turned to Ziva.

"Agent Payvan, it's good to see you well." He paused and appeared thoughtful for a moment. "I hope you don't mind if I continue referring to you that way. Old habits die hard."

She dipped her head and crossed her arms.

Clearing his throat, Tobias turned back and swept his gaze around the table. "I'm sure most of you know Agent Payvan. She'll be our guest until she's able to resolve some issues with the Federation, and I trust you'll all use discretion in sharing information about her presence here. In exchange, she has kindly agreed to assist us with our ongoing problem with the Ibarra Cartel."

The emphasis he put on the word 'agreed' struck Ziva as a way of not-so-subtly reminding her how much she now owed him after what he'd done for her, even though she was the one who had offered her services initially. Based on the looks some of the other thugs were giving her, they could also sense that element in his tone, and she made a point of keeping her shoulders as straight as possible while under their scrutiny.

Movement drew her attention to the other end of the table. Cole leaned forward, finally back to eyeing her like a trophy he was due to be presented with. Meeting and holding his gaze seemed to give him pause, but it didn't erase the sly smirk from his lips.

"I'll bet if we turned her over to the Feds, they'd be happy to take care of Manes and the Cartel for us," he said with a chuckle.

In that instant, the room fell dead silent. For a moment nobody even moved, then all eyes shifted warily to Tobias. The mobster's stone-cold gaze remained fixed on Cole.

The expression on the burly enforcer's face transformed instantly from smug to casually chagrined, then to all-out horrified. Ziva couldn't help but feel a twinge of amusement, but at the same time, the fact that someone of Tobias's stature could influence someone of Cole's in such a way sent chills down her spine. Never in her life had she expected to see the brutish man in such a state.

"I mean..." he said, swallowing hard and shifting a bit. He somehow managed to straighten and maintain eye contact with his boss, though doing so clearly made him uncomfortable. "Why keep throwing our own resources at Ibarra when we have an option like that? Losing resources has been our problem, hasn't it? She's not even one of us. We use her as a bargaining chip, and we won't even have to lift a f—"

The word 'finger' hadn't quite escaped his mouth when the plasma bolt sliced through the air and burrowed into his forehead. Everyone's focus remained locked on him as he stood upright for a split second longer, staring forward with vacant eyes and a slack jaw. Then his head lolled backward and he crumpled to the floor, a thin wisp of smoke trailing from the smoldering hole as he fell.

Ziva shifted her attention from Cole back to Tobias, who still stood with a pistol aimed at the place where his right-hand man had been standing. She risked a brief look past him and saw the man beside him standing with closed eyes and clamped lips, refusing to look at the empty holster on his own hip.

Tobias leaned over the table, gun still in hand. "Does anyone else have any helpful suggestions?" he muttered through his teeth. He stared straight down at nothing in particular, daring them to speak.

When no one responded, he turned and gently returned the pistol to his associate's holster, giving the man a pat on the shoulder. "I'm sorry you had to see that, Agent Payvan, though I suppose you're no stranger to death. I felt I needed to reiterate exactly how high the stakes are." He pivoted and looked over at her, though she got the sense he was addressing everyone in the room.

In his eyes, she saw something verging on remorse. Cole may have been a lewd bastard the majority of the time, but in all the years she'd dealt with the Mob, he'd been nothing but loyal as far as she knew. The fact that Tobias could put down one of his top lieutenants without so much as batting an eye, all just to prove a point, told her how desperate the man truly was right now.

She remained silent, not one for condolences but also unsure how the mobster might react to anything she had to say anyway. Tension was high and tempers were running hot around here, just as Serenity had warned her. With as far as the situation had deteriorated, she was surprised the Mob had been so quick to spare manpower for the battle with the Resistance.

"In case I haven't made it abundantly clear," Tobias said through still-clenched teeth, finally turning and leaning over the table again, "we will *not* be involving the Federation in this matter, and we will *not* be using Agent Payvan as a 'bargaining chip.' This woman is a precision instrument, capable of meticulously and efficiently performing a task. But such a fine tool is worth nothing if the hand that wields it is reckless."

For a solid ten seconds, no one stirred, no one spoke. Then, as if moving too quickly might bring their boss's wrath down upon them as well, the two men who'd been standing on either side of Cole stooped down and began to drag his body away. Tobias watched them until they disappeared into the shadows on the far side of the room, then, after hanging his head for the briefest of moments, finally turned back to Ziva. "What has Serenity told you?"

She brought her hands to rest on her hips and swept her gaze around the table. "The Ibarra Cartel has been making a push for your territory," she answered. "This Manes character is their leader and, dare I say, your rival."

The look of mild amusement on Tobias's face told her that her words had the desired effect. He was always making comments she perceived as subtle threats or challenges, so she was merely returning the favor. He struck her as someone who preferred it when people spoke plainly anyway.

"That's the gist of it, yes," he replied. "We've never done business with them, but for a long time, there was what many considered a mutual respect—even a truce—between our two circles. They've been on our radar for years, but there was always enough space between us that it was never necessary nor prudent to expend the resources to take them out of play. Things changed when Alastair Manes took power after clipping his old man a few months ago. We've lost contact with some of our outposts. Ibarra crews have been spotted in places they shouldn't be. There's evidence they may have had an indirect hand in the hijacking of some of our supply lines, including the one I hear Serenity told you about. That was before the younger Manes took over, but it wouldn't surprise me if he was already stirring the pot that long ago."

Based on the desperation and weariness he'd already displayed, Ziva guessed the situation was more serious than he was letting on. "You're sure this was all Ibarra-related? Sounds like a lot of speculation and coincidence to me."

Tobias nodded long and slow, his face hard. Without even looking, he reached to the control panel and activated the table's primary holographic function. Ziva found herself watching what appeared to be aerial footage of a decimated building, smoke still curling up from the center and flames still licking what remained of the walls. Several bodies were visible in the rubble, all but one of which appeared to have been killed by debris. The last man lay sprawled on his side, one hand outstretched toward a comm receiver that remained just out of reach. The signature Niiosian tattoos were visible on all of their necks, as shown in a series of still images depicting enhanced, magnified sections of the footage. In the close-up shot, Ziva saw that what had appeared to be a shadow under the sprawled man's head was in reality a large puddle of dried blood, and part of his tattoo had been disfigured by the massive slash cut across his throat. This had not only been some sort of airstrike; it had also been an execution.

"Your men," Ziva said, a statement rather than a question.

"Indeed," Tobias muttered, switching to another angle of the man whose throat had been cut. Someone had used his blood to write a message on the concrete floor in Standard.

All reigns come to an end. A.M.

She shook her head. "Alastair Manes."

"This was our outpost on one of the moons of Ribao. The warehouse was registered under a false name and was used to store some of our more...discreet products. It was manned by five men at any given time. Nobody was supposed to know we were even there."

He cleared his throat as if he were waiting for her to come to some sort of conclusion. Eyes narrowed, she took another long look at the still images and noted the timestamp. She lifted an eyebrow. "This is from just three weeks ago." *Just before I arrived.*

Tobias nodded. "Imagine returning home from helping an old friend with her little Resistance problem to find out that one of your clandestine supply drops—which happened to be *empty* at the time— had been destroyed in a precision airstrike and the only survivor had been taken out immediately after by someone who'd been sent for exactly that purpose." He turned and stared thoughtfully at the footage. "This was their first blatant attack against us, and it hasn't been the last."

That explained why he'd been willing to assist Haphez with that 'little Resistance problem'—the Mob hadn't experienced a devastating blow from Ibarra like this before. And perhaps Ibarra had also purposely chosen to attack while the majority of Niiosian forces had their attention directed elsewhere.

He drew a breath as if to continue, then hesitated a moment and swept his gaze around the table. One by one, each of the men gathered there stepped away. They moved to the far reaches of the room without a word, remaining present but leaving Ziva and Tobias relatively alone at the control center.

"I have always prided myself in my ability to run this organization in a civilized fashion," he muttered, staring blankly ahead as if his mind was elsewhere. "I only met the man in person once, but Oron Manes was the same way. He was old-school. He had etiquette. Principles. His son is the exact opposite. Overly ambitious. Temperamental. Even reckless in his quest for power. And he's willing to erase centuries of tradition to gain it."

Ziva couldn't help but compare this struggle between Niio and Ibarra to the one between the Federation and the Resistance. Haphez may not have had any stake in Federation matters, but they'd condemned the Resistance anyway because the Feds represented a crucial structural element in the galaxy which, if destroyed or even disrupted, would mean the end of everything Haphez and the other independent Fringe worlds stood for. The same could be said for Niio; it would be a mistake to ignore the fact that organizations like the Niiosian Mob and the Ibarra Cartel also represented pieces of galactic structure, regardless of the legitimacy of their operations. Allowing one of them—either of them—to grow too large or too powerful could disrupt that structure, just perhaps on a smaller scale. As with Haphez and the Federation, Ziva herself had no real stake in the Mob's affairs. The difference here was that Manes was vying for power and control while Tobias seemed content to maintain the status quo, at least as far as he was admitting. And there was the lovely little fact that she owed him a favor.

"Not only is Alastair Manes trying to take whatever he wants," the man went on, "but he is also annihilating anything and anyone he has no use for. He does not play by the rules, so as much as it pains me to say it, I'm planning on returning the favor."

She crossed her arms. "What exactly do you have in mind?"

"Your arrival here was timely, Agent Payvan. I had every intention of taking you up on the offer you made me when you were here looking for your team, but I must admit I had not anticipated needing to collect so soon. And now that you're here, I ask that you also fulfill the offer you made the night we first spoke here."

It was all Ziva could do to keep from saying what she was thinking: *Work for you for an indefinite amount of time doing the galaxy only knows what? No problem.*

"Not like I've got anything better to do right now," she said instead, putting conscious effort into sounding as indifferent as possible.

"We were talking before you arrived," he said, sweeping his gaze around the room at his men. "It's possible Cole was merely joking—very distastefully, I might add—about surrendering you to the Federation, but I couldn't risk him being serious, and I cannot afford to have anyone in my ranks treating this situation as anything but dire." He once again lowered his head, stroking his chin for a moment before recomposing himself. "Despite his folly, he was right about one thing: a lack of resources is currently our biggest problem. If we were to wage a full-scale war against Ibarra this very day, I'd estimate we have a fifty-fifty chance of winning or losing. If we lost, it would be the end of Niio as we know it. I don't like those odds, but I'm also not one to sit and twiddle my thumbs while Ibarra continues picking away at us. Make no mistake—we'll be on the offensive, but no one will ever know it."

"Let me guess," Ziva said. "You want me to covertly take out Ibarra personnel so the hits aren't directly tied to the Mob and Manes doesn't escalate before you have a chance to act. I deduced as much based on some of the things Serenity told me."

Tobias grinned. "You're a perceptive woman, Agent Payvan. Yes, your job would be to tilt the odds in our favor before we take any more drastic action. It's a process that could feasibly take multiple years— Manes may be ambitious but he knows better than to launch any full-blown attack against us before he has managed to whittle our numbers down in a similar fashion, so the goal will be to cripple the Cartel while also ensuring they're unable to retaliate against us as quickly as they'd like to."

"You have a good starting point?"

"I won't ask that you begin this project until you're back to full health, but I have some documents you may begin reviewing in the meantime." He pulled up some file clusters in the table's projection. "We may have never dealt with Ibarra or had issues with them up until now, but that doesn't mean I haven't had them thoroughly surveilled over the years. The majority of the people on this list are still playing crucial roles within the Cartel's ranks, though we've been unable to confirm some of them following the recent regime change, and with a leader as volatile as Manes, I think it's safe to say there will be more turnover in the coming months."

Ziva's eyes roved over the list. "So you want me to take all of them out."

"Correct. But quietly, if you would. Frame someone else. Make their deaths look like accidents. I'll leave the methods and timing up to your discretion, and although you volunteered your services, I'm willing to compensate you for each confirmed kill."

It wasn't like this work would be much different than what she'd always done at HSP. "Seems simple enough. But out of curiosity, why not just take Manes out directly? Cut the head off the snake."

The corner of Tobias's mouth curled upward. "I believe there's an old saying that has to do with knowing your enemy even better than you know your closest friends, and I would like to do just that. Ergo your duties will also include documenting what you see during your exploits. 'Gather intel,' as you might say. I want to know everything." His smirk widened into a full smile. "And call me old-fashioned, Agent Payvan, but I mentioned there's a certain level of etiquette in the way I like to conduct business. I would prefer to deal with young Alastair man-to-man for tradition's sake."

She assumed this was simply a polite way of informing her he wanted Manes for himself, and as much as she still thought it best to simply cut Ibarra off at the source, she respected his reasoning and merely shrugged in response.

"There is someone else you'd be well suited to deal with directly," the man continued. "His name is Jerrick Taan, a hitman, an assassin serving Manes in much the same way you'll be serving me in the coming days. He considers himself a messenger of sorts, as many of his recorded kills have been more for the purpose of fearmongering than any sort of gain. He has single-handedly been responsible for the most devastating blows to our ranks over the past few weeks. He is well-versed in a variety of weaponry but prefers to do his work with blades."

He paused and shifted his gaze back over to where footage from the warehouse was still being projected from the table. Suddenly Ziva understood.

"You seem to know a lot about him," she noted.

"I've had one of my best people tracking him for some time now. An expert, if you will. He has already done all the legwork and we have virtually all the information you'd ever need to know about Taan as a target. Your eventual mission will be to eliminate him."

"Why doesn't your so-called expert take him out?"

Tobias was quiet for a moment, lowering his gaze and placing his palms flat against the table. It was a completely foreign look after the iciness and apathy he'd displayed only minutes before in front of his men. "They're brothers. Half-brothers. Taan used to be one of us. We wanted boots on the ground at one of Ibarra's other compounds on Naris, just to keep an eye on things. Alastair Manes was overseeing operations there even while his father was in power. We still don't know how it happened, but the Cartel discovered Taan was Niiosian and captured him. Manes turned him." He looked her directly in the eye. "I'm not without mercy, Agent Payvan. I'd prefer to not send my man in to kill his own brother when morale is already in short supply around here."

He heaved a sigh and steeled himself, regaining some of the cold poise Ziva recognized. "Besides, as a former member of our family, Taan would recognize Niiosian presence from a light-year away. I can't risk losing the element of surprise when the time comes to strike. This is why a third party is preferable for this task." He looked her up and down approvingly. "Though I must admit Taan is a dangerous foe, especially after months of Cartel indoctrination. Elusive. Tenacious. Getting close enough to get the job done may take time."

Ziva nodded to herself and stood in silence for a moment, staring at the images of the Niiosian soldier who'd had his throat cut. Taking Taan out of play seemed logical from a tactical perspective, as he would no longer be able to pass Niiosian intel along to Manes. But it wouldn't solve the problem of lost resources; skilled bounty hunters and assassins were plentiful out here in the Fringe and would no doubt be delighted to come into the paid service of an organization like Ibarra.

She voiced this concern to Tobias. "In the grand scheme of things, I don't see how it will do any good to take him out. Manes will just get another assassin."

"Yes, he will."

Something about his tone just then caught her off guard, and when she noticed the way he was looking at her, a chill ran down her spine. Somehow she got the feeling she wasn't going to like what he was about to say.

"Tell me, how do you usually handle long-term undercover operations?"

"My team never did long-term undercover work. We performed precision strikes and recon. We'd be forced to role-play occasionally but never for more than a couple of days at a time."

Tobias blinked, unimpressed. "Humor me, then. How *would* you handle a long-term undercover operation?"

She hesitated, certain she knew what his questions were leading up to. "I would learn as much as I could about the target and their environment while I was still in friendly territory. I would prepare a role, and I would condition myself for it both physically and mentally. Then?" She sighed. "I would fully immerse myself in that role, shutting out anything and everything that wasn't part of it until the operation was over." *And then deal with the inevitable consequences later,* she thought.

The mobster beamed. "That's what I like to hear."

Chapter 27
Outskirts · Tabaco, Panuco

Aroska listened to the car start up and take off down the street, and he lay motionless until the whine of its engine died away. Even then, he remained silent, mostly because he still felt as though he couldn't breathe. Part of that was thanks to the impact of the plasma bolts striking the low-profile underlay he'd donned per Skeet's orders. He wondered if Ziva had felt pain on this scale when he'd shot her on the riverbank outside Haphor. Most likely not, considering he'd still been a couple of meters away. She'd had the barrel of the gun pressed directly to his chest, and that fourth shot had only been from about a meter. Plasma bolts may not have traveled with as much force as solid bullets, but from that close, they still packed a punch. His ribs were bruised—if not cracked—and he was positive his intestines had been displaced, were it anatomically possible. At least two of the rounds had burned most of the way through the underlay, scorching his skin and melting the vest's fiber mesh.

But his breath escaped him for another reason. Even with his eyes closed, he was left with a lingering image of the look on Ziva's face as she'd loomed over him. Anger. Fear. Confusion. Panic. It was like nothing he'd ever expected to see, and it had seemed completely genuine. He hesitated to say it *was* genuine, simply because he didn't want to believe she'd actually shot him. But here he was, still sprawled out on his back, with four smoldering holes in the front of his shirt that said otherwise.

That realization brought about a sense of despair that left him content to just lie there, despite the fact that every instinct screamed at him to get up, find cover, and contact Skeet and Zinni. But the sound of running footsteps snapped him out of his stupor before he could drift too far into it; he rolled halfway over, gritting his teeth against the pain that engulfed his midsection as he felt around for his gun. He felt like a fish out of water, flopping around and struggling to orient itself. Something metallic glinted in the corner of his eye. Ziva had tossed the weapon further than he'd realized, and he doubted he'd reach it before the footsteps arrived. At the moment he almost welcomed the thought of someone putting a bullet through his head if it meant this pain—both psychological and physical—would go away.

"Tarbic!"

He relaxed immediately in response to the familiar voice and collapsed again, head spinning as he turned and watched Skeet and Zinni's blurry forms rush across the street. The exertion, however brief and mild, irritated his damaged lungs, and he was overcome by a bout of violent coughing that left him clutching his abdomen in a futile attempt to alleviate the pain.

"What the hell happened?" Zinni cried, sliding to her knees beside him and yanking his arms away to give herself a better view of the impact marks.

Torn between fear and a sudden, overwhelming sense of anger, it took Aroska a moment to muster up a response. "She...shot me," he sputtered between coughs. Hearing the words out of his own mouth sent a fresh spasm through his chest, this one provoked more by emotion than the injuries. "*Frouchten hehle*, she *shot* me."

Skeet moved to recover the discarded gun while Zinni lifted Aroska's shirt to take a look at the damage. "Glad you were wearing this?" she said, running her fingers over the holes burned through the underlay.

"Doesn't feel like it did much good," he wheezed.

"Well, considering you'd probably be dead without it..." she muttered, her tone turning somber as she leaned closer. "It doesn't look like any of the shots broke skin, but you've got some superficial burns and probably some internal damage."

"No kidding."

"Can you walk?" Skeet asked. He remained upright, sweeping his gaze around the area, Aroska's pistol in hand. "We can't stay here."

It wasn't like he had any real choice. Zinni stood and offered her hand, and together she and Skeet managed to haul him to his feet. The underlay suddenly felt incredibly restrictive, though he didn't dare remove it yet for fear the tight garment was the only thing holding him together. He took a couple of shuffling steps forward and decided he could manage without assistance, though he kept one arm braced against his ribcage. He accepted his pistol when Skeet offered and held it ready at his side as the three of them set out for the ship, moving across the soft sand and assessing their surroundings as they went.

Aroska angled for the small medbay the moment he set foot in the vessel; Zinni followed while Skeet secured the boarding ramp and ensured all the *Saber's* stealth systems were fully operational. He set his weapon down and managed to shimmy out of his jacket on his own, but Zinni stepped in to assist with his shirt and then the underlay before easing him back into the bay's reclining chair.

The thought occurred to him that, despite being aware of his surroundings, he didn't really have any idea what was happening right now. He was on total autopilot, going through the motions he knew were required to survive but not doing much else. That final image of Ziva's face had yet to leave his mind. He'd felt so sure she would listen to him if he went after her, and even the initial walk across the beach had gone without a hitch. The change in her behavior had come on so suddenly, and like in the alley, he couldn't explain it. Something was wrong, and he wasn't sure how to deal with that, either physically with the team or mentally on his own.

Skeet appeared in the doorway, glancing from Aroska to Zinni as she began preparing a caura drip. He didn't look pleased, but there was a weariness in his demeanor that took the edge off the anger.

"I'm sorry, Skeet," Aroska said, leaning back against the chair's cushioned headrest. "I just thought..." He trailed off, unsure exactly *what* he'd thought. He'd chased after Ziva with the hope of gaining whatever information she'd been withholding, but when it came down to it, it had been a purely selfish endeavor.

"I know," Skeet said, his voice softer than expected. "I think we all let our guard down."

Did we though? Aroska thought. He saw Zinni steal a glance at the lieutenant as well. 'Letting his guard down' would not have been the most accurate description for the man's behavior in the armory throughout the past hour.

Zinni turned and held a scanner over his chest for a moment before administering several higher strength caura injections and attaching the drip line. "No broken bones," she murmured, almost as if to herself. Then she looked him in the eye and spoke in a loud, deliberate tone meant for more than just him. "You couldn't have known what would happen."

Aroska could tell she'd been growing impatient with Skeet during the conversation with Ziva as well. Perhaps impatience as a whole had been all of their downfall. They were impatient with each other and impatient with the lack of information, which had led to short tempers and hasty reactions all around.

More unsettling images of that vacant look in Ziva's eyes flashed through his memory. "No, I should have known. Something wasn't right—I saw it but didn't want to believe it."

"What do you mean?" Skeet said.

It struck Aroska as an odd question. The two of them had to have suspected something was amiss if they had come looking for him so quickly. Either that or they'd thought they could help him bring Ziva back. "I told you about what I saw in the alley, the hostile reactions and that vacant look in her eyes. I saw the same thing just before she left the armory—"

Zinni nodded in agreement.

"—and then again just before she...shot me. It was worse than the other times. Unnerving, to be completely honest."

Skeet moved further into the medbay and perched against the counter on Aroska's left while Zinni remained on his right preparing a dressing for the burns. "Start from the moment you left the ship," the lieutenant said. "Tell me everything that happened. Every detail."

Aroska launched into a thorough relation of events, mentally walking himself back through the trip across the beach, searching his mind for things he'd subconsciously seen but hadn't noticed in the moment. Ziva had almost seemed...resigned, maybe, as they'd walked together. Still evasive, certainly, but resigned. Everything had felt relatively normal right up until he'd given her an innocent peck on the forehead and she'd acted like she'd seen a ghost. Those people up the street had seemed too far away to be significant, but he wasn't sure what else she could have been looking at, assuming she *had* been looking at something and he hadn't imagined it. Now that he thought about it, he might have heard her car slow or even stop a few seconds after she'd sped away and left him lying in the dirt. Perhaps it had been where those people were.

"It was almost like..." he said, wincing at the pain in his chest as his breathing quickened, "...almost like she wasn't there. Like it wasn't her. She told me she was sorry two different times, like she didn't want to do what she did. But damn. She did it anyway."

The intelligence officer's brows remained drawn together as she worked. "Is there any way she could have known you were wearing the vest?"

Aroska sighed; the underlays were low-profile and composed of ultralight materials for a reason. "I suppose it's possible, but there was something about that look in her eyes. It was so purposeful, but so... blank. I couldn't read her at all."

Zinni gave him an almost-sympathetic look before glancing over to Skeet. "Thoughts?"

They were all once again in a situation of not wanting to jump to conclusions but also needing to take all the possibilities into account. Skeet seemed to recognize this as well and drew his hand over his face before running it back through his close-cropped hair the same way he'd always done when he'd worn it longer and wilder. "You think she was telling the truth about working for the Niiosians?"

The question had been directed mainly at Aroska, but Zinni piped in before he could muster up a response. "I think it was a reasonable explanation, and if it's true, it means our assumptions were mostly correct. But I felt like there were some gaps in her narrative. Things she didn't elaborate on. Details she left out. I still have almost as many questions as I did when we started."

Aroska had to agree, as much as he didn't want to. When Ziva had first begun her story, he'd been so excited about being right that he'd almost stopped listening altogether. But her continuous strange behavior was what had prompted him to chase her down. All he'd wanted were some answers, and he'd taken four rounds to the torso at point blank range for his trouble.

"I think," he said, drawing a sharp breath and diverting all his focus toward remaining still while Zinni began plastering his burns with something that made them sting. "I think regardless of what the circumstances are now, she started out loyal to the Niiosians. Going to Tobias was likely the only way she could have survived after the *Intrepid* blew."

"So she came here undercover, like she told us," Skeet said. "You think Manes got to her? You've seen how people around here are fanatical about him."

"Like brainwashing?" The thought nearly made Aroska ill, though the tangible ache in his ribs was somewhat nauseating as well. Ziva was one of the strongest people he knew, both physically and mentally. And yet...so very broken. He couldn't imagine what it would take to exploit that thoroughly hidden inner fragility, but if Manes was as manipulative as his reputation suggested, then perhaps it was something they needed to consider.

"It's a possibility," Skeet said, his tone finally bearing a shred of regret.

"If she was truly brainwashed, I'm not sure she'd be acting of her own accord," Zinni offered. "I'm not sure she'd have the faculties to save us at the docks or come here and warn us to leave. She would have followed orders and killed us."

Aroska couldn't help but notice the way she'd hesitated slightly before uttering the word 'killed.' The truth of it was that if Ziva had come aboard the ship with unfriendly intentions, it would have been three against one and they—theoretically—would have been able to take her down before she could cause too much damage.

Skeet tilted his head. "What are you thinking?"

"Maybe she did go to the Niiosians, and maybe she has been here on their behalf," Zinni answered. "But she's been here working for Manes for two years, at his beck and call and gaining his trust by doing unspeakable things I'm not sure I ever want to know about. That's a *long* time, way longer than any undercover op we've ever conducted. Maybe she's been so immersed in this Matia Moryi persona that she's having a hard time remembering whose side she's on."

It wasn't an ideal scenario, but Aroska liked it better than the first one. It accounted for the fact that Ziva still seemed to be thinking for herself, and some of the things she'd said to them made sense in that context. Talking about proving her loyalty to Manes, the way he'd come to favor Matia in her role within his organization...

"You're thinking some measure of cognitive dissonance?" he asked.

She nodded. "It's hard to tell how severe, but Ziva's goal is to obey the Niiosians and work against Manes. Matia's goal is to obey Manes and work against the Niiosians, or at least that's the premise Ziva developed for her. Those two things are just about as contradictory as you can get. But she's had to maintain this role like her life depends on it. Literally. Spend too long doing that and—" she shook her head "—it could be easy to forget who you even were before."

"But she knows us."

"And she kept telling us to leave before she did something she'd regret. She wanted to protect us but still be able to report back to Manes without technically failing her assignment."

She *had* seemed desperate for them to go away, which Aroska had just shrugged off as her trying to avoid the truth. But maybe she had told them the truth. Or maybe she wasn't completely sure what the truth was anymore.

"Then why did she shoot me?"

Zinni was quiet for a moment. "Maybe when things didn't go as planned, Matia took over."

If that was the case, then she was totally unpredictable. Aroska could once again picture the crazed look in her eyes, the way her face had been so twisted as she'd spoken to him. As much as he didn't want to accept it, all the signs told him she'd legitimately intended to cause him harm.

"Or," Skeet said, "maybe we need to acknowledge a third possibility: that she was lying about all of it, is really working for Manes, and deliberately tried to murder Tarbic."

Aroska and Zinni exchanged a glance. The intelligence officer heaved a sigh. "Don't be like this, Skeet," she said. "You've got to at least maintain a little hope."

"I'm just saying," Skeet replied, holding up his hands in surrender. Considering the subject matter, his tone wasn't nearly as condemning as it had been while Ziva was present.

"How would she have come into Manes's service, then?" Aroska said, wishing very much that he could just lie in silence for a while. "And why would she have saved us at the docks?"

For a moment the only sound in the room was the hum of the small machine mixing the caura treatment for the drip line. Then Skeet shrugged and shook his head, folding his arms and staring down at the floor. As Aroska had expected—and hoped—the suggestion had been more of a release of anger than an actual working theory.

"Well, I've been hearing a lot of 'maybe' here," he said, wincing as he attempted to adjust his position in the chair. No more assumptions. He wanted the facts, and he wanted very much to believe Ziva was still okay. If she wasn't, he dreaded to think of not only the countless hours but also the emotional energy he'd wasted seeking her out over the past four years. Then he hated himself for even thinking like that. Even if something had gone wrong somewhere along the line, they couldn't just give up on her. But this current feeling of confused rage—and, he had to admit, heartache—made it difficult to feel as optimistic as he once had.

"The fact is she shot you," Skeet said. "Whether she genuinely betrayed us, or has been turned into a mindless Ibarra drone, or is dissociating, we don't know."

"And we're once again in a position where I think we can only learn what we need to know from her," Zinni added. "Right back where we started, essentially."

"What do we tell Emeri, then?"

The room fell silent once more. With all the new developments the day had brought, Aroska had nearly forgotten this was even an ongoing mission. "*Sheyss*," he muttered. "I don't suppose we have the option of just not checking in."

The lieutenant shook his head. "We're under orders, Starcer's contract aside. We said we'd call in after the meet at the docks this morning, and we didn't. They were expecting an update hours ago."

Aroska sighed as best he could with the fresh compress on his chest, though he had to admit the caura treatment was already improving his comfort level by leaps and bounds. There was no obvious way around this.

"So what *do* we tell Emeri?" Zinni asked.

He shook his head. "The truth."

"That Ziva shot you?"

"That Matia Moryi shot me. Whatever the circumstances, that wasn't Ziva—not the Ziva we know, anyway."

All three of them spent a moment glancing between one another as though searching for affirmation that this was the right move. Finally, Skeet straightened and headed for the door. "I'll get the transmission set up, then."

CHAPTER 28
IBARRA COMPOUND · TABACO, PANUCO

The tiny drone hovered high and silent over the Haphezian agents' ship, transmitting a crystal-clear feed back to the Ibarra compound. That feed was projected via hologram in Manes's private office, a far cry from his other offices around the city where he allowed himself to be more accessible to the public. Now he sat in relative darkness and total silence, surrounded by modern comforts and some of the best technology Panuco had to offer, waiting for the drone's feed to show him what he wanted to see.

Matia had arrived on the scene several minutes earlier, lying in wait beneath the ship for a while before the boarding ramp had been lowered. He didn't know how she had managed to gain access, but from the moment she'd disappeared inside, all had remained quiet.

If he was dealing with anyone other than his best assassin, he would've killed her on the spot after learning what Blain Reed had heard on comm at the docks that morning. But he found himself in this instance driven by a sense of morbid curiosity. She would pay for killing his soldiers, make no mistake, but had she targeted them specifically, or had she simply reacted in the moment in order to protect the Haphezians? And if that were the case, did she know them? She'd most likely lied about there being a second shooter, so it was entirely possible she could have lied about other things. The question now was why. What was she hiding from him?

His attention was drawn back to the projection when the boarding ramp lowered again and Matia emerged. Once she'd figured out where the ship was docked, he would have liked to see her use heavy ordnance and simply destroy the whole thing from a distance, but going inside and taking out the agents in a surgical strike would give Ibarra an opportunity to check out the vessel and gain more information, whether about their intentions or about Haphez in general. He would send a team in and make sure the job had been done.

The drone reduced its altitude a bit, following Matia across the sand as she made her way back to where it had recorded her leaving her car. But then something moved in the corner of the feed. Manes's eyes were drawn to the spot; he did a double take and stood up, fixated on the man who had just come down the ramp and taken off after her. For a moment Manes feared he'd merely survived the attack and was going after her, but above the noise of the wind coming in off the sea, he could be heard calling something—not her name—out to her. She paused, waited for him to catch up, and then the two of them continued walking together.

Manes swore and swept his arm across the desk, sending its contents clattering to the floor. He moved around in front of it, pacing back and forth and ignoring the concerned knock on his door in response to the noise. "Stay on them," he growled into his comm, gaze locked on the hologram even as he moved.

The voice on the other end of the transmission gave him an affirmative and the drone dipped lower still. It was a small enough device that its soft buzzing couldn't be heard over the noise of the breeze and the rumble of the ocean, and it remained high enough that it would likely be mistaken for a bird at first glance. Still, its controller allowed it to maintain some distance behind the pair, moving it in a slow circle when they stopped and appeared to argue briefly.

Well, this confirmed not only that Matia had lied about knowing these people, but also that she had blatantly disobeyed his orders this time around. If this man was walking with her and hadn't turned outright hostile, it feasibly meant she hadn't killed the other two agents either. What she hoped to accomplish by sparing them, he could only imagine. Surely she knew the consequences for failure.

The drone followed as they continued on their way, alighting on the edge of an outbuilding's roof to watch as they approached Matia's car. They once again stopped to talk quietly, Matia's features steely and grim, the man's full of concern. "Can we get audio on this?" Manes demanded, unable to make out what they were saying.

"Not without getting close enough for them to see," the voice replied.

After a moment, it appeared the two Haphezians reached some sort of agreement. To Manes's shock, the man pulled Matia close, planting a gentle kiss on her forehead. He touched her as a lover might, or else someone who otherwise cared deeply for her. Matia had never struck Manes as having someone like that in her life, but perhaps it explained her actions...or lack thereof.

A second voice on the other end of the transmission swore. "I think we've been made."

The way Matia let her gaze linger on a point up the street confirmed this. "Let it play," Manes instructed, smirking at the thought of the emotional turmoil that must be going through the woman's head right now. He never would have imagined this was how he could break her, but now that the opportunity had presented itself, he couldn't resist.

So a moment later when she moved in to embrace the man and then drew his weapon and pulled the trigger, Manes froze in shock. He counted at least three discharges of the plasma pistol. The Haphezian agent collapsed into the dirt, his chest smoldering.

"Good girl," he whispered, though this action alone was no longer sufficient enough to get Matia completely off the hook.

She stood over the man and appeared to be speaking to him for a moment longer, though the tremors in her hands were visible through the drone's cam even from that distance. Then she fired one last round into the man's chest before casting the pistol aside and striding for the car.

"Bring her in," Manes instructed over the comm.

The drone watched as the car took off, leaving the dead agent lying on the ground. Then it lifted off the roof and followed, veering toward those two figures who waited up the street. Matia's car slowed as she approached them. Kimbra and Blain Reed stepped out of the shadows; the former moved out to ensure Matia stopped while the latter used a device to maneuver the little drone into his outstretched hand. The two of them piled into the car and the cam's feed cut out.

Manes turned and moved over to the control center in his office, bringing up the recording he'd been generating as the drone transmitted. He watched it in its entirety three times, starting from the moment Matia had emerged from the ship. Then he replayed the moment the man had chased her down several times, adjusting the pitch and separating sounds until the word he'd shouted became clear.

"Ziva!"

The name struck him as familiar. Most people in this part of the Fringe couldn't care less about what was going on in other independent systems across the galaxy, but if there was one lesson he'd learned from his father before slaying him, it was that anyone in this position of power should keep at least some track of galaxy-wide events for security's sake. Haphez had been of particular interest following the acquisition of the niobi crystals, though he hadn't paid the militaristic world much mind since then except for a brief and fruitless foray into Matia's past.

There'd been something though, a name that had cropped up in relation to the assassination of a Haphezian political figure just before the Cartel's black-market supply of genuine niobi crystals had been cut off. He checked his archives—*Ziva Payvan*. An agent with the Haphezian Special Police, the same agency Matia had speculated these agents here on Panuco belonged to. But now he wondered if it had truly been speculation or a cleverly placed truth to help reinforce her lies. He pulled up the mugshot that had gone out to regional news networks following the assassination, mentally projecting Matia's face beside it. Payvan still sported the dotted facial tattoos Kimbra had had carved from her face before fleeing her homeworld; her eyes were a deep crimson, the color of blood, and her jet-black hair was streaked with the same shade. But despite these cosmetic differences, this woman staring back at him had a familiar facial structure, one he was used to seeing scarred and smeared with dark reddish-brown war paint.

So she had lied about her true identity. Part of Manes had expected this all along. Kimbra had even insisted that Matia Moryi was a name with a hidden meaning, something involving an old phrase in the Haphezian native tongue, but he hadn't cared as long as the woman could perform. He'd argued that the benefits of recruiting an unknown outsider with no ties to the Cartel outweighed the consequences. At the moment, his first assumption was that she had taken up the alias and come to this sector of space in order to escape the authorities following the assassination she was wanted for. But she clearly knew these agents who had come here searching for her, appeared to still have good relations with them, and had refused to kill them until put under extreme pressure. Was she working with them? If so, why? And why had they been searching for her? Or had that all been a ruse?

He moved back and took a seat at his desk, folding his hands and letting all of these questions consume him until the security system alerted him that Matia's car had arrived at the compound. He instructed Kimbra over the comm to bring the assassin here to his office, a place he rarely took audiences but one of the only locations they could be guaranteed the utmost privacy.

Voices and heavy footsteps grew louder in the corridor. The door hissed open and Kimbra escorted Matia in; Manes caught a brief glimpse of Reed standing in shock just outside before the door shut in his face. The blonde woman grabbed a rolling chair from the far wall and shoved it forward so forcefully that it caught Matia in the back of the knees and forced her to take a short staggering step.

"Sit," Manes ordered.

She did, albeit with her weight forward and her hands resting on the armrests. She held his gaze for the duration, though he couldn't help but notice the fraction of a second her eyes darted toward the hologram of her face—her true face—still projected from the console behind him.

Kimbra took up position behind the chair with her arms folded across her chest, content for once to be somewhere other than hovering at his side.

The room fell silent as Manes stared into Matia's eyes, trying to picture them in that blood-red shade as he searched for any sign of the anxiety she'd showed immediately after shooting her comrade, for he was convinced that's who the Haphezian agent was. But now he saw nothing except her usual cold focus, perhaps minus the arrogant flair. Regardless of who she truly was, this was a woman who had spent years creating and reinforcing a shell, and it was up at full strength right now.

Manes stood and went to the console. "Ziva Payvan," he began. The name had a nice ring to it, and she made no immediate attempt to deny it belonged to her. Smart—it was pointless to do such a thing now.

"You lied to me," he said, staring into those red eyes in the hologram. Frankly, he was almost glad he'd never seen them in person; her piercing gaze was intense enough in yellow.

She remained silent until he turned back to face her, as though unsure whether she should respond. "I killed him like you wanted," she said, unable to conceal a slight tremor in her chin. "They're a skilled team—going in and taking on all three of them in such close quarters would have been suicide. Separating them was my only option. I can still take care of the others."

Perhaps that was all true, but she'd just shown that flicker of genuine emotion while recounting killing the agent, and that was the whole point. "No, you lied about knowing them," Manes said. He clasped his hands behind his back and strode around to the front of the desk, hovering before her. "You know good and well why they're here, don't you. You've been working with them."

He had to at least take solace in the fact that she had still displayed some shred of loyalty to him. Regardless of whether these people were her accomplices, she had followed orders and shot the agent. Perhaps she'd felt she had no choice upon realizing Kimbra and Reed were watching, and perhaps she was remorseful now, but the fact was she'd completed the task.

Matia's fingers tightened around the chair's armrests, but she made no other move to react, at least physically. Even with Kimbra in the room, she would still be capable of causing some damage if she chose to act, but there was no way she'd make it out of the compound— or even down the hall—alive. So no, she would not try anything here; her tendency toward self-preservation was too strong.

"I haven't," she said through her teeth, eyes burning. "I swear."

Another lie, no doubt. "They came here looking for you," Manes said, making a point of keeping his tone even. Raising his voice and threatening her would get him nowhere, he knew, and was likely the response she was expecting. Calm confidence would throw her off her game, make her believe she still had a chance. "You were Haphezian Special Police, hunted by your own agency after you murdered a Haphezian dignitary. But I have to wonder if all of that somehow got resolved, considering the...*amicable* relationship you seemed to have with these agents."

She looked over to where the drone's recording continued playing on a loop and watched as the man kissed her on the forehead just before she'd shot him.

"So you lied about who you were," he continued, "and you lied about knowing these people. The question now is why." He brought his face within centimeters of hers, reveling in the thought of how trapped she must be feeling. "They're here about the replicated niobi crystal tech, aren't they. And you led them straight to me."

The walls she was putting up seemed almost tangible. "I will say it again: I'm not working with them, and never have been."

"But you don't deny knowing them." He gestured toward the recording as it depicted her standing over the man's inert body in the street.

She only averted her gaze for a moment, but it was all the answer he needed.

"There wasn't a second shooter this morning, was there."

Her hesitation was brief. "No."

"Well." The corners of his mouth curled upward. "Let's see if we can find out what else you've been keeping from me." He moved back over to the console and began a query for her true name. He didn't know for sure what her role with HSP had been, but if the language in her wanted bulletin was any indication, much of the work she'd done was clandestine, and thus he didn't expect to find much public information. But he had some other resources at his disposal, ones that tended to possess information they had no real business possessing.

The initial search elicited no immediate results, but he'd by no means been expecting any. The Haphezians were known as a private, secretive bunch, and if she'd held any sort of covert position within their ranks, he'd find nothing further without putting some extra effort in. Frankly, he was surprised these people had been so quick to cannibalize her by releasing her name and photo following the assassination, but it was a perfect example of the ruthless guilty-until-proven-innocent model they followed. Kimbra had told him a little about that when explaining the circumstances surrounding her departure from her homeworld.

He expanded his search parameters to include some of those additional sources and cast a glance back at Matia. She kept her eyes on him, fingers still wrapped around the chair's armrests, body still rigid as if ready to spring into action at any moment. But she remained motionless, silent.

"I suppose your agency doesn't want anyone knowing any more than they have to," he said. Her stiff posture made him wonder if she was anticipating a specific search result, something that would tell him everything he needed to know. He doubted he would be so lucky, but he had to hope.

In that sense, it was almost startling when the console beeped, alerting him that the search had found something. He was still facing Matia, and though she still made no move to react, he saw her gaze shift toward the projection. He couldn't help but smile as he turned to see for himself what interesting information the query had yielded. But as much as he'd been looking forward to finding something, what he saw gave him pause.

The display before him showed a list, one that had been distributed by one of his intel networks but had originally been published four years earlier by a source he would never have expected: the Galactic Federation. For a moment, all he could do was stare at that title, that official seal, trying to wrap his head around why he could possibly be seeing what he was seeing. Haphez was neutral, independent, just like Panuco and all the other Fringe worlds. And yet, there was Ziva Payvan's name in a list of—he looked closer and gaped—

all known personnel who were part of the Resistance, the cluster of Core worlds that had rebelled against the Federation and had been all but defeated four years earlier. And of all things, she was listed among those who were considered Nosti, the Resistance's sect of telekinetic warriors.

He'd heard stories about the Nosti. His father had known a couple who'd hidden out on Panuco when the Federation had first attempted to purge them over two decades ago. Agility training and master swordsmanship combined with the ability to manipulate objects with their minds made them formidable foes in melee combat. The word was they could alter the path of a bullet or plasma bolt fired at them, and sometimes even deflect the projectile altogether. Supposedly object deflection was one of the first lessons Nosti trainees learned in hopes that it could be honed so thoroughly as to become a thoughtless reflex. He'd never seen Matia do or say anything that would lead him to believe she possessed such an ability, but then again, he'd never even considered the fact that she *could* possess such an ability. Perhaps there had been signs all along and he merely hadn't been looking for them.

He turned to study her once more. The only thing that had changed about her appearance was the fact that she had returned her attention to him and watched him with an unwavering gaze, waiting for a reaction. From that distance, he doubted she could see precisely what he was looking at, but the Federation seal was clear enough that he was sure she'd put two and two together.

"You're with the Resistance?" he said.

Behind Matia, Kimbra drew her weapon.

"I'm not," the woman answered, her voice low and monotone.

"Then what do the Feds want with you? You're hiding here because you're a Nosti, aren't you."

"I'm not," she said again, this time through clenched teeth.

Without warning, he hurled his communicator at her. She reacted to the movement but only managed to move her head a short distance before the device hit her in the face, leaving a red mark on her cheek. For a moment she only stared down at the floor, brows furrowed, but then she lifted her gaze back to him, and upon seeing the sheer hatred in her eyes, he was sure she would retaliate this time. But still nothing happened.

Well, she hadn't tried to deflect the comm, which by no means ruled out the idea that she could be lying but also made him more inclined to question the Federation's list. The majority of Fringe worlds were unwelcoming if not all out hostile toward the Resistance and the Nosti in hopes of avoiding Fed attention. If she truly was a Nosti, the chances were slim that she ever would have survived on Haphez, and he couldn't imagine these Haphezian visitors would be so friendly toward her now.

"Let me go after the other two agents," she said, as if reading his thoughts. "You saw what happened—I was already able to kill one of them, just like you asked. I can still finish this, Alastair."

Before he could stop himself, Manes's fist swooped through the air and struck her in the jaw. He couldn't recall her ever addressing him by his first name in the two years they'd been acquainted, or addressing him by name at all, for that matter. The majority of their interaction consisted of him debriefing her or giving her new orders while she waited in silence. Calling him by name had felt deliberate, perhaps an attempt at making a connection, keeping him engaged. Something someone with formal negotiation training would do.

He took a breath and composed himself. "No," he said, clasping his hands behind his back and beginning to pace in front of her, "I have a better idea." He looked up at Kimbra, who still stood with her pistol trained on the back of Matia's head. "Notify the dining hall that I'll be having two guests at dinner this evening."

Both women responded with equally perplexed looks, though Kimbra's morphed into a sly smirk as it dawned on her that he must have something interesting planned. Matia's did the opposite, shifting into a deeper confusion that was probably the closest thing to fear he was ever going to see from her. Her face was already turning dark red where he'd hit her.

"I told you I'd take care of them," she said, her tone still even. "I'm on your side here, I swear."

Part of him couldn't believe he was actually preparing to give her another chance, but it could hardly be considered a 'chance.' It was an opportunity to break her fully, to teach her the consequences for deceiving him. He still had yet to determine *how* she'd deceived him, but the fact was she had.

"We'll see about that," he said.

CHAPTER 29
SABER - TABACO, PANUCO

"She *shot* Tarbic?"

The life-size hologram of Emeri Arion shifted uncomfortably, and even with the soft flickering in the projection, the worry in his eyes was plain to see.

"He's fine," Skeet said. "Sore, but undergoing caura treatment as we speak."

"What the hell happened?"

The three of them had spoken a bit about how they would present this story to the director, trying to stick to the facts as much as possible while still protecting Ziva's identity...for now. Part of Skeet wanted to tell Emeri the truth and be done with it, but at the same time, he agreed with Aroska's suggestion that they keep referring to her as Moryi, if for no other reason than that he felt a great need to sort out this mess himself before getting Emeri completely involved. Besides, they still didn't have a good enough grasp on what the facts *were* for him to be comfortable with giving a full debrief.

"We managed to track Moryi down earlier this afternoon," Zinni said. "We almost had her, and we split up to try to hem her in. Unfortunately, that made each of us more vulnerable as individuals, and she was able to corner Tarbic."

It was the partial truth, anyway. They *had* split up, though not in any sort of tactical sense, and Ziva *had* taken Aroska by surprise...

"He took four plasma rounds to the upper torso," Skeet said. "Center of mass. Perfect kill shots if not for the underlay he was wearing. He's got internal bruising and some superficial burns where the rounds overlapped and ate through the underlay."

Emeri swore and dragged a hand across his face. "And Moryi?"

"Gone. But we think we know where she went."

'Think' was the key word there. The consensus was that she would have gone back to report to Manes about her encounter with them regardless of whether she'd been telling the truth about her role and intentions. The problem then was that none of them knew exactly where Manes was, and any excursion to find him would take them as deep into the core of the Ibarra Cartel as they could possibly get.

"So you have a good chance at apprehending her?"

Skeet stole a glance at Zinni, who kept her steely gaze on the director. "Yes," she said, "but with respect, sir, you told us we had the entire service term to find Moryi. What if we take the time to wait for Tarbic's injur—"

"I said you had the entire service term back before we knew what we were dealing with," Emeri said, cutting her off. "Moryi has now committed a direct offense against an HSP agent, which is more than enough grounds to bring her in. The Royal House is going to want her head. In fact, I'll be briefing them as soon as this call is concluded—I expect they're all going to be eager for some answers over there."

This time it was Zinni's turn to glance at Skeet. She'd made a valiant effort to buy them some time, and he offered her a subtle shrug that he hoped did an adequate job of saying 'thanks for trying.'

"Have you learned anything about her background?" Emeri asked.

"No," Skeet answered immediately. "She keeps her face painted to make her less recognizable, but she's definitely Haphezian. Don't think she's a Defective. It's hard to say for sure, but she moves and fights like she could be ex-agency." He felt Zinni tense beside him. "No indication of who she is or when or why she left home. None of us recognize her."

It was all he could do to keep from wincing as the words tumbled out of his mouth. *So much for sticking to the facts,* he thought.

He sensed movement behind him and turned to find Aroska lingering in the doorway of the comm room. The sergeant had managed to dress himself and was no longer keeping his arm braced against his ribs, but it appeared to be taking considerable effort for him to stand up straight, and his eyes were dull. Caura may have worked fast, but an hour wasn't long to have been undergoing treatment.

Zinni turned to look as well, and the fact that they both had their attention focused elsewhere was enough to clue Emeri in to what was happening. "Sergeant," he called, beckoning for Aroska to come closer so the projection could capture him. He did, stepping in between Skeet and Zinni and straightening as well as he could.

"How are you feeling?" the director asked.

"Frankly, sir, like *sheyss*. But also exponentially better than I did an hour ago, if that helps."

Emeri's lips flattened into a straight line. "Well, it's good to see you on your feet. I trust you'll be diligent with your treatment so you can be one-hundred percent functional as soon as possible."

"Absolutely."

"Good." The director's gaze shifted to Zinni and then to Skeet. "Did either of you witness what happened?"

"No, sir," Skeet answered, taking a split second to consider how to proceed without spiraling any deeper into the lies. "We knew Moryi and Tarbic were in close proximity, so we moved to close in on their position, but by the time we arrived, Tarbic was down and there was no sign of Moryi anywhere."

"If you were to re-acquire her, what are the chances you could recover the weapon she used against Tarbic? I imagine comparing the plasma signatures from the gun and the burnt underlay would go a long way toward prosecuting her."

Skeet remained silent for a moment, unsure how to divulge what was a rather embarrassing piece of information, but to his surprise, Aroska spoke up first. "We have the weapon."

Emeri crossed his arms, waiting for an explanation.

"She shot me with my own service weapon, then left it at the scene."

"How the hell did that happen?"

"She disarmed me, simple as that. I'm not proud of it."

Something in his tone told Skeet he wasn't just talking about physical disarming.

"Preserve the weapon for forensic analysis, then," the director said. "Fingerprints will tell us what we need to know."

"She was wearing gloves."

Emeri cursed. Several seconds passed as he merely stared at the three of them in silence. "Then Sergeant Tarbic, your personal testimony has just become the single most crucial piece of evidence in this case."

Beside Skeet, Aroska showed no outward reaction. "Yes, sir."

"In the meantime, Lieutenant Duvo and Officer Vax, you *will* re-acquire Moryi and take her into custody. Keep her sedated for the duration of the trip back if you have to. I want another update when you have her."

"Not me, sir?" Aroska said.

"You're in no condition to fight. Stay and continue your treatment. In the event of a catastrophe, you'll be available to deliver an official testimony that will be grounds for other teams to hunt her in the future." Emeri shifted toward Skeet. "If you're concerned about being down a man, I can send a team to back you up. There are two other ops teams doing independent service who could likely reach you within a day."

Skeet remained silent for a moment to create an illusion of deliberation, though there was no question in his mind. "That won't be necessary. We can handle it."

"See to it that you do, Lieutenant. We will be eagerly awaiting news of your success."

The transmission cut out abruptly, leaving the three of them standing awkwardly on the empty comm pad. Skeet had anticipated the director might exhibit some displeasure with the situation, but it hadn't made the conversation any easier. If they were dealing with Emeri alone, they might have some leeway, but the Royal House's involvement was going to complicate things. Nonetheless, he heaved a sigh. "Well, that could have gone better."

When he turned to Zinni, he found her staring him down, unimpressed. "What happened to sticking to the facts?"

"Believe me when I tell you I was asking myself the same question. I'll deal with the consequences later."

"Well, I'm not going to sit here and let you two go out there alone," Aroska said. "You're going to need all the help you can get."

Skeet considered this a moment. "No, do as Emeri ordered. If nothing else, Ziva thinks she killed you, or else Manes thinks she killed you. You need to stay 'dead,' and if we go out, you'll need to secure the ship. Manes's people no doubt know where we're docked now, and we need to relocate."

Aroska glanced down at the floor and nodded respectfully, wincing in pain as he stepped backward off the comm pad.

"Emeri doesn't know the whole story," Zinni said. "We have a better chance at getting through to Ziva than he or the Royal House realize. Whatever's going on with her, some of her old self is still there—we just have to connect with it."

Her dialogue itself was positive, but her tone and facial expression were far from it. It almost seemed to Skeet like the words were as much for her own benefit as theirs. She was right, of course, but he wasn't optimistic that it would be so simple, especially if they had to go into the heart of Ibarra territory to find her.

"Well," he said, "no sense in delaying the inevitable. Tarbic, get yourself hooked back up to your treatment and report to the cockpit. Zinni, gear up."

Ten minutes later, he and Zinni were standing beneath the ship, listening to the boarding ramp retract behind them. Neither of them knew where the vessel was headed for security's sake, and they'd stowed the car they'd been using in the cargo hold so as to erase all evidence of their presence from the beach. But they maintained comms with Aroska and would stay in contact as long as possible throughout their endeavor. The plan, if it could be called that, was to head back into the city and start by paying Ziva's apartment another visit in hopes of drawing her out. If she wasn't there and they had to wait, so be it; it would be a relatively safe and secure location where they could hopefully carry on a private conversation with her, keying on the shred of her old self that still remained. If they were unable to get through to her, Skeet carried a dose of sedative that would neutralize her long enough for them to procure a vehicle, rendezvous with Aroska, and get her off-world. He wasn't prepared to hand his old friend over to the Royal House as a traitor, even as confused and angry as he was with the situation, but removing her from this environment seemed preferable, at least until they could get some answers.

Zinni adjusted the strap of the compact backpack she'd donned and gazed across the sand as the ship lifted off and disappeared. They each carried a small loadout, intended for stealth and speed over brute force. Skeet felt almost naked without much of the hardware he normally carried, but if all went according to their shoddy plan, the less they had to carry, the better.

The two of them set off across the beach, passing the place where Aroska had been shot and continuing toward the heart of the city. A short walk brought them to a busier block, and they found themselves standing in front of a row of groundcars parked outside a cluster of buildings.

"Alpha Two, you clear?" Skeet asked as he surveyed the selection of vehicles.

"Just about," Aroska's voice responded in his ear. He'd set himself up with a mobile caura drip in the cockpit so he could continue his treatment even while piloting the vessel. "Just cleared the populated areas. Beginning the search for somewhere to set down."

So they were good on that front. Skeet glanced at Zinni, who shrugged and moved toward the nearest car. They'd considered returning to Ziva's place on foot to maintain a lower profile, but if their experience with Adler was any indication, Manes had eyes all throughout the city and someone was apt to report them regardless of their mode of travel. So they'd opted instead to use a vehicle and get there as quickly as possible; if everything went to hell, they might also be able to outrun anyone who gave them trouble.

Zinni worked her magic and breached the car while Skeet remained on the walkway, scanning their surroundings. There weren't many people outside, but a couple were already looking their way. It was difficult to tell whether they were merely curious about seeing someone break into a vehicle, startled by the mere sight of the Haphezian off-worlders, or whether they were Ibarra informants. He thought it wise to treat it as the worst-case scenario and went and slid into the now-unlocked car's passenger seat just as the engine roared to life.

Neither of them spoke for several minutes as Zinni maneuvered the vehicle toward the city center where they'd spent most of the morning. Skeet could tell she wasn't a fan of the way he'd handled the revelation of Ziva's presence here so far. Truthfully, after speaking with their long-lost friend aboard the ship, he'd begun to feel slightly more open-minded about the whole situation, but then she'd gone and shot Tarbic, sending him back to square one. He didn't want to believe she'd betrayed them or was so far gone that she was irredeemable, but as things stood now, she wasn't giving him much to go on.

"You're going to have to just talk to her," Zinni finally said, as if reading his thoughts. Damn, she knew him too well. "Regardless of where she stands, she's not going to listen to you if you go in and explode on her."

He knew this, of course, but in his opinion Zinni was being *too* open-minded about the whole affair. Not necessarily throwing caution to the wind, but certainly giving her feelings for her old friend more precedence than he would have liked. Objectively, he knew she was smart and experienced enough to not let those feelings dictate her actions—perhaps the issue was simply that they had differing opinions on the matter. She was right about one thing though: they couldn't afford to be divided right now.

He drew a breath and turned to respond but hesitated when he noticed the way her attention kept sweeping between the view ahead and that in the rear cam. Jaw set and eyes narrowed, she fixated on the cam a bit longer then hummed an affirmative to herself.

"What's up?" Skeet asked, wanting to look behind him but knowing better. Instead he watched through the windshield as they dipped down into a tunnel beneath a block of buildings, similar to the breezeway where Ziva's apartment was.

"This car put an awful lot of effort into catching up and cutting in behind us, and now they're just hanging back."

He leaned closer to her, doing his best to see the image from the rear cam without reaching to adjust it. A sleek black car with tinted windows hovered perhaps fifty meters back, blocking traffic on what had otherwise been a busy thoroughfare heading into the tunnel. It neither slowed nor sped up, and the cars backed up behind it didn't seem to mind the pace. That, or the pilots knew better than to challenge this newcomer.

"Do we have a problem?" Aroska asked over the comm.

Before Skeet could respond, two black cars identical to the one behind them swerved out of the oncoming lane an equal distance ahead, cutting them off. Zinni decelerated, bringing their vehicle sliding to a stop just shy of the newly formed roadblock. The car that had been following them slowed and parked horizontally just behind them, effectively hemming them in.

"I'd say we do," Skeet muttered in response to Aroska's question.

Four armed men piled out of each car, fanning out and forming a perimeter around their vehicle. Skeet's hand curled around the grip of one of the pistols he'd brought, but deep down he knew the best-case scenario in this situation was merely that he and Zinni would take out half these men before being gunned down themselves. And that was only *if* the men waited to open fire until they'd exited the vehicle, which was almost certainly not armored.

"What's our play?" Zinni asked quietly, her eyes darting back and forth between the thugs surrounding them.

Skeet refrained from answering for a moment as he watched one last figure climb out of a car in front of them, a large blonde woman who, unless he was mistaken, was Haphezian. She strode toward them, armed and clad in black leather, but paused several meters from their vehicle and held up an amplified communicator where they could see it.

"Not sure if we have any choice but to surrender," he muttered, gaze still fixed on the woman, "at least if we want to stay alive."

"Step out of the vehicle," the woman called out over the amped comm. "Surrender peacefully and you will not be harmed."

"Advise," Aroska said in the earpiece.

"Continue according to plan," Skeet answered. "We'll figure things out on this end. Get ready to sever comms."

He shot a glance at Zinni, who offered a resigned shrug and a nod. Then, with nearly perfect synchronization, they each opened the doors on their side of the car, casting their sidearms onto the ground before stepping out with their hands raised.

"Alastair Manes has requested the honor of your presence in his private dining room," the blonde woman said, her amplified voice echoing through the tunnel. "You will step forward and disarm completely. If you fail to comply in full, you will be shot."

"You catch that, Two?" Skeet said as quietly as possible, barely moving his lips.

"Affirmative."

He looked across the roof of the car at Zinni and nodded. As a unit, the two of them began to move forward, leaving a trail of blades and the other throwaway weapons they'd concealed on their persons. They halted a few strides from the woman and removed their communicators and earpieces, smashing them on the ground beneath their boots. Prompted by a nod from the woman, several of the men surrounding them closed in and began to pat them down, ensuring they'd obeyed their leader's instructions.

Without another word, the woman stepped back and extended a hand toward the car she'd arrived in, the doors of which still stood open. Zinni moved forward and climbed into the back seat first, with Skeet sliding in behind her. The interior was spotless and could even be considered luxurious, but that failed to bring him any added comfort.

"—intercepted them in traffic," the woman was saying into her comm as she got into the front passenger seat. "The third agent is gone, and their ship is no longer at the beach. They must have recovered the body, relocated, and traveled back into the city by car."

Well, at least that part of their plan was working, though Skeet wondered how long the charade would hold up. While gaining Ziva's cooperation was certainly the mission objective, self-preservation was currently at the top of his priority list, followed closely by protecting Aroska. As the car started up and the pilot maneuvered them out of the tunnel and toward the central Ibarra compound, he couldn't help but wish this whole operation could have been as simple as they thought it was when they left home.

CHAPTER 30
OUTSKIRTS - TABACO, PANUCO

"You catch that, Two?"

Aroska maintained a firm grip on the *Saber's* controls as he guided the vessel, his mind on autopilot while his focus remained almost entirely on his comm. The most important thing was that this invitation Manes had extended to Skeet and Zinni meant he wanted them alive, at least for now. That bought them some time. To do what, he wasn't sure just yet.

"Affirmative," he answered.

No one spoke on the other end of the transmission, though he could hear voices in the background and the sounds of wind and traffic. Despite being told to expect a cease in communications, it was still startling to hear a sharp crack followed by a brief, ear-piercing squeal and then silence. Not only had comms ceased, but he had a strong hunch that whatever had just happened ensured there would be no way to reestablish them.

But he could never be too careful. Fishing his own earpiece out, he crushed it on the floor, scrambled the comm channel they'd been connected to, then switched to a new channel despite having no one to talk to. If Ibarra had people like the kid the team had followed that morning who could trace multiple local comms, then moving the ship would be futile if their channel remained open for tracking.

Aroska sighed and scanned the landscape outside the front viewport. According to the nav computer, he was approximately twenty kilometers from the greater Tabaco metropolitan area, which was probably the ideal range in terms of both maintaining a safe distance and allowing them to escape in a timely fashion, something he was determined would still happen. He was at a higher elevation here than they'd been in the city; rather than grassy beaches, jagged cliffs dropped off on his port side, with the roaring sea crashing against the rocks far below. The *Saber's* instruments detected a rocky outcropping a short distance ahead and he veered toward it, setting the vessel down in an alcove that would conceal it from the naked eye, at least unless someone took a very close look. Hopefully it wouldn't come to that.

He ensured the landing gear was stable, killed the engines, made sure the stealth shielding was engaged, and leaned back in the pilot's seat, staring vacantly out the window. For a moment, he realized his mind was starting to go completely blank, and if there was ever a time when he needed to be thinking both clearly and quickly, it was now.

His attention shifted to the caura drip still attached to his arm. He'd been telling the truth when he informed Emeri he already felt much better, and now more time had elapsed as the treatment ran its course. Even as fast as caura worked, it hadn't been nearly long enough to heal the damage that had been done, but maybe it would have to be.

Rather than consider what he was willing to do in this situation, Aroska elected to narrow down his options by instead reflecting on what he *wasn't* willing to do. First things first—he wasn't willing to abandon Skeet and Zinni. Mission failure may have resulted in a team status downgrade, but if the two of them were killed, he'd be transferred and would be on his own just as he'd been after he thought he'd lost Jole and Tate. Objectively speaking, he knew such an outcome would not be favorable toward his well-being, but he also knew his mental state would be a thousand times worse if he had to look back for the rest of his career and wish he would have done something. Maybe it was morbid, but if *none* of them made it out of a rescue attempt alive...well then, they wouldn't have to worry about team status anymore, would they.

He also decided he wasn't willing to leave without Ziva. It wasn't a selfish goal this time, or at least not entirely selfish. If they left her behind—if they left Matia Moryi behind—without at least getting some additional information first, the agency would continue to send teams after her, teams who didn't know who they were dealing with and would expose her. Never mind the fact that the Royal House was going to want to hear his testimony about the shooting. Regardless of whether or not they were able to get Ziva off-world, he'd either have to lie or figure out a way to avoid talking altogether in order to conceal her identity. At the moment both of those options seemed absurd, but he'd deal with that when the time came. Part of him felt guilty for still wanting to protect her after what she'd done to him and the team, but if anyone could still gain her cooperation, it was them. And despite the bond she'd formed with Skeet and Zinni over the years, he had a feeling *he* would be best suited to engage with her directly.

And then, as much as he wanted to say he wasn't willing to hurt her under any circumstances, the objective part of his mind superseded that idea. If they couldn't get through to her, if she presented too much of a threat, if it *absolutely* came down to defending himself and his squadmates, he'd do what he had to do. The idea that he had to prioritize Skeet and Zinni's well-being over hers left a physical ache in his chest, something beyond the pain that remained after being shot.

By her.

So this was just how it had to be.

Taking everything into consideration, the solution was a simple one: he needed to set out after Skeet and Zinni, his treatment be damned, because without them nothing else mattered. He needed their support, and he suspected he'd need their help in gaining Ziva's cooperation, however that came about. Moving was still uncomfortable, but if sheer adrenaline didn't carry him through, then a few painkillers would at least temporarily ensure he forgot anything was wrong.

Drawing a deep breath, Aroska hefted himself out of the pilot's seat and dragged the mobile caura drip down to the medbay before detaching it, allowing the treatment to continue for a few more precious seconds. He wasted no time in retrieving a set of autoinjectors from one of the cupboards, two of caura and two of a local anesthetic. He lifted his shirt and applied one of each directly to his chest, then grabbed his jacket from where it still lay on the counter and slipped the others into the breast pocket. Next on the agenda was a fresh underlay; he equipped one from the armory, once again grateful for the garment's compressed fit, feeling as though it might hold him together when nothing else would.

He strapped on the drop leg holster he'd removed earlier and looked over the available munitions, bypassing the projectile weapons and selecting a new plasma pistol with more stopping power than the one he'd been shot with. If he was going to be infiltrating a restricted area, it would be best to stay quiet and not leave a blood trail in the inevitable event that he had to kill someone. He grabbed a pair of spare plasma cells and slid them into the cargo pocket on his other leg. A pair of blades completed the minimal ensemble, one on his belt and one in his boot.

The next step was the infiltration itself. He manipulated the projection controls on the armory table and brought up the map of Manes's compound Zinni had recovered from Mati...*Ziva's* comm console. None of the structures were explicitly labeled, but each had a numerical designation. He could only assume the large building in the center tagged with a number 'one' was Manes's private residence and no doubt the location of the dining room where Skeet and Zinni were being taken, assuming the invitation had been sincere. Every other structure within the compound's walls was connected to this one in some manner, whether directly or by what appeared to be narrow passages or bridges. He rotated the map and lifted it, examining the three-dimensional rendering of a series of underground tunnels. Like everything else, those tunnels connected to the main building but wound in a maze-like fashion beneath the compound, finally terminating at a symmetrical row of rooms near the outer wall. It wasn't a stretch to assume that space was a holding block or prison of some sort based on its layout. It looked like there was even an exit nearby...or for him, an entrance. Not only was it the simplest and most logical place to begin his infiltration, but he had a hunch he might find Skeet and Zinni there if they survived their dinner invite.

Not wishing to waste any more time, he transferred a copy of the map to a small viewscreen and slid it into his pocket as he headed out the door. The car the team had been using for the majority of the day sat in the cargo bay where they'd stashed it before parting ways; it had been a handy resource so far, and now it would be one last time. Perhaps twice if he—and, preferably, the rest of the team—was lucky enough to escape Ibarra's clutches.

Minutes later, the car sat at the entrance to the rocky alcove where the *Saber* was concealed. Aroska paused a moment at the pilot's door and watched the cargo ramp retract, satisfied by the faint echo of the additional security measures humming to life. Squinting against the harsh evening sun, he slid into the car and set out toward Tabaco, praying this wouldn't turn out to be the dumbest decision he'd ever made.

Chapter 31
Ibarra Compound · Tabaco, Panuco

The interior of the Ibarra compound was immaculate, or at least what little of it Skeet had seen so far—he and Zinni had both had hoods thrown over their faces immediately after getting into the Cartel vehicles, and they'd just been removed moments ago. It wasn't as though the compound's location was any big secret, so he imagined the hoods were just a scare tactic. A control tactic. He was determined it wouldn't work.

He and Zinni walked down a long, wide hallway composed of polished white stone, no doubt mined from one of the local oceanside cliffs of the same color. The big blonde Haphezian woman led the way; she had no *gesh punti* but the pale green in her eyes and hair was the same, eliminating the possibility that she was a Defective. Unless it was Skeet's imagination, she exuded a measure of hatred toward the two of them that surpassed what a simple prisoner escort should feel. She struck him as a wildcard, someone Manes could rely on to complete the most abhorrent of tasks and someone he and Zinni would need to pay special attention to in the coming minutes or hours.

They walked unrestrained but obediently kept their hands slightly raised as the woman had instructed upon their arrival. Neither of them were armed, but offensive action didn't necessarily require physical weapons. The problem at the moment was that they were surrounded by no less than half of the Ibarra soldiers who had intercepted them in the tunnel. If either of them tried to make a move, they'd both be dead before they knew what hit them.

The procession broke out of the long corridor and into an area that looked more like a home. A large staircase made of the same white stone curved upward to their left. Ahead, a set of heavy, meticulously carved wooden doors stood open, and a faint voice could be heard within the room. As they neared, the soldiers escorting them dispersed, with some taking up posts outside and some filing in ahead of them. The blonde woman strode in without hesitation, beckoning for them to follow.

Both Skeet and Zinni came to a stop just inside the door and took in the scene. An immense, round dining table sat before them, with an impressive buffet of food laid out across it. The next thing Skeet noticed was the man—no doubt Alastair Manes—seated across the table from where they stood. He couldn't have been more than a few years older than either of them, and he lacked the grizzled features Skeet had pictured. In a way, the fact that the man appeared well-groomed and suave made him more wary than he otherwise might have been.

About ninety degrees to Manes's right, Ziva sat with her palms flat on the table, an untouched plate of food before her, watching them enter out of the corner of her eye. She kept her head slightly bowed as though in submission, and she bore a bruise and small cut on her cheek that hadn't been there before. Her behavior was admittedly curious, and Skeet couldn't help but feel a twinge of concern, but it wasn't enough to trump the hot rage welling up in his chest as Aroska's narrative about the shooting replayed in his mind.

"Ah!" Manes exclaimed. He finished chewing a bite of food and wiped his mouth, then stood and indicated two empty place settings to his left, directly across the table from Ziva. "Wonderful of you both to join us. It's a shame all three of you couldn't make it."

Skeet had yet to remove his eyes from Ziva, and when he spoke, his words were directed at her rather than Manes. "That's what happens when you kill someone."

She looked up and met his gaze, lips parted as though she wanted to respond but didn't dare. Not that any excuse she mustered up could fix what she'd done. Still, she seemed shocked by what he'd just said. Maybe 'fearful' would be the more accurate description. Good. She had every reason to be.

Manes glanced from Ziva to Skeet as though amused by the clear hostility between them. "Well, we're here to share a nice meal, my friends, so I'm going to have to ask you to set your differences aside and make yourselves comfortable." His attention shifted back to Ziva. "We have a lot to talk about."

Neither Skeet nor Zinni made any move to comply, though Skeet took a step farther into the room, gaze still fixed on Ziva. He was angry—he couldn't deny it—and while part of him felt guilty about that anger being directed toward this woman who had once been his close friend, he had to remind himself she was the reason he was here. Whether she had control of her faculties or not, she had sold them out, had tried to kill Tarbic. If she'd been brainwashed by Manes and the Cartel, his anger stemmed more from the fact that he had no idea what to do about that. That *had* to be the explanation, mostly because he didn't believe she would ever do any of this willingly. But if she was acting of her own accord—he had a hard time even fathoming such a thing—then, quite frankly, he wondered how much effort they should even put into getting her out.

Regardless of her state of mind, one person was fully responsible for it. Skeet shifted his full attention to Manes, who had seated himself and was once more digging into his meal as if this truly were a dinner party. This man had taken his friend from him, had turned her into a completely different person. He may not have been the target of this mission, but Skeet suddenly wanted nothing more than to make him pay for what he'd done. He took another step forward.

He also couldn't help but notice the way Ziva reacted to the movement. He stole a glance her way, then returned his full focus to her when he realized she had slid forward to the edge of her seat. She kept her arms braced against the table, ready to rise at a moment's notice. Her eyes took in every centimeter of him, anticipating, calculating, preparing. All signs of her subdued, submissive behavior had vanished in an instant, the same way her behavior had shifted so drastically aboard the ship.

"Don't try it," she warned, voice low.

Skeet noted that she didn't appear to be carrying a weapon, which struck him as odd. But he'd never known anyone whose very body was a more perfect weapon, and he was unnerved by the realization that he didn't fully trust her not to hurt him if it came down to it. He was sure he could defend himself, but it wouldn't be pleasant.

"What are you going to do?" he demanded, unable to stop a slight tremor in his chin. "You going to *defend* him?"

"Lieutenant," Zinni said quietly from where she still stood just inside the doorway.

He spared a brief look in her direction. Chain-of-command formalities tended to be forgotten in an ops team environment, so he couldn't even remember the last time she had addressed him by his title. She was no doubt attempting to safeguard his identity by not calling him by name, and he realized he'd subconsciously been doing the same with Ziva. He released a quiet sigh and returned his attention to his own former lieutenant, wondering if there was any point in trying to protect her like that.

"I'd truly like to know," he said, putting conscious effort into keeping his tone even but fearful he was failing. Manes had clearly asked them here to toy with them—otherwise why not just throw them in prison or kill them outright?—and showing emotion or any other negative reaction would mean playing right into his game. Perhaps this was the whole point of the 'dinner invitation.' Humiliate them. Humiliate Ziva. Manipulate them. Manipulate Ziva.

He began taking short, slow strides toward the Ibarra leader, who at this point had set his utensils down and sat watching the situation unfold with an amused twinkle in his eye. Ziva stood abruptly, sending her chair skidding backward and drawing everyone's attention back to her.

"Stand down," she said, muscles tense and ready to be put to use. "I mean it."

"What the hell is the matter with you?" Skeet asked, the words leaving his mouth with less force than he'd intended. He glanced ahead; he had reached the empty place setting where he was supposed to sit, leaving the two of them equidistant from Manes in opposite directions around the table. He might reach the man first if he took a couple of running steps, but doing so would just get him shot. "They've brainwashed you. You don't realize what you're doing."

"You're wrong," she replied, matching his pace as she too began to move around the table toward Manes. "I know exactly what I'm doing."

The words were said with more conviction than he'd expected, and her eyes remained fixed solidly on him. She was present here in this room, not 'somewhere else' as Aroska had described it earlier aboard the ship. She meant what she was saying, and the thought wrenched his stomach into a knot.

As Skeet came within a meter of Manes, she advanced suddenly, positioning herself between him and the cartel leader. Her movements almost seemed to be in slow motion as Skeet's vision zeroed in on her and his mind entered a defensive mode that had become pure reflex after years of training. She reached to grab him, and his own arms moved to counter automatically. Somehow she seemed shocked by this and took a slight step back, though her weight remained forward and she held her arms loose, hands poised to form fists in an instant.

"You should have listened to me before," she muttered. "Don't make me do this."

His mind interpreted her words as a challenge of sorts. Driven by a renewed sense of anger and perhaps some morbid curiosity about just how far she'd go, he found himself taking a swing at her before he could stop himself.

"No!" he heard Zinni shout behind him. "Please!"

Ziva blocked his shot with ease, though he hadn't put too much effort into landing a direct hit. She caught his arm in the crook of her elbow, pinning it against her shoulder as she pivoted around behind him and drove her opposite elbow into his spine. With his arm now locked behind him, she slammed her heel into the back of his knee. Hundreds of counter attacks spun through his mind, but he allowed himself to sag to the floor, unwilling to play this game. Not here, anyway. Not now.

She kept his right arm locked above him and pinned his left to the floor with one knee, digging her other into the small of his back. Her shadow crossed over him, and he felt her warm breath against his ear. "Please don't fight this," she hissed.

Tears welled up in his eyes, the last thing he'd wanted—or expected—to happen here in front of Manes. It was without doubt exactly what the man wanted to see. But after being so angry with Ziva due to her evasiveness and actions against Aroska, being on the receiving end of similar actions was the final straw. He'd tried to give her another chance, had risked testing how far she'd go, and now he had his answer. It wasn't the one he wanted, but it was definitive enough. He wouldn't make the same mistake again.

With his cheek pressed against the cold, stone floor, he had a sideways view of Zinni, who appeared to have made it a couple of strides toward him before being forced to her knees and held at gunpoint by four different Ibarra soldiers. She kept her hands raised above her head and watched him with a combination of disgust and fear as several more soldiers moved in to surround him.

Somewhere behind him, Manes clicked his tongue and stood up. "As exciting as this is, this is no way to behave as a guest in someone's home." Then, to his men, he added, "Get them out of here."

Skeet's vision righted itself as Ziva slid off him and the thugs hauled him to his feet. They did the same with Zinni, and after a moment they were on their way back out the door, thoroughly restrained this time around.

"*All* of them," he heard Manes say just as they passed through the doorway.

A woman's voice—either Ziva's or the blonde woman's—exclaimed something in response, but the massive doors slammed shut and cut the sound off. The anger that had abated in favor of momentary sympathy for Ziva came flooding back, and it was all Skeet could do to keep from unleashing it against the soldiers surrounding them. But he allowed them to lead him without fuss and nodded for Zinni to do the same. Right now, he needed his full focus on whatever came next...and how they were going to survive it, with or without Ziva.

Chapter 32
Ibarra Compound · Tabaco, Panuco

The door slammed shut behind her. Though it looked ordinary, the sound of three separate locking mechanisms engaging reminded her that this door—this room—was anything but ordinary. She wasn't sure why Manes had chosen to put her in here rather than an average cell in the detention block. The most obvious reason was to keep her separated from Skeet and Zinni, though knowing him, it was to give her a false sense of security. Force her to cling to the hope he still trusted her, or force her to continue trusting him.

At the moment, standing completely rigid seemed like the only way to keep herself from all-out trembling. She hadn't expected her last-ditch attempt to regain Manes's trust to result in her own imprisonment, but then again, she wasn't sure *what* she'd expected. All she knew was that her actions had probably ensured Skeet and Zinni would never trust her again. If only Skeet had just *listened*. Subduing him had ended up being for his own good—Manes's people wouldn't have hesitated to put him down if he'd managed to get his hands on their leader. But she'd still hated every second of it. Perhaps what hurt the most was that he hadn't resisted at all, forcing her to play the role of the villain once again.

And then there was the matter of Manes discovering her Nosti abilities. Or at least he thought he had. He hadn't proved anything one way or the other with his little deflection test. Once upon a time, it might have worked; she recalled trying the same test with the Nosti agent HSP had captured in Haphor just before the battle with Ronan's fleet. But she hadn't even tried to use her Nostia since shortly after leaving Haphez, and the truth was she often forgot she even had the ability. Matia Moryi didn't have it, and she'd been Matia Moryi for a long time, therefore content to block it out of her mind. When Manes had thrown the comm, it hadn't even occurred to her to try to deflect it. She wasn't even sure how well she'd be able to use the ability these days; intense focus and meditation had always been the key to conjuring her Nostia when it had been a while since her last nostium infusion, and there certainly hadn't been time for that in the moment.

But all of these things were behind her now, and there was no point in dwelling on them any longer. She turned and surveyed the room for anything that could be used as a tool or weapon and wasn't particularly surprised when she found nothing. While comfortable, these holding rooms were sparsely decorated, the furniture heavy and cumbersome. They may have been designed to house Manes's more esteemed guests and clients, but they were also designed to transform into prisons at a moment's notice. Hence the three-point locking mechanism hidden inside what otherwise looked like an average door.

Taking a deep breath, she shut her eyes and brought her hands to rest on her hips, mentally running through her options. One thing was for sure: she didn't have time for this. It had been five days since she'd received and responded to the blip on her comm console...the blip from Tobias signaling that the Niiosian fleet was on its way. If everything had remained on schedule—and there was no reason it shouldn't have—he would be there knocking down Manes's door in what could very well be a matter of minutes. He and the same fleet that had played a pivotal role in the battle against the Resistance four years earlier. The problem was that *she* had fallen behind schedule thanks to the team's arrival, and this latest development had set her back even further.

She froze when the floor outside the door creaked long and slow, as if someone were approaching either hesitantly or stealthily. Perhaps both, if it was who she thought it was. Unlike Haphezians, most humans smelled too similar to differentiate by scent, but the smell of oil and the tinny sound of muted comm chatter were unmistakable.

She moved to the door and listened closer. No one moved outside, but the sound of the comms remained constant. "Blain," she said.

The floor creaked again as he shifted and drew nearer. Then the comm chatter ceased. "What's happening?"

"Open this door and I'll explain."

"Who are you?"

"That doesn't matter." She hesitated a moment. "I'm the same person you've known for the past two years." It wasn't a complete lie; despite the act and the disguise, out of everyone she'd met on Panuco, she'd been most genuine around him.

"I don't know the door code."

"Come on, Blain. Since when has that ever stopped you?"

He sighed, and Ziva heard a series of beeps as he remotely sliced into the door's security system. One by one, the heavy bolts inside slid away, and after a few seconds, the door hissed open.

The moment the opening was big enough to do so, she reached out, seized him by the collar, and dragged him inside before he could get a word in edgewise. He tapped at something on his viewscreen as he stumbled away from her, shutting the door behind him but leaving it unlocked. Whether it was for him to make a quick escape or for her, she wasn't sure.

The room fell silent as he sank back against the wall, hesitant to make eye contact. He appeared skeptical enough that for a moment she wondered if she'd be able to get him to listen to her, but the fact that he was even present here was a testament to something. If not open-mindedness, at least curiosity, something she hoped she could grab and run with. At this point, everything hinged on his cooperation.

"What are you doing here?" she asked quietly, moving in close to loom over him. She had no doubt there were cams hidden in the room; the feeds weren't usually monitored around the clock, but considering the circumstances, shielding him from prying eyes still seemed favorable.

"I had to know what was going on," he answered, his gaze flicking up to meet hers for a fraction of a second. "And...it's probably my fault you're in here."

Heat flooded her cheeks, but now was not the time to be angry with him for selling her out. She whirled away, lips pressed into a thin line to conceal gritted teeth.

"I told Manes what I heard on comms at the docks this morning," Blain continued. "I wanted to give you the benefit of the doubt—that's why I came to you first. But then those people showed up at your apartment...." His voice trailed off.

She'd assumed all of this before, and the fact that he'd been with Kimbra when the woman picked her up all but confirmed it. Still, there was something conclusive about actually hearing the words out of his mouth. She turned back to face him. "So, what, you here to apologize?"

"I'm here because you're the only person on this planet who gives a damn about me. When I went to Manes, I thought he'd be appreciative of the information I was bringing him, but...." He paused as though reflecting on how to admit an unpleasant truth for the first time. "As soon as he got what he needed, he sent me off with Comrade Soto to use me all over again, and...I just wanted to prove myself. So I went, even though I knew they were going to punish you. And then instead of punishing you, he tried to manipulate you into killing those people." He looked her in the eye. "They're your friends, aren't they. I saw you with that man, the one you ended up shooting. He means something to you."

At this point Ziva was still hesitant to confirm or deny. "Cut to the chase, kid."

"I'm saying that regardless of who you are, why you're here, or what you've done, you were right. I'm just a puppet. Everyone here is, regardless of what Manes tells them. After you came and asked me to patch you into those comms this morning, I tuned in to the strike team's conversation too. That man you took down at the docks? He was no snitch. He was there on Manes's orders, luring those agents into a trap meant to test you. Manes made him believe he was doing something for the good of the Cartel, but he was expendable, and it was all meant to manipulate you. I saw all of that play out, and now there's all of this, and...." By now he was trembling, once again reluctant to meet her gaze. "I don't know what to do, Matia. If that's even your real name."

She saw her opening and brought her face to within centimeters of his, ensuring she had his undivided attention. "You can help me get out of here and then let me get you off this rock."

He blinked as if the thought sounded preposterous, even after everything he'd just finished telling her. "I can't do that!" he hissed.

"Why not? You think you have any choice if they find out you were in here?"

He squared his shoulders. "Hey, I haven't actually done anything to help you. It's no secret we spend a lot of time together, so it's perfectly reasonable for me to come see you. Manes has nothing on me."

His tone was defiant, but the glimmer of fear was obvious in his eyes. "You keep telling yourself that, Blain," Ziva muttered. She turned and took several steps away, hands resting on her hips as she considered how to move forward.

Footsteps approached behind her and his hand settled on her shoulder. "Where I am I supposed to go?" he demanded, spinning her around to face him. His chin quivered and the early signs of tears glistened in his eyes.

Then she understood. Despite the newfound realization of his circumstances, this place—the Cartel structure, this way of life—was all he'd ever known. She doubted he'd ever even been off Panuco, so he had no idea how to function outside this environment and the niche he'd built within it, however toxic it might be. She'd caught herself a number of times over the past couple of years feeling grateful for something Manes or the Cartel had done for her, but she'd at least had the outside perspective necessary to remind herself none of it was real. Blain was the exact opposite, someone who had spent so long trying his very hardest to fit in that he hadn't believed the truth even when it was staring him in the face. Frankly she was surprised he was willing to admit it now.

Her first instinct was to promise him similar work once they reached their destination, without referencing Niio outright just yet. But while Tobias was a great deal more—dare she say it—*benevolent* than Alastair Manes, the thought occurred to her that inserting someone like Blain into Niiosian ranks would just put him right back where he'd started. On top of that, he'd be lacking the connections, however superficial, that he'd developed over the years on Panuco.

"You can go anywhere you want," she answered, hoping to reinforce the sense of independence she knew he craved. It was a better response than telling him she didn't know and they'd figure it out later, though both points were accurate.

He looked up at her with a desperation she hadn't seen in all the time she'd known him. She knew he respected her, but this was something more. It was an inquiry, a search for reassurance, a decision being made regarding trust. In this moment, he was just a scared kid, not the savvy, cynical young man she'd befriended.

She caught herself. Yes, in light of this current situation, she could admit he was her friend.

"What do you need me to do?" he finally said, his voice nearly a whisper.

As much as she wanted to melt with relief that he was willing to cooperate, there was no time for that. "Okay, listen," she said, lowering her voice in case the cams in the room accounted for sound. She placed her palms against the sides of his face, forcing him to look her in the eye. "There are some people coming who are planning to lay waste to this place, but they're also our ticket out of here. We need to be ready to leave the moment they arrive, and we're already behind schedule. There's a transponder code we can broadcast from the *Talon* to identify ourselves as friendly, but I'm going to need two copies: one for you and me, and one for my friends."

He was still trembling, unfocused. "Where do I get a code like—"

She rattled off the alphanumeric string she'd memorized and mentally repeated to herself every morning since leaving Niio. For a moment Blain seemed so stunned she was afraid she'd lose any ground she had gained, but eventually he managed a slow nod.

"Repeat that back to me," she demanded, shaking him.

He did, quelling her fears that he'd panic upon realizing just how long this plan had been set in motion. She was overthinking it; for all he knew she could have memorized the code that morning, and while he'd find out soon enough, he still had no idea who it was for.

Ziva stole a glance toward the door, listening for a moment to make sure nobody else had come around. "Second thing: I need you to hack into dock security. With all of this going on, there's a good chance Manes had Port Control lock down my docking bay. I need you to get in and check. If it's locked, open it. If it's unlocked, make sure it stays that way long enough for us to get out of here. Can you do that?"

"Yes, yes, I—I think so."

She tilted her head.

"Yes!" he said again, more conviction in his voice this time. "I can do it."

"Is the console at my apartment adequate?"

"Combined with some of my mobile equipment, yeah, it should be."

"Good. I want you to head straight there and get to work. I'll rendezvous with you there after I get my people out of here. Do you know where exactly they're being held?"

Blain adjusted the volume on his earpiece and listened for a moment. "Eastern cell block."

She nodded; the area was familiar enough, and she mentally mapped out the quickest route there. It shouldn't take her long to reach them.

"How's security?" she asked, eyes once again flicking toward the door.

"Considering how pissed Manes seems with you? Not that tight. He's got a few sentries on patrol but seems to be relying on surveillance for the rest. I think he's still trying to make up his mind what to do with you."

The corners of her lips twitched upward. "Best make myself scarce before he decides then, right? You go first, and I'll be right behind you."

Blain took a single step toward the door before hesitating, that same unsure look in his eyes once again. "I still don't even know what's going on here."

"How about I tell you the whole story once we're underway?"

He didn't look completely satisfied with that response, but he nodded nonetheless. "Here," he said, pulling out his knife, the very one she'd given him. He handed it to her. "You probably need this more than I do."

With that, he continued toward the door. Ziva held her breath as he hit the controls to open it, ready to see him get struck down by an Ibarra thug who happened to be passing by, or worse, one who had been lying in wait outside. She let out a quiet sigh of relief when neither of these things happened and watched as he cautiously peered in either direction down the corridor before throwing her one last glance over his shoulder and disappearing through the opening.

The door hissed shut once more, but the echoing *clank, clank, clank* of the locking mechanisms sliding home never came.

CHAPTER 33
IBARRA COMPOUND - TABACO, PANUCO

The series of underground hallways leading down to the cell blocks were a far cry from the polished, lavish areas of the compound she'd just left. They were hardly more than wide tunnels, with stone floors and earthen walls lit by garish yellow lighting panels. The prison was a bit of a trek from Manes's estate, still quite secure but out-of-sight, out-of-mind. It sometimes surprised her that the man had even been willing to set foot in this area when she'd been held captive here, lest he get his clothes dirty.

No, she took that back. She'd seen him beat people half to death and come away bloody without batting an eye.

If they hadn't discovered her absence from the holding room, they likely would at any moment. She'd made a point of moving as fast as possible, and with any luck, Manes's attention was sufficiently divided between her and the rest of the team, buying her a little extra time to maneuver. And hopefully Blain had made it safely away too. She couldn't imagine anyone would have hassled him on his way out—most of the high-ranking Ibarra crowd who frequented the compound were probably glad to see low-level street scum like him go—but her mind tended to jump to the worst-case scenario. That way she was rarely surprised.

She held the knife he'd given her loose but ready, the blade pressed flat against the inside of her forearm so it wasn't immediately visible to anyone who happened to stumble upon her. If she paused and really considered what she was doing, she was always stricken by a pang of guilt, so she tried not to think much about it. She legitimately wanted to get Blain away from this place; he didn't deserve this life, even if he thought he was doing fine. But that had always been a secondary objective. She'd known from the start that she'd eventually need to generate the transponder code that would enable her to rendezvous with the Niiosians without getting blown out of the sky, but waltzing into a docking station and demanding it without a sufficient explanation was never going to fly. So when she'd happened upon the gangly, naive young hacker a few weeks into her stint with the Cartel, she'd seen her opportunity. And with his expertise combined with her own observations while coming and going from Panuco, she'd gained a significant amount of intel about the planet's orbital defenses that she'd gradually transmitted to the Niiosians throughout her stay. While this little alliance they'd formed had of course strengthened and become more legitimate over time, taking him under her wing had initially just been a means of making sure he stayed alive until she needed him.

The thought occurred to her that, from an outside perspective, this all made her no better than Manes. The difference was that she was treating Blain like a pawn for his own good. By helping her, he was helping himself. She'd always guessed she'd be able to coax him into working with her regardless of how he viewed the Cartel, just because he'd gotten so close to her. The fact that he was now starting to doubt Ibarra's ways was certainly a plus.

Running footsteps echoed in the corridor somewhere ahead of her, prompting her to stop and listen. This was the only direction anyone else down here could come, and she wondered if someone was being sent to investigate the holding room. She took several quick, silent strides forward, pressing her back against the wall just inside a bend in the hall and flipping the knife over in her hand.

When the man rounded the corner at high speed, he crashed headlong into her outstretched arm, ramming his throat into her fist with almost as much force as she rammed her fist into his throat. The impact nearly took him off his feet and he stumbled backward, doubling over as he clutched at his crushed windpipe. She rotated her hips, driving her elbow into the center of his back with maximum force. He landed flat on the floor, where she plunged the knife into the base of his spine.

Yanking the blade free, she gathered up his communicator and pistol, chucking the former in the direction from which she'd come and sliding the latter into her empty holster before continuing on her way. Moving the body might help cover her tracks, but it would waste precious time; keeping up the pace and maintaining her head start might be just as beneficial. Besides, moving the body would do no good if there was a puddle of blood left behind on the floor.

She rounded another corner, positive the next bend in the corridor would dump her out at the intersection that led either outside or into the cell block. But another Ibarra thug stood between her and her destination, walking briskly away from her as if he'd been following his associate but had turned back for some reason. Her fingers brushed against her holstered pistol's grip. Projectile. Too loud. The knife would have to suffice.

Ziva didn't break stride, merely softening her footsteps as she closed in on him. He straightened and began to whirl around as she came within a meter of him, but she clamped one hand down over his mouth, pulling him back toward her as she simultaneously drove the knife upward into his neck, forcing the blade between the vertebrae and severing his brain stem. He went slack immediately, and she eased the knife back out.

She lowered the man gingerly to the ground in an attempt to remain as silent as possible as another set of approaching footsteps reached her ears, likely from the corridor that led outside. Chances were slim that she'd make it down to the cell block entrance without being seen.

The dead man still gripped a pistol in one hand. She relieved him of it and took his stun baton as well, listening as the footsteps drew within meters. She checked the pistol and managed to stand up and raise it just as a figure appeared from around the corner.

She'd expected to see someone pointing a gun at her; that much didn't surprise her. What she hadn't expected were the black jacket, pained expression, and wide amber eyes belonging to that person.

"Now where have I seen this before? This picture is getting a little old, don't you think?" Already surprised by the length of time she'd had him at gunpoint, she dropped the stun baton and raised her hand in surrender, then crouched and set the pilfered gun down as well, taking care to steer clear of the holstered one.

An odd tingle crept across her skin when Aroska didn't lower his weapon in response. The look in his eyes told her he didn't like the situation either, but after everything he'd just been through, she understood why he couldn't bring himself to put it down. She imagined she'd be doing the same thing if she were in his place. At least his finger hadn't moved to the trigger yet.

Keeping her hands raised and open, she took a step closer to him. "Look at me right now, Aroska. I'm not here to fight. Put the gun down."

Her stomach turned over when he still made no move to comply. His knuckles were white and perspiration gathered on his brow, giving her the impression that he was just as uncomfortable holding her at gunpoint as she was being held at gunpoint. She'd never expected him to display such resolve, at least not when she was on the receiving end.

Aroska's gaze flitted from her face to her empty hands to the pistol on the floor, then he warily reestablished eye contact. "You shot me," he said. "Left me for dead."

"Oh please," she scoffed. "You think I would have shot you if you weren't wearing an underlay?"

He gave her a blank look. "How'd you know?"

"I felt it."

She studied his face as it dawned on him. She'd felt it when he'd hugged her in the alley, and she'd double-checked just before pulling the gun on him in the street by the beach. Still, it had been a calculated risk—even with the underlay, shots at such close range could have caused irreparable damage. Maintaining a facade of indifference during Manes's interrogation had been incredibly difficult, and truth be told, she'd feared she'd made a mistake when Skeet had mentioned Aroska's death in the dining room. So despite the less than amicable nature of the current conversation, she was very glad to see him alive and well, relatively speaking.

He shifted uncomfortably. "And if I hadn't been wearing one? What would you have done?"

"I guess we'll never know."

"And what, you just hoped I wasn't carrying a projectile pistol?"

Now wasn't the time to admit she hadn't been one hundred percent sure. Four solid bullets at that range would have penetrated the vest. "I got a pretty good feel for it when I ripped it out of your hands in the alley," she replied, giving him a dismissive wave of her hand.

His eyes followed the movement of her arm, just as she'd hoped. She went for the gun the moment he diverted his gaze. He reacted more quickly than she'd expected, though if she was honest with herself, she hadn't expected him to react at all. He'd either been waiting for her to make a move—in which case she had to applaud his tenacity—or he'd simply been unwilling to let her disarm him again. His grip didn't falter even when she seized the weapon and pulled. She doubted he would ever actually shoot her, but she directed a good portion of her focus toward twisting the barrel down and away from her. A plasma bolt discharged just as she got it clear, burning through the space between them and burrowing into the floor just centimeters from her foot. Her eyes went wide and she looked up to find him equally shocked by what he'd just done. What he'd been *willing* to do.

An all-too-familiar animal instinct kicked in as her mind went into self-preservation mode. She let go of the gun with one hand and took hold of his shoulder, pulling him toward her and driving her knee up into his stomach. But in turn that brought him close enough to slam his forehead into her face; a *crunch* echoed inside her head as the cartilage in her nose cracked and a steady trickle of blood began streaming from one nostril.

Afraid of what he might do next, she tightened her grip on his arm and threw her entire body weight at him, forcing him to take a staggering step back. She ducked down and released his arm long enough to jab a well-placed fist into his already-fragile ribs. Using his grip on her against him, she took another quick step around him and let herself fall backward. He pivoted, off balance, and had no choice but to let her weight pull him down as well. Tucking her knees in, she braced her legs against his chest and rolled him over the top of her as she somersaulted. He landed hard on his back with a grunt of pain. She came to a stop on top of him, pinning him there with one knee as she wrenched the gun from his grasp.

Ziva flipped the weapon over, keeping her finger off the trigger but the barrel pointed directly at him nonetheless. He'd gone down more easily than she'd expected, no doubt still sore after his previous injuries and the hit she'd just landed. But the look on his face as he met her gaze was one purely of resignation.

Just like that, their roles had been reversed. She swallowed and studied her own arm as she rose to her feet. Her hand gripping the pistol. The barrel held steady. Aroska's face beyond that. Just like what she'd seen through tear-filled eyes earlier in the street. She didn't want to be holding him at gunpoint either, but she needed him to listen. If he had to think she was willing to shoot him for a moment, then so be it.

She wiped the back of her free hand across her nose and turned to spit out the blood that had found its way into her mouth. "Now pay attention," she snapped, listening for a moment to make sure their scuffle hadn't alerted anyone to their presence. "I told you to trust me, and you didn't."

Aroska stared up at her, breathing hard, one hand raised in surrender and the other clutching his midsection. His features were twisted slightly, as if he were trying and failing to ignore the pain that came and went with every breath. He smelled of caura treatment, but even a full round from an HSP ship's medbay wouldn't have been enough to heal cracked ribs, not in mere hours, anyway. All the pain he was feeling—both physically and emotionally—was her fault.

"You were going against everything you've ever known and believed in," he said, wincing a bit. "What were we supposed to think?"

"I had no choice!" she retorted, louder than she'd meant to. "They were watching, and I had to make them think I was following orders. But I was keeping you *alive*! You, Skeet, Zinni, *me*. I was keeping us all alive. You think I wanted to do that? You think I've wanted to do any of the things I've had to do here?"

"You didn't seem to have any problem with it."

"*Sheyss*, Aroska. I've been undercover for over two years, familiarizing myself with these people for even longer. I've been *this* close to the end, to finishing all of this. Then you all showed up and threatened to negate all the work I'd done. I couldn't let you do that, and I didn't want you to get hurt, so I had to keep you away. But you wouldn't listen. You wouldn't leave." She paused a moment, realizing how familiar the argument sounded.

The look on Aroska's face told her he was thinking the same thing. "How could I after you saved my life?" he murmured, more to himself than anything else.

His words gave her chills, and for the briefest of moments, the two of them were standing on the hill outside Salex where he'd uttered those same words, the landscape illuminated by the aeromids' bioluminescent bodies. The memory was interrupted by one from early that morning, though it felt like days ago; she could see Aroska through her scope, crouching behind a parked car while she'd put down the Cartel soldier who was about to take him out.

"I didn't want to get involved," she said, lowering the gun. "Manes ordered me to kill that informant just to see how you all would react, but when it became apparent that he had plans to either capture or kill you, I couldn't just stand by and let it happen."

"Manes used him—and us—to manipulate you."

The simple statement told her he was beginning to understand, but hearing the words from his mouth in addition to Blain's also sent a pang of shame rolling through her stomach. The extent to which she'd allowed herself to be used in order to get the job done was humiliating. "Manes was testing me, seeing if I would still follow his orders despite your arrival," she said. "I had to prove myself to him but also do whatever I could to protect you all, even if that meant withholding information. Every decision I made today was a conscious one. I appreciate you trying to redeem me and thinking you could save me, but I didn't need it. I knew what I was doing."

She took a moment to pause and listen for anyone approaching. They still seemed to be in the clear, but the longer they stayed there, the higher the chances were that someone with unfriendly intentions would stumble upon them.

"I told you to trust me," she said again with a sigh, wiping away a bit more blood as it trickled down over her lip. "I could see the bigger picture—you couldn't."

She tucked his gun into her waistband and extended her hand. Aroska watched it warily for a moment as he continued processing everything she'd just told him.

"I have a sneaking suspicion you and I are down here for the same reason," Ziva said. "The cell block is just down this corridor. I would know—I spent six weeks in it while Manes was vetting me."

Aroska finally reached up to take her hand, bracing his other arm against his ribcage as she helped him rise to his feet. There was a certain genuineness about the feeling of his hand in hers that allowed her to relax even as she strained to lift him. It was warm, calloused from years of handling weapons, just like her own. When she let go, he didn't, at least not right away. But then he took a slight step back and averted his eyes. No, he still wasn't convinced of her intentions.

Her gaze flitted from his face down to his hand then back up to his face before settling on his mouth and the way the corners of his lips turned down. For a moment, she considered kissing him just to show she was being sincere, but decided against it for fear that was all it would be. A show. He'd done the same thing to her on Chaiavis, and it had only made things worse. After all they'd been through, and after saying goodbye in that HSP holding room, a gesture like that needed to...mean more. Above all, it needed to wait until they'd made it out of here alive, until they'd had time to talk.

She reached for his gun, slowing her movements when she saw him glance at her and tense up again. "Here's the deal," she said, sliding it from her waistband and offering it to him stock-first. "I seem to recall telling you that you never know if you can really trust someone, but that's the whole point of trust." She pressed the grip into his hand when he tentatively reached for it. "This is me trusting you not to shoot me in the back."

He set his jaw and met her gaze as he took the weapon and held it in a relaxed grip at his side. "Just answer one question, and I promise I'll believe whatever you tell me," he said. "Are you really still working for Tobias?"

His tone seemed strangely merciful considering their confrontation and some of the comments he'd made just moments before. He asked the question as if, despite everything she'd done, working with the Niiosian Mob would somehow have made it all forgivable.

Ziva drew a deep breath. "Yes," she answered. "Everything I've done here has been with the intention of gaining Manes's trust so I can destroy this cartel from the inside. My job was to create fractures in the infrastructure, weaken its integrity. And when the Niiosians arrive, this place will crumble."

"You've killed innocent people!"

"Nobody out here is innocent!" She paused a moment and reminded herself not to shout. It was true; even Panuco's most docile civilians had either done work to further Manes's operation or would pledge their absolute loyalty to him if asked, just as all the Niiosians did with Tobias.

"I've had to kill Niiosian allies, yes," she said, fighting to keep her tone even, "but I've also managed to eliminate key personnel and resources within Manes's network. I let Pahl Starcer live because I needed someone on Delatori who's still loyal to Niio and never expected him to try to take matters into his own hands and go to HSP. I have been *trying*—" her voice wavered "—to do whatever I can to convince Manes I'm on his side while simultaneously protecting Niiosian interests and keeping myself *alive*."

Aroska still appeared hesitant, but based on the subtle relaxation in his shoulders, he believed her. She doubted he'd ever understand *why* she'd done any of it, specifically why she'd gone to Tobias in the first place considering the man was no model citizen himself, but regaining his trust was all she needed right now.

"Listen," she continued, "I know that's not much of an explanation, but this is not the time for discussion. Tobias is on his way here, and he could arrive at any moment."

"That's what you meant when you said something big was about to happen."

"Yes. I wanted to tell you earlier, but at the rate things were going today, I was afraid one or all of you would be captured, and I couldn't risk anyone else finding out."

Aroska scoffed. "You had that little faith in us?"

"Look at where we're standing right now, why we're down here."

He considered this a moment, then offered a nod of concession.

She took a cautious glance up and down the corridor. "We need to get to Skeet and Zinni before the Niiosian fleet shows up and levels this place on top of us. I'd appreciate it if you helped me get them out of here, but if you're not going to do that, I suggest you get out of my way."

He hesitated for only a split second before heaving a sigh and giving her a single nod. She dipped her head in return and drew her pistol, holding it at the ready as the two of them took off at a steady jog. The feeling of having a formidable ally at her side—even if relations were a little shaky—left her with a warm feeling inside her chest. Even on her own, she was confident, but this was something more, a different *type* of confidence she hadn't felt in four years. It was almost bittersweet though, considering the circumstances and all the uncertainty surrounding them, so it simultaneously left a sour feeling in the pit of her stomach.

They rounded a bend and found themselves in sight of the cell block door, as well as in the *sights* of the two soldiers standing watch outside. In a flash, they each had their weapons back up, and without even slowing, dropped the two men before either of them managed to get a shot off.

"Good aim," Ziva muttered, surprised when she heard the exact same words echoed in Aroska's voice. They spared each other a glance, and she saw what appeared to be relief on his face before he pulled ahead and went to work disarming the dead men. She'd almost forgotten how well they meshed in the field.

She dropped to a knee beside one of the bodies, recovering a coded key that would open the cell block. She inserted the rod into the correct port in the wall panel; the sound of the heavy metal door groaning open echoed down the corridor, reminding her of the days when she'd been confined within one of these very cells. The memory sent an unexpected chill down her spine, raising the hairs on the back of her neck as she and Aroska resumed their journey.

Most Ibarra prisoners were housed in larger communal prisons throughout Cartel-controlled cities, and thus many of these cells were simply used for storage. Manes used this detention block when vetting potential assets, as he had done with her, and when using prisoners as leverage to manipulate others, as he was doing now. Manipulation. There it was again.

Two cells at the far end of the hallway were closed, and she angled for them with renewed fervor. She found Zinni on her right and Skeet on her left, both alerted by the commotion and peering through the cell bars. For a split second, neither of them could do anything but stand there, dumbfounded.

"What the hell?" Skeet muttered. His expression shifted slightly from animosity to confusion upon catching sight of Aroska, but Ziva felt crushed beneath the weight of his gaze the moment he returned his attention to her.

She couldn't help but go on the defensive. "...am I doing here?" she finished for him, holstering her weapon and inserting the key into the control panel for Zinni's cell. "I'm getting you out of here. If you've got a problem with that, feel free to stay."

The heavy bolt slid away and Zinni's door swung open, squealing on rusty hinges just like the door on the next cell over where Ziva herself had spent those agonizing six weeks. The intelligence officer stepped out, her keen blue eyes displaying wariness more than anger. Despite what appeared to be cautious trust, she gave Ziva a wide berth as she moved around to receive one of the weapons Aroska had taken from the guards.

It was the best reaction she could hope for at the moment, and she turned her attention back to Skeet. "I'm going to open this door," she said, inserting the key rod but refraining from turning it just yet. "Can I trust you not to strangle me the moment you get out of there?"

Her stomach tightened when he didn't respond; his silence was a perfectly clear answer as far as she was concerned. Maintaining eye contact and sending him a warning glare, she twisted the key and braced herself for whatever he might do to her.

The moment the bolt slid clear, he lunged forward and shoved the door open. She ducked to the side to avoid getting struck in the face, but that only put her in prime position for him to seize her by the throat and push her across the corridor, where he pinned her against the bars of Zinni's cell. The impact drove the air from her lungs, and despite the fact that his grip wasn't overly tight, she still struggled to catch her breath. It took every ounce of willpower to remain still and not listen to the years of instinct that screamed at her to fight back.

Skeet himself was merely reacting the way he'd been trained to, the way *she'd* trained him to. He didn't want to hurt her—he'd made that clear when he'd wilted under her pressure in the dining room—but he simply didn't know how else to get his point across. There was a gentleness about the way he held her, or maybe *sincerity* was the better word. His grip was firm, but he wasn't holding her as tightly as he was capable. The fact that she was still conscious was a testament to that. This was a warning, a plea, a final chance to tell him the truth.

Out of the corner of her eye, she saw Zinni and Aroska ready their weapons and take aggressive steps forward, though who the aggression was aimed at was unclear. She held her hand out to halt their advance, not daring to break eye contact with Skeet. "I've got this," she hissed.

The raw emotion in his face was unlike anything she'd ever seen. "I don't even know what to say to you right now." His hands and arms had begun to tremble ever so slightly.

She worked her throat around and swallowed past his hand. "Skeet, you have to trust me."

"We can't keep doing this."

By 'this,' she assumed he was referring to the way she had on several recent occasions done something to betray his trust, intentionally or not, only to regain it and then somehow betray it all over again. It wasn't as though she'd *wanted* to hurt him or planned on breaking that trust, but she could almost understand his mode of thinking. He was doing the same thing she always did: basing his trust—or lack thereof—on analytical judgments of her past actions rather than any sort of gut feeling. And he was right in that she hadn't been giving him much to go on.

The desire to make him understand—in a very short amount of time, no less—sparked an entirely new line of conversation, and her plan to remain calm and collected fizzled then and there. "You think I wanted to reveal my Nostia to anyone?" she wheezed. "You think I wanted to run away and hide after Dasaro set me up, or that I wanted Ronan to come out of nowhere and target Haphez?" She reached up and took hold of his wrists with each hand, squeezing him as tightly as he held her. "Do you think I wanted to be stuck in this *sheyss* hole for the past two years, acting like a pawn for the scum of the galaxy?" Hot anger swelled within her chest and she gritted her teeth, enunciating every word: "I. Never. Asked. For. This."

He watched her, unblinking, his eyes searching every centimeter of her face for sincerity. "You chose to go to Tobias, Ziva," he said, his tone still accusatory but his voice quieter. Then he snorted in disgust. "Is that even true?"

After spending so long immersed in her Matia Moryi persona, hearing her own name still sounded odd. "It is," she retorted, "and considering the shape I was in after the *Intrepid* blew, I wouldn't be alive today if I hadn't gone there." She hesitated. "But you're right, I made that choice. I went there to get help and expected to do a few odd jobs for him in return for the information he gave me when I was looking for you and Aroska. Yes, I chose to help him combat Manes and took part in his plan to infiltrate Ibarra, but by the time I realized just how deep the situation went..."

...she'd gone right along with it anyway. As much as she wanted to say *it was too late to get out*, she knew deep down it was merely an excuse, a lie she'd been telling herself all along in order to justify the things she'd done. She could have walked away from the Ibarra Cartel at any point, Tobias and the Niiosians be damned. She could have escaped Niio before even beginning her infiltration of the Cartel, and, despite the fact that it likely would have killed her, she had to admit she could have just chosen not to seek Tobias's help in the first place.

He'd thought she was dead, as had the rest of the galaxy, and dead people couldn't return favors.

She swallowed hard when she realized there was no real explanation for why she'd done any of it, other than that she simply didn't know how to function when her life wasn't in shambles.

Now was the worst possible time to be dwelling on something like that, and she opted for a quick change of subject. "Listen," she said, her voice hoarse from too much talking and too little breathing. "I know I owe you—all of you—a better explanation, but we do not have time for this right now." The emotion was starting to manifest itself in the form of rage, and through clenched teeth she blurted the first thing that came to mind. "If you want nothing to do with me for the rest of your lives, fine. I don't give a damn. But right now, I need you to act like the professionals you are, use the skills we've developed as a team, and work with me here. You think you can do that?"

Skeet's grip on her loosened significantly, though he refrained from letting go until a few seconds later. He gave her one last look that clearly said *don't make me regret this* before turning and taking one of the other weapons from Aroska.

"I take it you have some sort of plan, then," he said, looking over the gun before sliding it into his empty holster.

It was all Ziva could do to keep from doubling over and gasping for breath, but now was not the time for such a display. She took a moment to focus on her breathing, massaging her throat with one hand as she contemplated a response. She wasn't sure if Skeet had meant to be condescending, but that was all she could hear in his tone. "I'm going to start sounding repetitive here, but we need to get out of here as fast as possible. And not just out of this compound—off the ground." She relayed what she'd already told Aroska about Tobias's imminent arrival and, to her relief, saw genuine concern in both Skeet and Zinni's faces. "I've got a contact with the resources we need, and he's hard at work as we speak. Tobias gave me a code to use to identify myself as friendly when he gets here—can I assume you need to recover your ship?"

"It contains HSP intel, so yes," Skeet answered.

"Good. I'm already having a copy of the code made."

"We can't just all leave together?" Zinni said, her eyes shifting to Skeet.

Ziva wondered if the intelligence officer was simply concerned for their collective safety or if she still considered her a security risk. "My vessel contains data and findings from every mission I carried out for Manes. The recovery of that material was part of my deal with Tobias. I'm docked at the port, so we'll have to split up."

Neither Skeet nor Zinni looked particularly impressed with that response, but they didn't protest. "Where did you leave the *Saber*?" the lieutenant asked, turning his attention to Aroska.

Tarbic consulted his communicator and passed the device over. "In an outcropping on a plateau about twenty klicks outside the city. These are the exact coordinates."

"Keep that with you," Ziva said, indicating the comm. "I'll send the transponder code as soon as I receive it."

"And I'll come with you," Aroska said. "You could use the backup."

She turned to him, ready to tell him she didn't need to be babysat, and caught a glimpse of the glance and subtle nod he threw at Skeet and Zinni. While she was sure he was indeed hoping to provide backup, she realized he was also offering to keep an eye on her.

The thought—the purely objective, factual thought—that she could kill him more easily if he was alone crossed her mind before she could muster up a response. It was almost disturbing how automatic that mentality had become over the past couple of years, and she immediately shook it off.

"Fine," she said. "We'll meet aboard the Niiosian flagship when it arrives."

"And if it doesn't, for any reason?" Zinni asked.

"Then we'll figure something out. We can track each other with those codes. We'll find a new rendezvous locale."

She cringed at how vague it all seemed and could only imagine what they were thinking. Or maybe that was the problem—she was paranoid, imagining it all, and they were ready to trust her and help her. No, logically speaking, that wasn't accurate. Her mind was a mess.

She looked up to find Skeet watching her as though she were a subordinate he needed to punish, a task that would bring him no great joy. The feeling was mutual; if he wasn't going to trust her, then she sure as hell didn't feel comfortable trusting him in return.

"Well," he finally said, "no sense in standing around here and getting caught."

"On that, we can agree." She beckoned for them all to follow her out of the cell block. "Come on—if they haven't realized I'm gone yet, they will soon enough."

Chapter 34
Ibarra Compound · Tabaco, Panuco

"I told you so."

Manes looked up at Kimbra, at the moment too busy mentally berating himself for that exact reason to be concerned that she would have the gall to speak those words. Not to mention it was the first time she'd said *anything* since they'd all left the dining room in a flurry nearly an hour earlier. Despite the momentary chaos and what he'd said to the Haphezian agent about his poor behavior, the situation had unfolded precisely as he'd intended. Actually, no, that wasn't quite accurate, because he hadn't expected Matia—Ziva—to react the way she had. And that was a good thing.

That was why he currently found himself at a loss as to what to do with her. She had lied about who she was, had lied about knowing who these agents were, and was quite possibly working with them in direct opposition to the Cartel, but he had no proof. He hated to lose one of his most prized assets if he had any other option; despite this deception and her occasional belligerence, she'd demonstrated a remarkable level of loyalty to him over the last couple of years. Ergo he was encouraged by her actions in the dining room, by the way she had subdued her own comrade without even being directly ordered to.

Still, she needed to be punished in some manner, and while the emotional suffering he'd engineered for her had been entertaining thus far, an example needed to be made, just as he'd said about Adler. Only this time, unlike that poor sap of a bartender, she was actually guilty of deceiving him. The last thing he wanted was for anyone else in his circle to think they could get away with such a thing.

"What exactly would you propose we do?" he growled as Kimbra paced back and forth in his darkened office. He was sure she was just itching for him to ask.

"You saw that Federation bulletin," she replied, immediately coming over to lean on the desk in front of him. "I'll bet they'd be happy to take her off our hands."

"They're hunting Nosti. She didn't use her powers earlier—there's no way to know whether she truly is one."

"Regardless, they've probably been looking for her for four years. Imagine their surprise when she shows up gift wrapped on their doorstep."

Manes brought his elbows to rest on the surface of the desk, steepling his hands in front of his mouth as he so often did while deep in thought. "Out of the question," he muttered, though as soon as the words were out of his mouth, he regretted saying them just yet. If anything in that bulletin was accurate, then it was true that the Federation might appreciate being informed of this woman's whereabouts, if not presented with her directly. The problem was just that for an independent world—particularly one like Panuco whose primary enterprises fell on the more nefarious end of the moral spectrum—it was considered bad form to do any business with the Federation. It wasn't as though the Ibarra Cartel had any direct quarrel with the Feds, but he knew for a fact that some of his clients did, and they were no doubt out there using his products to fight their battles. If too much attention was drawn to his operation, he had a hunch the Federation wouldn't have much trouble finding a reason to strip Panuco of its independent status and wipe it from the face of the galaxy.

"Think of what we could gain!" Kimbra went on. "If we use her as leverage, we can ensure the Feds leave us alone for good."

That was an idea, though he wasn't sure how much he trusted the galaxy's superpower to follow through such a bargain if they identified Ibarra as a threat. Besides, with the way Matia's reputation had spread throughout this sector of space, it wouldn't be hard for the Feds to figure out she'd been employed by the Cartel for two full years, and the last thing he needed was to be accused of harboring a Federation fugitive.

So as tempting as it was to take Kimbra's suggestion and run with it, he couldn't bring himself to do such a thing right now.

"I'm not going to turn her over to the Federation unless it's anonymously," he said.

Even in his peripheral vision, he saw Kimbra's scowl deepen. "But then what would we get out of it?"

"Exactly," he replied. "She could make a valuable bargaining chip, but we mustn't be hasty in our decision about how to spend her." It struck him that he'd completely gravitated away from the idea of trying to redeem her as an asset. Well, in a way, she would still be an asset. The question now was what he could get in exchange for her, and from whom.

Before he could put any more thought into the subject, an insistent chirp from his security console caught his attention. When nothing happened after that single chime, he turned to look at the console, perplexed. Kimbra was already on her way over, face scrunched in a similarly vexed manner as she waited for the alarm that should have come.

"What is it?" he said.

She shook her head and opened her mouth to respond, but a sudden cacophony of alarms and klaxons cut her off. The entire console was awash in flashing lights, signals from multiple systems throughout the compound—and the city—all vying for his attention. It took mere seconds for his communicator to start going off, and concerned voices called to him from outside the office door.

"What the hell is it?" he asked again, shouting above the noise.

"Orbital security breach," Kimbra answered. "Multiple contacts." She turned to him, wide-eyed. "It's Niio."

Manes swore and pushed against his desk with a shout of rage, sending the heavy piece of furniture skidding a meter across the floor. "How the hell did he get past our advance warning system?"

She didn't respond, but it had been more of a rhetorical question anyway. Here he'd been too preoccupied today with these damn Haphezians to notice an entire enemy fleet approaching his primary base of operations. But it was true that he should have received some sort of warning from Panuco's defensive systems; someone somewhere had failed, and he intended to find out who just as soon as these interlopers—both the Niiosians and the Haphezians—had been dealt with.

He went to the door and found several of his soldiers waiting in the corridor. "Scramble the ships," he ordered. "Divert all non-essential compound power to defensive measures."

They hurried off and he strode back over to Kimbra, all but shoving her out of the way to get a look at the security readings on the console. His thoughts drifted to Matia—it was her fault he'd been so distracted all day. He brought up the surveillance feed for the holding room she'd been placed in...and did a double take when it was shown to be empty. He swore again and slammed the heel of his hand against the screen, sending a series of cracks up the middle of it. Even with the distorted image, however, it was plain to see when he played the recording back that she hadn't gotten out on her own. She could be seen speaking at some length with another person, one who would have had no trouble cracking the room's security: Blain Reed, the young hacker.

"Pinpointing his location," Kimbra said before Manes even had to ask. She tapped at one of the console's other terminals for a moment, bringing up a map of the city with a blinking geo-locator that represented the comm signature she'd given the boy while he worked with her that afternoon. "He's in the Tunnel. He's at her apartment."

He could hear what she was saying, but the words were little more than an echo in his mind as he tried and failed to make contact with the soldiers he'd stationed down in the compound's prison block. He searched the security feeds until he found one that covered that area, and he could only stand and watch helplessly as Matia and another Haphezian man—somehow, the one he'd watched her shoot in the street—gunned down his soldiers and moved on toward the cells, which were now unlocked and empty according to the readings on the display before him. He'd been right to continue not trusting her, but now it appeared she had nevertheless gotten the upper hand.

Whatever the case, he did not need to be dealing with both of these problems at once, and the Niiosians posed the more immediate threat. He strode back toward the door and turned to address Kimbra one last time. "Send a team to deal with Reed, then shut down Moryi's takeoff clearance. She won't get far."

He left her at the console and walked out, determined that all of his enemies in this situation would be dealt with in turn, whether they were causing damage from within or without. Tobias Niio may have been his objective, but whoever Ziva Payvan was, whatever she'd done, she'd just made herself a sworn enemy of the Ibarra Cartel.

CHAPTER 35
COMMERCIAL SECTOR - Tabaco, Panuco

Ziva slowed and pulled Aroska into the shadows beneath a storefront awning when a dull rumble somewhere high above reached her ears. She couldn't see the source, but she didn't need to; the massive shadow currently washing over the filthy city could only be from a ship, a light cruiser of some sort based on the size. From here there was no way to know who it belonged to, but the distant whine of the anti-aircraft guns charging up throughout the main Ibarra compound told her everything. The Niiosians had arrived.

"*Sheyss*," she muttered, taking the briefest of moments to press her back against the wall and check the time.

"They here early?" Aroska asked, peering up at the sky with a look of incredulity that gave her the impression he was still somewhat surprised she'd been telling the truth about Tobias.

"I'm late," she retorted with enough of an accusatory tone to remind him she blamed him and the team for sending her schedule awry. Further argument, however, would only slow them down. The situation could still be salvaged, but they'd need to move faster than ever.

"We're almost to my place," she continued, checking the time once more and taking another glance up the street. "What are the chances you left my window open this morning?"

"It's unlocked."

"Good. We'll go in that way. It probably didn't take Manes long to realize I was gone. He'll no doubt send someone here if he hasn't already, and you can bet they'll have the Tunnel covered."

She beckoned for Aroska to follow and ducked into the next alley they came to, unable to help but consider the fact that it was one he'd chased her through just hours prior. If Manes was smart—and she knew he was—he might have someone covering her back window as well, but she imagined one or two thugs would be easier to deal with than whatever force he sent to knock down her front door. They'd moved quickly enough through the compound that they might be well ahead of that force anyway, and the Cartel no doubt had its hands full dealing with their new airborne visitors, but she thought it wise to stay prepared.

Regardless, with her favorite rifle already tucked safely away aboard the *Talon*, the only thing besides Blain she needed to retrieve from the apartment was her knife, which she'd also locked up following the shootout. Even if Cartel soldiers came looking for her there, she liked to think she and her male companions would be long gone by then.

They broke out onto the street and continued forward, taking in every detail of their surroundings as they moved. Most of the marketplace vendors were in the process of closing down their shops or had already vacated. The few civilians left in the area hustled away, some all-out running but many moving at a rushed walk. Most long-time citizens of Tabaco were used to the occasional skirmish with pirates or rebel groups and simply kept their heads down until the coast was clear, but Ziva doubted the average bystanders had any idea who they were dealing with this time.

She slowed as they neared the alcove that led to the Tunnel's back wall, motioning for Aroska to stop behind her as she cautiously peered around the corner. She could see her window from there and was relieved that the area around it appeared clear. But that didn't mean no one was lying in wait out of her line of sight.

Raising her weapon, she moved forward, eyes watching for movement and ears straining to hear any sounds that didn't belong. She swung the gun to the left, nothing but empty space in front of her. Aroska followed suit behind her, investigating the area to the right.

"Clear," they said simultaneously.

Ziva slid her weapon into its holster and stooped down to work the window open. "Stay here and keep watch," she instructed. "This won't take long."

Aroska appeared ready to protest, but the look was a fleeting one. He nodded and readied his pistol, turning his attention to the alley as she slipped through the window.

The interior of the apartment was still quiet, a good sign. Nevertheless, she froze and listened closer for several more seconds before easing the window shut and continuing forward. The drumming of fingers against a virtual keyboard reached her ears as she made her way from the bedroom to the living area, and she found Blain at work at her comm console. He spared her a glance over his shoulder, and the speed of his typing increased.

"I don't know if this is a good idea," he said.

"You don't want to spend the rest of your life here, kid," she replied. "Besides, you're past the point of no return now. Manes will kill you after what you did for me." She glanced toward the front door, unsure if the noises she was hearing outside were Tunnel tenants or Manes's men. She had to remind herself there was no real difference. "How's it coming? We don't have much time."

"Your transponder codes are ready," the young man answered, his focus directed solely toward the console. "The docks are under lockdown, just like you suspected. I was making good progress on getting into the system, but their security went haywire a few minutes ago and I've had some trouble getting back in. I think I'm almost there."

She barely heard him, preoccupied by the sound of running footsteps coming down the Tunnel. "Hurry," she instructed, voice quiet but firm. She lifted her weapon and stepped closer to the door, listening, listening.

A brief moment of silence preceded the unmistakable *beep* of a detonator. She had just enough time to duck halfway into a crouch before the door blew inward in a cloud of flames and smoke. She fired a round straight into the forehead of the first person through the opening, not caring who it was. The man's head snapped back and he fell into the rubble, but a second thug followed him so closely that she didn't have time to re-adjust her aim in the haze before he was upon her.

He was massive, one of the few Ibarra goons who actually surpassed her in height and whose sole purpose was to inflict pain. He hit her moving full speed and lifted her up, body-slamming her into the wall at the end of the short entryway. The pistol flew from her hand upon impact, and bright shapes danced in her vision as she gasped for the breath that had been punched from her lungs.

The man pinned her there, closing his meaty fingers around her throat. She curled both her hands into fists and brought them down hard against the back of his neck, then again against the sides of his head, but he barely budged. Sensing movement to her left, she turned to see if Blain could get to her gun and was shocked to find him already holding it in an unsteady hand. Without warning, he fired.

Again.

And again.

The thug's grip on her loosened immediately as his enormous bulk collapsed. Ziva sank to the floor, her legs like liquid, vaguely aware that her body had left a dent in the cheap plaster wall. She coughed as her lungs spasmed, attempting to process the relatively elaborate series of events that had just transpired over a period of mere seconds. No more of Manes's men were spilling through her front door—for now, anyway—and she needed to take advantage of that.

Blain stood frozen, shifting his wide-eyed gaze between the man he'd shot and the pistol in his own hand as if he didn't believe he'd actually fired it. Between coughs, she beckoned for him to hand it back and managed a nod of gratitude. The speed with which he'd reacted was admirable, but there would be time for proper thanks once they made it out of here.

The movement seemed to snap him out of his stupor. Maintaining his grip on the weapon, he shook his head and took a step toward her, innocently—ignorantly—offering it to her barrel-first...

Chapter 36
The Tunnel - Tabaco, Panuco

For a moment, Aroska wasn't certain whether the sound of the blast had been part of the overhead battle or somewhere on the ground—as the skirmish raged closer, it was harder and harder to tell. But some measure of instinct had him moving toward the window a split second before he heard a single gunshot and the telltale sounds of a brawl coming from within the apartment.

He bent down and lifted the filthy pane, cursing Ziva for having shut it in the first place. The moment the opening was clear, another three shots rang out from somewhere inside, prompting him to pick up his pace. Then just like that, the racket ceased as quickly as it had begun, leaving him hyper-aware of the amount of noise he was making as he struggled to fit through the small space for the second time that day.

His boots hit the floor and he paused to listen; somewhere out in the living area, he heard an agonized groan followed by a fit of coughing and sputtering. He considered calling out to Ziva but decided against it for fear of alerting any remaining hostiles to his presence. From the angle at which he approached the hallway, he could see what appeared to be the arm of an Ibarra soldier protruding from the apartment's entryway, its owner lying closer to the front door and out of sight.

Weapon raised, he stepped out of the bedroom and took in the entire scene, deafened by his own pulse as his mind prioritized everything he saw. At the top of the list was Ziva herself. She sat slumped against the wall, a dent and series of cracks above her and another dead thug beside her. She was moving, alive but in pain. Shattered plaster surrounded her on the floor, and fresh blood oozed from her head.

The second thing he saw was the scrawny young man the team had apprehended in this very apartment, the one who had sold her out to Manes. He loomed over her, gun in hand and pointed toward her head.

"Down!" Aroska shouted, taking aim and pulling the trigger without another thought.

The sound of his weapon discharging drowned out Ziva's voice as she lunged forward toward the boy. He twitched violently as the rounds tore into him and crumpled to the ground just out of her reach, leaving the gun to clatter harmlessly to the floor.

Aroska couldn't tell if the room actually fell silent or whether he simply couldn't hear anything over the sudden ringing in his ears. He could only stand there and watch as Ziva dragged herself over and clamped her hands down over the two smoldering holes in the young man's chest. She was yelling something, begging him to hold on, but it took only moments for him to stop responding.

"What were you thinking?" her voice finally echoed.

He wasn't sure. In his mind, he saw himself entering the room all over again, mentally replaying the last few seconds. This time, with everything moving in slow motion, he focused solely on the techie. Ziva hadn't flinched despite having the barrel of the pistol pointed directly at her. The boy had been trembling as he extended the gun toward her hand. Her outstretched hand.

Had he been offering her the weapon?

You killed him. Aroska wasn't sure if she'd spoken the words out loud or if his brain was merely conjuring up the phrase she was surely thinking.

So zoned out was he that he didn't even realize she was on her feet until she was in his face and the heels of her hands connected with his shoulders. He took a staggering step backward, ducking away as she came at him again. He caught her next swing with his free hand, pulling her in close and surprised by the utter dismay on her face. She didn't resist, but her features remained so twisted that he wondered if she'd even be able to comprehend anything he said.

"I thought he was going to kill you," he said, looking her in the eye despite the fury he saw there.

"You *killed* him," she repeated, struggling against his hold. He imagined if she really tried to break free, he'd be on the floor and maybe even unconscious.

"Listen to me," he said, releasing her. An odd tremor set in, brought on by the idea of having killed an innocent person, one who may very well have saved Ziva's life mere seconds before. It struck him that this boy was the contact she'd spoken of, the one who was helping them get off-world. The circumstances behind him assisting her after betraying her were, unfortunately, irrelevant now. "I swear, I thought he was going to shoot you. I was only trying to protect you."

It wasn't just his imagination when her chin wobbled and her eyes glistened. "Well don't," she snapped, taking a step back and thrusting her finger at him. "I don't *need* you to protect me. I don't *need* you to save me. All you ever do is *froucht sagh aht*."

"Ziva—"

"No! Do not speak!" She pivoted and stormed back toward the comm console across the room and took several seconds to study the display on the terminal. She swore in response to whatever it showed, pounding a fist against the side of the console before taking a moment to just hang her head. As much as he wanted to ask what he could do to help, Aroska heeded her command and remained silent. If this boy was indeed the contact who'd been helping them escape, there was a good chance the plan had just been botched. Judging by Ziva's reaction to the console display, that was exactly the case.

Finally, she snatched a comm unit from a shelf above the console and plugged it into the terminal. It emitted a beep after only a couple of seconds and she removed the device, taking a moment to send out a text-based transmission to Skeet and Zinni before tucking it into a soft pouch on her belt. She turned and opened up what appeared to be a weapons locker, removing a sheathed combat knife and strapping it to her thigh. Then, sparing the young man's body one last fleeting glance, she strode past Aroska with tears lingering in her eyes and headed for what remained of the front door.

"We have our transponder codes, but without him, my ship can't take off," she said. Her tone was surprisingly calm considering the outburst only moments before, but her demeanor was still stiff, her muscles tense as she stepped out into the breezeway. "We'll have to get clearance ourselves."

Aroska considered looking back at the dead boy one last time before rushing to catch up with her but thought better of it. He understood that she was unhappy with him for killing the young man in the first place—he was feeling guilty enough himself—but the extent of her reaction still surprised him. This was someone who'd become special to her, something he never would have expected to see, let alone in an environment like this.

By the time he made it to the door, she was already halfway to the tunnel entrance, moving at almost a full sprint, pistol in hand. He hollered for her to wait up but doubted she'd comply. The chase reminded him all too much of when he'd pursued her through the city that very morning, even in the sense that she was running away from him. He'd seen firsthand what kind of disasters ensued when she was upset and got too far out of his reach, and he wasn't about to let her get carried away and do something foolhardy when she'd been the one emphasizing the need to stay focused and work together to get out of there. He picked up his pace.

Ziva reached the end of the tunnel and paused, ready to shoot a group of passersby who turned in a different direction at the last second. Aroska pulled up behind her, taking a look up and down the street for himself. Like the thoroughfare behind the apartments, it remained relatively clear except for a few alarmed Panucan citizens rushing to take shelter. Nobody paid the two of them any mind, likely recognizing Ziva as Matia and putting no thought into her potential role in all of this.

"Listen," Aroska said, catching her by the shoulder just as she began to move again. "I know you're pissed, but don't check out on me now."

Her jaw twitched as she ground her teeth behind pursed lips. "I am not going to have this conversation with you right now. And if you try to initiate it one more time before we're off this rock, I'm leaving you behind." She turned and surveyed the street once more, peering upward as a trio of unfamiliar fighters roared by overhead. "Now," she continued without even looking at him, "my ship—the *Talon*—is kept in a cluster of secure underground docking bays near the main compound. Without the clearance override, we'll have to go straight to the dock control station to unlock the bay ourselves. And hope we don't get caught in a Niiosian crossfire while we're at it." Finally, she threw him a glance over her shoulder. "Got it?"

It was amazing how she could project such an air of composure when he knew how much fury was boiling just beneath the surface. It was a skill he'd finally begun to hone over the past four years, though he had yet to meet anyone who was as good at quashing their emotions as she was.

He nodded and the two of them took off.

Chapter 37
Ibarra Compound - Tabaco, Panuco

"Status?" Manes demanded as he stormed into the compound's defensive control center.

Several sets of eyes spared him glances from around the room, but no one made any immediate move to respond. The space was already warm thanks to all the computer systems performing in overdrive, and everyone present had a glistening sheen of sweat on their foreheads as they worked feverishly to control the anti-aircraft guns, maintain shielding, and monitor the status of airborne forces. Most of the people here were ex-military, engineers and combat analysts who had done this same sort of work before coming into the Cartel's service, and thus they were some of the most disciplined individuals under his command. The fact that nobody had answered him yet—both from a professional standpoint and in terms of the severity of the situation—was unacceptable.

"Tell me what the hell is going on!" he roared, seizing a nearby vacant chair and pitching it across the room.

It went skidding across the floor toward a man who appeared to be in charge, based on his position at the largest console. He rose from his station and wiped his brow, swallowing hard. "Defenses are holding, sir."

"But?"

"But the Niiosians have our forces effectively pinned down. Without an advance warning, they were able to get on top of us—"

"And *how* did that happen?"

"Frankly, sir, we've been trying to keep this place from getting obliterated and haven't had time to look too closely. But the only way unauthorized vessels could have made it past the defense grid is if the system didn't recognize them as such. Either the parameters were changed in the system's core code or the Niiosians figured out how to broadcast as Ibarra ships. The grid never went offline—we'd be able to tell if it did. Nobody knows exactly what happened."

Well, that sounded all too familiar. Regardless of whether the Niiosians had breached their system or someone had let them in, heads would roll.

"What can be done at this point?" Manes asked. Every preparation he'd made since taking power had been for this exact moment, yet he just never seemed to be quite ready. Coincidence, or not?

"As I said, they have us pinned down. I believe we have the means to hold them off—" the man gestured toward a readout displaying the status of the state-of-the-art shielding over the compound that had never been needed before today "—but at this point I think a full offensive would be a mistake. We're too enclosed and don't have any room to maneuver under the umbrella they've created. Based on their attack patterns so far, they weren't expecting this degree of planetside defenses, but without any sort of resistance, they *will* eventually be able to break through those defenses. My recommendation would be to...fall back."

"You mean evacuate."

"To preserve the Cartel's interests, yes."

It was tempting to shoot the man merely for telling him something he didn't want to hear, but deep down, Manes knew that wouldn't accomplish anything and would only eliminate what could very well be one of the Cartel's most valuable resources at the moment. The thought of retreating made him physically ill; the sheer principle of it was disagreeable enough, but add on the fact that he'd be running away from the very battle he'd spent over four years equipping for and he almost couldn't bear it. For a moment he could only stand there paralyzed by anger.

On the other hand, this was far from the scenario he'd pictured when he'd imagined usurping Tobias Niio and expanding the Ibarra Cartel into Niiosian Mob territory. The objectively smart thing to do in this situation *would* be to fall back to one of Ibarra's other bases of operation, regroup, and try again. He had contingency plans, but had of course hoped to not require them. He hated the fact that evacuating was something his father might have done. He'd killed the man for a reason.

"Shall I give the order, sir?" the control room supervisor said.

Manes took one more second to mull the situation over before looking the man in the eye. "Send word to my private dock. Have my ship prepared. Then give the signal." He swept his gaze around the room, addressing everyone present. "Initiate Operation Recovery."

He strode back out the door with a flourish of his long leather coat and made it halfway down the corridor before Kimbra appeared, breathing hard.

"The team I sent to the apartment isn't responding," she said, holding up her communicator as she fell into stride beside him.

"How many men did you send?"

"Two. Should have been more than enough to take care of the kid."

Yet another blow. "Not if Moryi went there," he muttered.

Kimbra scoffed. "I've been telling you for months, we should have—"

He whirled on her abruptly, his hands curling around each of her wrists as he pinned her to the wall. "Please, tell me more about what we should have done," he snarled, ignoring a lock of greased hair that came loose and fell into his face.

Her eyes took on a more defiant quality than they normally did when he lashed out against her, but she refrained from reacting. He let go just as quickly as he'd taken hold of her and continued on his way; another couple of seconds passed before he heard her footsteps rushing to catch up.

"Where is Matia now?" he asked as the two of them exited the control center and found themselves in a courtyard just east of his private residence in the center of the compound. Night approached, though rather than the cool breeze and scent of the sea, the air was filled with the roar of ships and the stench of smoke. The shielding above the compound rippled as stray plasma bolts struck it, but it appeared to be holding. They angled toward the hangar where his personal vehicles and private ship were docked.

"Don't know. In case you haven't noticed, we've had other problems to deal with."

He didn't break stride but cast a warning glance over his shoulder.

She cleared her throat. "Last confirmed sighting was the prison block. Surveillance showed her leading the Haphezian agents out the back tunnel, and it appeared she and one agent split off from the other two."

"You recalled her departure clearance?"

"Locked down her docking bay and those surrounding it the moment our vessels took off."

"Good. Send a team—a *full* team—to stake out the *Talon*. She is not to leave this planet alive. Once she's been dealt with, they are to recover her vessel and rendezvous with the fleet. When the Niiosians are no longer a factor, we may yet be able to learn what she was doing here and whether her actions have produced any long-term consequences." He stepped into the hangar, where his ship was already idling. Several of his men stood at the base of the boarding ramp, weapons at the ready.

"You seriously want to waste resources on—"

"If she thinks she can get away with what she has done simply because I have other problems to deal with, she is gravely mistaken. Send a team after the other Haphezian agents as well. They can't have gotten far, and they will all pay."

"Fine," Kimbra muttered as they ascended the ramp into the ship. The hangar's roof began to slide open, and the vessel lifted off.

Manes went to a viewport as they soared above the compound, letting her voice fade into the background as she began relaying orders over comm. All throughout the city, other Ibarra vessels began to ascend, many of them under the protection of the force field. As a unit, they surged toward the coast, with several lingering behind to throw themselves into the Niiosians' sights if necessary. Manes's ship shuddered as it passed through the shield on the far edge of the compound then barreled upward, gaining altitude at full speed with its shields at full power.

"Sir!" one of his men called, passing him a data pad. "Operation Recovery is ready for execution."

Manes took the device and looked it over, wishing desperately that it hadn't come to this but glad, for once, that so many of his precious resources remained on Delatori rather than in his own warehouses. Not caring much who might still be on the ground, he entered a command on the data pad. Far below, a series of carefully planted charges received that command, and he watched through the viewport as his home and every storage and manufacturing center throughout the city went up in flames.

CHAPTER 38
TABACO SPACEPORT · Tabaco, Panuco

The door hissed shut behind them, reducing the clamor of explosions and gunfire to a muffled rumble. Hurried footsteps drew Ziva's attention to her left; she crouched, took aim, and fired two rounds into the chest of the docking supervisor who appeared from around the corner with a pistol pointed her direction. Without a word, she continued forward and swept her weapon around the adjacent room while Aroska moved in the opposite direction and checked the far side of the main control area.

"Clear," he called, moving back toward her. "What are we looking for?"

"Main terminal," she replied, sweeping her gaze around the room until it fell on an active display the supervisor must have been using. She strode toward it. "Here."

She studied the readouts on the console, identifying her docking bay among the twenty or so others this particular station controlled. Manes had assigned her a bay on the outer edge of the cluster, reserving the inner ones for vessels with a more direct role in Ibarra's operations. This had always irritated her, as it meant she had to walk further to reach the Tunnel and the relative safety of her apartment. But now it was a relief. The two of them could stick to the outer passages and skirt around, avoiding the brunt of the security measures. At least in theory.

Her hand hovered over the controls as she considered the best course of action. She felt Aroska draw up beside her to get a look at the console himself; she curled her free hand into a fist, resisting the urge to turn and punch him in the throat as another image of Blain's scrawny, mangled body flashed through her mind.

"What's our play?" he asked, the mere sound of his voice grating on her nerves.

"It looks like all of these bays are on lockdown, not just mine," she replied, redirecting her focus to the terminal. "So, choice number one: we unlock all the bay doors, but if those bays are occupied, we risk allowing more ships to scramble for pursuit. Choice number two: we keep all the other doors locked and only grant clearance to the one we want, but there's a risk of being specifically targeted. Chances are they'll see the breach and send all their reinforcements to our location. Neither option will make for a clean getaway."

He appeared thoughtful for a moment. "So it boils down to whether we'd rather fight our way out ship-to-ship or man-to-man. I think I'd opt for taking our chances on the ground."

"Right, because you haven't seemed to have any trouble gunning people down today."

She returned her focus to the screen before he could get a word in edgewise, but a low rumble caught her attention. That rumble grew into a muted roar somewhere outside, and the ground trembled beneath her feet. Across the room, she could see out the window as a building down the street erupted in a ball of fire. Unless she was mistaken, it was one of Ibarra's weapon storage depots, and it hadn't been hit by Niiosian ordnance.

"*Sheyss*," she whispered, abandoning the clearance controls for a moment to check the terminal for organizational alerts. Sure enough, a warning had gone out mere minutes earlier proclaiming that Operation Recovery was going into effect. While she'd never officially been made privy to the particulars of the order, she'd made it her business to learn the details anyway, as its implementation would almost certainly mean her entire mission here had been blown. She'd just pictured herself still being on relatively civil terms with Manes and leaving Panuco with him, then still being able to eventually lead Tobias to him. If the Ibarra facilities were already being destroyed, it more than likely meant Manes was already gone. A quick check revealed a takeoff order at his private hangar just a couple of minutes ago.

She swore again and slammed her palms against the terminal,

furiously poring over it to see if there was any possible edge she could still give the Niiosians, just in case it wasn't too late. The AA guns surrounding the compound were obvious and should have been easy for Tobias's ships to target, but a force field signature she didn't recognize shielded them and many of the escaping ships from Niiosian fire. Of course Manes would have a secret defensive measure like that; it was in his nature but also fit in splendidly with everything else that had been going wrong for her today. She silently cursed Aroska and the rest of the team again. If the day had gone as she'd envisioned it for the past several months, she'd have had time to not only discover the shield but disable it before quietly leaving the planet with Blain just prior to Tobias's arrival.

"What is it?" Aroska asked.

She merely waved the screens away and returned to the clearance controls, where she selected her docking bay and transmitted a unique clearance code to the terminal that awaited her there. At the rate she was going, she was going to be in just as much trouble with Tobias as she was with Manes.

"We have to go."

CHAPTER 39
CITY CENTER · TABACO, PANUCO

Zinni shrank back against the nearest building when the whine of a disabled aircraft reached her ears. Skeet crouched beside her, and they watched as a small fighter—maybe Ibarra, maybe Niiosian, it didn't really matter—plummeted into the street just ahead of them. Thankfully, the majority of the Niiosians' bombardment was focused on the Cartel's main compound and not on Tabaco itself, but that didn't mean the two of them were safe from a stray plasma bolt or a spray of armor-piercing rounds. They were still close enough to the compound's outer walls that neither were in short supply.

"Go, go," Skeet said as soon as the fireball from the downed ship started to disperse.

Black smoke billowed from the aircraft's rear end, creating a screen that concealed them as they continued on. The immediate area was almost totally clear of civilian traffic; those not directly involved with the Cartel had probably noticed Ibarra was the target of this attack and had opted to vacate. This both relieved and unnerved Zinni. Anyone remaining in the streets was likely an Ibarra soldier and would be easy to pick out, but it also meant she and Skeet had no one to blend in with and would be equally visible. The key then was to move fast. They needed transportation.

It had been over fifteen minutes since they'd parted ways with Ziva and Aroska, and she was just beginning to worry that something had gone wrong when the comm Tarbic had given them beeped. She paused her thorough surveillance of their surroundings just long enough to look down at the screen. "The transponder code came through."

"Let's hope it works," Skeet muttered.

His tone wasn't nearly as hostile as it had been throughout the day or even in the cell block, but there was still a measure of cynicism she could do without at the moment. She still had numerous questions for Ziva, but after the woman had shown up in the prison with Aroska in tow, some of the distrust and hostility had dissipated. Or maybe a more accurate explanation was that any remaining distrust was in response to historical matters—being left out of the loop and all—rather than fear that Ziva had betrayed them. But she wasn't convinced Skeet was on that level just yet.

They moved in silence for another ten minutes, slowly working their way toward the outskirts of the city and the beach where the *Saber* had been docked earlier. While nowhere near as large as any of the cities back home on Haphez, Tabaco was still substantial enough that going anywhere on foot made for slow progress. In the grand scheme of things, the beach, the shipping yard, and even the marina where Adler's bar was located weren't far from the compound, but they didn't have time to be strolling along.

As if on cue, a sleek black groundcar not unlike the ones that had apprehended the two of them earlier slid to a halt in the road just ahead. Two Ibarra thugs leaped out and recovered automatic weapons from the storage area in the back, sweeping them up and down the street.

"They were just spotted in this area," one of them said to his partner. "They don't leave this planet alive. Manes's orders."

Skeet placed a hand on Zinni's shoulder and the two of them slipped around the next corner, out of sight of the soldiers. "Petty bastard, isn't he?" he muttered. "Didn't realize we'd hurt his feelings that bad."

"Maybe he's got something against Haphezians," Zinni said, thinking of the way the big blonde woman had regarded them after their capture.

"Not sure if he would have been employing two of them if that were the case."

Before she could think of a snappy response, the *boom* of an explosion filled the air, followed by several subsequent *booms* from the direction of the compound and surrounding area of the city. The sound echoed off nearby buildings and made it feel like the very air was vibrating. Both of them whipped around, catching sight of smoke and the glow of flames rising up against the dark evening sky.

"The hell was that?" Zinni hissed.

Rather than respond, Skeet took her by the arm and hustled her into the alley behind the building they'd been standing beside. Upon listening closer, she could hear the thugs moving their way, discussing what they could see of the explosions. Taking advantage of the men's distraction, the two of them ran down the alley on light feet, circling around to the far side of the building and finding themselves within meters of the still-idling car. A quick look around the corner confirmed the men still had their backs turned. Zinni shot a glance at Skeet, who was already watching her with a look that silently confirmed they were thinking the same thing.

Without a word, the two of them made a beeline for the car, with Zinni sliding through to the passenger seat and Skeet taking the helm. The sound of the door slamming shut immediately drew the thugs' attention, and they turned their weapons on the vehicle.

"Skeet!"

The sudden acceleration pinned Zinni to the seat; the bullets began to fly, but it only took a split second to close the gap between themselves and the soldiers. The car slammed into the first man, throwing him several meters up the street. The second was tossed into the air and came crashing down against the windshield, tumbling over the engine compartment. Skeet wrenched the controls around and had the car spinning in the opposite direction before the man had even hit the ground.

"*Sheyss*," he said, glancing back and forth between the rear cam and the view ahead as they sped away. "I think that guy was on comm. We may have to deal with reinforcements."

"With everything else they've got going on?" Zinni scoffed, peering out through the cracked windshield at the battle still raging in the sky.

"Well, I wouldn't have thought they'd send anyone after us to begin with, but here we are."

She merely shook her head and consulted the communicator. "Okay. Get us to the beach—there was a road that led up into the cliffs east of the city. I'll navigate from there."

No sooner were the words out of her mouth than a black car identical to theirs came screeching around the corner a block ahead. Skeet swore and accelerated toward the other vehicle, coming within meters of a head-on collision before throwing the controls to the right and slipping into a narrow side street Zinni guessed wasn't even intended for vehicles. Pedestrians who had taken cover from the battle dove out of the way or ducked into doorways. In the rear cam, she saw the other car start to enter the alley before reversing and turning back the way it had come. She doubted they'd seen the last of it.

"Hold on," Skeet said.

She turned back around and saw that they were approaching a wall a few meters tall with a small doorway through which more pedestrians were fleeing. The car's engine whined as Skeet took them into a climb steeper than the machine was designed for; they lunged over the wall and dove back into the street on the other side, with the car's rear end bouncing sharply off the ground before the repulsors righted it.

"Take a right here!" Zinni cried, glancing to their left in search of the other car. It was nowhere to be found, at least not yet. If they could stay far enough ahead, they might be in the clear.

Skeet obeyed and steered them onto the wider thoroughfare. They found themselves weaving in and out of other vehicles, some of which were still moving, some of which had been abandoned in the street while their owners sought safety. The surrounding environment was beginning to look familiar, and the route eventually opened up into the shipping yards in which they'd fought for their lives just that morning. It seemed like a lifetime ago.

Still no sign of the car that had been tailing them, but the Ibarra soldiers no doubt knew the city inside and out and might still manage to catch up. For the time being, Zinni returned her attention to what lay ahead, both in the physical and more abstract sense. Assuming they survived this—and that Ziva and Aroska survived—there were some conversations that needed to take place. Confessions and apologies from all parties involved. The emotional dissonance created by being overjoyed to see Ziva alive and being angry at her for past transgressions left an ache in her stomach. She'd also felt a rift building between herself and Skeet throughout the day, mostly due to disagreements over how to deal with Ziva. Perhaps that issue would resolve itself if they were able to reconcile with their old friend, but it was certainly something that needed to be addressed.

"You know she was probably telling the truth the whole time, and we didn't believe her," she said out of the blue. Even in the dining room, she could look back and see how Ziva's seemingly antagonistic actions had actually been in their best interest. She'd needed to maintain her Matia Moryi charade long enough to keep Manes's trust, and if Skeet had been allowed to attack the man, they all would have been killed instantly. By protecting Manes, she'd been protecting *them*.

She looked over at Skeet when he didn't respond. "You're going to have to face her at some point."

"I know," he said quietly, his eyes still flitting over to the rear cam every couple of seconds. "I just...I'm just trying to wrap my head around all of this."

They rode in silence for the next several minutes, cutting across the shipping yard to the farthest reaches of the city then gliding along the beach that had served as their base since the night before. Out here, signs of the overhead battle were almost nonexistent, and a full moon was just cresting the sea off to their left, washing the landscape in silvery hues. Zinni spotted the road she'd seen earlier and directed Skeet up it, and soon they found themselves tearing across a rocky plateau.

She looked skyward, studying the distant flashes over the city. Large silhouettes hovered at a much higher altitude, no doubt Niiosian cruisers that were too big to bring planetside. Some of the smaller vessels appeared to be breaking off from the battle and heading back up to where the fleet waited.

"We'd better hurry," she said.

Just before she turned away from the window, something else caught her eye: four pairs of lights moving at high speed over the beach they'd just crossed. The moonlight illuminated a great cloud of sand billowing in their wake.

"And we're about to have company."

Skeet took a brief look for himself in the rear cam and accelerated again. "How far out are we?"

"Far enough that we probably won't make it before they catch up," she answered, consulting the coordinates Aroska had provided. She turned in her seat and leaned into the back compartment, squinting in the poor light to see what the car's original users might have left in terms of armament. If this car was anything like the ones that had transported her and Skeet to the compound, there was bound to be a decent selection.

Her hand came to rest on a scoped rifle; the scope wouldn't do her much good in this light and with all the movement, but at least she knew the weapon had decent range. She pulled it out, selecting one of the corresponding mags as well, and moved back into the front, sitting backwards in her seat. By the time she got the window open, leaned out, and had the rifle steady, the dust cloud was visible over the crest of the hill and the lead car's spotlights had broken the plane of the plateau.

"They're gaining," she announced.

"See what you can do about that," Skeet said.

She drew a deep breath and released it slowly, taking aim for the dark void between the nearest set of spotlights. She fired twice in quick succession. Red-orange light trailed behind the rounds as they sliced through the air, surprising her. *Tracers.*

Based on the rounds' visible trajectory, it appeared she had hit the car, but aside from wavering briefly, it was still coming. She fired another pair of rounds for good measure, then a couple more at a different vehicle, and achieved similar results.

"*Sheyss*, they must be armored," she said, sliding back into the car. That explained why the man Skeet had run down had only cracked the windshield rather than shattering it.

"Fix it, Zinni," Skeet ordered, eyes wide and knuckles white as he gripped the controls and focused fully on what was in front of him.

She abandoned the rifle and threw herself further over the seat, taking a closer look at the remaining hardware in the back. There was a selection of pistols she imagined they might want to take with them when they reached the *Saber*, but the only other remaining weapon was a hulking black thing with a cylinder in the far corner. She hefted it out, pleased to see it was what she thought it was: a grenade launcher. The projectiles it fired sat encased in soft foam, and she inserted five of them into the cylinder, praying that would be enough to get the job done.

"Slow down a little," she instructed, returning to the window.

"You sure?"

"Damn, I hope so."

He obeyed, decelerating gradually as she fed the launcher through the window and shimmied out. She braced one leg under the car's front console and settled squarely on the narrow window rim, leaning out as far as possible and steadying the hulking weapon with both hands. The Ibarra cars were closing in fast, and she once again took aim for the lead vehicle. Fired.

Thunk.

It was hard to tell what happened first. A brilliant explosion lit up the plateau as the Cartel car went up in flames, and the launcher's substantial kick knocked her backward off her precarious perch. Without a free hand to grasp anything, she felt herself begin to fall and flailed her legs in a desperate attempt to find purchase within the car. The vehicle swerved, its repulsors kicking up a cloud of dust, and one of her shoulders bashed against the outside of the door. Hanging there nearly upside-down, she thought she'd managed to hook her foot under the dash again but realized after a split second that Skeet's hand was now clamped around her ankle.

"Keep it up!" he hollered.

She grunted and engaged her abdominal muscles, pulling herself into a more upright position and taking aim for another car as the thugs continued to close the distance. She fired. The grenade struck the vehicle dead center, sending it careening into the one beside it. Both cars erupted in a ball of flame as the device detonated.

One more, she thought, once again relying on her core and her free leg to haul herself up higher and hopefully relieve some of the pressure on Skeet. She rested her elbow on the roof of their car, taking a couple more precious seconds to steady her aim as she zeroed in on the final Ibarra vehicle. Its engine roared as it came up on them, and rapid muzzle flashes accompanied the distinctive *rat-tat-tat-tat* of automatic weapons fire from the passenger window. Two could play that game, certainly, but Zinni was determined to win. And she had the bigger gun.

She fired one more time, bracing herself with all her strength to keep the kick from knocking her backward again. It wasn't a direct hit, but the force of the detonation upended the pursuing vehicle and sent it tumbling across the plateau in a cloud of smoke. Then, aside from the roar of their own car's engine, all fell quiet.

Zinni released the launcher and let it fall into the dirt. Skeet let go of her ankle, and she slid back into her seat, breathing hard. He increased their speed once more as he angled for their destination, throwing her an astonished glance accompanied by something that looked like the beginning of a smile. She felt a wide grin spreading across her own face and began laughing out loud before she could stop herself. It was the only reasonable response to the adrenaline surging through her veins.

"I think that was one for the books," she said, huffing a sigh.

The sound of both their laughter filled the car as they sped off into the night.

Chapter 40
Tabaco Spaceport - Tabaco, Panuco

Ziva flattened herself against the doorframe of a service room and risked a look behind her as another barrage of plasma fire flew down the passage. Aroska used a pair of shipping containers for cover a few meters back; behind him, the bodies of several Ibarra soldiers they'd already encountered were still visible, strewn and mangled on the floor. This group that waited ahead surely had to be the last wave. The subterranean landing bay that housed the *Talon* lay just beyond them, and one more push was all it would take to get there. She was glad—she'd run out of ammunition for her own weapon long ago, and the plasma charge in the carbine she'd taken off a dead thug was dying fast.

The fetid scent of hot stone filled her nostrils as a bolt of sizzling energy clipped the corner of the wall mere centimeters from her face, leaving an ugly black scar on the beige material. She coughed and leaned out, squeezing off several suppressive shots as she attempted to take a headcount. Only two men were visible from where she stood, but unless they were both using fully automatic weapons, the volume of fire led her to believe there was at least one more shooter.

It was like Aroska had read her mind. "Got three," he called as she ducked away from another hail of plasma. Taking advantage of the fact that her brief appearance had captured the thugs' attention, he raised his own weapon, using one of the containers to steady his aim, and fired off three quick shots. The dull *thump* of a body hitting the floor could be heard somewhere ahead. "Make that two!"

Two soldiers would be simple compared to what they'd already dealt with. Ziva checked the carbine's charge one last time, estimating that it would be adequate. She adjusted her grip on the weapon and took in a couple of deep breaths, beginning a mental countdown in preparation to press forward.

Movement in the corner of her eye drew her attention back to the floor just before she stepped from her hiding place. A round, metallic object the size of her fist hit the ground and bounced, rolling forward with a *clank, clank, clank*. Her eyes grew wide.

Her body moved before she even realized she'd given it a command. "Grenade!" she exclaimed, ducking low and sweeping the explosive away with her foot before it had even come to a stop. The device sailed down the corridor past Aroska, erupting in a ball of fire just meters beyond him. The roar of the explosion was deafening in the narrow passage. A low rumble followed as cracks crisscrossed up the wall and down the ceiling. Lights flickered and debris rained down, sending a great cloud of dust and smoke billowing toward the docking bay.

Ziva shut her eyes and dove to the floor, flattening herself as best she could to escape the stifling cloud. Keeping one hand clamped over her nose and mouth, she raised her head and peered toward the bay, blinking rapidly as smoke filled her eyes and made them smart. Whether due to the cloud or her blurry vision, she could no longer see the two thugs. In a way, this was good—it meant they couldn't see her either. But she was reasonably sure the path behind her was now completely obstructed. The moment the dust cleared, she and Aroska would be exposed.

She could hear him somewhere behind her as she felt around for her weapon. His breathing was ragged and shallow, and he cried out at intervals, obviously in pain. A moment of silence. The sound of him struggling with something. Another groan and a loud curse. "Ziva!" he called.

One second, she replied silently as her hand came to rest on her carbine. She rose into a kneeling position and remained motionless, sighting up one of the two shadowy figures moving around in the haze through the doorway ahead. A break in the cloud gave her a clearer view of her target. She pulled the trigger just as he raised his own weapon toward her, sending him to the floor with a new hole in his head. She swung the barrel a couple of degrees to the left and did the same to the other figure, this one still just a dark shape. There was a shriek of pain as her plasma bolt struck something, though she had a feeling it hadn't been a direct hit. Still, it bought her some time.

When she saw no activity ahead after a few seconds, she slung the carbine's strap over her shoulder and turned back toward the pile of rubble, able to see Aroska moving around as the dust continued to clear. He lay on his back, having made it halfway out of his hiding spot before one leg had become pinned by rubble. He propped himself up with one arm, clawing desperately at a particularly large chunk of stone before collapsing onto his back again and sucking in a raspy breath.

"Damn it, get this thing off of me," he wheezed.

She stepped away and studied the rubble for a moment, conscious of the fact that she could very well just leave him there after what he'd done to Blain but simultaneously determined not to. She opted to start with some of the smaller pieces on top of the primary offender, tossing them aside and coughing as she stirred up more of the chalky dust. Aroska had already managed to clear away a few small chunks in his struggle, leaving minimal work for her. There was no guarantee moving the large piece wouldn't destabilize the entire pile, but they were running out of time.

"Ready?" she said, placing both hands against the rock and establishing a solid foothold.

Aroska nodded and sat up as best he could, his face streaked where streams of sweat had cut through the dirt. He gritted his teeth and placed his own hands on the stone, and together they pushed.

Ziva did her best to ignore his agonized groan as the chunk tipped and rolled free, focusing instead on keeping several newly loosened pieces from falling onto him. He began to scramble backward the moment he was free, coughing and sputtering and clutching his abdomen to support his injured ribs. He looked pallid, though it was difficult to tell whether his skin was actually *ashen* or just covered in *ash*.

"Ah, *sheyss*," he panted, doing his best to get his good leg under him. The other dragged limply behind him, his foot twisted at an impossible angle. A protrusion that could only be shattered bone jutted under his pant leg about halfway up his shin, and bloodied flesh was visible through the torn material.

After all she'd seen throughout her career and elsewhere, it was amazing that such a sight could still repulse her to such an extent. Angry about everything that had already transpired that day, angry that *this* had now happened, and angry that she was the one stuck dealing with it, she reached down and grasped his arm, yanking him upward. "Tarbic, get on your feet!"

He slipped and sagged further to the floor, struggling for purchase on the uneven ground.

In that instant, some of the raw rage was replaced by something else: panic, perhaps at the thought of not knowing how to help him, perhaps at the thought of getting buried alive down here. Either way, it provided an additional burst of motivation to get moving. She stooped down and took him under both arms, looking him straight in the eye. "Get *the hell up*, Aroska!"

That seemed to be enough to snap him out of his stupor. He clenched his jaw and nodded, slipping one arm around her shoulders and bracing the other against his torso. They rose as a unit and Ziva began leading him toward the bay, struggling for balance as he gimped along. He lifted his injured leg and shuffled forward, reaching out to support himself against the wall as they moved. His foot and ankle flopped lifelessly, and his boot and pant leg were both slick with blood.

She hadn't realized how little attention she was paying to her surroundings until she saw him look up and open his mouth to exclaim something. Her gaze shifted toward the docking bay in time to see the second man she'd shot drag himself into view just inside the open blast doors. His left arm and shoulder hung lifeless, reminiscent of overcooked meat where her plasma bolt had struck. With his good hand, he flipped the primer switch on a second grenade and lobbed it toward them.

She was halfway through the process of bringing the carbine around when Aroska shoved her forward with a surprising amount of force considering his current state. She stumbled and hit the floor just as she heard the grenade do the same somewhere behind them.

With the pile of rock blocking the hall, the roar of the device detonating in the reduced space was even more crippling than before. Another section of the wall crumbled, and the blast transformed the preexisting fragments of rubble into lethal projectiles as it propelled them in all directions throughout the confined space. A piece of scalding stone struck Ziva in the forehead. She threw her arms over her face and curled up tighter as ash, shale, and burning material poured down over her. An attempt to draw a deep breath resulted in a lungful of dust, and she felt her throat spasm and constrict. The ground shook as blocks of ceiling crashed to the floor, though she could hear none of it over the ringing in her ears.

The only other audible sound was a steady hum, though she wasn't sure if it was the vibration of the structures around her or simply a figment of her imagination. She remained still until she could no longer feel debris pummeling her body, and even then, it was a struggle to get moving again. Her eyes stung, full of dirt and the galaxy only knew what else, and piles of sand a centimeter deep slid from her arms and legs as she rolled over onto her stomach. The strap of the carbine caught, and she squinted through the smoke, able to make out the silhouettes of two rocks the size of her head that had pinned the weapon to the ground. The nearly depleted plasma cell had been cracked clean open, officially rendering the gun useless.

Head spinning and ears still ringing, she pushed herself into an upright position and staggered over to brace herself against what remained of the wall. As tempting as it was to gasp for breath, she knew it was pointless to do so; turning and spitting out the wad of gunk that had accumulated in her mouth was an acceptable compromise for now. A steady stream of blood oozed from the split on her forehead where the rock had impacted, immediately growing thick and sticky in the filthy air. She wiped at it just enough to keep it out of her eyes, then she pressed forward, keeping her aching body low and moving as lightly as possible.

Part of her—a part she almost didn't recognize after four years of focusing solely on self-preservation—felt guilty about leaving Aroska behind and in unknown condition. Another part—the ever-present calculating logistician—reminded her that *neither* of them would survive another explosion if the remaining thug got his hands on another grenade. From the looks of things, he hadn't been in great shape, but a cursory glance through the doorway revealed that he'd still managed to crawl away.

He hadn't gotten far. She had a clear view of him the moment she stepped into the bay, where the cloud of smoke and dust had more room to disperse. With the overhead door still closed, everything was shrouded in shadows, but he was definitely hobbling, having likely been struck by debris himself. He clutched a pistol in his good hand and used it to hold his mutilated left arm steady as he came to a stop below the *Talon* and began fiddling with the security controls on the locked boarding ramp.

She wasted no time in striding after him, determined he wouldn't receive the privilege of escaping, especially not in her only ticket out of there. He didn't seem to realize she was coming until she was already upon him, and by then it was too late. His weapon was torn from his grasp before he could even turn to face her, his legs swept out from underneath him, his head in her hands. She wrenched his skull to one side, and with a dull *crack*, the struggle he'd begun to put up was immediately put to an end. She cast his limp form aside and lowered the boarding ramp herself.

Her legs were carrying her back toward the access corridor before she was even able to put conscious thought into what came next. A hot, thick haze still filled the hallway; anything that could burn was burning, and it was impossible to determine what damage had been caused by which blast. The whole space was one big mess of destruction, and Aroska was somewhere in the middle of it.

She paused in the doorway and took in one last gulp of the relatively clean air in the bay before pressing forward into the corridor. The lighting panels in this section of the hall had been destroyed in the blast, but the glow cast by the burning refuse was adequate to guide her. Broken wires dangled from the ceiling, spitting sparks and smoke. As the dust cloud continued dissipating, it became clearer just how unstable the area was. They needed to get out of there.

Something crunched under her boot and she looked down to find her broken carbine. This was the place where she'd fallen. Using it as a reference point, she scanned the area just ahead and slightly to the right, catching sight of Aroska's arm and part of his torso almost immediately. For a moment she could only stand there and marvel at what little distance there'd been between them, and the thought occurred to her that she would have gotten buried as well if he hadn't pushed her forward.

"Damn it, Aroska," she muttered, wiping the blood and muck from her face again as she stumbled toward him. "Why do you do this to me?"

She half-fell, half-knelt beside him, the edges of her vision blurring as her mind zeroed in on only what was directly in front of her. It was a comforting feeling, this hyper-focused mode, a constant, reliable, familiar thing in this situation with so many unknowns. She went to work on the pieces of rubble obscuring his face and found that his head had mercifully been nestled into a space between two rocks. Nonetheless, his face was bloodied almost beyond recognition, his eyes closed, his jaw slack.

"*Sheyss*," she whispered, her hand immediately going to his neck and probing for a pulse. "*Sheyss, sheyss.*" She drew in a breath and held it in order to still herself, letting it all out in the form of a relieved sigh when she detected a slight rhythm. He was alive, though unresponsive to the point that the thought didn't bring her much comfort.

"Tarbic," she said, shaking his shoulder with one hand as she scooped rubble out of the way with the other. "Aroska, come on."

An image flashed through her mind in response to her own words, an impossibly distant memory that seemed a lifetime ago. So much had happened since then—new missions, new foes and allies, a new life and identity—that for a moment she wasn't even sure if it was real, but the longer she pictured it, the clearer it became. She saw herself standing over him as he lay strapped to that cold table in the harvesting room at Dakiti, shaking him and attempting to rouse him just as she was now. He'd been partially coherent then, had come to his senses after some prompting. She blinked and the image of that crisp, white room vanished, replaced by the real scene. The real hazy, filthy, precarious scene with the angry orange glow where he wasn't waking up.

She felt a sudden tightness in her chest, something more abstract than the choked-out feeling caused by the smoke. The breath she tried to take caught in her throat, and she was startled by the sound—some strange cross between a cough and a whimper—that emerged. For several seconds that felt like an eternity, she could only sit there without the faintest clue how to proceed, and the feeling of losing control petrified her.

Then her own voice echoed through her head. *Get on your feet.* It was the same tone she'd just used with Aroska minutes before. *Get the hell up.*

She coughed past the lump in her throat and scrambled into a more upright position, taking a moment to survey her surroundings again with a clearer head. The facts: the majority of Aroska's body was pinned under a pile of rubble that also cut off any alternate means of escape. He was unconscious and injured, so even if he was free, he wouldn't be able to move on his own. All their remaining opposition was dead, so they had a clear path to the ship if she could get him out, but therein lay the problem. She studied the rubble, sure she could eventually move it all by hand, but she lacked both the time and the space to rearrange it. Taking all of this into consideration, she could pinpoint only one option, one she wasn't convinced would work.

Establishing as solid a foothold as she could, she focused on the pile and extended her hands, willing the rocks and debris to move with her mind. As much as she was unsurprised by the lack of response, it still inspired a renewed sense of panic. There was no familiar tingle at the base of her skull, only a heavy throbbing that increased in intensity the longer she stood there.

She dropped her arms and shook them out, taking a couple of deep breaths. She was certain a lack of focus and calm state of mind were the primary problems here; it had only been four years since her last nostium infusion, so the timeframe should have had no bearing on her ability to conjure her Nostia. But she was also out of practice, and that last infusion had been with the Resistance's experimental formula, which put her at a definite disadvantage. Perhaps sheer willpower would do the trick.

No, not perhaps—it *had* to work. This was the only way.

Without another thought, she raised her hands and pushed again, as if she could take her own mind by surprise if she worked fast enough. Every already-aching muscle in her body went rigid, and as much as she wanted to look down toward Aroska, she forced her gaze to remain on the pile.

"*Frouchten* move," she whispered through clenched teeth.

Then she felt something deep within her head, hardly more than a tiny tickle, as if vocalizing her thoughts had helped ignite a spark. It was so faint that for a moment she feared she was only feeling what she wanted to feel, but then came the pain, that same dull ache that slowly sharpened into the familiar stabbing sensation she remembered from before the Resistance attack.

And then the rubble began to vibrate.

Shocked, she nearly stopped, but she dared not lose momentum. That pain, however uncomfortable, meant something was working, and she pushed with renewed fervor, straining until her whole body trembled.

"Move!" she commanded.

A low rumble filled the hallway as the vibration intensified and the chunks of stone began to knock against one another. Certain her muscles would snap, she pushed harder. Her ears popped. She could feel the tendons in her neck bulging. Something warm and wet began to dribble from her nose down over her lips, and the metallic taste of blood filled her mouth.

Taking a step forward, she swept her hands around in a lifting motion, ordering the rubble upward toward what remained of the ceiling rather than backward down the corridor where it had no room to maneuver. Only then did she risk a look at Aroska. One by one, the pieces of debris trapping him began to rise, quivering unsteadily in mid-air as she struggled to control them. And only then did the irony of the situation occur to her. Here she was once again using a forbidden ability to save the life of a man she was currently at odds with, lest they both end up caught in friendly fire. Last time she'd just managed to do it *before* he got hurt.

Unsure how much longer she could keep the floating rubble stable, she lunged forward, willing it to stay airborne for just a split second longer as she took Aroska under the arms and yanked him toward her. He came free with little resistance, and she flung herself over him, shielding his face with her torso and throwing her arms back to protect her own head as all the debris came crashing down just behind her. Then everything fell still once more.

The sudden release of tension left the pounding in her skull as the most prominent sensation. She blinked several times in hopes of righting her swimming vision, but she was rewarded only with sharp pinpricks of light, black fog, and a sudden roiling in her stomach. She crawled off of Aroska and retched into the dirt, certain she could no longer move.

So when she found herself staggering across the docking bay and stumbling backward up the boarding ramp with him in tow, she wasn't sure how she had gotten there, or how it was possible. Her body was in complete autopilot mode, reacting unprompted to years of training and instinct while her conscious mind remained numb. Again, she was glad—she only hoped it knew what it was doing.

She collapsed onto her back at the top of the ramp, dragging Aroska up just far enough to keep him from rolling back down. Satisfied that he was stable, she rushed for the cockpit—mere strides away—and initiated the ignition sequence before sprinting back out to the control console in the bay. The takeoff order she'd sent from the docking station remained intact, quashing her fear that the Ibarra soldiers had somehow locked the bay down again before she and Aroska arrived. The thought occurred to her that they would have needed to leave it unlocked in order to escape themselves.

Not wanting to waste another second, she pulled the bright red lever on the console. The heavy aperture above her began to twist open, releasing all of the smoke and dust in the bay and allowing her to really breathe for the first time in what felt like hours. But right now, there was no time to enjoy it. The moment the shielded door opened all the way, the ship would be vulnerable.

Sounds of the overhead battle echoed through the bay as she hustled back up the boarding ramp, hauling Aroska's limp body a bit further toward the pilot's seat before sliding into the chair and swiveling to face the control board. The vessel's repulsion system was already at one hundred percent power, and she began the lift-off procedure immediately. Feeling around on her belt for her padded supply pouch, she removed the communicator she'd brought from the apartment and plugged it into the *Talon's* comm board, immediately broadcasting the Niiosian transponder code and praying it worked. Praying Skeet and Zinni's worked too.

The orange glow of fire had turned the night sky a deep purple, and bolts of plasma sliced through the air from all directions. She double-checked the shields as the ship broke the plane of the bay and began its ascent into the madness. There was something liberating about being back aboveground, about leaving Tabaco and Panuco behind, but she dared not let that sense of relief take hold. They weren't in the clear yet, and she imagined she had only caught a small glimpse of just how far the situation had deteriorated. She had no doubt that her problems were only beginning.

She braced herself and shot forward at full speed.

To be continued...

The story concludes in

EMBERS

ZIVA PAYVAN LEGACY • PART 2

Like what you read? Tell someone about it!
Taking the time to leave an honest review is immeasurably helpful
for any author, new or established. Your opinion helps other
people make informed decisions about their reading options and
allows the book to reach its target audience.

Your ratings and reviews are greatly appreciated!

About The Author

EJ Fisch is a long-time action junkie and fan of the science fiction genre. She'll readily admit that she has a vivid imagination, which can be both a blessing and a curse. She has been writing as a hobby since junior high and began publishing in the spring of 2014.

When she's not busy writing or working her day job as a data analyst in the medical field, she enjoys listening to music, working on concept art, reading, gaming, and spending time with her animals. She currently resides in southern Oregon.

Fracture is her fourth novel, Book 4 in the Ziva Payvan series and Book 1 of the Ziva Payvan Legacy duology.

Find EJ Fisch on your favorite social media site!

Keep up with news, catch sneak peeks, and more at:
www.ejfisch.com

Questions? Comments? Use the resources above or email at:
ej@ejfisch.com

Your thoughts about the characters and storylines are always welcome and appreciated!

www.ingramcontent.com/pod-product-compliance
Lightning Source LLC
Chambersburg PA
CBHW031548240626
47153CB00002B/430